Praise for the Runelords

"The breathless third installment of Farland's second Runelords quarter . . . Enchanting parallel-world landscapes and charming minor characters."
    —*Publishers Weekly* on *The Wyrmling Horde*

"David Farland has written a series that rivals the best of Terry Brooks, Terry Goodkind, and Orson Scott Card." —*SFRevu* on *Worldbinder*

"The suspense is real, the action is nonstop, and the characterizations continue to convince. . . . [This is] a series that has put Farland on high-fantasy readers' maps." —*Booklist* on *The Lair of Bones*

"Fans of Robert Jordan and Terry Goodkind will enjoy Farland's Runelords."
    —*RT Book Reviews* on *The Lair of Bones*

"The author's imaginative approach to magic, coupled with a richly detailed fantasy world and a cast of memorable heroes and villains, adds depth and variety to this epic tale of war and valor."
    —*Library Journal* on *Wizardborn*

"Sure, *Brotherhood* has incredible edge-of-your-seat, nail-biting battle scenes—the finale being an exceptional example—but Gaborn's struggle to make a decision, and then facing the consequences, is equally thrilling."
    —*Starlog* on *Brotherhood of the Wolf*

"When I reached the end of this first volume, *The Runelords*, and saw grace arise from a devastating battlefield where too many great hearts lay dead, Farland had earned the tears that came to my eyes. It was not sentiment but epiphany."
    —Orson Scott Card, author of *Ender in Exile*

TOR BOOKS BY DAVID FARLAND

The Runelords
Brotherhood of the Wolf
Wizardborn
The Lair of Bones
Sons of the Oak
Worldbinder
The Wyrmling Horde
Chaosbound

To contact the author, e-mail DavidFarland@xmission.com,
or visit his website at www.runelords.com.

CHAOSBOUND

The Eighth Book of the Runelords

❧ DAVID FARLAND ❧

TOR®
fantasy

A TOM DOHERTY ASSOCIATES BOOK
NEW YORK

CHAOSBOUND: THE EIGHTH BOOK OF THE RUNELORDS

Copyright © 2009 by David Farland

A Tor Book
Published by Tom Doherty Associates, LLC
175 Fifth Avenue
New York, NY 10010

www.tor-forge.com

Tor® is a registered trademark of Tom Doherty Associates, LLC.

ISBN 978-0-7653-6140-0

First Edition: October 2009
First Mass Market Edition: January 2011

Printed in the United States of America

0 9 8 7 6 5 4 3 2

For my daughter, Nichole: may all of your fantasies

come true—at least the pleasant ones!

❧ BOOK I ❧

THE FLOOD

❧ 1 ❧

SIR BORENSON AT THE END OF
THE WORLD

*Great are the healing powers of the earth. There is
nothing that has been destroyed that cannot be
mended . . .*

— *The Wizard Binnesman*

At the end of a long summer's day, the last few beams of
sunlight slanted through the ancient apple orchard outside the ruins of Barrensfort, creating golden streams
among the twigs and branches of the trees.

Though the horizon was a fiery glowering, sullen and
peaceful, from the deadwood linnets had already begun
to rise upon their red and waxen wings, eager to greet
the coming night.

Sir Borenson leaned upon the ruins of an old castle
wall and watched his daughters Sage and Erin work amid
the tallest branches of an apple tree. It was a hoary thing,
seeming as old as the ruins themselves, with lichen-
covered boughs that had grown to be as thick as many
another tree.

The wind had knocked the grand old tree over two
summers ago, so that it leaned at a slant. Most of its

limbs had fallen into ruin, and now the termites feasted upon them. But the tree still had some roots in the soil, and one great branch thrived.

Borenson had found that the fruit of that bough was the sweetest to grow upon his farm. Not only were the golden apples sweeter than all of the others, they ripened a good four weeks early and grew huge and full. These apples would fetch a hefty price at tomorrow's fair.

This was not the common hawk's-day fair that came once a week. This was the High Summer Festival, and the whole district would likely turn out up at Mill Creek, for trading ships had come to Garion's Port in the past few weeks, bringing spices and cloth from faraway Rofehavan.

The fallen tree left a hole in the canopy of the orchard, creating a small glade. The grass grew lush here. Bees hummed and circled, while linnets' wings shimmered like garnets amid streams of sunlight. Sweet apples scented the air.

There can be beauty in death, Sir Borenson thought, as he watched the scene.

Erin climbed out on a thin limb, as graceful as a dancer, and held the handle of her pail in her mouth as she gently laid an apple in.

"Careful," Sir Borenson warned, "that limb you're on may be full of rot."

Erin hung the bucket on a broken twig. "It's all right, Daddy. This limb is still healthy."

"How can you tell?"

She bounced a bit. "See? It has some spring in it still. The rotten ones don't."

Smart girl, for a nine-year-old. She was not the prettiest of his brood, but Borenson suspected that she had the quickest wit, and she was the most thoughtful of his children, the first to notice if someone was sad or ill, and she was the most protective.

You could see it in her eyes. Borenson's older offspring all had a fierceness that showed in their flashing blue eyes and dark red hair. They took after him.

But though Erin had Borenson's penetrating blue eyes, she had her mother's luxurious hair, and her mother's broad face and thoughtful expression. It seemed to Borenson that the girl was born to be a healer, or perhaps a midwife.

She'll be the one to nurse me through my old age, he mused.

"Careful with those apples," he warned. "No bruises!" Erin was always careful, but Sage was not. The girl seemed more interested in getting the job done quickly than in doing it well.

Borenson had wadded some dry grass and put it in the buckets, so that the girls could pack the apples carefully. The grass had tea-berry leaves in it, to sweeten the scent. Yet he could tell that Sage wasn't packing the apples properly.

Probably dreaming of boys, he thought. Sage was nearly thirteen, and her body was gaining a woman's curves. It wasn't uncommon here in Landesfallen for a girl to marry at fifteen. Among the young men at the Festival, Sage could draw as much attention as a joust.

Marriage.

I'll be losing her soon, too, Borenson thought. All of my children are growing up and leaving me.

Talon, his oldest, was gone. She'd sailed off to Rofehavan more than three months past, with her foster siblings Fallion, Jaz, and Rhianna.

Borenson couldn't help but wonder how they had fared on the journey. By now they should have made landfall on the far continent. If all was going as planned, they were crossing Mystarria, seeking out the Mouth of the World, beginning their descent into darkness, daring the reavers' lair.

Long ago, according to legend, there had been one true world, bright and perfect, shining in the heavens. All of mankind had lived in joy and peace, there in the shade of the One True Tree. But an ancient enemy had tried to seize control of the Seals of Creation, and in the battle that ensued, the world shattered, breaking into millions and millions of shadow worlds, each less perfect, each less whole, than that one world had been.

Fallion, a young flameweaver, said that he knew how to heal the worlds, bind them all into one. Borenson's older children were accompanying him to the underworld, to the Seals of Creation, to help in his task.

Borenson wrenched his thoughts away. He didn't want to consider the perils that his children faced. There were reavers in the underworld, monstrously large and powerful. Best not to think of that.

Yet he found it hard lately to think of much else. His children should have landed in Rofehavan. If their ship had made good time, they might soon reach the Seals of Creation.

A new day could be dawning.

"Father," Erin called, "Look at this apple!" She held up a huge one, flashed her winning smile. "It's perfect!"

"Beautiful!" he said.

You're beautiful, he thought, as he stood back and watched. It was his job to take down those buckets that were full.

There was a time a few years ago when he would have been up in the tree with her. But he was getting too fat to climb rotting trees. Besides, the arthritis in his right shoulder hurt. He wasn't sure if it was the long years of practice with the war hammer or some old wound, but his right arm was practically useless.

"I'm growing, I'm growing old.
My hair is falling and my feet are cold."

It was a silly rhyme that he'd learned as a child. An old gaffer with long silver hair used to sing it as he puttered down the lanes in the market, doing his shopping.

Borenson heard a sound behind him, a suspicious rustling of leaves.

Barrensfort was not much more than a pile of gray rocks. Two walls still rose sixty feet from some old lord's tower, a broken finger pointing accusingly to the sky. Once it had been a great fortress, and Fallion the Bold had slept here sixteen hundred years ago. But most of the rocks for the outer wall had been carted off long ago. Borenson's fine chimney was made from the rounded stones of the old wall.

So the courtyard in the old fortress was open to the sky. In a hundred years the rest of the walls might fall in, and a forest would likely grow over the spot.

But for now, there was only one large tree here, an odd tree called an encampment tree. It looked nothing like the white gums common to the area, but was perhaps a closer relative to the stonewood trees down by the sea. It was large, with rubbery gray bark and tiny spade-shaped leaves. Its limbs were thick with fronds that hung like curtains, creating an impenetrable canopy, and its branches spread out like an umbrella. A good-sized tree could shelter a dozen people.

When settlers had first come to Landesfallen, nearly a thousand years earlier, they had used such trees as shelter during the summers while building their homes.

Unfortunately, Sir Borenson had three such trees on his property, and for the past several years he'd had problems with squatters coming to his land and living in them—particularly during the harvest season. They'd steal his fruit, raid his vegetable garden, and snatch shirts from his clothesline.

Borenson didn't hate the squatters. There were wars and rumors of wars all across Rofehavan. But he couldn't allow them to stay on his land, either.

He whirled and crept toward the tree.

It's probably nothing, he thought. Probably just some rangit or a sleepy old burrow bear.

Rangits were large rabbitlike creatures that fed on grass. They often sought shade during the heat of the day.

A burrow bear was a gentle beast that ate grass and vegetables. It had no fear of mankind whatsoever, and if Borenson found one, he'd be able to walk right up to it and scratch its head.

He went to the tree, swatted aside the long trailing fronds, and stepped beneath the canopy.

There was a burrow bear—its carcass sitting upon a spit, just waiting for someone to light a fire beneath it.

Inside the shadowed enclosure, entire families squatted: mothers, fathers, children—lots of young children between the ages of three and six. There couldn't have been fewer than twenty people in all.

They crouched, the children with wide eyes and dirty

faces peering up at him in terror. The stench of poverty was thick on them.

Borenson's hand went to his dagger. He couldn't be too careful around such people. Squatters had attacked farmers before. The road to Sand Hollow had been treacherous all summer.

He half-expected someone to try to creep up on him from behind. Borenson was vastly outnumbered, but he was an expert with the dagger. Though he was old, if it came to a fight, he would gut them to a man.

One little girl who could not have been eight pleaded, "Please, sir, don't hurt us!"

Borenson glanced at one of the fathers. He was a young man in his mid-twenties with a wife and three little children clinging to him for protection.

By the powers, what can I do? Borenson wondered. He hated to throw them off his property, but he couldn't afford to let them remain, thieving.

If he'd had the money, he'd have hired the men to work. But he couldn't support these people.

He said, "I thought it was the borrowbirds that ate my cherries, fool that I am."

"Please, sir," the young man apologized. "We didn't steal anything."

Borenson shook his head. "So, you've just been hunkering down here in my fields, drinking my water and helping get rid of the excess burrow bears?"

Back in the shadows Borenson spotted a young man clinging to a pretty lass. His jaw dropped as he recognized his youngest son, Draken, holding some girl as skinny as a doe.

Draken was only fifteen. For weeks now he had been shucking his chores, going "hunting" each afternoon.

Borenson had imagined that it was wanderlust. Now he saw that it was only common lust.

"Draken?" Sir Borenson demanded. Immediately he knew what had happened. Draken was hiding this girl, hiding her whole family.

"It's true, Father," Draken said. "They didn't steal the cherries. They've been living off of wild mushrooms and garlic and trout from the river, whatever they could get—but they didn't eat from our crops!"

Borenson doubted that. Even if these folks spared his crops, he lived on the borders of a small town called Sweetgrass. Surely the neighbors would be missing something.

Draken was clutching his girl with great familiarity, a slim little thing with a narrow waist and hair as yellow as sunlight. Borenson knew that romance was involved, but one glance at the poor clothing of the squatters, the desperation in their faces, and he knew that they were not the caliber of people that he would want in his family.

Draken had been trained in the Gwardeen to be a skyrider, patrolling Landesfallen on the backs of giant graaks. Borenson himself had taught Draken the use of the bow and ax. Draken was warrior-born, a young man of great discipline, not some oaf of a farm boy to sow his seed in the first pretty girl who was willing.

"I thought I taught you better," Borenson growled in disgust. "The same discipline that a man uses on the battlefield, he should use in bed."

"Father," Draken said protectively, leaping to his feet, "she's to be my wife!"

"Funny," Borenson said. "No one told me or your mother of a wedding. . . . You'll not sleep with this tart."

"I was trying to think of how to tell you—"

Borenson didn't want to hear Draken's excuses. He glared at the squatters, and then dismissed them. "You'll be off my property in five minutes." He let them imagine the penalty for failure.

"Father," Draken said fiercely. "They're good people— from Mystarria. This is Baron Owen Walkin and his family—his wife Greta, his daughter Rain, his sons and their kin."

Borenson knew the Walkin name. He'd even met a Baron Walkin twenty years ago, an elderly man of good report. The Walkins had been staunch supporters of the king and came from a long line of stout warriors. But these starvelings looked nothing like warriors. There was no muscle on them. The patriarch of the family looked to be at least ten years Borenson's junior, a thin man with a widow's peak and fiery red hair.

Could times really be so hard in Mystarria, Borenson wondered, to turn true men into starvelings? If all that he heard was true, the barbaric warlords of Internook had invaded the coasts after the death of the Earth King.

Ten years back, Borenson's family had been among the very first wave of refugees from Mystarria. He was out of touch with his homeland.

But the latest rumors said that the new overlords were harsh on their vassals, demanding outlandish taxes, abusing women.

Those who back-talked or stood up to the abuse would find themselves burned out of their homes—or worse.

As a baron loyal to the Earth King, Walkin and his kin would have been singled out for retribution.

Borenson suddenly realized just how desperate these people really might be.

"I . . ." Draken fumbled. "Rain here will be a good wife!"

Rain. Borenson made a mental note. His own wife Myrrima was a wizardess who served Water. Borenson thought it no coincidence that his son would fall for a girl named Rain.

He sought for words to voice his disappointment, and one of the poor folk in the group—the matriarch Greta—warned, "Beware what you say about my daughter. She loves your son. You'll be eating your words for the rest of your life!"

What a confounded mess, Borenson thought. He dared not let these people stay on his land, yet he couldn't in good conscience send them off.

If he sent them off, they'd have to make their way into the interior of Landesfallen, into the desert. Even if they found a place to homestead, it was too late to plant crops. The Walkin family had come a long way—just to starve.

Outside in the orchard, Erin called, "Father, I need another bucket!"

"Where are you, Father?" Sage called.

That's when he was struck.

Something hit Borenson—harder than he'd ever been hit in his life. The blow seemed to land on the back of his head and then continue on through his whole body, rattling every fiber of his being.

White lights flashed in his eyes and a roaring filled his ears. He tried to turn and glance behind him, but he saw no one as he fell. He hit the ground and struggled to cling to consciousness, but he felt as if he'd been bashed by a reaver's glory hammer.

He heard the squatters all cry out in alarm, and then he was spinning, spinning . . .

Borenson had a dream unlike any other. He dreamt that he was a man, a giant on a world different from his own, and in the space of a heartbeat this man's life flashed before his eyes.

Borenson dreamt of simple things—a heavy-boned wife whose face was not quite human, for she had horny nubs upon her temples and heavy jaws, and canine teeth that were far too large. Yet he loved her as if she were beautiful, for she bore him stout sons who were destined to be warriors.

In his dream, he was a warrior himself—Aaath Ulber, the leader of the High Guard, the king's elite forces. His name was a title that meant Berserker Prime, or Greatest of All Berserkers, and like his wife, he was not quite human, for his people had been breeding warriors for two hundred generations, and he was the culmination of their efforts.

He dreamt of nights spent on guard duty on a lonely mountain with only a spear for company, and days hunting for fell enemies in the dank forests, thick with morning fog. He dreamt of raids on wyrmlings: pale manlike monsters that were larger even than he, monsters that fed on human flesh and hid from the sun by day in dank holes. He dreamt of more blood and horror than any man should see in a lifetime.

Last of all, he dreamt that he saw a world falling from the heavens, plummeting toward him like a great star that filled the sky. As it drew near, all around him his people cried out in wonder and horror.

He saw blue water on that world, vast seas and great lakes. He saw the titanium-white tops of giant clouds, swirling in a great vortex. He saw a vast crimson desert, and green lakes and hills. He saw a terminus, a line dividing night from day, and the gloriously colored clouds at its edge—great swaths of rose and gold.

Around him, people were shouting in alarm and pointing into the air. He was on the streets of Caer Luciare, a mountain fortress, and his own daughter was looking up and crying, "This is the end!"

Then the falling world slammed into his.

When he woke, Sir Borenson was still falling. He was lying on the ground, but it was dropping away. He cried out, and all around him the squatters shrieked in fear, too.

He slammed to a halt and his whole body smashed into the ground, knocking the air from his lungs.

Though the skies had been clear, thunder roared in the heavens.

The squatters under the tree were still shouting. The mother of one family begged, "Is everyone all right?"

"Earthquake!" someone said. "It was an earthquake!"

Sir Borenson had never felt anything like this. The ground wasn't trembling or rolling. Instead, it seemed to have just dropped—perhaps hundreds of feet.

Borenson peered at the group. His heart raced. The ground was wet and smelled of seawater, and his clothes were sopped.

Other than that, he felt somehow disconnected from his body. All of the old aches and pains were gone.

"Father!" Sage shouted. "Father, help! Erin's hurt!"

Borenson leapt to his feet and stood for a moment, dazed. The dream that he'd had, the dream of Aaath Ulber, cast such a huge shadow in his memory that he felt unsure just who he was.

He blinked, trying to recall where he was. Memory told him that he was on the mountain, on Caer Luciare. If he turned around he would see his girl.

But this was no mountain. He was under the tree.

He glanced at the squatter children in the shadows. Two women and a couple of children seemed to have fainted. A knot of children were trying to revive them, and suddenly one little girl peered up with terrified eyes. She shrieked, and others glanced up at him and followed suit. They fell over themselves in their hurry to back away.

Borenson looked down at the tots, wondering if he had blood on his face, wondering what frightened the children, and it seemed that he looked from too great a height.

"It's all right," he told them. "I won't hurt you."

He raised his hands. They were meaty things, huge and heavy. More importantly, there was a small spur of bone protruding from each wrist, something that no human should have.

His hands were the hands of Aaath Ulber.

He was wearing war gear—metal bands with targets on his wrists, heavy gray mail unlike any forged on his world.

He reached up and felt his forehead—the bony plates on his temples, the nubs of horns above that were more pronounced than those of any other warrior of the clans, and he knew why the children cried in terror.

He was Aaath Ulber and Sir Borenson, both men sharing one enormous body. He was still human, as humans had looked on that other world, but his children and wife here would not recognize him as such.

"Father!" Sage shrieked out in the orchard. She wept furiously.

Borenson turned and stumbled through the curtain of vines.

The world that appeared before him was a disaster.

Strange vortexes whirled in the sky, like tornadoes of light, and thunder crackled in the clear air.

Water covered much of the ground—seawater and beds of red kelp. Crabs scuttled about while starfish and urchins clung to the mud. Bright coral stuck up from a ridge of rocks that hadn't been in the glade moments ago. Everything was sopping wet.

An enormous red octopus surged over the grass desperately, just up the path.

The walls of the old fortress leaned wildly, and everywhere that he looked trees had tilted.

Sage was under the huge apple tree, weeping bitterly and calling, "Father! Father, come quick!"

Part of that old rotten tree had fallen during the disaster.

Borenson bounded to her, leaping over an enormous black wolf eel that wriggled across the trail.

Sage stood solemnly, looking down at her little sister. Erin had fallen from the tree onto a rotten limb; now she lay with her neck twisted at a precarious angle.

Erin's mouth was open; her eyes stared up. Her face was so pale that it seemed bloodless. She made little gaping motions, like a fish struggling to breathe.

Other than that, her body was all too still.

In the distance, a mile away, the village bell in Sweet-grass began ringing in alarm.

Sage took one look at Borenson and backed away from him in horror. She gave a little yelp and then turned, fumbling to escape.

Draken had come out from under the encampment tree, and he rushed up to Erin.

He tried to push Borenson away. "Get back, you!"

He was small, so small that his efforts had little effect. "It's me, your father!" Borenson said. Draken peered at him in shock.

Borenson reached down and tried gently to lift Erin, to comfort her, but felt the child's head wobble in a way that no person's should. The vertebrae in her neck seemed to be crushed. Borenson eased her back into place.

If she lives, Borenson thought, she might never walk again.

Erin peered up at him, took in the horror of Boren-son's face, and there was no recognition in her eyes— only stark panic. She frowned and let out a thin wail.

"Stay calm, sweet one," Borenson said, hoping to soothe her. But his voice came out deep and disturbing— more a bull's bellow than the voice that Erin was used to. "It's me, your father."

In the distance a war horn blew an alarm. It was his wife Myrrima sounding a call from the old ox horn that he kept hung on a peg beside the fireplace. Two long blasts, two short, three long.

It was signal for retreat, but it wasn't a simple retreat. He was supposed to go somewhere. He had not heard that call in so many years that it took a moment to dredge up its meaning.

Draken was at his side now, reaching down to lift Erin, trying to pull her into his arms. He was just as eager to help the child as Borenson was, just as frightened and dazed.

"Don't touch her," Borenson warned. "We'll have to move her with great care."

Draken peered at him in terror and disbelief. "What? What happened to you?"

Borenson shook his head in wonder.

In the distance Myrrima shouted, "Erin? Sage? Borenson?" She was running toward them; he could tell by her voice that she was racing through the orchard. "Everyone, run to high ground! Water's coming!"

That's when Borenson felt it: a tremor in the earth, a distant rumbling that carried through the soles of his steel boots.

The realization of his full predicament struck him.

On Aaath Ulber's world there had been no continent where Landesfallen stood—only a few poorly charted islands on the far side of the world.

Borenson had taken meetings with King Urstone many times. The wyrmling hordes had all but destroyed mankind, and some of the king's counselors advised him to flee to the coast and build ships to carry refugees to the Far Isles.

But it had seemed impossible, and the king had worried at what would happen if his people were ever found there, cornered on some desert island.

On Aaath Ulber's world, this whole continent was underwater, Borenson realized. In the binding of the worlds, the two became one. That's why there are sea animals here on dry land—it wasn't dry on both worlds. Now the land has fallen. The sea is rushing in to cover it!

"Run!" he shouted to Draken and Sage. "Run to high ground! The sea is coming!"

He peered down at little Erin. He could not move her safely. Nor did he dare leave her here.

He wasn't sure how much time he had. Minutes? Hours? No, he could feel the land trembling. He might not have even minutes. The sea was rushing toward him in a flood.

We may all be doomed!

The squatters came boiling from under the tree, then stood gaping, gasping and crying in astonishment. Nothing could have prepared them for what they saw—kelp and coral and creatures of the sea all suddenly appearing where once there had been dry ground.

"Run!" Borenson urged them.

The valley here along the Hacker River was long and narrow, a mile or two across.

On both sides of the valley, stark red-rock cliffs rose up. In only a few places could those cliffs be scaled.

"There!" Borenson shouted. "Up that hill!"

The squatters were shrieking, the children yelping in fear. At least one woman was still unconscious, and young men carried her. Others limped about groggily. The men were gathering bags while mothers tried to herd their children.

Draken looked back toward the house. "Shall I save the horses?"

"Save your sister!" Borenson shouted. "Get to high ground."

The earth continued to rumble, growing louder by faint degrees. Draken grabbed his sister Sage by the elbow and took the girl Rain by the hand. The three rushed off.

It was nearly a mile to the ridge. They'd be minutes running toward it, long minutes climbing.

Borenson looked down at Erin. "Daddy?" she said. Her eyes scanned left and right, unseeing, unable to focus.

"I'm here," he said. "Mother is coming. You'll be all right."

Myrrima had some skills as a healer, as did all water wizards. Her kiss could calm a troubled mind; her stroke could draw away a man's pain. But Borenson didn't think that she could mend a broken neck, not in the time that they had.

Perhaps the flood won't reach us, Borenson dared hope. How far did the land sink? Certainly it won't all be underwater. We are fifty-two miles from the sea.

He imagined that some sort of balance must have been reached in the binding of the worlds. Perhaps his homeland would only sink halfway into the sea.

He heard his wife crashing through the brush of the overgrown orchard. This part of his land was ill-kept.

"Myrrima," Borenson bellowed. "Over here!"

She came running a moment later, leaping over a rock covered in coral, rushing between two trees, panting from exhaustion. She wore her deep blue traveling robe over a white tunic and leggings. The years had put a little weight on her, but not much. She did not run fast. No longer did she have any endowments of speed or brawn. The Dedicates who had given her their attributes had all been slain long ago, shortly after they'd fled Mystarria, as had his Dedicates.

Yet as a wizardess she would enjoy a longer life than Borenson, and in the past ten years she seemed not to have aged a year.

Myrrima stumbled to a halt, not even recognizing him. The woman had had the sense to bring his war hammer, throw together a bundle of clothes. Now she backed away with fear in her eyes.

Her body language said it all: Who is this giant, crouching above my child?

"Myrrima," Borenson said. "It's me—your husband."

Wonder and confusion warred in her face. Myrrima peered down at Erin, there gasping for breath, and she seemed to cave in on herself.

"Erin?" she called, daring to scrabble closer. "My little Erin!" Myrrima dropped to her knees, still panting for breath, and kissed Erin's forehead, then began to stroke her. "My baby! My sweet baby?"

"She fell," Borenson explained, "in the binding of the worlds."

"Mother?" Erin called. She peered up, unseeing.

"I'm here," Myrrima whispered. "I'm here for you."

There was a protracted silence. Borenson became more aware of the rumbling beneath his feet, the squawking of borrowbirds. The animals felt the danger, too.

"We have to get her to safety," Myrrima said. She eyed Borenson with distrust. "Can you move her gently?"

Borenson let out a little wail of frustration. His giant hands were so powerful, yet so uncouth. They were ill-suited for such delicate work.

"Can you hold back the water?" he begged.

Myrrima shook her head in defeat.

Borenson worried that nothing that he could do would save the child. Perhaps he could not even his save his family. How tall would the waves be? Forty feet tall, or four hundred?

Myrrima shifted the child slightly, lifting her just enough so that Borenson could slip his fingers beneath Erin. As gently as he could, he slid one palm beneath the child's body and another beneath her head.

With great care he lifted. The girl seemed so small in his arms.

I am of the warrior clan, a voice whispered in his mind. This child weighs nothing.

It was Aaath Ulber's voice.

Borenson put one arm beneath Erin, like a board, and began to carry her as swiftly and as delicately as he could.

The grass was wet, the ground uneven. Strange sea creatures dotted the land—enormous crabs creeping about with claws ready, rays gasping for air. Colorful coral rose up in shades of tan and bone and red, all surrounded by clumps of summer grasses.

Borenson hurried, trying not to jar his daughter, careful not to slip. He kept glancing to the ground then back to Erin's small face, contorted as it was as she struggled to stay alive.

Is she even breathing? Borenson wondered. He watched her chest rise a little and then fall again.

Yes, she breathes.

Up ahead, Owen Walkin's people lumbered along. All of them moved slowly, painfully, as if some great illness had befallen them.

Suddenly, Borenson felt as if he were watching them from outside his own body. The people looked small and puny. "Run, you feral dogs!" he roared.

People of such low breeding don't deserve to live, he thought.

It was not a thought that would ever have presented itself to Sir Borenson.

Aaath Ulber was talking.

Though the others were weak Borenson felt strong, stronger than either he or Aaath Ulber had ever been. In some ways, he felt as if something vital had always been missing and now he had found it.

He reached the river, which had gone strangely muddy. A pair of giant rays were flapping about. The water was not deep this time of year, nor was it swift. But the rounded stones beneath the surface were slick.

Borenson sloshed through, Myrrima at his side, and made it more than halfway before he slipped.

He caught himself, but Erin's little head swiveled to the right.

"Aaaagh!" Myrrima gave a cry, then reached out and tried to hold Erin's head securely in place. They attained the far bank, raced up wet stones. A patch of slick red kelp hindered him, but he finally made it to the base of the ridge.

The squatter families ahead toiled up the long slope. The ground trembled mightily now. The flood was coming.

Borenson marched boldly, passing the squatters, holding Erin as securely as he could. He studied Erin's face; she gasped for breath. Her complexion was as white as a pearl, her skin seemingly translucent. He could make out the tiny veins and arteries that colored her skin, blue and red. Her pupils had constricted to pin-points.

She's in shock, he realized. She's strangling for lack of air.

There was no way to save her. Perhaps all of his efforts had been in vain. Yet he clung to hope.

With giant strides he passed through the clot of squatters, surged uphill. The air filled with a distant roar and birds squawked.

He'd climbed three hundred feet. He peered to the east and saw a gray cloud in the distance—a haze of dust and spray.

He had to get higher. With a burst of speed, he charged uphill, cuddling Erin, trying to hold the life inside her.

At last he reached the ridgetop and peered toward the sea. Just to the west lay Sweetgrass, its village bell ringing wildly. The whole earth was roaring, and beyond the town a massive wave surged through Hacker River Valley.

The squatters, Myrrima, and Borenson's children trudged up, their faces stark with shock and amazement; they stopped next to Borenson and peered at the rushing waters.

The sea came far more swiftly than Borenson would have imagined. This was not some puny wave making its way along a sandy beach.

It roared—a sound that shook the world in a continuous boom as if all the thunder that had ever been suddenly voiced itself at once.

The ground was trembling now, and loose stones began to bounce down from some red-rock cliffs above. Borenson glanced up fearfully, but none of the stones came near.

The valley spread below, and Borenson had an eagle's view of the river snaking along, the green fields to either side. He could see his own pleasant home with its newly thatched roof and barns, with his sheep and cattle in his pens, and his yellow dog Mongrel standing out in front of the house, woofing at the confusion.

His neighbors' homes lay east and west. He saw the Dobbit family rushing about near their cottage, Farmer Dobbit racing to free his livestock, seeming only now to recognize the danger.

Old widow Taramont, half blind and crippled by age, was puttering at the door to her home, calling for help.

Farther west, townsfolk were stirring. A young girl raced down the road beside the river; dozens of folks were charging behind her, hoping to outrun the great wave.

Then the sea came.

The flood surged into the valley and followed the course of the Hacker River as it snaked through the hills. A wall of water two hundred feet high blasted through the canyon, thundering over the village, crushing houses, Borenson's barn, sweeping neighbors away.

It crashed into the ruins of the old fortress, knocking down stone walls that had stood for sixteen hundred years.

The sea ripped up trees and sent them rumbling in a wall before it. Borenson saw flashes of pale bodies, victims of the flood, mingled among the ruins.

The water thrashed below, raising a fine mist that wetted Borenson in a muddy rain. Then the wall hurried on, filling up the valley as the sea sought its new bounds, creating a long irregular inlet.

A rainbow formed in the mist above the ruin, a cruel joke of nature.

For a long moment Borenson searched for signs of life. The water was filthy, as dark as loam. Bits of bark and even whole trees came bobbing to the surface, along with patches of thatch roof.

He waited breathlessly to hear someone shout for help, to see a pale body thrashing in the dark waves.

But nothing moved down there—not so much as a wet cat. The weight of the water had crushed the townsfolk, snuffing out their lives as completely as if they were but the tender flames of candles.

It seemed forever that he stood rooted to the ground.

Borenson recognized what had happened. Fallion had done it! Fallion had bound two worlds together—the world of Borenson and the world of Aaath Ulber.

For some reason when the worlds had combined, Borenson and Aaath Ulber combined, too. Yet he wondered why none of the others around him had been similarly transformed.

It was said that other people lived on shadow worlds; it was as if when the One True World splintered, the folk of the One True World had splintered too.

It was believed by some that every man was therefore incomplete and had shadow selves upon far worlds.

Borenson had always thought it idle speculation.

But somehow in the binding Borenson had bound together with Aaath Ulber, his "shadow self." Two men, each living his own life upon a different world, had fused into one body.

The notion was staggering. He didn't have time to comprehend it. He couldn't even begin to fathom the implications.

He wondered why Fallion had bound only two worlds. Why not all of them? Why not bind a million, million worlds all at once, and re-create the perfect world of legend?

Perhaps it's an experiment, Borenson imagined. Fallion is testing his powers.

He worried. If Fallion had bound two worlds together, then that meant that he had already made it to the Lair of Bones deep in the Underworld.

Considering the devastation that Fallion had wrought here, what must Fallion be going through now? There might have been cave-ins in the tunnels. They might have filled with water.

For all that Borenson knew, Fallion and his friends were all dead.

If this binding had been a trial, it had gone horribly awry. Chances were that the experiment might never be repeated.

Only then did the magnitude of the destruction begin to sink in. Here in Landesfallen, the vast majority of the people lived in cities along the coast, while a few others lived in river valleys like this one.

If we had been on the coast, Borenson realized, we'd all be dead.

Without my crops, he considered, we may be dead anyway.

Young Draken peered at the crashing waters and spoke some words that Borenson had not heard in many long years. "The Ends of the Earth is not far enough. . . ." He turned and glanced at his father. "Do you think *he* knew?"

The boy was referring to the warning that the Earth King had uttered when he died, the words that had sent

Borenson fleeing to Landesfallen. At Garion's Port, fifty miles to the west of here, two huge stones flanked the bay, stones called the Ends of the Earth. And upon his death, the Earth King Gaborn Val Orden had warned Borenson that the Ends of the Earth were not far enough. Borenson had known that he had to flee inland.

Had Gaborn sensed this flood? Borenson wondered. Could he have known what would befall us, ten years in the future?

Borenson sighed. "He knew. His prescience was a thing of legend."

The refugees all fell in exhaustion and lay panting, peering down at the flood. The ground still shook, and the water thundered. But the sound was receding.

The starvelings seemed to be floundering in despair. Driven from their homes, and now this.

I'm as poor as them, Borenson thought. Poorer, for at least they have a few sacks full of belongings.

Borenson sat down on the rocks; Myrrima knelt at his side. Draken and Sage followed, and all of them focused on Erin, weeping, their eyes full of concern.

Borenson's youngest daughter was fading. There was nothing that anyone could do. Perhaps Myrrima's touch and her kisses could ease the child's passing, but Myrrima could not save her.

For several long minutes Erin gasped, struggling only to breathe, too far gone to speak.

Then at last her eyelids fluttered, and Erin's piercing blue eyes rolled back into her head. Her chest stopped rising, and now a gurgle escaped her throat as her chest fell one last time. It was a sound that Borenson associated with strangling.

Life fled from her.

Borenson sat cradling his sweet daughter Erin; Myrrima cried in despair.

There was nothing left to do but mourn.

A vast gaping void seemed to yawn wide and black in Borenson's soul.

There is no beauty in death, he realized.

❧ 2 ❧

THE CROW RIDER

The eyes of the Great Wyrm are upon you, though you see her not, for she can ride the mind of the rat and the roach, the crow and the owl. She is aware of all of your doings, and will take vengeance for those who are weak, and offer blessings to those who serve her well.

—From the Wyrmling Catechism

In the cool light of predawn, a carrion crow searched a tidal pool, tilting her head to the right to listen for prey and to get a better look into the pool. The water was flat and as clear as crystal. In the shallows the crow spotted myriads of anemones, bright starbursts of green and purple, while orange starfish grazed along the rocks among gray-blue barnacles. In the deeper water an ugly sculpin fish, mottled in shades of muddy brown, lay finning in the sand. The crow held back from gulping it down, for the fish was full of bones that could lodge in her chicks' throat.

She was seeking for soft young shrimp that might be trudging about in the shallows, but saw a cockle in the sand, its heart-shaped shell wide open. She grabbed it in her beak, but it snapped closed instantly.

So she hurled it against a rock until the shell shattered. Then she held the cockle under one talon while she pulled the sweet meat free with her beak.

Suddenly the carrion crow felt a cool touch, a wind that hinted at winter, and looked up in alarm, ruffling her feathers. She cawed in warning to others of her kind, though the beach was empty, and then peered about, her black eyes blinking as she searched for the source of her fear.

There was a shape above her, hiding beneath a twisted pine on a craggy ledge. It was not moving. It was large and white of skin, much like the wyrmlings that the crow sometimes saw marching along the ridge in the predawn. But it was ill-shaped, and though it had sockets for eyes, she saw nothing in its eye holes but empty shadows.

Suddenly the bloated figure dropped, its ugly white skin deflating, like a bubble in the water that has popped. In that instant, a shadow blurred toward her, and the crow recognized the source of her fear. . . .

Crull-maldor lunged from the shadows, abandoning her cloak of glory, her malevolent spirit but a darker shade among the morning shadows, and she seized the crow. She did not grab it with physical hands, did not rend it with teeth or fingers. Instead, she took it with her mind and her will, forcing her spirit into the tiny shell of its body, grasping hold of its consciousness.

Almost, Crull-maldor could imagine the voice of her ancient master Yultonkin warning, "Do not be too eager to seize the mind of a bird, for birds are prey to many, to the hawk and coyote, the bobcat and the mink, and if you should die while your two minds are joined, you may never be able to return to your flesh."

So once she had seized control of the bird's mind, Crull-maldor blinked, peering about for signs of danger, looking out from the eyes of the crow.

The world was distorted. The crow's eyes were set upon the side of its head, and so it had a vast field of vision, and it could focus with only one eye at a time. The crow saw a wider spectrum of colors than Crull-maldor could with her own eyes. The crow saw the blacks and whites and reds that a wyrmling can see, but it also saw greens and blues and yellows, and everything had a crystalline clarity that Crull-maldor envied.

So Crull-maldor scanned for danger.

The beach was a wasteland, rocky and uninviting. A few huge walruses could be seen in the distance, surfing in upon some waves to spend the day swatting at sand flies on the beach. But there was little else. Few gulls. No hawks or foxes.

The lich had little to fear in the way of predators, she knew. The powerful spells that let her cling to life allowed her to exist only by siphoning off spiritual energy from creatures around her, and as she drew off that energy, the plants and animals around her weakened and succumbed. Most of the Northern Wastes were barren of life not because they were infertile, but because the presence of her kind drew so much from the land. There were no fine trees here anymore, and fewer herds of caribou and musk oxen than there had once been. Crull-maldor and her disciples had sucked the life from such creatures long ago. Now the lifeless land left her weak. Nearly all that survived within fifty miles of here was a few tenacious gorse bushes, insects, and the larger creatures that haunted the beaches.

Now comfortable, Crull-maldor gobbled the tender yellow innards of the cockle in one swallow. It tasted of sand and shell and salt. The savor was not altogether pleasing, but she would need sustenance this day.

The carrion crow leapt into the air, then flew up into the pines. Crull-maldor loved the sense of freedom that came with flying.

The bird was eager to return to its nest, regurgitate the cockle into the mouth of her babes. But Crull-maldor wrestled for control, forbidding it.

It was a struggle, a constant struggle, to take control of living things. Even after a hundred and eighty-two years of practicing the skill, Crull-maldor found her hold upon this beast to be tenuous.

Yet she held on to the crow with her mind. Seizing it with claw and talons would not have been half so cruel, for the crow ached to return to its nest.

As the sun rose, a luminous pearl climbing up from the sea, the carrion crow found itself leaping into the air, and flying out over the waters to the south.

Crull-maldor dominated the crow completely now, and peered out through its eyes, scanning the distant horizon for ships.

All that she saw were a few large wyrmling fishing vessels, their square sails the color of blood.

The crow would tire and falter long before it reached the distant shore, some two hundred miles south, Crull-maldor knew. When it did, Crull-maldor would let it fall and drown. Until then, she felt the exhilaration of flight. . . .

Such was her lot, day after endless day. There is a price to be paid for working in the service of evil, and the lich lord Crull-maldor was paying it. She was too powerful in the ways of magic for others to kill. Indeed, she had mastered dark magics known to no one else. Thus, she held the exalted position of Grand Wizard of the Wyrmling Hordes, and was far too dangerous for her political rivals to want around. So one hundred and eighty-seven years ago, the emperor Zul-torac had "promoted" her, sending her to lead the garrison at the wyrmling fortress in the Great Wastes of the North.

As such, it was her duty to protect this land from intrusion, to keep the humans from ever returning. Her armies occupied the wastes, and it was her job to feed and clothe them. Thus, her hunting parties scoured the lands in the far north hunting for caribou, seals, and great white bears. Her fishermen plied the coastal waters, taking the great serpentine leviathans that chased schools of fish to the north each summer.

She also commanded scores of miners and workers: smiths to forge weapons, armorers to carve mail from the bones of world wyrms, sorcerers to manufacture goods that could be used as tribute to the empire—cloaks of glory that would let a lich walk in the sun, artificial wings, and wight wombs to shelter and nourish the spirits of the newly dead.

But though Crull-maldor was Lord of the Northern Wastes, and thus had an exalted title and rank, hers was an appointment that would take her nowhere. She had no opportunity for advancement, no hopes of ever returning to the great fortress at Rugassa. Serving well at her post would earn her no reward. She had been disposed of utterly, and forgotten.

In more ways than one, she was the living dead.

Yet always there was the hope that the emperor Zul-torac would fall from grace, and that the great Creator—Despair—would need someone to replace him. Crull-maldor knew that it would happen eventually, and in that moment, if all went well, Despair would remember Crull-maldor's name. It was only a matter of time, but Crull-maldor lived in hopes of that moment.

Thus, she did her master's bidding.

By night the wyrmlings of her garrison would usher out into the wastes, keeping watch over the ocean shores lest a cohort of humans try to settle. Theirs was a futile watch, for it had been fifty-eight years since a human had been seen.

By day, while her wyrmlings toiled, Crull-maldor kept her own watch.

She climbed higher into the air. The seas were glassy calm for as far as the crow's sharp eyes could perceive.

Killer whales were spouting as they herded a school of salmon along, and a few gulls rode the calm waters. Crull-maldor spotted a young leviathan undulating over the waves. Nothing else moved.

There were no humans riding on the waters.

But the lich had more than one reason for riding this crow. Crull-maldor was seeking to extend her skills, to learn to ride in the minds of creatures perfectly.

She wanted to learn not only to control others, but to avoid detection while doing it.

In particular, some who were strong in arcane powers would be able to detect her presence. Her ancient nemesis, the emperor, was always wary, always watching.

Someday, she thought, I will ride a crow into the southern lands, and there I will spy upon my enemies.

Each day she risked it. Each day she grew in skill. Yet each day she was rebuffed.

So now she blanked out her mind, seeking to hide her thoughts, her intent, and concentrated simply on the mechanics of flight: flapping the crow's wings, breathing steadily, ignoring hunger and thirst.

More than an hour into the flight Crull-maldor was attacked.

For those who had the ears to hear, a high-pitched growl of warning, like the snarl of a jaguar, sounded in alarm in the spirit world. At the cry, thousands of other voices rose up, iterating the same warning, as an army of liches went on the defensive. The emperor's minions struck out blindly, sending thousands of spirit darts that rose up from the southern horizon, each a fiery nimbus that streaked through the sky like ball lightning, hissing and crackling, each discernible only to the eyes of Crull-maldor's spirit.

One dart struck, and the crow's wings cramped. Dazed by the attack, the bird fainted. As the crow plummeted toward the sea, Crull-maldor fought for control, flapping furiously.

Distantly, Crull-maldor heard Zul-torac's simpering laugh. The emperor never tired of his petty games.

The emperor was jealous of Crull-maldor's powers, her ability to "ride" others, to project her thoughts into the minds of lesser creatures. He was also afraid of her.

Each day, Crull-maldor tested his strength—as she ranged farther and farther across the waters. Each day, she drew a little closer before one of his spies discovered her.

Crull-maldor fought to still the crow's wings, let them catch the air. She soared for a moment as she strengthened her tenuous hold upon the bird.

"Be gone, little Crow Rider," the emperor whispered to Crull-maldor's spirit. "Go find yourself a statue to defecate on. You may never return. You may never again lay your eyes upon the mainland."

"Every man's days are numbered, my emperor," Crull-maldor shot back, "even yours. Especially yours!"

The wind was wet and heavy under the crow's wings, making flight a labor. The bird regained consciousness, and began to flap with difficulty as Crull-maldor gave it its head.

The lich waited to hear more of her old enemy's banter. Perhaps he would send another hail of spirit missiles, hoping to strike down her mount, hoping that the crow would drown while Crull-maldor's spirit was still harnessed to the beast. But there was an unaccustomed silence.

Suddenly the crow spotted something in the heavens: a bright light, like a new moon glowing above.

Crull-maldor wondered if it was some new form of attack, and the crow slowed on the wing, cocked its head to the left to peer upward, and soared for a moment.

The orb grew in brilliance and expanded as it rushed toward the earth. The crow's heart beat wildly, and Crull-maldor loosed her hold enough to let the crow wheel and head inland.

In seconds the orb filled the heavens, and Crull-maldor gazed up in wonder.

She saw a world falling toward her, vast and beautiful. Brilliant white clouds swirled over a cerulean sea. There was a vast red continent—a desert, she suspected, and white-capped mountains. Still the world plummeted toward her, growing in her field of view.

It's like a falling star, Crull-maldor thought, one that will crush the whole world! What a beautiful way to die.

She spotted rivers running like veins of silver through greenest jade, and saw vast forests of emerald and jasper.

Then the world struck, and tumult filled the skies.

The crow cawed and flapped wildly, its heart pounding, but there was no physical blow, no massive assault of rock hurtling down from the heavens.

Instead, Crull-maldor felt energy sizzling through her as bolts of static lightning suddenly roared through the heavens. Atoms fell in a cold drizzle, pounding through her head and back, as if to force the crow down into a watery grave. Eerie lights blazed in the heavens, pinwheels of white fire, and a mist exploded up from the sea.

Then the new world stopped falling, and every atom locked into place.

Something slammed into the crow, a shock more mental than physical, and it began dropping toward the water. The pain of the blow fogged Crull-maldor's eyes, and for a moment she fought to see. Crull-maldor seized control of the small animal, steadied its wings, and went into a blind glide.

Then it seemed as if a film fell away from her vision, and a new world was revealed: ships plied the waters below her, fishing vessels bobbing on the sea as fishermen threw their nets, schooners racing south with sails full of wind. Even from a distance, Crull-maldor recognized the forms of humans.

Dozens of vessels spread out along the coast in every direction, and off to her left a city sprawled along the arms of a bay. Where once there had been nothing but rocks and scree scattered over the barrens, now there were vast fields and forests in the distance.

Crull-maldor fought down mounting excitement.

Somehow two worlds had collided. She'd seen a world falling from the heavens. In an instant everything had changed in ways she'd never imagined.

The barrens were now filled with people, with life— life that would sustain her, make her strong. To her right, she spotted more cities all along the coast. The humans were vast in number. She guessed that hundreds of thousands now lived in the Northern Wastes. Maybe millions, she realized.

Yet as wondrous as this all seemed, as she flew along Crull-maldor had a second insight: all morning long she had been struggling to retain control of her crow. Now, she flew steadily, strongly, and hardly even noticed the crow's struggle to escape her grasp.

I have greater power in this new world, Crull-maldor realized.

Crull-maldor could not yet guess what had wrought such a mighty change, but she planned to find out.

She turned the crow, went riding on the morning thermals toward her fortress to the north. She would need to consult the elders in the City of the Dead.

❧ 3 ❧

RAIN IN THE DARKNESS

It takes a strong man to do what must be done, regardless of how unpleasant the deed might be. As a Walkin, I expect you to be forever strong.

—Baron Owen Walkin

Rain turned into iron that day. While some in her family seemed content to just sit and wallow in despair, Rain vowed to survive this disaster. So she went to work.

She helped carry her aunt Della up the ridge before the flood took the Hacker River Valley; then she spent the rest of the morning doing what she could to make the children comfortable.

First she found some shelter beneath an exposed cliff near a streamlet where the grass was thick enough for a bed. She helped lay the family's blankets on the wet ground, and then tried to start a fire.

This turned out to be no easy task, for kelp and coral mingled among plants on the ground and seawater had soaked everything. So Rain took some of the children to find dead branches in a ravine up among the red-rock, but found more sea urchins and brightly colored anemones than good dry wood.

Still, she pulled off the bark from some sticks, exposing the dry pith. Soon a wan blaze sputtered in the open air.

In no time at all the children ran about and began to

gather food. They found lobsters and eels lying on the ground, with octopuses and halibut—rare treasures from the sea.

These they cooked above the fire, making the biggest feast that Rain could recall having eaten in many years.

With his belly filled, her father Owen went out to explore. Like everyone else, he felt strangely exhausted, and walked with less energy than a man twice his age.

Something has happened to us, Rain thought. Some sort of wizardry has sapped our vitality.

Rain felt so weary that she feared that if she stopped moving, she might just lie down and die. They all felt so.

Rain's aunt Della said it best when she woke from her faint. Rain asked, "How do you feel?"

Rain's mother Greta had offered, "It's okay to say it. You feel like cow shit. We all feel that way."

But Della, never one to be outdone, countered, "No, I feel like cow shit that's been trampled on by the rest of the herd."

Then she just lay in the shadows, the sweet grass for her bed, and asked, "What happened?"

Rain delighted in saying, "Nothing much. Half of Landesfallen has sunk into the sea, flooding everything, and we managed to drag your lazy carcass up the cliff. I was sure that you were faking, just trying to get out of work. Oh, and for some reason, there are starfish and crabs and kelp growing everywhere, and Sir Borenson turned into a giant eight feet tall—with horns."

Della propped herself up on an elbow and peered around, looking at the growths of coral clinging to the rocks above her. The Borenson family sat in a little knot, about a hundred yards away, hovering around Erin.

"Is that girl dead?" Della asked.

Rain nodded, and a look of dread crossed Della's face. She hadn't asked about her own children. "Did any of ours . . . ?"

"No," Greta answered, "thank the Powers."

Della began asking questions, the same questions that everyone else had. What happened? How could this happen? What shall we do?

Rain had no answers. The flood could be explained easily enough by an earthquake. But the change to Sir Borenson? The strange tornadoes of light?

Her mind revolted from wondering or worrying about it.

Instead she watched the Borensons, her heart aching for them. She longed to go to Draken, put her arms around him and comfort him. But she dared not do it in front of his father and mother, particularly that father, now that he had changed into something . . . monstrous.

Her face reddened, and she looked away.

She couldn't look at Borenson without feeling guilty. He'd said that they'd stolen cherries, and it was true. The children in her family had gone out in the early mornings, rampaging through the trees, filling their bellies.

The Walkins had done their best to hide it even from Draken. Rain had begged her parents to make her brothers and sisters stop, but Rain's father had downplayed the deed, saying that the children's need for food outweighed Borenson's rights as a landowner.

At least Rain had been able to keep the children out of the Borenson's garden, though the neighbors' gardens hadn't fared as well.

We are thieves, she thought. Borenson was right. But me and my family will be thieves no more.

Today, making such a vow was easy, she knew. There was no one to steal from, nothing to take.

But winter was coming, and her family would be forced to find shelter somewhere upriver, in a town. Hard times would surely follow. What would they do then?

When Owen Walkin came back from his little scouting trip, the only report that he could muster was "There's a whole lot of fish and whatnot on the other side of the hill."

He knelt on the ground. His face looked gray and weathered in the morning sun, and his eyes were dazed. "What do you figure happened?" he asked no one in particular, as if perhaps the Walkin clan had somehow managed to answer the riddle in his absence. "I mean, I mean nothing adds right. The great wave could be explained, but . . . the fish on dry ground . . . and what happened to Draken's dad?"

He was still in shock.

"Don't worry," she said. "We'll figure everything out."

Owen put his head in his hands, shook it. He peered up at his brothers and his sons. "I've been thinking. Everyone down in Sweetgrass got washed away. Everyone in the whole valley got washed away. . . ."

"Yes?" his brother said.

"They should be floating to the surface soon," Owen said meaningfully. Then he added, "We should be the first to the harvest. . . ."

The idea sickened Rain. She wasn't a grave robber. She'd been raised as a proper lady of the court. Ever since Warlord Grunswallen had Rain as his bed servant, her family's estate had been falling endlessly.

Her father and his brothers had waylaid Grunswallen in the streets, leaving him in a bloody heap.

The whole family had fled their homes that day, taking what riches they could. Three months of travel got them out of the country. The family hadn't had enough gold to buy passage to Landesfallen, but her father had come up with it somehow.

Rain dared not ask where he'd stolen the money. Hopefully, no one had died for it.

Petty theft had become a way of life; all of the younger children in the clan were doing it. But robbing from the dead?

What I was, she thought, I am no more. And I do not like what I am becoming.

Rain felt unclean, and remaining in her father's presence made her feel even filthier. She got up and walked over to the Borenson family.

She felt like a traitor by doing so, as if she was switching camps.

When she reached the Borensons, she stopped for an instant and hugged Draken, wrapping one arm around his back and giving him a squeeze. She dared not show more affection openly.

The giant, Sir Borenson, stood talking softly, his voice a deep rumble, like distant thunder. She peered up at him, at the nubs of horns above his temples. He hardly looked human.

If anyone can understand how people can change, Rain thought, he should be able to.

Draken's mother Myrrima smiled at her. "So," she said, as if some mystery had been solved at long last, "you're the reason that Draken has taken up 'hunting' so suddenly. I thought that there might be more to it than a taste for burrow bear."

"Yes, milady," Rain said, giving a small curtsy. She was a proper lady of the court after all.

"No need to curtsy here," Myrrima said. "My husband is a baron over nothing in Landesfallen."

The family was standing in a cluster, though they had moved a few paces away from Erin's body. No one spoke for a long moment. Instead, they stood with heads hanging, deep in thought, and Rain realized that she had broken in on a family council.

She waited for someone to ask her the inevitable question "What do you think happened?," but no one did.

"Okay then," Sir Borenson said. "Now that we're settled, I'll head inland to search for survivors, and Draken can go seaward." He did not say it, but Myrrima would obviously stay here with their daughters.

"How long will you be gone?" Myrrima asked.

"As long as it takes," Borenson said. "If we find anyone who is hurt or in need, we'll take care of them as best that we can. But it might be a while before we can make it back to camp."

Myrrima listened to his words, worry evident in the creases on her face. "I'll keep a fire going."

Rain felt glad to hear of their quest. She cringed at the thought that some poor child, cold and broken, might be washed up along the shore. With the fury of the flood, it seemed a vain hope that anyone might have escaped, but it was a hope that she had to cling to.

The group broke as Sir Borenson and his wife went off to speak in private. Rain took that moment to stop and hold Draken's hand. She stood gazing into his dark eyes.

"My father will be heading toward the coast, too," she said, realizing that she would have to warn her father, let him know that he should couch his pilfering from the dead as a rescue mission.

"I'll be glad for the company," Draken said.

For nearly two hours now her clan had left Draken's family alone, giving them time and space to grieve for little Erin. Rain had been reticent to get close.

She almost asked Draken, "What do *you* think happened?" But the words died on her tongue. Her head was hurting from wondering so much, and she knew that he couldn't possibly have an answer. Indeed, at any moment, she expected him to ask the question.

But he never did. He merely stood, gazing into her eyes.

Suddenly she understood. "You *know* what happened! You know why there are fish on dry ground!"

He squeezed her hands, looked toward her family. "I have a guess. . . ."

"What is it?" she demanded.

"I can't say. I am honor-bound not to speak of it. Someday, when we're married, perhaps. . . ."

Rain understood secrets. Draken had his secrets, she had hers.

"When we're man and wife," she said, "I want no secrets between us."

She clung to his hand as if she were drowning. She knew that she'd have to reveal her own secrets to him someday. How could she tell him what Warlord Grunswallen had forced her to do?

Draken nodded. Rain glanced back toward her father's camp; her father, Owen, rose from a crouch, along with his brother Colm.

She excused herself from Draken's presence and warned her father of the Borensons' intentions.

Moments later, Sir Borenson and most of the other men set out from camp, splitting off in two directions. For long minutes Rain stood watching Draken as he trundled away.

I'll wait for him, she thought. I'll make my bed near the Borensons, so that I'll awaken when he returns.

Late that night Sir Borenson came stumbling in to camp, closer to dawn than to midnight. Myrrima had been awake all night, thinking about the implications of the great change that had occurred.

Her husband had told her little before he hurried off on his rescue mission. He'd told her how he had merged with another man in the binding of the worlds, but he had cut the conversation short when Rain entered their camp.

So when he returned that night she asked, "Why don't you tell me what you are afraid to say in front of the others?" Myrrima studied his face by starlight, waiting for an answer, but the giant only hesitated, searching for the right words.

The night was comfortless. Stars glimmered cold and dim through a strange misty haze. All afternoon, Myrrima had preened Erin's body for burial—washing her face, primping her clothes, braiding her hair in corn rows. It was the custom back in her homeland in Heredon to stay up at night with the newly dead, for their spirits often hovered nearby on that first few nights, and one could hope for one last glimpse during the long vigils, one last chance to say good-bye.

Borenson had been gone for hours, scrabbling along the shore, calling for survivors. When he'd walked into camp, he reported, "Mill Creek is gone, washed away." His voice was hoarse from overuse, from calling out.

He sat beside her little fire, his head hanging, gazing into the ash-covered embers, their dull red light too dim to reach his face.

Myrrima had anticipated that the town would be gone, but she suspected that her husband was weighed down by some greater worry. He had secrets, and she knew from the way that he got up and began to pace that he was fighting to find the right words to tell her.

Myrrima had knelt all evening with Sage, and together they wept. They'd mourned Erin and all of the friends and neighbors that they had known. They'd considered their lot and mourned for themselves.

She worried for her oldest daughter, Talon, who was off in Mystarria, and for Fallion, Jaz, and Rhianna—whom she loved as much as if they were her own offspring. The suspicion that she had lost Talon and the others was growing minute by minute.

I lost more than a child today, Myrrima knew. She dared not say it yet, but she feared that she had lost a husband.

Oh, when she looked at the giant, she imagined that she could see the old Borenson. His features were there, somehow hidden in all of that mass of flesh, the way that one can sometimes look at a knot of wood on a tree and imagine seeing a half-hidden face in it.

But she estimated him to be over seven and a half feet tall now, and he could not weigh less than four hundred and fifty pounds.

She could never be intimate with such a monster, not like a husband and wife should be. They could never be tender or close.

She suspected that Borenson had something to tell her, something that would cause her more grief, so Myrrima asked the question that was most upon her mind. "Why don't you tell me what you were afraid to say in front of the others?"

"Where do you want me to start?" Borenson begged, shrugging. It was a peculiar gesture, one that he used to signify that he would hold nothing back.

"Start with your life on that shadow world," Myrrima said. "You had a family, a wife, I suppose?"

"Her name is Gatunyea," Borenson said in that deep voice. It was as if a bull were trying to approximate human speech. "We lived in what you would call Rofehavan, in the north of Mystarria, in a city called Luciare. She bore me two fine sons, Arad and Destonarry, and I have a daughter close to Talon's age named Tholna."

Myrrima sighed. There was so much that she didn't understand. If two men had merged into one, why did he appear here and not in Mystarria, or somewhere between the two lands? "I see. . . . Do you think that they are still alive?"

"I'm alive," he said. It was all the argument he could give. "You're alive. Our children survived. Things have changed in the binding, but I suspect that my . . . other family is still out there."

Now Myrrima spoke the hardest words that had ever come from her mouth. "You need to go to them. You'll need to find out if this wife of yours survived. If she is alive, she and the children will be beside themselves. You must reassure them."

They both knew what Myrrima was really saying. He was a giant now, and he was no longer suited to be her husband. There was a chance that he still had a wife out there. It only made sense that he go to her.

"Myrrima," Borenson said with infinite sadness.

"We both know the truth," Myrrima said, struggling to be strong, to hide even a hint of the loss she felt. "You have changed in the binding. Though I'll love you forever, some things are impossible."

She could not make love to such a man.

"You know me," Borenson said. "I may look like a monster on the outside, but I am the same man who has slept at your side these past twenty years. My love for you—"

"You have another woman, one who must be sick with grief. Your children must be wondering where you are. . . ."

Borenson hung his head, reached out and stroked her cheek with one finger.

He would have to sail back to Rofehavan, she knew. But that was easier said than done. They had no boat. Perhaps they could buy passage on a ship, but they had nothing to buy passage with. Their only shelter for the night was a bed of ferns at the base of a cliff.

A great feast they'd made in the midafternoon, but by morning all of the sea life would be going to rot.

Myrrima had to wonder how they'd survive the coming week, much less make it back to Rofehavan.

She didn't even want to think about going back.

Myrrima had always felt so strong, but something was wrong. Her muscles ached as if from fatigue, a weariness that made her fear sleeping, lest she never wake again. To stand or move took immense effort. The numbing weariness wasn't just upon her, but upon her children and the Walkins, too—seemingly everyone but Borenson.

"It could be months or years before I make it back to Rofehavan," Borenson confirmed. "All of Garion's Port is drowned. A ship might come in time, but even if it does, I may not be able to buy passage. . . ." He took a deep breath, as if to broach a topic that he dared not discuss, and then released it again, his head shaking from side to side.

All of his old mannerisms are there, Myrrima realized. It is as if my husband is wearing different flesh.

"Say what is on your mind," Myrrima begged.

"I want you and the children to come back to Rofehavan with me," Borenson said. "I dare not leave you here without food or a home—" Myrrima began to object, for even if she wanted to go back to Rofehavan, finding a ship might be impossible.

"Hear me out!" Borenson begged. Myrrima fell silent as he struggled for words.

"I have been thinking," he said, "for long hours. Not everything is clear to me yet, but much *is* clear.

"I believe that Fallion bound two worlds together as an experiment, to see what would happen in such an event, and I believe that his experiment failed.

"We could be in grave danger, more danger than you—or Fallion—yet know.

"You wonder why I have joined with my shadow self and you have not? I have an answer: On our former world there were millions and millions of people, strewn all across Rofehavan and Indhopal, Inkarra and Landesfallen. But on the shadow world where I came from, humankind was all but wiped out. There were only forty thousand of us, living in one vast enclave upon a mountain deep within the borders of what you call Mystarria. Our enemies had all but destroyed us.

"I think that you did not join with your shadow self," Borenson said softly, "because you had no shadow upon that world to join with."

Dead, Myrrima realized. On that world my shadow self was dead.

It made sense. She felt more dead than alive right now. The strange exhaustion that had come upon her . . .

"On the shadow world," Borenson continued, "there are creatures called wyrmlings. They are giants, larger than I am. They're fierce, and they eat human flesh. They've hunted mankind nearly to extinction."

"Are there other creatures from that world that we do not have on ours?" Myrrima asked.

"A few," Borenson said. "The birds and squirrels are different, as you will see."

"Are there other monsters besides wyrmlings—things that we should be warned about?"

The giant shook his head no. "The wyrmlings," Borenson continued, "number in the millions. They hide in great tunnels and warrens beneath the ground by day, and only come out to hunt by night. A large wyrmling stands up to nine feet tall and can weigh seven hundred pounds."

"So they are like the arr, or like sea apes?" Myrrima asked. The arr was a race of giants that had once lived in the mountains throughout Rofehavan. They were like apes in form, but much larger.

"They look more like men," Borenson said. "Legend

says that they once were men, but they began to breed themselves for size and strength, just as my people do. In time they changed."

Myrrima shook her head. "How can that be?"

"Are not the beagle and the mastiff both brothers to the wolf?" Borenson asked. "Do not the pony and the warhorse both come from the same stock? It is the same with people. Some say that humans and wyrmlings share common ancestors, but I do not believe it. When you see one, you will know. They have no love or compassion. All that is in them is fierceness and hunger.

"They live for one reason, hoping for only one reward," Borenson said, and he paused for a moment, as if unsure is he should speak more, "they hope that their evil deeds will be great enough so that a locus may feed upon their souls."

Myrrima gasped. A locus was a parasite, a being that fed upon men's spirits. Once it attached to a human host, it controlled him. It rode him the way that a man rides a horse, turning him this way and that. A man who had lost his soul to a locus became a crazed thing, ruthless and vile.

"They *want* this?" Myrrima asked. It was a horror beyond imagination.

Borenson frowned, as if searching for the right words. "They have been trained to want it, for generation after generation. They are taught to believe that the soul of a man dies shortly after the death of the body, and that his spirit is like a mist that fades and dissipates. They have been taught to believe that only a locus is immortal, and if it feeds upon them, consumes their spirit, it will live on."

Borenson paused. A star shot overhead, and in the

distance out among the rocks a herd of rangits suddenly began to bound away, startled by some noise, thumping as their huge bodies landed upon the compact ground. Cicadas were buzzing up among the trees. Myrrima wondered where Draken was, when he would return. The night was half gone, and dawn was mere hours away. She hunched up a little, hugging herself for warmth. It was a summer night, but dampness made it feel cool.

She sniffed. The Walkins' fire just up the trail had gone out, leaving only the scent of ash. The night flowers of a nearby bush had opened so that the shadows under a ledge were filled with a wonder: white petals like wild peas that glowed with their own inner light; the shadows were filled with numinous stars.

A great uneasiness began to assail Myrrima. If what Borenson said was true, then a new horror had arisen in Rofehavan, something so monstrous that it boggled the mind.

She could not quite fathom it. She could not imagine people engaging in a breeding program that spanned generations. The mind revolted at the thought. One could not help whom one fell in love with. Her son was proof of that. Draken was hardly more than a boy, but he had found this girl Rain, and he wanted to marry her. He seemed totally devoted to her.

She tried to adjust her thinking, and the dangers presented by the wyrmlings seemed clear.

Yet Borenson spoke of returning to Rofehavan, and of taking her family back there.

"You want to go and fight!" she said.

The giant set his jaw, the way her husband used to do when he was determined upon some course. "I have to go back and fight—and you must come with me!"

Myrrima wanted to argue against his plan. She'd fought in wars before. She'd fought Raj Ahten's armies, and had slain reavers in battle. She was the one who had slain a Darkling Glory at Castle Sylvarresta.

Sir Borenson had been a mighty warrior, as had she. But they'd both lost their endowments long ago.

"No," she said. "We're too old for another war. You once told me yourself that you would never fight again."

"We don't always join the battle," Borenson said. "Sometimes the battle joins us."

"We don't even know that the wyrmlings are alive," Myrrima objected.

"You have sea anemones on the rocks above your head and crabs walking on dry ground," Borenson said. "How can you doubt that other creatures from my world—the wyrmlings—survived?"

A new realization struck Myrrima. "You think that the wyrmlings will come here?"

"Eventually," Borenson said. "They will come. Right now, it's nighttime. The wyrmlings' home is spread across the hills near Mystarria's old border with Longmot, while fortresses dot the land. The wyrmlings have come out of their lairs for the night—and discovered a new wonder: humans, small folk the size of you and Sage. What do you think those monsters will do with them?"

The very notion struck Myrrima with horror. Yes, she sympathized with the plight of her people. But she also recognized that there was no saving those folks tonight. Whatever happened to them would happen. It would take months for them to travel to Rofehavan, even if she decided to go.

Every instinct warned against it. She was a mother now, with children to protect.

"I can only hope that the folk of Mystarria will band together, form some sort of resistance."

"They might," Borenson said. "But I don't know if they stand a chance against the wyrmlings. You see: The magics of the shadow world worked differently from ours. The wyrmling lords are not . . . entirely alive. The wyrmling lords are wights. Their lord, the Dread Emperor Zul-torac, is no more substantial than a mist."

Myrrima wondered at this. If wyrmlings were ruled by wraiths . . .

"We had no magic to fight them," Borenson said. "The wraiths flee from the sun and the wyrmlings make their home in lightless holes; our men feared to seek out their lairs, for even if by the power of our arms we could hope to win against the wyrmling hordes, we could not fight their dark masters."

"Couldn't you cast enchantments upon your weapons?"

"There are no water wizards in their world," Borenson said. "With cold steel we might be able to wound a wight, but that was the best that we could hope for, and even in wounding one, we would most likely lose our own lives."

"I see," Myrrima said. She was a wizardess, Water's Warrior.

"We can hike from here down to Garion's Port," Borenson said. "There are lots of traders plying the waters this time of summer. One will find us."

"Perhaps," Myrrima said, "but where will they land? Garion's Port is submerged. All of the landmarks that showed where it was are underwater."

"Still, the ships will come," Borenson said. "With any luck we can hail one, buy passage."

"We have no money."

"Look at me," Borenson said. He lifted her chin, forcing her to behold his might. "I can do the work of four men. You can work, and Draken can too. I suspect that we can buy passage with our sweat. Maybe not on the first ship that passes, but eventually. . . ."

Myrrima wondered. If a ship came from Rofehavan, it would be looking for a port so that it could sell its goods. Its captain would be hoping to take on food and stores, not hire a family of destitute beggars to go limping home after a profitless voyage.

Still, Borenson voiced his hopes. "This flood may have wrecked the coasts, but ships that were on the high seas will still be intact. With any luck, we can reach Mystarria before the winter storms."

"Two months, or three, with any luck," Myrrima agreed. "It might take that long to hail a passing ship. We'll have to hope that some captain will have mercy on us."

"I did not say that the trip would be easy," Borenson agreed, "but staying here would be no easier. We have no crops, no land, no seeds or implements to till the ground. Summer is half over. We'll be eating wild rangit for the winter, you'll be sewing clothes from burrow-bear skins, using nothing more than a sharp bone for a needle.

"At least if we reach Rofehavan, we can hope to find a port somewhere. We can live like civilized folk."

Myrrima didn't like feeling cornered. She wanted to make a rational choice, not get bullied into some fool-headed course. "Even if we make it," Myrrima said, "what do you hope to find? If what you say is true, then all of Rofehavan will be overrun. Here we may struggle to eat, but at least we won't have to fight hordes of wyrmlings.

Our folk haven't the strength to fight such monsters, not without blood metal."

Blood metal was forged to make forcibles, the magical branding irons that Myrrima's people used to transfer attributes—brawn, grace, speed. Each branding iron had a rune forged upon it that controlled the attribute it could harness. As a vassal was branded, the forcible drew out the desired attribute, so that when the iron next touched a lord, the lord would gain the vassal's power. The spell lasted so long as both of them remained alive, and the forcible was destroyed in the process.

Thus a lord who had taken endowments from his vassals became more than a man, for he might have the strength of ten men, the speed of five, the intelligence of three, the sight of five, and so on. Using such implements, Sir Borenson had become one of the greatest warriors of his generation.

But the blood-metal mines in Kartish had played out ten years back. There were no runelords of great stature anymore.

"Oh, there will be plenty of blood metal," Borenson assured Myrrima. "Upon the shadow world, folk had no use for it. Rune magic as we use it was unknown. But there is a large hill near Caer Luciare, a hill riddled with blood metal. And if there is one hill, there may be others.

"Let us hope that the folk of Rofehavan will put the metal to good use—that by the time we reach those green shores, the wyrmlings are subdued."

Myrrima's mouth dropped. It seemed to her that the world could not get more twisted, more turned upside down.

She saw clearly now why he wanted her to return to Mystarria: to fight a great war.

Home, she thought. There is land aplenty back in Mystarria. All we have to do is take it back from the monsters.

"I'll come," Myrrima said, though she could not help but worry.

Borenson said softly, "Good, I would appreciate it if you would tell the children and the Walkins of our plan. They might take the news better from you."

"All right," Myrrima said. But she couldn't just leave it at that. "You need to understand: I will enchant weapons for you, but I will not let you take my children into war."

Borenson said, "Draken is old enough to make up his own mind. Unless I miss my guess, I can't talk him out of marrying that slip of a girl, and if he so chooses, you won't be able to stop him from going to war."

He was right, of course. She couldn't stop Draken, and she wouldn't stop her husband.

Borenson peered to the west, filled with nervous energy, as if eager to be on his way across the ocean. He looked off into the distance, where the shadows of trees and brush melded with the shadows of red-rock. "I wonder what is keeping Draken?"

"Fatigue," Myrrima guessed. "We're all so tired. I suspect that they wandered as far as they could, and decided to settle for the night."

"I'd better go and find him," Borenson said, "make sure that he's okay."

"In the dark?"

"I've hunted by starlight all of my life," Borenson said. "Or at least Aaath Ulber has. I can no longer sleep by night: that's when the wyrmlings come out."

In a moment he was off, trundling along a winding

trail that dipped and rose. The trail was made by game, mostly—wild rangits and hunting cats. But men used it from time to time, too. Several times a week she had seen horsemen up here. During the rainy season, the ridge trail wasn't as muddy as the old river road.

So she watched him trudge away, a lumpy malformed monstrosity fading into the darkness.

I'll follow him to Mystarria, she thought, but if I have my way, I won't be going to fight any wyrmling horde. I'll go to win my husband back. I'll go to find Fallion and plead with him to unbind the worlds.

Rain lay in the deep grass beneath the shadows of the cliff, as silent as the boulders around her. She'd heard Borenson trudging home in the dark, tramping through the dry leaves that she'd swept onto the trail.

She didn't understand everything that the giant had said, but she understood enough. The Borensons would be going away.

Rain chewed her lip, thought about her own family. Her father had killed men for her benefit. He'd stolen and lied to bring her family here, where they might have some hope of living in peace and safety.

She tried to imagine what it would be like to sail back to Mystarria with the Borensons, and she couldn't envision it. It would be a betrayal to her father, to people who had sacrificed everything for her honor.

There is only one thing to do, she decided. I'll have to convince Draken to stay here, with me.

After Borenson left, Myrrima tried to sleep. There was a patch of sandy ground among the rocks, where a little sweet clover grew. Myrrima had gathered a few ferns and laid the leaves out as a cushion. That was all that the family had for a bed, and she huddled with Sage for warmth, their bodies spooned together. The child felt so cold.

Today was supposed to be the High Summer Festival, and because it was high summer, Myrrima didn't feel much need for a blanket. Yet sleep failed her.

The Walkins were all spread out in a separate camp, perhaps a hundred yards up the trail. While their fire died, Myrrima lay like a dazed bird, her mind racing from all that Borenson had told her.

While she rested there, eyes hardly blinking, she saw a girl tiptoeing down the trail, making not a sound. A mouse would have been hard-pressed to walk as quietly.

Rain is coming to see Draken, Myrrima thought. She can't bear to leave him alone.

Somehow, the realization gladdened her. Draken had lost so much already, Myrrima hoped that he would find a lasting love.

A cool wind blew over her, and Myrrima felt a sudden chill. It was cold, so cold.

Just as quickly, she realized that it wasn't the wind. The cold seemed to be inside her—reaching down to the bone. And the young woman coming toward her made too little sound. She was leaping over rocks, marching through deep grass and dry leaves.

Myrrima recognized the young woman now. It was Erin. It was the shade of her daughter, glowing softly, as if with some inner light. Yet her form was translucent.

Myrrima pushed herself up in a sitting position, heart racing. To be touched by a shade might mean her death. Myrrima's every instinct was to run.

Yet she longed to see her child one last time.

"Ware the shade!" someone in the Walkin clan hissed in the distance. It was an ancient warning.

Erin came, passing near Myrrima's bed. Her feet moved as if she was walking, but her body only glided, as if carried on the wind. She was dressed just as she had been in death.

She went past the edge of camp, over to her own still body, and stood for a moment, looking down, regarding it calmly.

Myrrima dared hope that the shade might notice her. Very often, the dead seemed only vaguely aware of the living, so Myrrima didn't expect much. But a loving glance would have warmed Myrrima's heart. A smile of recognition would have been a lifelong treasure.

The spirit knelt above her body, reached down a finger, and stroked her own lifeless chin.

Myrrima found tears streaming down her cheeks; she let out a sob, and hurriedly shook Sage, waking her, so that she too might see her sister one last time.

Then Erin turned and peered straight into Myrrima's eyes. Instantly the child drew close, covering eighty feet in the flutter of a heartbeat, and she did something that no shade on Myrrima's world had ever done before: Erin spoke, her child's voice slicing through the air like a rapier. "What are you doing here, Mother? You should go to the tree."

Myrrima's throat caught. She was too astonished to speak. But Sage had risen up on one elbow, and she spoke: "What tree?"

Erin looked to Sage. "The Earth King's tree: one of you should go there before night falls again. Before night falls forever."

A sob escaped Myrrima's throat. She longed to touch her daughter. "I love you."

Erin smiled. "I know. You mustn't worry. All of the neighbors are here. They're having a wonderful festival!" She pointed east, up toward Mill Creek.

As if carried on the wind, Myrrima suddenly heard the sounds of the fair: a joyful pandemonium. Minstrels strummed lutes and played the pipes and banged on drums. She heard the young men cheer uproariously as a lance cracked in a joust. There were children screaming with wild glee. In all her life, Myrrima had never heard such sounds of joy.

Then Erin peered at her again, and said, "Go to the Earth King's tree!"

With that, the shade dissipated like a morning mist burning beneath the sun. Yet though Erin's form was gone, Myrrima still felt the chill of the netherworld.

Sage climbed to her feet and stood peering off into the east. "Why does she want us to go to the Earth King's tree?"

Myrrima had no idea. She knew where the tree lay, of course. It was an oak tree—the only one in all of Landesfallen, up on Bald Hill, past the town of Fossil. Legend said that before the Earth King died, he'd traveled the world, seeking out people, putting them under his protective spell.

When he'd reached Bald Hill, he was an old man, failing in health. So he'd used the last of his powers to transform himself into a tree. Thus he stood there still, in the form of an oak, watching over the world.

"He's coming back!" Sage suddenly exulted as an odd notion took her. "The Earth King is returning!"

Myrrima stood, studied her daughter's clear face in the starlight, saw wonder in Sage's eyes.

"He can't be," Myrrima said calmly. "Gaborn is dead."

But Sage was too enamored of the idea. "Not dead," she said, "transformed. He's a wizard of wondrous power. Don't you see? He knew that his life was failing, so he turned himself into a tree, preserving himself, until now—when we need him most! Oh, Mother, don't you see?"

Myrrima wondered. She was a water wizardess, and often during the changing of the tides, she felt the water's pull. If she were to give in to it, go down into the river and let herself float out to sea, in time she would grow gills and fins, become an undine. And as the centuries slowly turned, she would lose her human form altogether.

But could she gain her old form back? She had never heard of such thing, never heard of an undine or fish that resumed its human shape.

Gaborn had been the Earth King, the most powerful servant of the earth in all of known history. If he'd had the power to transform himself into a tree, then perhaps he could indeed turn himself back.

"It's more than twenty miles from here to Bald Hill," Myrrima said. "I don't think I have the energy to walk that far in a single day."

Sage said matter-of-factly, "Father can do it."

❧ 4 ❧

THE WHITE SHIP

The generous man is beloved of his family and of all those who know him.

—Emir Owatt of Tuulistan

Borenson loped for seventeen miles in the darkness before he found Draken. The lad was with Baron Walkin and one of his brothers.

The giant reached them just at the crack of dawn, as the sun rose up in the east as pretty as a rose. Wrens flitted about in the brush beside the water, while borrowbirds whistled their strange ululating calls from the white gum trees.

The three had stopped at a huge bend in the channel where the ruins of a ship had been cast up among the dead trees and bracken. The ship must have been taking on stores at Garion's Port. The hull was more than breached—the whole ship had cracked in half. The men had begun salvage efforts, pulling a few casks and crates from the water around the wreckage. But when they had grown tired, they had then set camp by the shore.

Borenson found Draken groggily nursing a small fire while Baron Walkin peered out into the water and his brother slept beneath a bit of tarp. Borenson jutted his chin toward the wreck and asked Draken, "What's the report?"

"The only people that we found were floaters. Other than that, all we really found was this wreck."

Borenson was saddened to hear that there were no survivors, but he hadn't expected better news. So his mind turned to more immediate concerns. "Anything of value on it?"

"Not much. There were some casks of ale floating about, and bales of linen. We found a few empty barrels floating high. We got those. As for the ship, we thought that the brass fittings on the masts and whatnot might be of worth. But after our long walk, we grew too tired to try to haul it all home. We thought that we might use the empty barrels and some other flotsam to make a raft, and then pole it upstream with the tide."

Borenson walked over to Baron Walkin to get a better view of the wreck. Dead fish floated in the still water beside the ship's hull, their white bellies distended and bloating. After a moment, Borenson recognized that something large and hairy floating against the wreck was a goat.

"Do you think we could use the wood from the ship to make a smaller vessel?" Borenson asked.

Baron Walkin peered up at him curiously. "There's not enough left of it, even if we had the right tools. Besides, if we did manage to get something floating, where would you sail to?"

"Haven't decided," Borenson averred.

"I'm afraid there's not much here to salvage," Baron Walkin said. "There are a few more casks floating inside the wreck. If you dive up into it, you can see them, but it's hard work, and risky, trying to get them out. Broken beams, shifting tides. A man takes his life into his hands every time he dives into that mess."

"Have you seen any other wrecks?" Borenson asked, "More lumber?"

"About two miles farther on the sea meets the land," Baron Walkin said. "That's as far as we got. The whole coast is submerged."

In his mind's eye Borenson consulted a map. The Hacker River wound through the hills here, but gently turned. That meant that most of the wreckage from the tidal wave should wash up south of the new beachfront—perhaps only five or six miles to his south.

"You didn't try searching for Garion's Port?"

"We were too tired," Draken said, stepping up beside the two. "The land is pretty rugged. The water just sort of comes in and surrounds the trees, and the rocks are something terrible."

Borenson bit his lip. Draken looked done-in, too tired to go for a rigorous hike. But Borenson felt optimistic. He'd searched in vain through the night for survivors. The tidal wave had just been too brutal, but he hoped to find a couple more wrecks like this one—perhaps with enough material to patch together a real ship.

"You gents see if you can get those barrels pulled out by noon," he said. "I'm going to go down the coast a bit to see what I can see. . . ."

Baron Walkin peered up at Borenson, gave him a warning look. "Don't order me about," he said. "I'm not your manservant. I'm not even your friend. My title—such as it is—is every bit as vaunted as your own."

Walkin wasn't a big man. Years of hard work and little food had robbed the muscle from his frame, and Borenson had a hard time trying to see him as anything more than a starveling. But the baron held himself proudly in the manner of the noble-born.

But nobility was a questionable thing. Sir Borenson had made himself a noble. He had won his title through his own deeds, while Owen Walkin had gained his title by birthright. Such men weren't always as valiant or upright as their progenitors.

This man believes that I owe him an apology, Borenson realized, and perhaps he should have one. After all, our children do want to marry.

"Forgive me," Borenson said. "If anything, your title is of more worth than mine, for yours was a prosperous barony, whereas I was made lord of a swamp—one where the midges were as large as sparrows and the mosquitoes often carried off lambs whole."

Baron Walkin laughed at that, then eyed Borenson for one long moment, as if trying to decide whether Borenson was sincere, and at last stuck out his hand.

They clasped wrists and shook, as befitted lords of Mystarria. "I'll forgive your insults, if you'll forgive my children for eating your cherries."

"I'd say we're even," Borenson laughed, and the baron guffawed.

With that, Borenson went striding off.

Draken watched the giant lumber away, and fought down a knot of anger. In the past few weeks, he had gotten to know Baron Walkin well, and he liked him. Walkin was a wise man, hospitable. It was true that the family had fallen on hard times, and Draken pitied the family. But Walkin had a way of looking into a man's eye and recognizing his mood that seemed almost mystical, and though he had little in the way of worldly goods, he was as generous as he could be.

"What do you think he's after?" Draken asked as the giant loped away, following an old rangit trail.

"He's heading for Rofehavan, unless I miss my guess," Walkin said, then peered at Draken meaningfully. "You'll be welcome to stay and make your home with us, if you prefer."

Draken thought for a long moment. He was in love with Rain, that much he knew. In the past six weeks, he hadn't had a day when he'd gone without seeing her. Already he missed the touch of her skin, and he longed to kiss her.

But he was torn. He had already guessed what had happened. Fallion had bound two worlds. Draken didn't know what that meant precisely. He didn't know why his father had changed, but he knew that something was terribly wrong. The binding should not have brought such a mess.

Draken had been trained from childhood to be a soldier. He knew how to keep secrets. And Fallion's whereabouts and mission were a family secret that he hadn't even shared with Rain. So he had to go on pretending that he didn't know what was wrong with their world.

But he was worried for Fallion, and he felt torn between the desire to go to Rofehavan and learn what had happened and to stay here with Rain.

"I don't know what to do," Draken admitted.

"Let your heart guide you," Baron Walkin suggested.

Draken thought for a long minute. "I want to stay with you, then."

The baron waited and asked, "Why?"

Draken tried to find the right words. "I can't abide

the way my father spoke to Rain. He owes her an apology, but he'll never offer it. He won't apologize to a girl. He's a hard man. All that he ever taught me was how to kill. That's all that he knows how to do. He knows nothing of kindness, or love."

"He taught you how to raise crops, didn't he? How to milk a cow? It seems to me that he taught you more than war."

Draken just glared.

"You're being unfair," the baron said. "You're angry with him because you think he will try to keep you from the girl you love. That's natural for a boy your age. You're getting ready to leave home, start off on your own. When that happens, your mind sometimes plays tricks on you.

"The truth is that your father is raising you the best way that he knows how," Baron Walkin said. "Your father was a soldier. From all that I've heard, he was the best in the realm."

"He killed over two thousand innocent men, women, and children," Draken said. "Did you know that?"

"At his king's command," Walkin said. "He did it, and he is not proud of it. If you think that he is, you misjudge him."

"I'm not trying to accuse him," Draken said, "I'm just saying: A foul deed like that takes its toll on a man. It leaves a stain on his soul. My father knows nothing about gentleness anymore, nothing about mercy or love.

"In the past few months, I've begun to realize that about him. I don't want to be around him, for I fear that I might be forced to become like him."

Baron Walkin shook his head. "Your father taught you to be a soldier. Every father teaches his son the craft he knows. He is an expert at warfare, and that craft can serve you well.

"But don't think that your father doesn't know a thing or two about love. He may be hard on the outside, but there's kindness in him. You accuse him of killing innocents, and that he did. But killing can be an act of love, too.

"He killed the Dedicates of Raj Ahten, but he did it to serve his king and his people, and to protect the land that he loved."

Draken glared. "From the time that I was a child—"

"You had to flee Mystarria with assassins on your tail," the Baron objected. "What loving father wouldn't teach a child all that he needed to know in order to stay alive?

"And once you were six, you went into the Gwardeen and served your country as a graak rider. You've hardly seen your father over the past ten years.

"Take some time to get to know him again," the baron suggested. "That's all that I'm saying."

Draken peered into the baron's brown eyes. The man's long hair was getting thin on top, and a wisp of it blew across his leathery face.

"You surprise me," Draken said. "How can you look past his appearance so easily?"

"Every man has a bit of monster inside him," Walkin said, flashing a weak grin.

In the distance, Draken could still see the giant loping along, leaping over a fallen tree.

Perhaps the baron is right, Draken thought.

He'd only been home from his service among the Gwardeen for a few months, and the truth was that he'd felt glad of the change. From the time that he was a child, he'd lived his life as a soldier. Now he wanted to rest from it, settle down.

Draken felt so unsure of himself, so uprooted. He wasn't certain that he had really ever understood his father, and right now, he felt certain that he did not know him at all—not since the binding of the worlds. That hulking brute rushing down the trail, that monster, was not really Sir Borenson.

Of that Draken felt strangely certain.

Borenson's long legs took him swiftly to the beach two miles inland, where he stood for a moment on a tall promontory and gazed out over the ocean. The waters were dark today, full of red mud and silt. The sun shone on them dully, so that the waves glinted like beaten copper.

But he did not see the ocean, did not focus on the white gulls and cormorants out in the water. Instead he saw a wall. The ocean was a wall.

It's a low wall, he thought, but it's thousands of miles across, and I have to find a way over it.

He turned and followed a line of small hills.

As he loped along, he found wildlife aplenty. The rangits were out in force, grazing beneath the shadows of the trees, and as he approached they would leap up and go bounding through the tall grass.

The borrowbirds flashed like snow amid tree branches, their white bellies and wings drawing the eye, while their pink and blue crests gave them just a hint of color. They landed among the wild plum trees at the shaded creeks and squawked and ratcheted as they squabbled over fruit.

Giant dragonflies in shades of crimson, blue, and

forest green buzzed about by the tens of thousands, and tiny red day bats that had lived among the stonewoods until yesterday now flitted about in the shadows of the blue gums.

The sun beat down mercilessly, spoiling the dead fish and kelp that lay all about.

So for a long hour Borenson hiked, sometimes struggling to climb rocky outcroppings where perhaps no man had ever set foot, and other times wading between hills in water as quiet as a lagoon.

He'd seen how Draken had turned his back on him there in camp. The boy had been leaning toward Baron Walkin.

They're getting close, Borenson realized. Draken feels more for him than he does for me.

Borenson felt that he was losing his son.

In his mind, he replayed an incident from yesterday. Rain Walkin had been up, stirring the cooking fire. The other Walkin children had been scurrying about, hunting for any fish or crabs that might be worth scavenging.

Borenson had nodded cordially to the waif Rain, doing his damnedest to smile. But all he had accomplished was a slight opening of the mouth—enough to flash his overlarge canines.

The girl had frowned, looking as if she might cry.

I must have looked like a wolf baring its fangs, Borenson thought.

"Good day, child," he'd said, trying to sound gentle. But his voice was too much like a growl. Rain had turned away, looking as if she wanted to flee.

Borenson had felt too weary to cater to her feelings.

I'll have to apologize to that girl for calling her a tart,

he thought. The prospect didn't please him. He hadn't decided completely whether she was worth an apology.

Besides, he wasn't sure if she would accept it.

There are many kinds of walls, Borenson thought. Kings build walls around their cities, people build walls around their hearts.

As a soldier, Borenson knew how to storm a castle, how to send sappers in to dig beneath it, or send runelords to scale it.

But how do you scale walls built of anger and apathy, the walls that a son builds around his heart?

When my family looks at me now, they only see a monster, he realized.

Borenson's size, the bony protuberances on his forehead, the strangeness of his features and his voice—all worked against him.

My wife is already distancing herself from me. I would never have thought that Myrrima would be that way.

Children will shriek when they see me.

Even Erin recoiled from me as she died, he thought. That was the worst of it. In the end I could give her no comfort, for she saw only the outside of me.

They don't realize that on the inside I am still the same man I always was.

At least Borenson hoped that he was the same.

Borenson felt alone. He worried that he could no longer fit in among his people. He wondered what would happen when he sailed into Internook or Toom. How would people receive him?

With rocks and sticks, most likely, he thought.

But then it occurred to him that he might not be unique. Perhaps others from Caer Luciare had merged with their shadow selves. Men like him might be scattered all across Mystarria. . . .

He sighed, wondering what to do, and trudged over a ridge, seeking footholds among the rocks and bracken. Dead crabs and fish still littered the ground, but these had been left from the binding, not from the tidal wave.

The flood had been violent, of course. The tidal wave had uprooted huge trees and sent them hurtling in its path, and floating debris had been carried along and piled high—kelp, brush, buildings, dead animals and trees—creating something of a dark reef for as far as the eye could see. In some places, the flotsam rose up in a huge tangled mass of logs and ruin.

Gulls and terns could be seen out perching on the debris, as if silently guarding it.

Most of the flood victims would be caught in that tangle, he imagined, and in many places the tangle was a hundred feet high, and it was hundreds of yards from shore.

He had not gone five miles when he knew that he had found some wreckage that had washed inland from Garion's Port. He climbed a tall rocky hill and scaled a pinnacle of weathered red stone, then stood looking down for a long moment.

The blue gum forest was not particularly thick, and now it was all submerged. Trees stood in water as if they had all gone a-wading. Amid some trees he spotted a little wreckage—an old woman floating belly-up, her skin appearing as white as a wyrmling's hide.

Not far away was a bit of an oxcart, and just beyond that floated the ox that might have been pulling it.

The woman looked naked, much as many of the folks

last night had been when he searched upstream. At first Borenson had wondered if perhaps they'd all been caught bathing. But apparently the violence of the flood had a way of stripping the soggy clothes from a corpse.

He waded out into water that was chest-deep, until he reached the old woman. Then he checked her for valuables. The woman's pants still clung to one leg, and he pulled them free. They looked too small for Myrrima, but Sage might need them. He found a ring on the woman, too—gold with a big black opal in it.

"Forgive me," he whispered as he wrenched it from her finger. "My family has need."

He didn't know how much it might be worth, but he hoped that it might buy passage if he managed to hail a ship.

Then he pushed the woman back out into the waves, in the manner of his folk, giving her to the sea, and waded back to shore.

He continued south for a mile, scavenging as he went, trying to get as close to the huge mounds of wreckage as possible.

Garion's Port had been among the largest cities in all of Landesfallen. It was a popular place for ships to take on stores. The supplies were typically packed in waterproof barrels and then sealed. Borenson hoped that a few barrels might have survived intact, but he saw nothing like that.

Upon a hill he thought he spied the hull of a ship, and so he stripped and swam out to it, nearly a mile, but it turned out to be nothing more than the curved trunk of a gum tree floating in the water. He returned to shore feeling downcast.

A few times he called out, trying to hail any survivors, but his throat was too far gone for much shouting. He saw a few floaters—mostly children and animals— and he wondered why he did not see more.

He lost hope, but kept on trudging doggedly, until the coast suddenly veered back to the east. He stopped atop a small knoll and stood for a moment, staring breathlessly out into the water, not believing his luck.

There, not three hundred yards from shore, a white ship lay amid a tangle of trees, looking as if some vast giant had just lifted it out of the sea and set it there.

It is too whole to be a wreck, Borenson thought. Someone has beached it.

"Hallooo aboard!" he cried. "Halloo in there!" He waved his arms and stood on the hill for a long moment, waiting for someone to come topside and give answer.

The wind was still, the water as calm and flat as a pond.

Perhaps they're scavenging, he thought.

Borenson took off his armor and clothes, and then laid them on the bank. He swam through the water until he reached the pile of flotsam. He climbed up on the logs, fully expecting that at any moment someone from the ship would pop a head up and find him standing there naked.

But as he neared the ship, he called again, and no answer came.

His prize was just dancing on the water, light as a swan. The prow had beached upon some logs, but other than that, the ship looked whole. There were no sails, but that could be fixed. The Walkins had been sleeping beneath a bit of sail just up the beach.

Borenson climbed over the railing, walked around.

The vessel was small indeed, no more than thirty-five feet in length.

It was a small trader by the looks of it, or perhaps a large fishing vessel, the kind used for plying the waters along the coast—not one of the big ships meant for crossing the ocean. It looked odd, for the ship was all gleaming white, reflecting the sunlight.

Borenson appraised it.

This ship is new-made! It hasn't even been painted properly. There is only an undercoat!

He could not believe that his fortune would hold.

He climbed down belowdecks.

The ship had two cabins—one for a captain, the other for a crew of four—but Borenson found that the captain's quarters were not made for a man of his proportions. With only a six-foot ceiling, he could not enter without crouching. He would never have fit on the slat of board that made the bed.

Much better was the hold. The entry was wide enough so that he could climb in easily. The ship had a deep belly, with a wide berth for cargo, and Borenson imagined that he and a dozen more people could make do inside.

But the vessel hadn't escaped the flood completely free of damage. He found water seeping into the hull, and the wood was warped. The ship had been cast into a rock perhaps, or hurled into a tree.

He studied the breach. The seep was not bad, he decided. The ship had apparently been in dry dock when the flood hit, probably up on a cradle, waiting for a new coat of paint. Because it was so light, without crew or cargo, it must have floated high in the water, rising above the flood.

The interior of the vessel had been pitched, and that stopped most of the leakage, but the truth was that when any ship took its maiden voyage, it always had a few cracks. Given a couple of days the wood would swell, and most likely the hull would seal itself. If it didn't, Borenson decided, it wouldn't take much work to pass a few buckets of water topside each day, to drain the bilge.

When he was done inspecting, Borenson felt so moved that he dropped to his knees to thank the Powers.

I have a ship! he told himself. I have a ship!

❧ 5 ❧

A NIGHT IN THE CITY OF THE DEAD

The Great Wyrm provides for all your wants: meat to cure the pangs of hunger, ale to ease a troubled mind, the wine of violence in the arena to entertain. All of these are found in the city. There is no need to ever leave.

— *From the Wyrmling Catechism*

Crull-maldor peered down from a spy hole in the wyrmling's citadel at the Fortress of the Northern Wastes. A band of human warriors two hundred strong had encircled her watchtower, and now they stood below, blowing battle horns, bellowing war cries, and shaking their fists at the tower as they encouraged themselves for battle.

These were small men by wyrmling standards. They were not the well-bred warriors of Caer Luciare that she'd known in her world. These small folk wore armor made of seal skins, gray with white speckles, and had bright hair that was braided and slung over their backs. They bore axes and spears for battle, and carried crude wooden shields. They had dyed their faces with pig's blood, hoping to look frightening.

Crull-maldor fought back the urge to laugh. No doubt they thought they looked fierce. Perhaps they even were fierce. But they were small, like the feral humans that had gone to war with the wyrmlings three thousand years ago.

She admired their fortitude. No doubt they had seen the giant footprints of the wrymlings and had some inkling as to what they were up against.

But none of the wyrmlings had shown themselves. Sundown was long hours away. It was late afternoon, and the dust particles in the air dyed the world in shades of blood. The sun cut like a rapier, leaving stark shadows upon the world.

The enormous stone pinnacle of the fortress's watchtower, standing three hundred feet tall and crafted from slabs of rock forty feet thick, drew the small humans like flies to a carcass.

They had been coming all morning—first children eager to explore this strange new landmark, then worried parents and siblings who were wondering what had befallen the children. Now an angry mob of warriors prepared for battle.

Human settlements surrounded the towers. No doubt by nightfall the small folk would begin to muster a huge army.

Still, the warriors below did not want to wait for reinforcements. So they sang their war songs, gave their cheers, lit their torches, and rushed into the entrance.

At Crull-maldor's back, the wyrmling Lord Aggrez asked, "What is your will, milady?"

Wyrmling tactics in this instance had been established thousands of years ago. The tunnels at the mouth of the cave wound down and down. No doubt the humans imagined that it led straight up to the citadel, but they would have to travel miles into the wyrmling labyrinth to find the passage that led up.

Along the way, they would have to pass numerous spy holes and kill holes, ranging through darkness that was nearly complete, down long rocky tunnels lit only by glow worms.

"Let them get a mile into the labyrinth," Crull-maldor said, "until they find the bones and offal from their children. While they are stricken with fear and rage, drop the portcullises behind them, so that none may ever return. I myself will lead the attack."

Crull-maldor peered at the lord. Aggrez was a huge wyrmling—nine feet in height and more than four feet across the shoulder. His skin was as white as chalk, and his pupils were like pits gouged into ice. He frowned, his lips hiding his overlarge canines, and Crull-maldor felt surprised to see disappointment on his face. "What troubles you?"

"It has been long since my troops have engaged the humans. They were hoping for better sport."

Twenty thousand warriors Crull-maldor had under her command, and it had been too long since they had fought real battles, and too long since they had eaten anything but walrus and seal meat.

"You want them for the arena?" Crull-maldor asked.

"A few."

"Very well," Crull-maldor said. "Let us test their best and bravest."

Though Crull-maldor did not lead the way, she followed. This would be her people's first real battle against a new enemy, and though the humans were small, she knew that even something as small as a wolverine could be astonishingly vicious.

So she went down into the tunnels, to the ambush site. The metal tang of blood was strong in the air, and filled the hallway. Dozens of the small folk had already been carried down to this point, deep under the fortress. Their offal lay on the floor—piles of gut and stomachs, kidneys and lungs, hair and skulls.

The humans had been harvested, their glands taken for elixirs, the meat for food, the skins as trophies. Not much was left.

Now Crull-maldor chose a small contingent of warriors to lead the attack, and they waited just down the corridor from the ambush site, silent as stone.

It took the human warriors nearly half an hour to arrive. They bore bright torches. Their leader—a fierce-looking man with golden rings in his hair and a helm that sported the horn of a wild ox poking forward—found the bones of his children.

Some of the men behind him cursed or cried out in anguish, but their leader just squatted over the pile of human refuse, his face looking grim and determined. His face was dyed in blood, and his hair was red, and torchlight danced in his eyes.

Quietly, each wrymling raised a small iron spike and plunged it into his neck. The spikes, coated with glandular extracts harvested from the dead, filled the wyrmlings with bloodlust, so that their hearts pounded and their strength increased threefold.

The wyrmlings roared like beasts, and the rattling of chains in the distance gave answer. The portcullises slammed into the floor behind the humans, metal against stone, with a boom like a drum that shook the world.

Half a dozen wyrmling warriors led the attack, charging into the human hosts, bearing long meat hooks to pull the men close and short blades to eviscerate them. They hurtled heedlessly into battle.

The human leader did not look dismayed. He merely hurled his torch forward a dozen paces to get better light; in a single fluid move he reached back and pulled off his shield.

The wyrmlings roared like wild beasts; one shouted "Fresh meat!" as he attacked.

Instantly the human warlord snarled, and suddenly he blurred into motion. Crull-maldor had never seen anything like it. One instant the human was standing, and the next his whole body blurred, faster than a fly's wings, and he danced into the wyrmling troops, his fierce war ax flashing faster than the eye could see.

Lord Aggrez went down, lopped off at the knee, as the warrior blurred past, slashing throats and taking off arms. In the space of a heartbeat he passed the wyrmling troops and raced toward Crull-maldor.

The human warriors at Caer Luciare had always been smaller than wyrmlings, yet what they lacked in size they made up for in speed. But this small warrior was stunning; this went far beyond anything in Crull-maldor's experience.

The women and children had not shown such speed. There was only one explanation—magic, spells of a kind that Crull-maldor had never imagined.

The warrior raced toward her, but seemed not to see her. Her body was no more substantial than a fog, and she wore clothing only for the convenience of her fleshly cohorts—a hooded red cloak made of wispy material with the weight and consistency of a cobweb.

Thus her foe did not see her at first, but was peering up at the great wyrmlings behind her. In the shadows of the tunnel, she was all but invisible.

The humans' champion bellowed—fear widening his eyes while his mouth opened in a primal scream. He charged toward the wyrmlings behind her, and suddenly his breath fogged, and terror filled his eyes.

He felt the cold that surrounded Crull-maldor. It stole his breath and made the blood freeze in his veins.

He shouted one single word of warning to the warriors behind, and then Crull-maldor touched him on the forehead with a single finger.

Her touch froze the warrior in his tracks, robbed him of thought. He dropped like a piece of meat, though she had brushed him only lightly.

The rest of the human warriors backed away in fear, nearly in a rout. Crull-maldor knelt over her fallen foe for a moment, sniffed at his weapons. There was no enchantment upon them, no fell curses.

She rose up and went into battle, floating toward the rest of the warriors. None raced with their leader's speed. None bellowed war cries or tried to challenge her.

They were defenseless against her kind.

Crull-maldor was the most powerful lich lord in her world; she feared nothing.

She did not wade into battle on legs, but instead moved by will alone.

Thus she drove into ranks of the small humans. They screamed and sought to escape. One man tried to drive her back with a torch, and the webbing of her garment caught fire. Thus, for a few brief moments she was wreathed in smoke and flame, and all of the humans saw the hunger in her dead face and the horror of her eyes, and they wailed in despair.

Then, invisible without her cloak, Crull-maldor waded into the human troops and began to feed, drawing away the life force of those who tried to flee, or merely stunning those whose ferocity in battle proved that they would make good sport in the arena.

There were no more warriors like the mage that had confronted her. She found herself hoping for stronger resistance. She found herself longing for a war that promised great battles and glorious deeds, for only by distinguishing herself could she hope to gain the attention of Lady Despair, and thus perhaps win the throne.

But she was bitterly disappointed.

As the last human warrior crumpled to his knees and let out a mewling cry, like a child troubled by nightmares, Crull-maldor told herself: There are millions of humans in the barrens now. Perhaps among them I will find a worthy foe.

* * *

Her wyrmling troops feasted upon fresh man-flesh that evening, and then prepared a few captured humans for the arena, stripping them naked lest they have any concealed weapons.

That was when Crull-maldor found the markings upon the humans' champion. His skin bore scars from a branding iron, and upon the warrior's flesh she saw ancient glyphs, primal shapes that had formed the world from the beginning.

Crull-maldor studied a glyph—actually four glyphs all bound into a circle. The largest was the rune for might, but attached to it were other smaller glyphs—seize, confer, and bind.

The lich lord had never seen such scars before, but instinctively she knew what they meant. It was a spell of some nature, a type of parasitical magic, which caused attributes from one being to be imbued upon another.

This is a new form of magic, she realized, one with untold potential. She suspected that she could duplicate the spells, even improve upon them, if she knew more. With mounting excitement she pored over the champion's other scars: speed, dance, resilience. Four types of runes were represented, and Crull-maldor immediately knew that she could devise others that the humans had not anticipated.

Suddenly, the humans and their new magic took on great import in her mind.

She did not know if she should reveal what she had found to the emperor. Perhaps he already knew about this strange magic. Perhaps he would never know—until after Crull-maldor had mastered it.

So far today, she had not heard from the emperor. Certainly he had witnessed the great change wrought upon the world. Other wyrmling fortresses would be reporting the sightings of humans.

But if things were amiss in the capitol at Rugassa, Crull-maldor had not been forewarned.

Probably, she thought, the emperor will not tell me anything. He hopes that I will fail, that I will embarrass myself, so that he will look better in return.

It had always been this way. Their rivalry had lasted for more than four hundred years.

But at the moment, Crull-maldor suspected that she had the upper hand.

I could just tell him that humans have come, she thought, and not warn him of the dangers of confronting them.

She liked that. A half-truth oft served better than a lie.

But she decided to wait. She didn't need to report the incursion instantly.

Little of import happened that day. One of the wyrmling captains reported a strangeness: some of her subjects claimed to recall life on another world, the world that had fallen from above. They wished to leave the fortress, head south to their own homes.

Crull-maldor ordered that all such people be put to death. There was no escaping the wyrmling horde.

So she waited until after sundown, when the long shadows stretched into full darkness and bats began to weave about the citadel in their acrobatic hunt.

Stars glowered overhead, the fiery eyes of heaven, and a cool and salty breeze breathed over the land.

With the coming of night, the spirits of the land rose from their hiding places.

A second human army was gathering for the night,

soldiers from far places riding horses to the towers. Crull-maldor did not want to leave her wyrmlings defenseless, yet she needed to gain information.

So while the armies began to surround her fortress, Crull-maldor dropped from the citadel and went floating beneath the starlight, weaving her way between boulders, drifting above the gorse and bracken.

Field mice felt the cold touch of her presence, and went hopping for their burrows.

Hares thumped their feet to warn their kind. Then they would either hold still, hoping that she passed, or race for the shelter of the gorse.

Nothing substantial had lived here—until today. Nothing substantial could have lived here. Crull-maldor had been cheating death for centuries, living as a shade, a creature that was nearly pure spirit. But to hold on to the spark of life, to stay in communion with the world of fleshy creatures, required tremendous power, power that could only be gained by drawing off the life force of others.

Thus, on a normal night, as she wound her way through the bracken, Crull-maldor would have touched a rabbit here, drained a bush there, or cut short the song a cricket as she passed.

She would have left a trail of death and silence in her wake. But tonight she felt sated, for she had fed upon the spirits of men.

Her mind was not upon the hunt for food that evening, but upon the hunt for information. Her eyes could see beyond the physical realm. Indeed, she was so far gone toward death that she could not easily perceive the physical world anymore, unless she happened to be riding in the mind of a crow or a wolf.

Now she passed through the wilds in a daze, as if moving through a dream.

More immediate, more real to her, were the perceptions of her spirit. She could see into the dead world easily, a world that had always been a mystery to mortals.

They lived here in the Northern Wastes, the dead did—in these so-called "barrens." Most of the time, the dead prefer to isolate themselves from the living, for living men often hold powerful auras that confuse and trouble the dead.

So the dead had built cities that seemed to be sculpted from light and shadow. Great towers rose up all around her in shades that the mortal eye cannot see—the rose colors of dawn, the deepest purples of twilight, and shades of fire that no mortal can imagine.

Soaring arches spanned the streets, with flowering vines cascading from them, while great fountains spurted up in broad plazas that seemed to be paved with a pale mist.

What a living wyrmling imagined was only a barren waste was in fact the home to millions.

But tonight in the spirit world, much had changed. There had been one city here yestereve. Now Crull-maldor saw towers everywhere, rising above the plains. Hosts of human dead had come.

Their women shrieked for joy and children laughed, while minstrels played in far pavilions.

The spirits of the dead celebrated here, the shades of humans and wyrmlings mingling together, oblivious of the living world—just as the living world was oblivious of them.

So the lich lord wafted above streets of mellow haze, into the House of Light, and there came upon a great convocation of elders, mixed with scholars from the human world.

Crull-maldor did not see them with her physical eyes; instead she perceived their spirits, like spiny sea urchins created from light. Each spirit was a small round ball with thousands of white needle-like appendages that issued out in every direction.

Each spirit had the memory of its fleshly form draped over it like a cloak, showing dimly remembered exteriors. Thus, the balls of light hovered about inside the shells of wyrmling lords and men.

Crull-maldor went to the most glorious among them—a human woman who shone with tremendous brilliance, a symbol of her wisdom and power.

Then the lich lord seized the woman. Crull-maldor sent a tendril of light coiling out from her own spirit, and penetrated the woman's field. The lich took the woman by the umbilicus and twisted, causing the woman untold pain.

Once again, Crull-maldor found the act to be surprisingly easy. A spiritual attack upon such a powerful being should normally have required great concentration. But now it felt like child's play.

"Tell me what you know!" Crull-maldor demanded.

The woman shrieked, and the color of her spindles of light suddenly changed from bright white to a delicious deep red. She recoiled, and all of the tendrils around her nucleus shrank in on themselves, the way that the arms of a sea anemone will do when something brushes against it.

"What would you have of me, great lord of the dead!" the woman cried. Her name was Endemeer, and she had once been a vaunted scholar.

"What has happened to my world?"

"A great sorcerer has come," Endemeer said. "He has bound two worlds into one, two worlds that were but shadows of the one true world that existed at the beginning of time.

"He has bound flesh to flesh in those who live; and he has bound spirit to spirit among the dead. . . ."

Immediately Crull-maldor knew that the scholar spoke correctly. This world that she had said once existed, Crull-maldor had heard of it from some of the greater spirits she had tortured.

But until now, Crull-maldor had not believed in it. She had suspected that it was a place found only in one's imagination.

It explained everything so simply, yet it had tremendous ramifications.

Crull-maldor had not yet revealed to the emperor her news about the humans in her land. She knew now that she could not hide the news. This great change impacted entire continents.

Humans are abroad in the land once again, Crull-maldor thought, and where there is conflict, there is also opportunity.

Crull-maldor immediately sent an alarm, a flash of thought to the emperor Zul-torac. *Our wyrmling scouts have found humans in the Northern Wastes. They came with a great change that has twisted the earth.*

The emperor sent back a terse reply, and she felt his thoughts crawling through her mind, seeking to infiltrate it. She set a barrier against them, so that he could not read her mind, and he replied. *I know, fool! Deal with them.*

His thoughts fled, dismissing her.

Crull-maldor grinned. As she had hoped, he had not had the foresight to tell her how to deal with them.

The scholar Endemeer whimpered and tried to escape Crull-maldor's grasp. The lich lord merely held her, eager to wring more information from her.

"Tell me about the humans' new magic, the glyph magic."

Crull-maldor sent her own tendrils of light plunging deep into those of her captive. Each tendril of light was like a strand of human brain. It stored wisdom and memories. As Crull-maldor brushed against Endemeer, she glimpsed the memories stored upon Endemeer's tendrils.

Grasping the ones that she wanted, Crull-maldor ripped the tendrils free. It was like tearing apart a human brain. The tendrils' light immediately began to dim, so Crull-maldor shoved them into her own central bundle, transplanting the memories. By doing so she stole the spirit's knowledge. It was a violation as reprehensible as rape, a type of murder.

So Crull-maldor hunched over her prey, ripping light from Endemeer. In the City of the Dead the lich lord discovered the deepest secrets of the runelords.

❦ 6 ❦

A CALL TO ARMS

It is only when a man gives up his life in service to a greater cause that he can attain true greatness.

—*The Wizard Binnesman*

War horns rent the air; Myrrima startled awake, heart pounding.

She cocked an ear, alert for sounds of danger, and heard the screams of horses dying in battle, along with some warlord shouting, "Man the breach! Man the breach, damn you!"

A drum pounded and sent a snarl rolling over the hills like the crack of thunder. Deep voices roared in challenge in some strange tongue, voices unlike any that Myrrima had ever heard.

Blinking the sleep from her eyes, Myrrima climbed from her bed there in the lee of the rocks, the warm ferns crushed from her weight, and peered out in alarm in the cool morning mist, trying to find the source of danger.

But there were no armies clashing in the distance, and as she woke it seemed to her that the sounds faded, as if they could be heard only in dream.

She stood panting, trying to catch her breath, clear her head. She blinked, looking around. Erin's body still lay there on the grass not a hundred yards off, her face pale, her lips going blue. Sage was sleeping soundly in the ferns.

Nearby, the Walkin clan was still sleeping, too. Myrrima was the only one who had wakened.

Her heart ceased to hammer so hard; she stood for a moment, thinking.

It was only a dream. It was only a dream. All of Borenson's talk last night stirred up evil memories of battles long past. Or perhaps her vision of Erin that she'd had not more than a couple of hours ago had conjured an evil dream.

Whatever the cause, the sounds of battle had faded. Myrrima sat in a daze, wondering.

"What is it, Mother?" Sage asked, stirring from her sleep.

"Nothing," Myrrima whispered. She searched about camp. Borenson and Draken were still gone.

Yet as she sat in the early dawn, she heard the sound of water tinkling in the streamlet nearby, the discreet cheeping of small birds in a thicket.

Other than that, the morning was utterly still. The sun was just rising in the far hills, painting the dawn in shades of peach and rose. It was that time of morning when everything is still, even the wind.

Yet there she heard it again—the deep call of a war horn in the distance, and the sound of men clashing in battle.

She strode toward it with a start and cocked her ear. The sound seemed to be coming from the far side of the old river channel.

Straining to hear, she crept over to the cliff, her feet rustling dry grasses, and stood for a moment. The sound had faded again, but she could hear it now—a deep rumbling in the ground, as if horses were charging into battle, the blare of horns. She could almost smell blood in the air.

She peered across the channel. Its waters were dark and muddy, filled with filth and jetsam. Mists rising off of it made the far shore nearly impossible to make out. Could there be a battle over there? But who would be fighting?

Yet as she stood at the edge of the cliff, peering about, there was no sign of troops in the distance, and the sound seemed now to be coming from below her, from the still waters in the channel.

Myrrima clambered carefully down the steep slope a hundred feet, until she stopped at the water's edge.

The sounds of war came distant now, so distant. She wondered if she was listening to the remnant of a dream.

Suddenly, out in the water a body floated to the surface not forty feet from shore, a woman with wide hips, someone who would have made her home in the village of Sweetgrass. Thankfully, Myrrima could not see her face, only her stringy gray hair.

The corpse bobbed for a moment, and then the sounds of battle suddenly blasted in Myrrima's ears.

"Internook! Internook!" a barbarian cried. "Hail to the Bearers of the Orb!" Men cheered fiercely all around her, and she heard them running, mail ringing and jangling.

She peered off in the mist, and let her eyes go out of focus, and then she saw it: a castle a hundred miles north of the Courts of Tide, its battlements all lit by fire. It was dark there, and she could not see the enemy—except for a mass of great beasts out beyond the walls, giants with white skin and startling white eyes, wearing armor carved from bone.

"To battle!" some warlord cheered. "To battle!"

And then just as suddenly as it had come, the vision ended, as if a portcullis gate had slammed down, holding the vision at bay.

Is this a vision of the future? Myrrima wondered. But a certainty filled her.

No, it is a battle happening now, far across the ocean. Dawn had come to her home here in Landesfallen, but night still reigned on the far side of the world. As Borenson had warned, the wyrmlings were greeting their new neighbors.

The vision, the sounds, both seemed to be coming from the water, and that is when Myrrima knew.

She had wondered whether to follow Borenson across the ocean into his mad battle.

But water was calling to her, summoning Myrrima to war.

Borenson will find a ship, Myrrima realized. Water will make a way for us to reach that far shore. My powers there will be needed.

A giant green dragonfly common to the river valley came buzzing over the water nearby, a winged emerald with eyes of onyx. It hovered for a moment, as if gauging her.

Myrrima knelt then at the edge of the old river channel and laved dirty brown water over her arms, then tilted her face upward and let it stream, cold and dead, over her forehead and eyes. Thus she anointed herself for war.

* * *

There had been a time in Myrrima's life when she'd made a ritual of washing herself first thing each morning. As a child she'd loved water, whether it was the sweet drops of a summer rain clinging to her eyelashes, or the tinkling of a freshet as it darted among the rocks. It was her love of water that gave her power over it. At the same time, water had power over her, too—enough power so that she often felt pulled by it, and she found herself wanting to go lie in a deep river, so that the water could caress her and surround her and someday carry her out to sea.

Six years back, she had purposely given up the ritual, afraid that if she did not, she would lose herself to water.

But this morning was different. Worries wormed their way through her mind, and she had seldom felt so tired.

So when she reached camp, she found Sage and led her to the nearby stream. It was only a trickle at this time of year. A little water roamed down from the red-rock above. In the winters the rain and snow would seep into the porous sandstone, and for centuries it would percolate down through the rock until it hit a layer of harder shale. Then it would slowly flow out, and thus seeped from a cliff face above. Myrrima was so attuned to water that she could taste it and feel in her heart how long ago it had fallen as rain.

Not much water escaped the rocks, barely enough to wet the ground. But there was a boggy spot where the streamlet stole through the moss and grass.

Wild ferrin and rangits often came to drink here, and so had trampled the grass a bit.

So Myrrima took Sage and with stones and moss

they dammed the small stream, so that it began to rise over the course of the morning.

Rain came to help them, bringing some clay that she had found nearby. As they padded clay between the stones of the dam, Myrrima told the young women of Borenson's plan to return to Mystarria.

"It may be a dangerous journey," Myrrima said. "I can understand why you would not want to go. I hesitate to ask you, Sage. Landesfallen has been your home for so long, I will not force you to come."

"I don't remember Mystarria," Sage said. "Draken sometimes talks about the vast castle we lived in, all white, with its soaring spires and grand hallways."

"It wasn't grand," Myrrima said. "I suppose it must have seemed so to a tot like him. Castle Coorm was small, a queen's castle, set in the high hills where the air was cool and crisp during the muggy days of summer. It was a place to retreat, not a seat of power."

"I should like to see it," Sage said, but there was no conviction in her voice.

"Much has changed in Mystarria, you understand?" Myrrima said. "It's not likely that we'll ever live in a castle again."

Rain had just brought some mud, and she halted at the mention of Mystarria, her muscles tightening in fear. The girl knew how much the place had changed far more than Myrrima did.

"I understand," Sage said.

"I don't think that you do," Rain told them. "When we left last year, the place was in turmoil. There is no peace in that land, and I think that there never shall be again. The warlords of Internook have been harsh masters, harsher than you know. When my father fled the land, he left a prosperous barony. But months later we heard that all of the people in the barony—women, children, babes—were gone. One morning the warlord's soldiers came and marched them all into the forests, and none came back. But that evening, wagons began to arrive filled with settlers who had shipped in from Internook, and the houses in the cities were filled, and farmers came to reap crops that they had not sown.

"The warlord Grunswallen had sold our lands months before his soldiers began the extermination. My father had sensed that it was near. He said that he'd felt it coming for days and weeks. He'd seen it in the superior smirks that the Internookers gave us, in the way that they heaped abuse on our people. My family fled just two days before the cleansing occurred. . . . I thank the Powers that we were able to exact a small token of vengeance against that pig Grunswallen. The Internookers wear hides made of pigskin because they are pigs in human form."

Myrrima peered up at Rain; she worried that the young woman would turn Sage away from the course.

Perhaps that would be best, Myrrima thought. I don't want to take Sage into such unstable lands. I don't want to make life-and-death decisions for my child.

"There are other dangers, too," Rain said. "The mountains and woods are full of strengi-saats, monsters that hunt for young women so that they can lay their eggs in the women's wombs. You cannot go out by night. The soldiers do a fair job of keeping them away from the towns and the open fields, but each year the strengi-saats' numbers grow, the monsters range closer into the heartland, and the nights grow more dangerous."

Sage looked to Rain. "You don't think I should go?"

Rain stammered, "No—Perhaps there is no right choice. But I think that if you go to Mystarria, you should know what you're up against.

"And since the change in the world—who knows what things will be like in Mystarria now?" Rain hesitated and then explained to Myrrima: "I heard your husband talking last night about creatures called *wyrmlings*. . . ."

Myrrima's heart skipped. If the girl had heard about the wyrmlings, then she'd heard much that Myrrima would wish to keep secret. "What else did you hear?"

"I know that your son Fallion is responsible for this . . . *change*." Rain hesitated, her keen green eyes studying Myrrima for a sign of reaction. "But I don't understand it all. Draken told me that his brothers and sisters had all gone back to Mystarria; I'd already known that Fallion was a flameweaver, but I've never heard of a flameweaver who had powers like this." She shrugged and swept her arms wide, pointing to a ledge nearby where an outcrop of rock was still covered in coral.

"Who else have you told?" Myrrima asked.

Rain had been keeping her voice soft, and she glanced over the deep grass to where the folks in her own camp were beginning to stir. "No one. Nor shall I tell. I think it is best if no one here ever learns who is responsible for this . . . debacle."

Myrrima found a knot of fear coiling in her stomach. She was worried for Fallion and Talon, for all of her children. What would people think if they knew? Half of Landesfallen had sunk into the sea, millions of people were dead. Certainly, one of their kin would seek vengeance against Fallion, if they knew what he had done.

Yet Myrrima's worries for her children went far beyond that. Fallion had planned to go deep into the Underworld, to the Seals of Creation, to cast his spell.

With all that had happened, Myrrima could not help but fear for Fallion's safety. She worried that the tunnels he'd entered had collapsed. Even if the structures had survived, they had been dug by reavers, and it was well known that every time a volcano blew or a large earthquake struck, the reavers grew angry and were likely to attack during the aftermath, much like hornets whose nests have been stirred up.

Fallion had gone to heal the world; Myrrima felt almost certain that he had paid for his trouble with his life. No good deed ever goes unpunished.

Sage had listened to Myrrima's words, to Rain's warnings. Now she peered up at her mother with blue eyes blazing. She had deep red hair and a face full of freckles. "I want to go with you. There's nothing holding me here. Everyone that I knew is gone. I want to find Talon and Fallion, make sure that they are all right. . . ."

Myrrima looked to Rain. "And you? Will you come with us?"

Rain hesitated. "I don't think so. I don't see why you have to go looking for trouble. If the wyrmlings come, we can fight them on our own ground."

Myrrima knew that Rain would try to convince Draken to stay here with her. Myrrima didn't know how to feel about that—whether to be angry or to hope that she succeeded.

So Myrrima hummed to herself until the shallow pool filled to a depth of a few inches. The Walkin children came by and all stood peering into the water eagerly, until Myrrima began to draw runes of healing and re-freshment upon the water.

She bathed then, laving the clean water up over her own head, letting it wash over and through her. She peered up, and wished that she knew what the best course to follow might be. Dare she really take the children back to Mystarria, expose them to such dangers? Or could she possibly stay here? It would be easy to enchant some weapons, cast spells upon them that would vanquish un-clean spirits. She could send them with Borenson.

When she finished her mind felt cleared of all doubt. She had to go with Borenson. She would need to en-chant weapons not for one man, or even a hundred, but perhaps for thousands.

More importantly, she felt renewed, filled with en-ergy. The bath seemed to wash away the curse that had sapped her strength.

So she bathed Sage now. As she laved the water over the girl, she asked her master for a small blessing upon Sage: "May the stream strengthen you. May the mois-ture renew you. May Water make you its own."

As the last handful of water streamed down Sage's face, she gasped as if in relief, and then broke into tears of gratitude for what her mother had done.

She reached up and began to wipe the tears away, but Myrrima pulled her hand back. "Such tears should be given back to the stream," she said.

So Sage stood there in the stream, and let her tears fall into its still waters.

Afterward, Myrrima invited Rain into the pool, and offered to repeat the cleansing ceremony with each of the Walkin women and children.

For two long hours Myrrima stood in her blue traveling robes, her long dark hair dangling over one shoulder. Between each ceremony she would have to stoop and trace runes of cleansing and healing on the surface of the pool while water-skippers danced around her fingers.

One by one she washed everyone in the group.

Those children who had been cleansed instantly began darting around camp, their lethargy much diminished, while the womenfolk seemed at last to come alive.

Noon had just passed and Myrrima was thinking about lunch when a call went up from the Walkin children.

"There's a ship! There's a ship in the channel!"

The sighting aroused a bit of excitement, and the Walkin children raced to the lip of the cliff and peered down into the polluted water below.

Myrrima had been trying to keep the children away from the old river channel all day, afraid of what they might see floating past. But now the whole Walkin clan stood on the shore and waved.

"We're rescued, Mother!" Sage was calling.

Myrrima walked to the bank and stood peering down.

It wasn't one boat—it was nine, or one boat and eight rafts. They were paddling over the water, following the course seaward.

Three dozen men manned the vessels. "Halloo!" they called, waving bandanas and hats.

Myrrima drew closer, but one of the Walkin women strode forward and acted as voice.

"Need help?" one of the men called from a boat. "We're from Fossil!" another shouted from a raft. "Is anyone injured?" a third cried.

The men paddled, doing their best to row the clumsy vessels in unison, and a fine tall man with a blunt face and long brown hair hanging free stood up in the boat.

"We've got a child dead," the Walkin woman, Greta, shouted. "She's beyond anyone's help."

"Do you need food or supplies?" the tall man asked.

"We got away with nothing more than what's on our backs," Greta said. "We had fish and crabs for dinner last night, but we daren't eat it today."

The boat floated near and finally bumped against the shore not far below them. "Where are your menfolk?" the leader called.

"They went west, searching for survivors," Myrrima answered.

The leader gave them a suspicious look. Then he put on a pleasant face and called up, "I'm Mayor Threngell, from Fossil. We don't have much in the way of supplies, but you're welcome in our village. There's food and shelter for any that need it."

He searched the faces of the Walkins as if looking for someone familiar. "Are you locals?"

The Walkins hardly dared admit that they were squatters. "New to the area," one of them answered. "We're looking to homestead."

Myrrima had met Mayor Threngell two years back at the autumn Harvest Festival; she recognized him now. "I'm local," she said. "Borenson's the name. Our farm was destroyed in the flood."

The mayor grunted, gave her a cordial nod. "Go east, not twenty miles. It's not an easy walk, but you should make it. You'll find food and shelter there," he affirmed. But the welcome in his voice had all gone cold, as if he wasn't sure that he wanted to feed squatters. "Tell your men when they get back. Tell them that there is to be no looting of the dead, no salvage operations. This land is under martial law."

Myrrima wondered at that. Law here in the wilderness was rather malleable. Vandervoot, the king, had lived on the coast. Most likely, Myrrima imagined that he was food for crabs about now. This mayor from a backwater town could hardly declare martial law.

More than that, she could see no justice in what Threngell proposed. Here he was: a man with land and horses, crops and fields, demanding that folks who had nothing take no salvage from the dead. But she knew that often lords would find reasons why they should grow a little fatter while the rest of the world grew a little leaner.

"Under whose authority was martial law declared?" Myrrima asked.

"My authority," Mayor Threngell said, a warning in his voice.

ACTS OF LOVE

Rage can give strength during battle; but he who sur-
renders to rage surrenders all reason.

—Sir Borenson

Sweating and grunting, Borenson used a log as a lever to pry the bow of the ship up so that it groaned and scraped.

For two long hours he'd been trying, with Draken, Baron Walkin, and the baron's younger brother Bane to get the ship free. It was grueling labor—pulling wreckage from under the vessel, setting up logs to use as rollers under the ship, setting up other logs to use as pry bars, shoving and straining until Borenson felt that his heart would break.

Now, as the ship began to nudge, he realized that all of their labor might have been for nothing. The rising tide had lifted the back of the ship. Had the tides been extra high, he imagined that they just might have borne the ship out into open water. But the tide wouldn't rise high enough today, so he shouted, "Heave! Heave!"

As one, all four men threw their weight into their pry bars, and the bow lifted into the air. Suddenly there was a groaning as the roller logs took the weight of the ship, and it began to slide backward into the ocean.

Bane Walkin let out a cry of pain, shouting, "Stop it! Stop it!"

But there was no stopping the vessel now. It rolled backward and splashed into the ocean, spewing foam.

As the bow slid away, Borenson spotted Bane—fallen, clutching his ankle. His foot had obviously gotten caught between the ship and a log.

Borenson rushed to Bane's aid, and had the man pull off his boot. Draken and Baron Walkin knelt at his side. Gingerly, Borenson twisted the young man's ankle. It had already begun to swell, and a bruise was setting in. But the man was lucky. At least he still had his foot.

"Good news," Borenson teased. "We won't have to amputate!"

Bane gritted his teeth and tried to laugh, though tears had formed in the corners of his eyes.

"Well, at least we won't have to be hiking home," Baron Walkin said, and he turned and looked at their ship, bobbing proudly on the waves.

Borenson grinned. I have my ship!

So it was that the four men claimed their prize. With a sail and rope salvaged from another wreck, they set sail nearly at noon. A breeze had kicked up, making small whitecaps on the waves, and with a little trial and error they managed to set out, plying the waters north. The ship had no proper wheel, but instead relied upon a rudder, so Borenson manned it from the captain's deck while Baron Walkin and Draken trimmed the sails. Bane merely sat on the prow, nursing his foot. He'd wrapped it in wet kelp to keep down the swelling, and now he held on to his rubbery green bandage.

In less than an hour they reached the mouth of the channel and turned inland, then retrieved their salvage from the earlier wreck.

Borenson had just loaded the last of the crates and

barrels aboard when Draken raised a cry of warning. Borenson looked upstream. Several rafts and a small boat paddled in the distance, perhaps a mile out upon the water.

"Rescuers!" Bane Walkin said.

Borenson doubted it. The men were rowing toward them, hard.

Borenson didn't like the look of it. "Let's get under way, quickly."

"Agreed," Baron Walkin said, face grim. He nodded toward the wreckage floating nearby. "Looks like we're done with the salvage. It's going to turn into a free-for-all out here."

Draken untied the knots that bound the ship to a tree and shoved off, pulling himself topside at the last moment, while Borenson raised the sails, then took the tiller from Baron Walkin.

As the wind swiftly began driving the ship up the channel, the rafts began to spread out, as if to intercept.

"Give them a wide berth," Borenson suggested, "until we know what they're about."

He pushed hard on the tiller, taking the ship directly north, toward the far shore, some four miles in the distance, while Walkin tacked the sails.

The men in the flotilla waved frantically, trying to hail the ship. There were more than thirty of them.

"Halt!" one man shouted from the boat, his voice carrying over the water. "How long have you had that ship?"

Borenson recognized Mayor Threngell from Fossil. He was a nodding acquaintance. Borenson knew of only one reason that he would ask that question.

"Four years!" he cried out in return, knowing full

well that the mayor wouldn't recognize him, not with the change to his form.

"Bring her about!" the mayor cried. He and his men waved frantically.

"What?" Borenson called. He cupped a hand to his ear, as if he couldn't hear. Then Draken and the Walkins all waved back, as if to say "good day."

"That's the mayor from Fossil. You think he'll give us trouble?" Draken asked under his breath.

Borenson felt embarrassed to have such a lack-wit for a son.

"Of course they'll give us trouble," Baron Walkin said. "A ship like this is worth twenty thousand steel eagles, easily. Everything else out there in the water is just leftovers. He'll be out to steal it before sundown."

"He'll have to catch us first," Borenson said.

Borenson didn't think that the ship was worth twenty thousand eagles—it was worth far more. Fossil had always been a nothing town, out in the middle of nowhere. But now with the flood, with the water moving inland, it was in prime position to become a port city, perhaps the largest in Landesfallen.

Mayor Threngell would have figured that out by now. But a port was nothing without ships.

This ship might be Fossil's only tie to the old world, to trade between the continents. Threngell would see that, in time, too. He'd bring his mob to take the ship.

Borenson realized that he'd need to make his escape quickly, before the mayor had time to act.

The Walkin and Borenson families didn't have much in the way of stores, but a plan began to form in Borenson's mind. He could sail up the old river channel to Fossil and buy a few supplies. Those men in their rafts would have a hard time rowing forty or fifty miles up-stream, especially now that the tides and turned, and with the lowering of the tide, it would be pulling the rafts back toward the open sea.

But no matter how he figured it, there was no way to avoid the mayor and his lackeys completely.

Fortunately, the mayor and his men weren't well armed. If it came to a fight, Borenson wasn't above showing them a trick or two.

It was early afternoon when the ship sailed to camp at the base of the cliff. Draken leapt out of the vessel as it neared shore and swam to a half-submerged tree, tying the boat up to dock.

The entire camp swarmed down to see the ship, the children leaping about excitedly. It was a great treasure, a valuable find. The only person who didn't come down, it seemed, was Rain, and she was the one person that Draken most wanted to see.

So while the Walkins showed off the white ship with its makeshift sails and a few barrels and crates of odd salvage, Draken scrambled up the cliff.

He found Rain preparing dinner for the clan, roasting some hapless burrow bear.

"These are for you," he said, setting a pocketful of plums on a large rock that served as a table. He'd picked them this morning, and had been saving them all day. "They grow along the creeks."

Rain fell into his arms, and Draken hugged her. He realized that she had been waiting for him, staying back up here while the others buzzed around the ship.

Holding her, touching her, felt like coming home.

She was a slender girl, so narrow of hip that it often

surprised him when he put his arms around her to feel
how little of her there really was. She had pale blond hair
tied back in a sensible style, and copious freckles. Her
jaw was strong, her lips thin, and her green eyes looked
as if she was a woman who would brook no argument.
She did not wear a dress, but a cream-colored summer
tunic that was wearing thin, over a pair of tight woolen
pants.

After a long kiss, Rain whispered, "Has your father
told you the news?"

"What?" Draken asked.

"He plans to go back to Mystarria, to fight some
war. Your mother told me all about it. She asked if I
would come with you."

Draken was surprised to learn the news this way,
rather than hear it from his father. Now Rain whispered
hurriedly, giving what few details she could. Mostly, it
seemed that she had only guesses and suppositions, but
the news was grave indeed.

"Do you want to go?" Draken asked, fighting back
his worry. He didn't want her to. He didn't want to
take her into danger.

She thought long and hard. She'd told him much of
how they had fled Rofehavan in the first place, but he
knew that she still had secrets.

The brutish warlords of Internook had taken over the
coastal cities of Mystarria, and they were harsh taskmas-
ters. They'd driven the peasants mercilessly, and every
few months they would march through the villages and
demand a levy, taking the finest of the family's sheep and
cattle, seizing anything of worth, and dragging off the
fairest virgins in the city.

For the past three years, Rain had spent her days and nights in hiding, as much as she could.

Townsfolk died, driven to starvation, and each time some land opened up, a family of barbarians from Internook would show up and lay claim to it.

Soon, neighbors were spying upon neighbors, telling which family might be hiding a cow in the woods or a daughter in the cellar, so that the levies would be paid.

As a baron, Owen Walkin had commanded respect among his people, but the time had finally come when hope failed him, and he'd taken his family and run off, crossing through cities and countryside by night, until they reached the land of Toom.

He'd fled just in time, as Rain told it, for two days later the entire barony was destroyed, its citizens forced to march into the forest and never return.

Rain finally answered, "We had it hard enough escaping from Mystarria the first time. I'm not eager to go back. I don't think I could ever go back. Stay here with me—please."

Her voice had become soft and urgent at the last, and she begged him to stay with her eyes more than with her words. She clutched his hands, as if begging him to stay forever.

Dare I stay? he wondered. His mother and father were going away, going to fight. He couldn't imagine leaving them to their own devices.

A moment later, Borenson came lumbering up the cliff and stood for a moment. He seemed to weave on his feet, and Draken realized that he had to be exhausted. As far as he could tell, his father had gotten no sleep since yesterday morning.

But the giant stood blinking his bloodshot eyes and peering at Rain and Draken as if judging them. At last he sauntered over and said to Rain, "I want to apologize for my harsh words yesterday. I . . . was distraught."

Rain put her hands on her hips and gave him an appraising look. "Yesterday when you were a man, you insulted me. Today when you're a monster, you ask forgiveness. I think I like the monster better."

Borenson guffawed and broke into a genuine smile. "Then you would be the first."

A clumsy moment followed. Rain looked down at the ground, gathered her courage, and said, "You need to know something. I'm in love with your son, and he loves me. We didn't set out for it to happen. It just did. He was kind to my family, and I saw his goodness. . . . Anyway, I begged him to tell you, but he was afraid of what you would think. He was hoping that we might find some land nearby, get settled, and then introduce us. We have not done anything unseemly, except . . ."

Borenson's brow furrowed, as if he expected her to admit to some infidelity. "Except what?"

"Except that we hid on your land. My father and brother found some odd jobs with your neighbors. We didn't dare speak to you. We were ashamed that we had fallen too far. . . ."

Draken knew that his father was not a man to stand on station. He had been born a butcher's son, and had made himself the first knight of the realm.

Borenson finally reached down and hugged her briefly. "Welcome to the family."

"Thank you," she said. She pulled away, blinked a tear from her eye, and studied his face.

"Myrrima says that you're going back to Mystarria. She's invited all of us to come along."

"Will you be joining us?" Borenson asked.

Rain frowned, looked to Draken, and let out a deep sigh. "I don't know. The family is against it. There is not much for us here, but if what you say is right, by going back to Mystarria we would be marching out of the rain to get into the storm. . . ."

Draken squeezed her hand, begging her to be discreet. He wanted to talk to his father at length before making a determination.

"You wouldn't have to go all the way to Mystarria," Borenson suggested. "We'll make stops along the way. There is good land in Toom to be had."

"There was ten years ago," Rain objected, "but refugees took it. 'There's plenty of good ground left,' they say, 'if you'd like to grow rocks.' But since everyone in Toom has more than they want, rocks are awfully hard to sell."

"I wouldn't recommend that you stay here in Landesfallen," Borenson said. "There is food to be had, if you work hard enough. But the coastal cities are all gone, and with them went the smithies, the chandlers, the glassblowers, and so on. You'll find yourselves lacking for comfort."

"My mother has considered that, and she says that while 'We may find ourselves wanting for some necessities, there is one thing that we will have in abundance here—peace.'"

"Perhaps," Borenson agreed, "for a time. But who knows how long it will last? The wyrmlings will come eventually, perhaps in an hour or a manner that you are not prepared for. I prefer to take matters into my own hands."

Rain peered up at him, gauging his size. "Do you really think that there's blood metal to be had in Mystarria?"

"I've seen it with my own eyes."

She nodded. "You'd make a fearsome lord."

It was true, Draken thought. Borenson looked strong now, terrifying.

What's more, Draken realized, his father knew the secret fighting styles of the assassins from Indhopal, and had mastered the weapons of Inkarra. He'd been a strategist for kings.

Sir Borenson had gained fighting skills that the wyrmlings had never seen before. With his size, Draken imagined that his father would be a fearsome opponent.

Rain turned to Draken. "So, what all did you find on your trip?"

"Two casks of ale, four barrels of molasses, a barrel of rice, a barrel of lamp oil, and some crates. The crates were packed . . . with women's linen undergarments."

Rain laughed. "Well, then we shan't want for underwear."

Draken knelt on the ground and pulled out a small pouch, dropping some jewelry into his hand. "I also got this," he whispered. There were two rings, one all of gold and one with a ruby. There was also a silver necklace and a couple of coins—steel eagles out of Rofehavan. "I got us wedding rings!"

Borenson bit his lower lip, peered down at the rings disparagingly. "Put them up, lad. No sense in letting the children see."

The blood rose on the back of Draken's neck. He'd

taken salvage from the dead, and now his father was embarrassed by it.

But at that moment, Baron Walkin came into the camp and dumped the contents of his own coin purse onto the ground, spilling out dozens of rings and coins.

"Have a look at this!" he called to his wife and children. "Look what the men brought home. There's enough gold and coin here to buy a small farm!"

Walkin's brother Bane stood precariously above the loot on his injured ankle, beaming, like a boy who has just brought his first stag home from the hunt.

Borenson peered at the baron in surprise, then glanced back at Draken. He suddenly saw the way of it. He'd sent Draken out to search for food and supplies, but the Walkins had spent the night looting dead bodies. Draken didn't tell what had happened; Borenson simply saw the shame burning in his face.

What's more, the Walkins had made a race of it— looting the bodies before Draken could reach them.

An unholy rage suddenly welled up in Borenson, his face flushing. He strode forward and stepped on the Walkins' loot. "This isn't yours," he said. "The people of Mystarria—that you once swore to serve—need it. In the name of the king, I lay hold of it."

Walkin's fist clenched in anger, and he squatted with back bent, but tried to restrain himself.

"You have no right to speak for the king," Owen Walkin growled. "Nor for Mystarria. There is no king in Mystarria anymore. There is no Mystarria—just a rotting carcass being carved up by scavengers."

"Fallion Orden still lives," Sir Borenson countered. "He's the rightful king. He has returned to Mystarria. I'm sailing back to serve him."

Baron Walkin peered up at Borenson, eyes gleaming with anger. Draken suddenly realized that his father had challenged a desperate man. The baron had lost everything in the world, and so he had nothing to lose.

Instinctively, Draken pulled Rain back away from the two men.

"I've been meaning to talk to you about that," Baron Walkin said dangerously. "My brother and I risked our lives for that salvage, and my brother almost lost a foot. It's half ours—at the very least. And I have a right, too. My family is starving. Whatever loot me and the boys find, we intend to keep."

Borenson growled deep in his throat, a warning sound that Draken had only heard from dogs.

Sir Walkin needed no translator. He reached down and drew a dagger from his boot, backed up a step, and took a fighting stance.

Draken studied him. Walkin might have been a fighting man once, but he wasn't practiced at it.

Borenson gave a fey laugh. "I had almost forgotten how much trouble the in-laws can be. . . ."

Baron Walkin grinned, began to circle to his right, his eyes glittering with bloodlust.

"I give you fair warning, little man," Borenson said. "You can't win this fight."

Walkin grinned, a surprisingly fey smile. "That's what they all say."

"I could cut you down faster than you know."

"You make that sound easy," Walkin warned.

Walkin feinted, trying to draw Borenson in, searching for an opening.

Borenson laughed grimly. "You can have the crates of linen. Those alone are worth a small fortune."

The baron shook his head no, eyes glimmering dangerously.

At first Draken had thought that the baron was only posing, that he wouldn't dare attack.

But now Draken could see Walkin thinking. There was a ship to win, and treasure—enough booty to secure his future in this wilderness. This might be his last chance to make such a boon for himself. If he didn't take the loot now, he might have to watch his children starve this coming winter.

There were riches worth dying for—or killing for. Walkin imagined that he had no choice but to fight.

What was it that Baron Walkin had said earlier? Draken wondered. "Sometimes killing can be an act of love"? Suddenly Draken realized that the baron was talking from experience. He'd killed to provide for his family before.

"I'm sailing that ship to Mystarria," Borenson warned. "Any trade goods we find will go to pay for supplies and safe passage through Internook's waters. If you want, you can have your share *after* the voyage is done."

"That's a fool's plan," Walkin said. "I'm not going back to Mystarria. Warlord Bairn has a price on my head."

So Walkin had decided. He wanted to take it all.

The women in Walkin's camp stood with open mouths, stunned at this sudden turn.

Myrrima shouted at the baron and Borenson, "Stop it! Both of you stop it right now." She stepped between them.

But she hadn't properly gauged the situation. She still hoped that this was some petty squabble. She didn't realize yet that Walkin had just decided to kill them all. That would be his only choice—to get rid of any witnesses who might tell what he'd done. It wouldn't be hard to dispose of the bodies. Nearly everyone in Landesfallen was floating up on one beach or another.

Walkin grabbed Myrrima, pulled her in front of him as a shield, expertly shoved a blade against her throat, and warned Borenson, "Drop your weapon!"

Rain screamed, "Father, what are you doing? Let her go!"

Draken released his grip on Rain's bicep, drawing his own blade. The time for talking was coming to an end, and he knew how to fight. He wasn't going to try to use the woman that he loved as a shield, so Draken stepped back, lest one of the Walkin men tried to circle behind him.

Borenson smiled grimly. "You see, son, how he repays your hospitality? This man is every bit the brigand I thought that he was."

"Honor is a luxury that only the rich can easily afford," Baron Walkin said.

"Father—" Rain tried to argue.

"Stay out of our way!" Walkin growled, but Rain stepped between the two men. It was a courageous thing to do. Or maybe it was foolish.

Borenson still hadn't drawn his own knife.

Myrrima grabbed the baron's knife wrist and tried to break away. There was a time when Myrrima had enough endowments to snap the man's arm, but she'd lost them all years ago, when the warlords of Internook overthrew Mystarria.

Rain lunged, grabbed her father's wrist, and tried to

free Myrrima. In the scuffle the baron's knife caught Rain on the forearm. Blood gushed.

Some children cried out in alarm while Rain staggered back, put her hand over the gash, and tried to staunch the blood.

Sudden resolution shone in Baron Walkin's eyes. He decided to kill Myrrima. He grabbed her chin and pulled her head back, exposing her throat.

At the sight, Sir Borenson's eyes lost focus. His face darkened and contorted in feral rage.

With a snarl the giant lunged so quickly that Draken's eyes could hardly register the attack. Big men weren't supposed to be able to move that fast.

No, Draken realized, *human beings* can't move that fast!

Borenson grabbed Walkin's knife wrist. He twisted, as if to disarm the man, but perhaps misjudged his own strength. Walkin's wrist snapped like a tree limb, a horrifying sound.

Borenson gripped Sir Walkin by the left shoulder and lifted him into the air. He shook the man like a rag doll, whipping him about so hard that it looked as if Walkin's head might come off. For a full ten seconds Borenson roared, a deep terrifying sound more befitting a lion than a man.

The scene was totally riveting, and time seemed to slow. Borenson roared and roared, staring beyond the baron, while women shouted for him to stop.

The baron shrieked in pain and terror. His eyes grew impossibly wide. Borenson seemed beyond hearing, beyond all restraint. He dug his enormous thumbs into the Baron's shoulders, plunging them through soft flesh like daggers, gripping the poor man so hard that blood blossomed red on the baron's tunic.

Then Borenson bellowed and pulled his hands apart, ripping the baron in two.

Blood spattered everywhere, glittering like rubies in the sunlight, and Draken saw the blue-white bones of the baron's ribs. Half a lung and some intestine spilled from the baron's ribcage.

Borenson continued to roar as he shook the man, raising him overhead, and at last he hurled Baron Walkin sixty feet—over the cliff.

Walkin hit some rocks with a cracking sound; a second later he splashed into the water.

Borenson whirled on the rest of the Walkin clan, muscles straining, as he roared another challenge.

No one dared move. Borenson stood huffing and panting.

The giant had taken leave of his senses. He glared at the crowd, as if searching for another enemy to rend in two. Gore dripped from his hands.

Instinctively, Bane backed away, as did the other Walkins.

The children shrieked in terror and cringed, gibbering in fear. Rain just stood in shock—both at what her father had done and at Borenson's response.

Even Draken feared what Borenson would do next.

Then, slowly, Borenson began to come to. He stood peering about at the crowd, his eyes jerking and refusing to focus. He raised his hands, peered at the gore dripping down his arms, and moaned.

Draken could not quite believe it. He could look back now and recognize the instant that his father had lost control. And Draken knew that his father had regained it. But in between, his father had been . . . gone, acting on pure instinct. He wasn't even a spectator in the battle.

Owen's wife Greta stood motionless, her face drained of blood. She gaped at Borenson as if she'd just wakened from one nightmare to a greater nightmare, and then in a small voice said, "Grab your things, children. We have to leave. We have to leave *now*!"

She was shaking, terrified. She dared not turn her back on the giant, for fear of an attack. So she glared at him as the children gathered around.

Borenson did not move to stop her.

Weeping and fearful glances came from the children. Bane's wife berated him, commanding him to "Do something!" while another young woman muttered insults under her breath, calling the giant an "ugly arr," and an "elephant's ass."

Rain stood for a moment, looking between her family and Draken, unsure which way to choose.

"Stay if you want," Myrrima pleaded with Rain softly. Rain hesitated, turned to look at Myrrima with tears streaming down her cheeks. The horror of what had happened was too great for her to overcome. She turned and began to follow her clan.

Draken called, "Rain!"

Myrrima told him, "And *you* can go if *you* want."

Draken stood, in the throes of a decision. He knew that he couldn't follow. Rain and her family, they'd never accept him now. Besides, he wasn't sure about them anymore. The baron had been willing to kill them all.

The entire Walkin clan scuttled away, grabbing their few bags of goods, fading off into the shadows thrown by the rocks.

Borenson grumbled, "There will be other women, son. Few are the men who fall in love only once in their lives."

"She's special," Draken said.

Borenson shook his head, gave the boy a suffering look, and said, "Not *that* special."

Draken whirled and growled at his father, "And you have the nerve to lecture me about discipline!" Draken stood, trembling, struggling to find the words that would unleash all of his anger, all of his frustration.

Borenson turned away, unable to face him.

Borenson said, "I am a berserker, bred for two hundred generations to fight the wyrmlings. They come at us with axes and harvester spikes stuck into their necks. I meet them with my rage.

"Even among those bred to be berserkers, only one in ten can do it—set aside all the pain of battle, all of the fear and hesitation, and go into that dark place where no soul ever returns unscathed. . . ."

Borenson watched the Walkins, shook his head, and said under his breath. "They'll be back. We should leave here—soon."

"They won't be back," Myrrima said. "They're more afraid of you than you are of them."

"Fear only makes a coward more dangerous," Borenson intoned.

Borenson stood, trembling at the release from his rage. His whole body seemed poised for battle, every muscle rigid. Draken had seen well-bred hunting dogs act that way.

"I had no choice but to kill," Borenson told Myrrima. "The man put you in danger."

Myrrima shouted, "You roared at children! No one

does that. I not only don't know *who* you are anymore, I don't know *what* you are." She hesitated. "Aaath Ulber, that's what they called you on that other world?"

"It means Berserker Prime, or Greatest of the Berserkers," Borenson said.

"*Aaath Ulber* then," Myrrima said in disgust. "I shall call you Aaath Ulber from now on."

Draken could see in the giant's expression that he knew what Myrrima was doing. By calling him a different name, she was distancing herself from him.

For a moment, all fell silent. Draken fixed the new name in his mind.

Pure grief washed across Aaath Ulber's face, but he took Myrrima's rebuke. "Right then, Aaath Ulber it is."

Draken stood between the two, bewildered. Draken was afraid of Aaath Ulber, terrified by what he'd done. The violence had been so fast, so explosive.

"Walkin deserved his punishment," Aaath Ulber said evenly. "If that man was still alive, I'd kill him again. He planned to kill me, and then he would have done you."

"How can you be so sure?" Myrrima demanded.

"I saw it in his eyes," Aaath Ulber said.

"So, you can read minds on your other world?" Myrrima asked.

"Only shallow ones." Aaath Ulber smiled a feral smile. He tried to turn away Myrrima's wrath with a joke. "Look at the good side of all of this," he said. "We won't be squabbling with the in-laws over who gets to eat the goose's liver at every Hostenfest feast."

❧ 8 ❧

FILTH

Many a man who labors to remove the dirt on his hands from honest toil never gives a thought to the stains on his soul.

—Emir Owatt of Tuulistan

There was work to be done before the Borensons broke camp. There were empty casks that needed to be filled with water. The family would need to take a trip to Fossil to fetch supplies.

And there was a child to be buried.

Myrrima had been waiting for Aaath Ulber to return so that the whole family could join in the solemn occasion. She'd wanted to have time to mourn as a family. She had never lost a child before. She'd always thought herself lucky. Now she felt as if even her chance to properly mourn was being stripped from her.

Fallion bound the worlds, Myrrima thought, and now my family is being ripped apart.

She told Aaath Ulber how Erin's spirit had visited near dawn, and told him of the shade's warning that they must go to the Earth King's tree.

Aaath Ulber grew solemn, reflective. He looked as if he wished that he had been here to see it, but the chance had been lost and there was no bringing her back.

"She spoke to you?" he asked in wonder.

"Yes," Myrrima said. "Her voice was distant, like a faraway song, but I could hear her."

"A strange portent," Aaath Ulber said. "It makes me wonder. I am two men in one body. Is Erin now two spirits bound together? Is that how she found this new power?"

Myrrima shook her head, for it was something she had no way of knowing.

"And if spirits also bind," Aaath Ulber said, "does that mean that within my body, the spirits of two men are also bound?"

Somehow, this idea disturbed him deeply. But there was no knowing the truth of it now. It was a mystery that no one could answer, so he asked, "Shall we bury Erin in water, or in the ground?"

Myrrima considered. She was a servant of Water, and always imagined that she would want to be buried in water herself. And on Sir Borenson's home island, it had been the custom to send the dead floating out to sea.

But the water in the old river channel was filthy, and Myrrima didn't want her daughter floating in that. Besides, if Myrrima ever returned to Landesfallen, she would want to know where her daughter's body might be found.

Myrrima said, "Let's plant her here, on dry ground, where she can be near the farm."

Aaath Ulber did not begrudge the task of digging a grave, even though he had no tools. The giant went to a place where the ground looked soft, then began to dig, using a large rock to gouge dirt from the earth.

Myrrima and Draken rolled the empty barrels out of the ship's hold; she opened each one and smelled inside.

Most of them had held wine or ale, so these were the ones that she moved to the spot where the small stream seeped down the cliff. She began to fill each barrel with water for their journey, and as she did, she fretted, making long lists of things she hoped to buy in the small village of Fossil: rope, lamps, wicks, flint, tinder, clothes, needles and thread, fish hooks, boots, twine, rain gear, medicines—the list was endless, but the money was not.

So she wrestled the empty barrels to a rock where the clean water cascaded down the cliff and began to let them fill. It was a slow process, letting the water trickle into the barrels. As she did, she found that her hands were shaking.

She paced around the barrels, nerves jangling. She felt that she should go after the Walkins and try to offer some apologies, make amends.

But nothing that she could do would ever undo the damage. Baron Walkin was dead. Perhaps he deserved it, perhaps not. Myrrima strongly suspected that if Aaath Ulber had just stopped to negotiate, approached things more rationally, the tragedy could have been averted.

But Aaath Ulber had killed the baron, taken all of the Walkins' money, and left them with nothing.

They came to our land with nothing, she thought, and with nothing they walk away.

It sounded fair, but Myrrima knew that it wasn't.

Draken went up the cliff, heading toward the brush. "We're going to need plenty of firewood," he said. It was one more thing that they'd need, and Myrrima dreaded the chore. Bringing in enough for the long journey would take hours, and she knew that they couldn't wait that long—the mayor of Fossil and his men were probably already rowing frantically toward them.

"Just get enough for a day or so," she shouted. "We can stop up the coast and take on firewood."

Sage came to the barrel and crouched next to it. The girl was trembling, and tears filled her eyes. She was only thirteen, and had never seen anything like what Aaath Ulber had done to Owen Walkin.

She needs comfort, Myrrima thought. I could cast a spell to wash away the memory. . . . But that would be wrong. She's going to need to learn how to deal with such things if we go back to Mystarria. "Are you all right?"

Sage shook her head no. She peered into the water barrel, her eyes unfocused. "Daddy tore that man apart."

Myrrima had a rule in life. She never blamed a man for what he could not control. Thus, she would never ridicule a foolish man, even if he was only a little foolish. She'd never belittle the halt or lame.

But what of Aaath Ulber? Was he guilty of murder, or was what he'd done outside his control?

She didn't want to exonerate him to Sage. But she'd seen how Aaath Ulber's mind had fled when he attacked. He wasn't in control. What's more, Myrrima suspected that he couldn't control himself.

"I think . . . he was protecting us," Myrrima said. "He was afraid of what Owen Walkin might do. I suspect . . . that he was right to kill him. I just wish that he hadn't been so brutal. . . . To kill that man so, in front of us, his wife and children—"

"I feel sick," Sage said. Her face had a greenish cast, and she peered about desperately.

"If you need to throw up," Myrrima said, "don't do it here."

But Sage just sat for a moment, holding all of the horror in. "So . . . Aaath Ulber was born to kill that way."

Myrrima had seen the rage in Aaath Ulber's eyes, how his own mind revolted after the deed. "There were men like him even in our old world, men whose anger sometimes took them. It's . . . Aaath Ulber's rage is an illness, like any other. I don't like it. I don't approve of what he did. But I cannot fault him for it. If you fell ill with a cough, I would not condemn you. I wouldn't find fault. Instead I would offer you herbs for your throat, and with a compress I would wash your fever away. I would seek to heal you. But I fear that curing your father might be beyond my ability. I know only a few peaceful runes to draw upon him. I can try, but I suspect that the only cure lies in Mystarria—in the hands of Fallion. We must find him, and get him to unbind the worlds."

"Did father start the fight?" Sage asked. "Draken said that it was 'all his' fault. Father started it."

Sage had lost so much in the past day. She still needed a father. So Myrrima decided to let the girl hold on to the illusion that she still had her father for as long she could.

Myrrima asked, "What do you think?"

"Draken said that when Daddy first found the Walkins, he insulted them. He called Rain a 'tart.' So father started it, and Owen Walkin tried to finish it."

Myrrima traced the logic. "It wasn't Aaath Ulber who started this," Myrrima said, "it was the Walkins. They're the ones who were squatting on our farm. We thought it was the birds eating our cherries, but now you and I both know better."

"Draken was letting them live there."

"Because he loved their daughter," Myrrima said. "But Draken didn't have the right to let them squat. It wasn't his farm. You wouldn't go give away our milk cow, would you? That is what Draken was doing. He should have come forward and asked your father's permission. Nor should the Walkins have allowed it."

Myrrima did not want to say it, but she half-wondered if the Walkins had thrown Rain at Draken. Perhaps they'd hoped that the two would fall in love. Perhaps they'd encouraged Draken's affection, knowing that his father was a wealthy landowner who might provide a parcel for an inheritance. It was, after all, a time-honored tradition among lords to increase their lands that way. But in Myrrima's mind, it was also damned near to prostitution.

"Your father was in the right to throw them off," Myrrima said. "We've had this talk about squatters before. It isn't a kind thing to do, but it is needful."

"But the Walkins had children in the camp," Sage said. "Some of them were just babies. They shouldn't have to starve just because . . . their parents make mistakes."

"That's the way of it," Myrrima said. "When parents make mistakes, children often suffer." She thought of Erin, and even of Sage. What would her children be called upon to bear because of her actions?

She dared not say it, but now she was reminded of how much she feared Aaath Ulber's plan. He was going to take the whole family back into a war.

"The ship doesn't really belong to Father," Sage said. "It doesn't belong to anyone. Father shouldn't be able to just take it."

"Aaath Ulber is a soldier at war," Myrrima pointed

out. "When a lord is in battle, he often finds that he may
have to commandeer goods—food for his troops, shelter for his wounded, horses to draw wagons. He takes a
little in order to help the many. That is what your father
was doing with the ship. Owen Walkin knew that. He
was a soldier, too. Baron Walkin broke his oath."

Sage peered into the barrel. It was nearly full, and
light reflecting from the water's surface danced in her
blue eyes.

Sage was aptly named, for even as a babe she had
seemed to have a thoughtful look to her. "Father has
changed," Sage said. "I don't know who he is anymore.
He doesn't think like we do, or else how could he do
what he did to Sir Owen?"

"I suspect that you're right," Myrrima said. "Aaath
Ulber's people have been at war with the wyrmlings
for thousands of years. In that war, his people lost
everything—their lands, their friends, their freedom to
roam. On Aaath Ulber's world, he had a choice of only
a few women that he could wed. He was expected to
marry a woman from the warrior clans, a good breeder.
In his world, he was expected to give up everything in
the service of his people—even love."

"I think that people who give up love," Sage said,
"must be a different kind of people. A person who would
give up love for the war effort would give up anything
else. I think he just expected Walkin to give up the ship.
He didn't think to ask for it, because in his world there
would have been no need to ask."

Myrrima studied her daughter, surprised at the depth
of the girl's insight. "I think you're right. You should
remember this. You and I both know your father, but

we have yet to learn what kind of man Aaath Ulber really is."

Rain still loved Draken; that much she felt sure of as she walked away from the Borenson camp, using a wad of grass as a poultice to stanch the wound to her arm. The cut wasn't wide, but it was deep.

Yet the image of her father's death hung over her, blinding in its intensity, so that as she plodded down the uneven trail, she often stumbled over rocks or tree roots.

Her thoughts were jangled, her nerves on edge.

There was a road of sorts here along the rim of the mesa—uneven and narrow. Teamsters sometimes used it in winter, Draken had told her. But there were no houses here, no other sign of life. Instead ragged bluffs of rock—sometimes iron red and sometimes ashen gray—rose all around in a jumble; in places the rock lay exposed for mile after weary mile. The soil was so shallow that little but rangit grass could grow in the open, and most of the shade could be found only beside the occasional stream.

I love Draken, she kept thinking, and she wanted to return to him. But she couldn't bear standing in the presence of Aaath Ulber. His actions had driven a wedge between her and Draken, and Rain feared that she had lost him forever.

Just as importantly, she couldn't bear the thought of abandoning her mother now. The Walkin clan was so poor. Rain was the oldest of seven children. Life would be hard enough here in the wilderness, but without her father, it would be much tougher now. Rain felt that she owed it to her mother to stay.

Which left her only one choice: She had to convince Draken to stay.

She found herself walking slowly. The Walkins soon became strung out, Rain's mother leading the way, her back stiff and angry, her strides long and sure.

The mothers carried their infants, the fathers the toddlers, and every child above the age of five had to walk. But the little ones could not travel in haste, and could not go far. After a mile, they began to lag.

So Rain kept up the rear guard, making sure that they were safe. There were wild hunting cats up here on the bluff, she knew, cats large enough to take down a large rangit or run off with a child. She'd heard them not two nights ago snarling in the dark as she tried to sleep.

So she lagged behind. Her aunt Della soon came to walk at her side. Della was ten years Rain's senior, and already had five children. Her tongue was as sharp as a dagger, and she felt compelled to honestly speak any cruel thought that came to mind.

"You're not thinking of going back to Draken, are you?"

"No," Rain said. The word was slow to come from her mouth.

"You can't go back to him. It's because of *you* that we're in this mess."

The notion seemed odd. "What do you mean?"

"If you hadn't gotten caught by Warlord Grunswallen, Owen never would have had to kill to defend your honor."

Rain felt determined to defend herself. "As I recall, I was churning butter in the basement when I got 'caught.' It wasn't my fault. Someone—one of our neighbors—reported me."

"But why?" Della demanded. "Obviously, you offended someone. They wanted to see you gone."

Rain knew that wasn't true. "I had no enemies, only faithless townsfolk who hoped to gain some advantage for themselves."

"Or maybe someone just disliked the way that you always go around with your nose in the air, acting like you're better than they are! Here I am, the pretty little lady—to the manor born."

Della wasn't the most pleasant woman to look upon. Nor was she ugly. But it was plain that she felt ugly inside.

"I've never done that," Rain said. "I've never been a snob. Mother taught me to hold my head up high, to look others in the eye. That isn't the same as being proud."

Della opened her mouth, and then stopped, a sure sign that she had something truly devastating to say. "Going back to that boy would be a poor tribute to your father. He died to save your honor."

That was the problem, Rain decided. He hadn't died to save her honor. She'd seen the look in his eyes before the fight began. He was willing to kill Aaath Ulber—and Draken, and anyone else who got between him and his money.

"Father saved my honor," Rain said candidly, "but took little thought for his own."

"He was trying to feed his family," Della said. "You'll understand what he was going through someday, when you've spent enough nights awake worrying about how to feed your little ones."

He could have tried to work it out, Rain thought. Della's trying too hard to defend him. Suddenly she understood something. "You think it's my fault that my father is dead?"

"He died to save your honor," Della insisted. She stumbled over a root and caught herself, switched her babe to the other shoulder and patted its back, trying to soothe it to sleep. The babe was only nine weeks old. It was a colicky thing that spent most of the night crying. Now it raised its head, as if to let out a wail, but instead just lay back down to sleep.

I'd be colicky too if I had to drink Della's sour milk, Rain thought.

She tried to track Della's logic. When Rain had been caught and taken to Warlord Grunswallen's manor, Owen had waited for the man to leave his home, and had then ambushed him in the market, overpowering his guards.

He'd tried to avenge Rain's honor, but he'd struck too late. The fat old warlord had already bedded her.

Still, Owen had known that his deed would bring retribution on him and his family, so the whole family had fled that day, taking boats downriver for thirty miles, reaching a town in the full night, and then creeping overland for days.

They hadn't stopped to purchase food for a week, hadn't met with a stranger. They'd traveled only at night.

When they did resurface, two hundred miles from home, they heard rumors of how Owen Walkin's entire realm had been "cleansed."

At first, Rain imagined that it was their fault, that Grunswallen's men had taken revenge upon the entire realm. But all of the bards agreed—the lands were cleared in the morning, and new tenants began to arrive by noon.

That could only have meant that Grunswallen had sold their lands months earlier—perhaps as much as a year in advance.

He'd simply become more rapacious as the time for the cleansing neared. Taking her as his slave was simply one last mad act among a long list of crimes.

So Rain's father had saved her. In fact, he'd saved his entire family, and Rain felt grateful to him. But she did not feel guilty about the manner of his death.

She hadn't wished it upon him. She hadn't sensed it coming. She would have averted it, if she could.

"You say that my father died for my honor, but it seems to me that he died for all of us—just trying to get by."

"*You* shouldn't have stepped in!" Della said. "Your father couldn't fight that giant—and you!"

Now Della's true feelings came to the fore. Rain felt angry. She'd tried to talk her father down, stop him from committing a senseless murder. She'd hoped to remind of him of his honor.

But now she saw the true reason for Della's rage. She suspected that Owen had been slow to react precisely *because* he feared hurting his own daughter.

Maybe she's right, Rain thought.

She halted a moment, feeling ill, overwhelmed by the questions that raced through her mind.

Della's youngest boy was trudging along ahead. He turned back and whined, "I want some water."

"There's water ahead," Della urged.

The road before them wound over a long stretch of gray rocks that could not support even a gorse bush or a blade of rangit grass. The sun beat down mercilessly. Rain's mother had forged far ahead of the rest of the group, and was now approaching a line of gum trees and wild plums, a sure sign that there was a creek. They had come perhaps two miles from the Borenson camp.

Suddenly Rain's mother burst into a sprint, stretching her legs long as she pounded down the road. She looked as if she was breaking free, running from all the troubles of her past.

"There she goes," Della said, as if she'd been expecting her to run. "Off to town. That mighty Lord Borenson is going to hang when she gets through with him."

Rain's mother was heading toward Fossil. It would be a long run—twenty miles—but she could make it in a few hours.

The blood burned in Rain's face, shame and rage warring in her.

She worried how her mother would twist the tale. She couldn't hope to gain much sympathy if she told the truth, so she'd have to lie: tell the townsfolk how a giant had killed her husband, a cruel beast who was intent on robbing a bit of salvage from her poor family. She'd neglect to mention what her husband had done.

But there was one thing that Rain felt sure of. No matter what happened, Aaath Ulber would not get a fair hearing. People would see his size, his strange features, and cast their judgment based on that.

Most likely the law would demand that he hang. Whether for the killing or for the robbery, it did not matter. The penalty was the same for both. Justice here in the wilderness was stark and sure.

Rain hurried her pace until she reached the line of trees.

They came upon a relatively broad creek, perhaps

eight feet across. White gum trees grew along its banks, as did wild apples and plums. Rain crossed it and looked beyond—across a broad expanse of more gray rock, interspersed with fields of rangit grass. She studied her surroundings.

The fruit trees were the same breed as found in the Borensons' old orchard. Most likely, burrow bears or borrowbirds had eaten the fruits in ages past, and then shat out the seeds here on the ridge. In this manner the fruit trees had gone wild along the creeks.

"This looks like a good place to camp," Bane said. He was now the oldest of the Walkin brothers. So he urged the families to set camp beneath some trees, while the children went about searching for food.

An hour later, half of the children were asleep and Rain was wading in the creek, lifting rocks so that the children could catch crayfish, when Draken showed up.

One of the children saw him and raised a warning shout, as if he might have come to attack the camp.

As he came in out of the sun, beneath the shelter of some woody old peach trees, he called out, "Is Greta here?"

No one answered at first. Rain didn't want to tell him. But finally she answered, "She's gone . . . to Fossil."

She watched his face fall, saw the fear building in his eyes.

Della laughed, "Your father is going to swing, if the town can find a tree big enough!"

Several of the children chimed in, "Yeah, he's going to hang."

Draken withstood the insults. "When she returns," Draken asked, "will you give her this? It's the salvage that Owen found last night."

He held out a piece of white linen all bundled together.

Rain knew that he was trying to make things right. She suspected that he had come here on his own, defying his father.

"We don't want your blood money," Della called out. "Besides, there isn't half enough to buy us off."

Rain's thoughts raced. Della didn't want his money but she wanted him to double his offer?

Reverently, Draken set the money on the ground. "I'm not trying to buy you off," he said. "This is for Greta . . . and her children. I was hoping she could use it to get some land and some food, so that the children don't starve."

No one stepped forward to take the gold. He stood for a long moment, gazing at Rain, and she merely remained by the creek, her heart breaking.

"Just so you know," he said, "it wasn't my father who did this. Anyone could tell you, my father was a fair man. But since the change . . . well, you can see . . . Aaath Ulber . . . my father isn't himself."

Draken stood shaking, peering into Rain's eyes. He was forty feet away, but seemed afraid to draw any closer.

"You'd best get out of here, little man," Della called.

Draken peered into Rain's eyes, and with all that was in him begged, "Come with me!"

Rain just shook her head. He was asking too much of her. She turned and raced off into the trees, tramping loudly, blinded by tears. When she was in the deep shadows, she swiped her face and turned to see Draken out in the sunlight, trudging over the barren rock on stiff legs.

"Your da is going to hang!" Della shouted, and the

children offered up similar catcalls, even as one of them grabbed up the little bundle of gold.

Rain felt confused, broken. Draken had tried to do something noble, had tried to make things right. But her family was just being mean and vindictive.

We were nobles once, she thought. Now we are reduced to being beggars and thieves, liars and robbers.

She loved Draken; that much Rain knew.

He was decent and strong. As a child he'd served as a Gwardeen, a skyrider flying on the backs of giant graaks. She admired his courage, his devotion to the people he'd served.

She knew that in all of Landesfallen, she'd never find another man that she shared so much in common with. Both of their fathers had been barons in Mystarria. Both of them had fled to the ends of the earth to start a new life.

Suddenly she realized that their fathers had even shared a common flaw. Draken felt humiliated by his father's actions, just as Rain was embarrassed by what her father had become.

If Draken were more like my father, would I love him better? Rain wondered.

The answer was obvious.

I would not love him at all, she realized. I would think him mean and lowly, unworthy of affection.

She felt deeply troubled by the realization. The problem was that her entire family was changing, becoming the kind of people that Rain could not respect or tolerate.

For long minutes she sat in the deepest shade there in the grove. She saw a flash of red above as a day bat went winging about, hunting insects.

At last she got up, and began walking west, toward Draken, and hopefully toward a brighter future.

She passed by the edge of camp, and worried what her family would say. It seemed that all eyes followed her—the children's, her aunts'.

She'd reached the blinding sunlight and the path over the rocks before Della spat, "I hope you die with them!"

Rain considered many replies before she turned and said, "Della, I hope that you have a happy and prosperous life, and that all of you can find peace."

Half an hour after Draken left, Myrrima realized that he'd stopped bringing in firewood. She knew instantly where he had gone.

She wasn't sure if he'd return to her.

Aaath Ulber had finished digging the grave for Erin, and now he put her body in. He gave a worried glance to the east, looking up the trail for Draken, and finally acknowledged that his son was gone by saying, "I reckon we lost another one."

Then he went down to the ship and made ready for the voyage by wrestling the big water barrels onto the deck and stowing them in the hold. It was a job befitting a man of his size. Myrrima estimated that each barrel weighed nearly three hundred pounds. She and Sage together could hardly budge one.

The family gathered at Erin's grave, and each of them spoke for a moment, talking about the best and brightest memories of her that they would treasure.

When it was Myrrima's turn, she spoke of the blue dress that Erin had made for her last Hostenfest with material that she had bought herself. Erin had sewn it in secret, out in the barn, and when she had brought it out as a gift, Myrrima had feared that it would be ill-fitting or badly sewn. So she was astonished to find that it fit perfectly, and that Erin had sewn it as well as any seamstress in town might have done.

Aaath Ulber talked about how Erin had always been one to do her chores. He told her once when she was six that it would be her job to feed the pigs, and every day after that she would be up at dawn mixing the mash for them. He'd never had to tell her again.

Sage told of a time when Erin was only a toddler, and wanted a horse. The family didn't have one, so Sage took Erin out into the fields until they found a burrow bear. Sage had used a bit of dried plum to tame the creature, simply offering it fruit from her pocket until it followed her around, and then she put Erin on its back so that she could ride.

Myrrima laughed at the tale. She'd never heard it before, and she wondered how many other secret acts of kindness Sage had done for her children.

With a heavy heart, she looked off to the east, hoping that Draken would return, but she didn't see him. It was past time to go.

So she reached down and grabbed the first handful of dirt.

"Wait," Aaath Ulber said. "He's coming!"

From his higher vantage point, Aaath Ulber could see better. He gave a shout. "Hurry up!"

Draken raced into camp a minute later, looking shaken and guilty.

Myrrima called, "You couldn't get Rain to come?"

Draken shook his head.

Aaath Ulber asked in his deep voice, "Did you give them the gold?"

Draken nodded, face pale. He was ready to take whatever punishment Aaath Ulber proffered.

Aaath Ulber grunted. "I saw you take it," he admitted. "It won't make things right between us, but Greta will thank you for it, come winter."

"Greta wasn't there," Draken said. "She's running ahead, to tell the townsfolk in Fossil what happened."

Myrrima worried. The townsfolk would be quick to sympathize with the poor widow once they heard her tale. The best that Myrrima could hope for was that they could get into town, grab a few supplies, and then escape before Greta made it there.

Then, of course, she had to worry about the mayor and his men, coming to seize the ship.

"So much to do, so little time," Aaath Ulber mourned. He began shoving dirt over Erin's grave.

Moments later the family was on the ship. Draken unmoored it, and together they hoisted the sail.

They weren't sixty feet from shore when they heard a shout from the cliff up above.

Rain raced downhill, reached the shore, and leapt out into the water. The men struggled for a moment to drop the sail as Rain swam out to meet them. The ship drifted farther and farther from shore faster than Rain could swim. The ship was nearly a quarter of a mile out when at last Draken was able to pull Rain into the boat, sopping wet.

She hugged Draken and wept, and Aaath Ulber said dryly, "You didn't happen to bring a change of clothes, did you?"

She just laughed and cried and shook her head no.

Myrrima felt happy, for a moment. Happy for Draken, happy for Rain, happy that she hadn't lost another child.

But instantly Aaath Ulber pointed out, "We'd better get under way, lest Greta reach town before we do and get us all hanged."

The race was on.

Myrrima shook her head sadly at a sudden realization. It wasn't her husband that she was worried about: it was any townsfolk who tried to stop him.

❧ 9 ❧

RETURN TO THE OAK

Every man serves himself, and that is the proper duty of man. But once in a while, if we are to live in good conscience, we must serve something greater than ourselves. Give freely to the Powers that Protect, and humbly proffer that which you have to those who are in need.

—Jaz Laren Sylvarresta

The trip to Fossil took too long for Aaath Ulber's comfort. He wanted to speak to no one, and no one wanted to speak to him. He was glad to have Rain aboard ship, though there was a wall between them. He wanted to offer his sympathy, but he knew that she would have none of it.

I have become a monster, he thought. I have lost myself.

At home in Caer Luciare, it was considered a boon to be born a berserker. His gift was a prize. But here in Landesfallen, the gift had become a curse. He'd always told his children that they should retain control of themselves.

But how could he ask it of them, when he himself was out of control?

Aaath Ulber had no answer except one: I shall try to do better in the future.

But he felt weak, bereft of comfort. His children had seen him at his worst, and he knew that his life could never be the same. They wouldn't trust him.

So he set his mind to other matters.

Right now, he felt an urgent need to get out on the open ocean, set sail for Mystarria. He yearned to know what had befallen Fallion, and he wanted to get home to Caer Luciare—to the wife and children that must be wondering about him.

But it wasn't his mood that made the trip feel slow. An afternoon breeze was blowing up the channel toward the village, and ship could have made good time but for the debris floating in the water.

Only a day before the Hacker River Valley had been filled with orchards and woods, cities and homes. Now the debris was rising to the surface. Whole trees lay hidden in waters the deep brown color of dark ale. Bits of bark and wood floated everywhere, along with the occasional cow or burrow bear or dead fish or person. Beams from barns and homes littered the surface of the channel, along with bits of thatch, here a stool, there a chest that held some young girl's dowry.

Often their little ship plowed over a sunken tree, and

Aaath Ulber would hear it scraping the hull—or he'd hit a submerged body and feel it bumping along.

Aaath Ulber held his tongue, not wanting his children to know what made that noise.

So the ship sailed at quarter-mast, moving sluggishly, so that Myrrima and Sage could direct Aaath Ulber around the larger logs.

It would take months for the old river channel to get clear of debris, Aaath Ulber suspected. The Hacker River was just a trickle at this time of year. The water would move the logs and sticks around, send them surging inland when the tide rose, suck the debris back out to sea as the tides fell. The winds would have their way with it, too, blowing it toward one shore or another, depending upon the day.

In time it would wash high up on the beach, or it would sink into the depths, or it would simply wash back out to sea.

But for now the refuse was everywhere. In some places where the channel turned, the winds had already sent it into still eddies, and there the flotsam was so thick that it looked as if one could hike across it.

Already it had begun to smell foul as dead animals oozed into the flow. Aaath Ulber could hardly bear to look at it, for fear of whom he might see.

"Can I come to the Earth King's tree?" Sage asked her mother.

"If your father will take you," Myrrima answered.

Aaath Ulber raised a questioning brow. He'd thought that Myrrima would go to the tree.

"I think it best if you aren't seen in town," Myrrima reasoned.

Aaath Ulber couldn't argue against that, nor did he want to. He'd need Draken, Rain, and Myrrima to go through town and purchase whatever supplies they could lay their hands upon, and they would need to reach good bargains, for his money would not spread far.

With this in mind, he promised to take Sage with him. She smiled at the thought, and began to chatter incessantly about her theory: the Earth King was going to rise again!

Aaath Ulber didn't believe such foolishness. He wasn't even sure that the young oak tree there at Fossil *was* the remains of the Earth King. It made sense, in a strange way. When a flameweaver was killed, the elemental in it took the form of towering flames and did its best to consume all that it could. When a wind wizard died, it released a tornado. When a water wizard passed, she typically gave herself to the sea. So it made sense that Gaborn would find some way to quickly return to the earth.

But Aaath Ulber refused to put too much stock in such speculation.

So they sailed in the late evening toward Fossil, and finally came to a place where the flotsam was so thick, Aaath Ulber did not dare go farther.

He moored the boat to a tree, and the family walked. A mile upstream, the vast tidal wave had deposited a huge wall of tangled trees and wreckage. Some of the local children from Fossil were out exploring in the mess.

Town was a mile beyond. By the time they reached it, the sun had nearly fallen.

Aaath Ulber gave Myrrima his coin pouch, such as it was. He wasn't sure what a merchant might make of the steel discs from Caer Luciare. Myrrima had her own coin pouch as well, but it had been a lean year, and the family had been counting on the harvest to pay for supplies.

"First things first," Aaath Ulber warned as he pressed his coin bag into her hand, "Hooks, needles, twine, matches, a good ax—"

"I know," Myrrima said. Aaath Ulber bent down and gave her a kiss on the head, a clumsy gesture. It felt like kissing a child.

Fossil was not a large village, just a couple of hundred cottages all huddled on the banks of the river. It had a single inn and a great house that was used for the village moots.

Myrrima, Draken, and Rain took the old River Road to town; Aaath Ulber and Sage crept through some orchards, thus skirting the village altogether.

A couple of dogs barked at Aaath Ulber, and a horse nickered, as if it was time for feed, but otherwise the village paid him no regard.

Aaath Ulber and Sage reached a crossroad, heading north and south.

Night was beginning to fall. The air had gone still in the hills, which were thick with boulders. Among the short dry rangit grass, crickets had begun to sing. It was but two more miles.

With the coming of night he made a run for the tree, while Sage raced at his side. Running felt good. Once he got a steady pace, he reveled in the race, and became lost in thought. Sweat streamed down his face and back, while his heart hammered a steady rhythm. He cleared his mind and focused only on breathing.

Birds peeped querulously from the gorse along the road as he ran, while ferrin and rangits darted from his path.

Half an hour later, the evening sun was falling behind the hills, a rose-colored pearl that limned the horizon. The old dirt highway ran right up to the side of Bald Hill, and Aaath Ulber could see the tree on its crown a mile away.

"There's your tree, Sage," he huffed. "It hasn't turned into a man."

"There's someone beneath the tree, though," Sage pointed out.

Her eyes were sharper than his. He saw nothing, until after a few minutes he spotted movement, a lone figure in the dusk. But then it seemed that the figure vanished again, perhaps by walking to the far side of the tree.

He put on a burst of speed, went climbing to the top. The hill was covered with dry grasses. Cicadas buzzed in the dusk.

He crested the top of the hill, came to the tree, and halted. The setting sun smote his eyes, backlighting the tree in shades of rose and blood.

No one was standing beneath it. Aaath Ulber peered around its base, just to be certain.

Sage gazed up at the oak silently, as if communing, and Aaath Ulber stood for a long moment, letting the sounds of nature wash through him. The tree's leaves shivered in a small wind, and elsewhere in the vales below he could hear the breeze rustling through dry grasses.

He noted motes of dust caught in the wan light, small green motes that seemed to be dripping from the leaves. The ground beneath the tree seemed unnaturally bright, and as if golden sunlight caught it, sunlight that wasn't there.

Aaath Ulber felt a thrill as a voice suddenly filled the silence within him, a voice that he recognized from long ago.

"A great evil is rising in the west," the Earth King Gaborn Val Orden whispered. "I've sensed the change coming all summer. The crickets heralded it in their songs, and the mice worried over it. The enemy will commit a sacrilege against the earth."

"Master," Borenson said, dropping to one knee and lowering his head in token of respect. He had visited this tree before, a few years back. He'd sat beneath it on an afternoon and longed to hear Gaborn's voice. But he'd left feeling empty and unsatisfied.

Now there was no denying what he heard. Gaborn's voice came soft but clear. Aaath Ulber peered into the tree itself, and saw a ghostly form. Gaborn's arms were raised up, contorted into limbs, and his elongated hands were lost in the branches. His face had the greenish hue of an Earth Warden, but his eyes had changed most of all. They seemed to be filled with starlight and kindness.

"A war is beginning, a war not for this world alone, but a war that shall span all of the heavens. Your enemy will embark upon a terrifying course, one that you cannot yet see. Their armies will race through the heavens like autumn lightning.

"Only you can stop them, my old friend. There is little that I can do to help."

"Command me," Aaath Ulber said, "and I will do all that is in my power."

"I once told you how some had murdered my chosen. Do you recall?"

Aaath Ulber bowed his head, wondering why that knowledge would be important. He remembered the day clearly when Gaborn had visited him, revealing how some monstrously evil people had carried out plans to murder those under his protection. It was a secret that Aaath Ulber had never revealed. "I remember."

"Good," Gaborn whispered. "The time is coming when others must learn this secret. But your goal is not to kill unless you must. Your challenge is to help Fallion bind the worlds," the Earth King whispered. "Only then can they be healed. Deliver him to the Seals of Creation."

"It shall be done," Borenson said, and for a moment his worries for Fallion were alleviated. The Earth King would know if his own son was dead or alive.

The tree's leaves suddenly rustled in a stray breeze, and for the moment the tree fell silent.

"Beware the subtle powers of Despair," the Earth King whispered. "It will seek to break you."

Aaath Ulber trembled. He recalled the sound that Owen Walkin's carcass had made as it bounced over the cliff.

"I am already broken," Aaath Ulber admitted. "I fear that I am already lost."

The image of the Earth King was fading, retreating back into the tree, like an old man turning toward his bed for the night.

"The journey will be long," the Earth King whispered. "You must find yourself along the way. A broken man is hard-pressed to heal others."

The image of the Earth King dissipated altogether, and the very last of the day's sunlight seemed to dim all at once, as if the candle of heaven had been snuffed. The golden glow at their feet, the motes of green dust in the waning light, all were gone.

Sage reached down to the ground and grabbed a single acorn. "We should keep this," she said reverently, "as a remembrance."

Aaath Ulber placed a large hand on her shoulder and nodded his agreement, and together they turned and marched downhill in the dusk.

They had not gone a hundred feet when they heard a loud crack, followed by a crash. They turned to see the great oak split in half.

Aaath Ulber thought, Now Gaborn is gone forever.

When Sage and Aaath Ulber reached the outskirts of Fossil, it was past dusk. Smoke wafted above the chimneys, and Aaath Ulber could smell meat roasting on the fire.

I should go into town, he told himself. The time will come when I must win people over. I must figure out how to inspire them to follow me to war—or at the very least, give up their endowments.

I'm big and strange to look upon, but I'm not that strange.

So he sauntered to the town square in front of the inn, with Sage on his heels, and found a surprise: A rider had reached the village, a girl of seven or eight who rode upon the back of a huge white sea graak.

The townsfolk had gathered around it, and now they stood with torches. The graak shone an unearthly orange in the firelight, and stood regally, fanning its wings, the skin at its throat jiggling—a sign that it was hot after a long flight. It was a male, with a long white plume upon its forehead—a bony ridge that ended with a fold of skin like a fan. The blue staring eye of the Gwardeen was painted upon the plume.

The rider, a petite thing, had her hair tied back and wore the ocher tunic of those who manned the citadel in the Infernal Wastes.

Several men had gathered round the beast, hoping for news. Myrrima, Draken, and Rain were among the crowd, bearing cloth sacks filled with produce. Rain had a pair of goats tethered together. Little Sage raced up to her mother, excited to see what might be in the sacks.

Aaath Ulber stopped in the shadows of the inn and stood listening.

"The southern coasts are worse," the girl was saying. "The ocean swallowed all of the land for six hundred miles, from what we can tell. The South is flooded."

The sheriff of the town was a big man whose name Aaath Ulber could not recall. He had obviously been hoping that the disaster was some local affair.

"Do they know what caused this?" There would be no answer, of course. The appearance of fish and coral reefs on dry land was unprecedented.

The girl shook her head.

"Right," the sheriff said. "We're on our own then." He turned to some of the townsfolk. "We'll—" The sheriff caught sight of Aaath Ulber in the shadows.

"Here now," he demanded, "who's there? What's your business?"

Aaath Ulber had been dreading this moment. He turned and glanced behind him, as if unsure that the sheriff was talking to him.

The sheriff didn't recognize Aaath Ulber, of course, but Aaath Ulber had known him as a nodding acquaintance.

Aaath Ulber stepped out into the torchlight, and there were a few exclamations of shock from the men. Some of them reached for their knives almost by instinct, and even the graak reared up and flapped its wings, letting out a croak of warning. A black dog that had been wagging its tail and watching the crowd suddenly began to bark at Aaath Ulber, ranging back and forth, its tail between its legs.

"I came for a drink at the inn," Aaath Ulber said, "and to buy goods—if it pleases you." None of the men spoke for a moment, so he added "What's the matter—you've never seen a giant before?"

The sheriff eyed Aaath Ulber suspiciously. Always in the past he had been a jolly fellow, eager to please. He said coldly, "I decide whom we will trade with in this town—or not. Do you have a name?"

Aaath Ulber might have said that he was Sir Borenson, but he did not want to confuse the man. "Aaath Ulber," he answered, "a poor giant, traveling from afar. Do not mistrust my appearance, for though I am the size of a great boar I am as gentle as a burrow bear."

Aaath Ulber smiled at his own description, no doubt baring his oversized canines.

On any other evening, that answer might have served as an invitation to tell a tale or two, but the sheriff was in no mood for tales. He studied Aaath Ulber, taking in the curious hornlike growths on his temples; the bone spurs on his wrists; and the unearthly gray metal of his armor. He demanded, "Where do you hail from?"

Aaath Ulber dared not lie; yet the truth was stranger than any tale he could have devised. A half-truth served better. "Near Mystwraith Mountain on the far borders of Indhopal is the home of my ancestors."

"I have never heard of it," the sheriff said. Of course, Aaath Ulber knew that the folk here in Landesfallen had little contact with strangers. Indhopal was on the far side of the world; he doubted that anyone in this town had ever set foot there. The world was full of wonders, and so he thought to add one more.

"Our people are few in number now, fewer than the frowth, fewer than the arr. Like the hill giants of Toom, our numbers are dwindling. My people are called the Bawlin. In ancient times we bowed to the kings of Mystarria, and the most famous of our number served as a guard in the court of King Orden. I myself fought reavers under the banner of the Earth King, and saw the fall of Raj Ahten."

Aaath Ulber of course could tell stories of the Great War all day; they'd even be true.

There were approving nods from some men, and one chimed in, "I've heard of them giants."

The sheriff gave Aaath Ulber a stone-cold look for a long moment, as if weighing some argument in his mind, then said softly, dangerously, "Seize him!"

"What?" Aaath Ulber roared. "On what charge?"

"Suspicion," the sheriff said. "There are no songs of a giant like you fighting beside the Earth King, and if you had done so, there would have been a song. Hence, I know you to be a liar."

Aaath Ulber studied the man. The sheriff was looking for any foolish excuse to jail him—that much was evident.

Men fear power, and Aaath Ulber's size and bearing marked him as being more powerful than others.

A couple of men strode forward, armed with nothing more than torches and a pitchfork. One of the townsfolk reached for his knife.

Myrrima stepped in front of him, blocking their path. She demanded, "Are there any songs of Myrrima and her bow, who slew the Darkling Glory at Castle Sylvarresta?"

The men drew to a halt. They all knew her name even if they did not know her in person. Some whispered, "It's Myrrima!"

"I can vouch for this man," she said. "Indeed, I fought beside him in the service of the Earth King. Any who seek to hinder him will have to deal with me and my husband!"

The townsfolk withdrew a pace. Sir Borenson's reputation was more than enough to cow them.

At that, she turned toward the boat, and Aaath Ulber decided to forgo his chance at a beer and head for safety.

Aaath Ulber strode along in Myrrima's wake. None of townsfolk tried to stop him.

Hah, Aaath Ulber thought, not one of them has the heart to fight.

Suddenly there was a mewling cry from the darkness up the road. A woman shouted, "Murder! Murder most foul!"

Greta Walkin staggered from exhaustion as she rounded a thatch-roofed cottage. She stood for a moment in the road, panting. Sweat streamed down her face, staining the armpits and neck of her blouse. She had obviously run for miles. A dog barked and ran out to meet her.

When she saw Aaath Ulber, she froze in her tracks. Her eyes widened and she pointed. "Murderer!"

Suddenly the villagers were thrown in a panic. The hue and cry had been raised. Ancient law required all the men in town stop whatever they were doing and apprehend the suspect.

The sheriff himself drew his long knife.

Aaath Ulber stepped back; bloodlust threatened to take him.

Villagers ringed about him, a couple waving their torches as if he were a wolf that they sought to keep at bay.

Aaath Ulber felt his heart racing, heard blood thundering in his ears. The shouts of the men seemed to come from far away, as if they were in a tunnel.

At any moment the berserker rage would fall over him, unless he did something to avert it.

The Earth King's warning rang in his ears: "You must find yourself. . . ."

Aaath Ulber lunged and swung his fist lightly, smashing the sheriff in the forehead. The whack echoed from the stone walls of nearby cottages, and the sheriff staggered back, blood flowing from his broken nose. He stood for a moment, dazed, staring at the blood in his hands.

As his nose began to swell, he wheezed for air. The sheriff didn't know it yet, but he was out of the fight.

Several men had drawn daggers now, and ringed Aaath Ulber. One man rushed in blindly jabbing his pitchfork. Aaath Ulber simply leaned away, then as his opponent drew close Aaath Ulber grabbed him by the collar and sent him flying. Another took advantage of the opening at Aaath Ulber's back and lunged in with a knife swinging low, trying to hit an artery in his leg. Aaath Ulber simply kicked the man backward.

Aaath Ulber was going to grab the nearest man, but Myrrima shouted, "No more!"

She rounded on the townsmen. "I am Water's Warrior!" she shouted. "A curse on all who dare hinder us! Your crops shall dry up, and your livestock will starve. Your manly parts shall wither, and every child that shelters under your roof will waste away with a pox!"

A wizard's curse was not to be taken lightly. Perhaps only a horde of reavers could have given the men greater pause.

They looked at one another, and someone muttered, "I'm done here." Then they began to back away, fading into the darkness.

Greta fell to the ground just outside the circle of men and lay sobbing beneath the upraised wings of the enormous white graak. "Murder!" she cried, begging for justice.

To Aaath Ulber's surprise, Rain strode forward and addressed the townsfolk. "I saw what happened," she said. "The man who died was my father—but he did not die honorably. He had slaughter on his mind, and robbery as his goal. It was not murder, as my mother here well knows. I loved my father dearly, and once he was a good man, but killing Aaath Ulber here would not serve justice. If my father had had his way, there would be four people dead now, not just one."

The men of the town looked back and forth, as if to decide what course to pursue. At last the sheriff threw his own blade down. "It's not worth it," he said, spitting upon the ground, giving water to the earth, thus to ward off Myrrima's curse.

The rest of the men backed off a pace, each spitting in turn, even as Greta lay crying "Murder! Murder!"

A couple of the men were still on the ground, panting and bloodied.

All of the townsfolk cast hateful looks Aaath Ulber's way.

Had I been alone, Aaath Ulber realized, I would have had a fight on my hands.

Myrrima headed for the ship. Aaath Ulber followed at a measured pace, while the children rushed to join them. Aaath Ulber worried that at any moment a dagger might come flying at his back. He dared not run, dared not appear guilty.

For two hundred yards he avoided the temptation to glance behind. At last he cast a fleeting glance over his shoulder. The townsfolk were all gathered in the shadow of the enormous white graak, the torchlight glimmering red upon it. The men had a bitter air of defeat about them.

Aaath Ulber wanted more supplies, yet his instincts warned against ever returning to the village.

He thought sarcastically, A fine job I did of winning these men's hearts.

❧ 10 ❧

THE NARROWS

Ultimately, greater freedom comes when we honorably fulfill our obligations than when we seek to escape our responsibilities, for the man who fulfills his obligations will have a clear conscience, while he who hides from responsibilities will forever be weighed down by regret.

—*Gaborn Val Orden*

The sun had died, sinking into an evening mist that drifted in from the sea. Rain ran along the road blindly, feeling as if the Powers that be had decided to shut off the world from all light.

"Get to the ship, quickly!" Myrrima warned the others. Rain, Draken, and Myrrima had purchased what supplies they could—a pair of lamps, some twine and rope, fishhooks, fresh rutabagas and apples from farmers, eggs, cheese, honey, and ham.

Rain carried a pair of sacks, not even sure now what they held, while Sage led their pair of goats out of town, toward the ship that was moored in the distance.

The townsfolk stood in a knot in front of their great house, some of them jeering and shaking their fists at Aaath Ulber while he strode away, glaring and baring his teeth.

The young graak rider flapped off on her great white

monster, heading toward the ocean, and as Rain watched, she could see its wings blotting out the first new stars, flapping gently as it rode through the heavens.

They followed the road south through town, and every minute Rain expected to encounter some resistance, but for two miles they hurried, breathless from carrying their load of food.

When they reached the ship, Draken was first aboard. He disappeared into the cabins for a moment, then stopped and looked down into the hold, trying to make sure that no one had boarded in their absence.

"All clear," he called, and then climbed down into the hold, carrying a huge bag of turnips. He came up and Rain handed him her load, while Aaath Ulber set his own bundle aboard.

Then Rain and Myrrima helped Sage wrestle the goats over the threshold and the group tried to set sail.

The wind had died in their absence, and the ship moved sluggishly, serving as a perch for a pair of gulls that thought the prow was a fine place to roost.

The tide was still going out. This far up the channel, there were no waves, just a gentle retreat of the water, and here so close to the end of the bay, the water was filled with flotsam. Much of it had the consistency of sawdust, for there were ground-up bits of bark and twigs everywhere, but some of it was made of logs, and amid this mess she could see things more vile floating in the water—the pale bellies of dead fish, the hair of dark animals, a woman's bloodless hand.

So the group sat upon the deck as the ship drifted, gently floating toward the sea.

Rain doubted that the boat would drift far any time

soon. The channel was nearly half a mile wide here, and the Hacker River had been but a trickle so late in the summer. The current was almost nonexistent.

"A night breeze will come soon," Myrrima offered. She did not say it with hope but with certainty, as if already she felt it breathing upon her.

Rain peered to the south as the gloom deepened. She knelt on the deck, her arms thrown over the railing. Her mind was a muddle. She wanted to be with Draken, but she worried about her brothers and sisters.

Just as importantly, she worried what her family would think of her. Myrrima came and stroked her back.

"Are you having regrets?"

"I'll miss my family," Rain admitted. "But I fear that they won't miss me—not after what I said in town."

"You spoke the truth," Myrrima said.

"Some people hate the truth," Rain said, "and they hate those who tell it even more."

"Not all truths are equally pretty," Myrrima said. "Sometimes a truth is too hard for people to bear. Your mother will mourn Owen, but she will miss you, too."

That brought tears to Rain's eyes. She hoped that it was true.

"It's my little brothers and sisters that I worry about the most," Rain said. "They need someone to look after them. And they'll always think of me as the sister who ran away."

"Perhaps the future will bring you back together again, in brighter days," Myrrima said.

Rain shook her head. She was going back to Mystarria, where there was most likely a price on her head. She was going to war, and she could not see that the future held any light for her at all. It was darker than the skies above.

Rain could hardly imagine how they would handle the ship with just four adults and a child. This looked to be a grueling journey.

"There is still time to go back home," Myrrima said, "if that is what you truly want."

Rain didn't have any good choice here. Whether she stayed or went, she'd lose something she valued more than life itself.

She sat for a moment, twisting the ring on her finger. It was an old thing, passed down from her grandmother. The band was broad, of cheap silver, and the large stone in it was blood-red jasper. It was the only heirloom that she had from the family.

She shook her head. "You should have seen the looks they gave me when I left. I've never felt such hatred. And if I stay, it would just grow, until my aunt Della drove me out once and for all. It's better that I leave."

The whole crew fell silent. Aaath Ulber sat on the captain's deck, manning the rudder. He had not slept in well over a day, and finally he began to snore wonderfully loud.

And in half an hour the wind came, rushing down the hills from the deserts of Landesfallen, fanning out above the cool water. It was not much of a breeze, but it filled the sails fitfully, so that they luffed for a moment; then the new wood of the timbers creaked as the ship began to ease forward.

Rain worried. They hadn't had time to take on much in the way of supplies, and she didn't know where the company might be able to take on more. If she understood correctly, islands that had once supported passing ships might well be underwater.

But Rain had more immediate concerns. The river channel was still filled with debris, and in the starlight whole trees could lie hidden beneath the ale-dark waters. So Draken and Rain each lit a little lantern, and she sat on the prow, her feet dangling near the waves, and helped guide the vessel.

Her efforts did little good, for often now they would scrape or bump against hidden obstacles.

Aaath Ulber came awake, and sat on the captain's deck. He expertly steered the ship, pulling down on the shaft so that the rudder lifted and did not catch on hidden trees. He seemed to relish the touch of the rudder, the water gliding beneath him.

With a thoughtful expression Aaath Ulber made slowly for the sea.

Myrrima voiced the concern that Mayor Threngell would try to stop them, but Aaath Ulber said, "There's little that they can do. Their little rafts can't form much of a blockade. Even if a couple of them do get close enough so that they try to board, I'll just throw them back in the water."

They rode the waves for nearly thirty-six miles, until they rounded a wide bend. Here, two monolithic hills of stone created a narrow passage less than a quarter of a mile wide—the perfect spot for an ambush.

Ahead, guttering torches lit the water, a string of them billowing smoke. Men upon rafts held the strait.

At the sight of the ship, they gave a warning shout and stood upon their rafts, waving cudgels—knotty limbs pulled from the water.

"They don't know who they're dealing with!" Aaath Ulber growled, and he set course straight ahead—aiming to plow through the midst of them. But the channel ahead was filled with debris—dead trees and bits of houses, all thrust up from the water so thick that it looked like rugged ground, broken by rocks and ruin.

"Father," Draken cried, "they've blockaded the river!"

Rain recognized what had happened. The townsmen had tied logs together and strung them across the narrow strait, forming a dam. And as the tide had retreated, the dam had collected tons of debris.

"Turn the ship!" Myrrima shouted, but it was too late. The ship rammed the debris, scraping against tree trunks and the roof of a house, then ground to a halt as completely as if it had struck a beach.

They sat there.

"Those clever little schemers," Aaath Ulber muttered. "I thought they'd wear themselves out trying to catch us, but they came up with a better plan."

"Prepare to be boarded!" Mayor Threngell called. "Lower your sails!"

Rain saw him, two hundred yards off, on the far side of the debris; he had a torch in one hand. He stood at the edge of his boat and peered about nervously, trying to figure out how to make his way across the flotsam.

Aaath Ulber chuckled at the man's predicament. The mayor and his men didn't have proper weapons, and crossing the logjam looked all but impossible.

Aaath Ulber got up from his seat, strode to the prow, and pulled his old war hammer from its sheath on his back. "Leave them to me," he said, urging Rain and the others to retreat a pace so that he would have room to swing his weapon.

Rain heard Myrrima begin to pray under her breath, calling upon Water. Need drove her, and compassion.

She spoke to the Power that she served, whispering, "If indeed you want me to go to war, then I beg of you, open a path before us."

Peace filled Rain like an ocean, and suddenly Myrrima stood, as if she had made up her mind what to do.

She went to the prow of the boat and raised her hands, summoning water into her service. Draken stood at her back, holding his lantern aloft, and Aaath Ulber stood at her right.

"Come the tempest, come the tide!" she shouted.

Nearby, the water began to swirl beside the boat, as if a huge hole had opened up in the ground and was draining the ocean away. Debris swirled in the vortex. It began to whirl faster and faster, and the sound of roaring water filled Rain's ears, as if a mountain river thundered through rocks.

"Whoa!" Draken shouted; Sage cried, "Mother?"

It was obvious that neither child had ever seen Myrrima make such a display of power before.

The ship creaked and wobbled, and waves began to build, lifting the flotsam so that it swelled and bucked.

Then suddenly water spouted up from the vortex, twisting and rising into the air.

Myrrima reached out and grasped the column of water, taking it into her hand, so that a plume of water twisted a dozen feet in the air, whirling from her palm, as if it were a staff.

She pointed her watery staff toward the logjam in front of the ship and shouted, "Come the tide!"

Suddenly a rushing filled the air, and all around her the water began streaming seaward. Water from the sound leapt up and flowed over logs and bracken as if a river had suddenly flooded.

Mayor Threngell saw what Myrrima was doing; his eyes went wide. "Run!" he shouted to his men. "They've got a water wizard!"

In the logjam, debris strained toward the open sea, and strange groaning sounds and rumblings erupted. The enormous pressure of the rushing tide suddenly snapped ropes that held the dam in place.

The ship lurched forward, logs and debris rumbling against its hull as it began to break clear.

The great raft of debris went rushing seaward, and now the townsmen on their various watercrafts began to scream and do their best to push themselves away from logs that rumbled toward them.

Myrrima stood with her watery staff still swirling in her hand. She threw the whirling staff back into the surging tide. It danced upon the surface a moment, like a waterspout, and the water at its base began to swirl faster and faster.

"Bring up the dead!" Myrrima called to the waves. The whirlpool churned and foamed, became a waterspout rising into the air; from the foam a body surged, a dead man large and pale, his eyes already plucked out by fish. The water made a moaning noise as it rose, as if the dead declared their pain.

Then a young girl surged into the waterspout, and in an instant dozens of other corpses bobbed into the air as if eager to be free of their watery grave, and all of them spun about in the plume, rising fifty feet in the air, as the moaning in the waters continued to build.

There had recently been a village here, a thriving hamlet. It had had tidy streets and quaint shops. A man in town had made stained-glass windows for a living, and every shop and house along the street was provided with a window to advertise his wares. Rain had envied the folks who'd lived here.

Their corpses rose, faces blue from the depths, hideous and terrifying, whirling as they swirled up the waterspout and then went flying through the air like fat dolphins.

The mayor and his men groaned in wordless terror and sought to escape, paddling away in a hurry, as horrid corpses began to splash around their boat in a gruesome hail.

Suddenly the ship burst through the last of the flotsam, groaning and scraping as it ran over a submerged log.

The Borenson family broke free of the narrows and headed out into the open sea.

❧ 11 ❧

WHISPERS

Beware the sound of whispers as you breach a wyrm-ling stronghold. As a lich lord sloughs its physical shell, it loses its vocal cords. Thus it can never speak above a whisper.

—Aaath Ulber

An hour before dawn, heavy fog from the sea besieged the watchtower at the wyrmling fortress so that its single black stone pinnacle floated above an ocean of clouds. Crows circled the tower, cawing, troubled by the movement below.

All around the tower, the clouds were lit a sullen red from beneath. Hundreds of bonfires ringed the tower so that the fog glowed like dying embers.

From the fires below voices rose up, human voices cruel and cold, singing songs of war:

> "Behold! Thy fate is in my hands,
> I'll hear no coward's plea.
> I come from cold and distant lands,
> To bring sure death to thee!"

Though the black basalt walls of the great tower looked smooth and unscalable from a distance, it was assailable—for a small man with clever fingers and a few endowments of grace and brawn.

So the runelords came, nine of them, eeling up through the fog, as swift as lizards, barefoot and unarmored, garbed only in sealskin, their long blond locks braided and dyed in blood. They bore sharp daggers in their teeth and carried ropes coiled over their backs.

With three or four endowments of metabolism each, they seemed to race up the nearly vertical slope.

Few were such runelords among the warriors of Internook. These were old men, cunning warlords who had lived in wealthier days. Most of them had little left in the way of endowments, for the majority of their Dedicates had died over the past decade. But they came nonetheless, for they were bold men, and fierce, and endowments of attributes alone do not a warrior make.

The first runelord neared the top of the tower, reached back with one hand, hurled a grappling hook over the lip of a merlon, and scrambled up.

A wyrmling guard saw the hook and rushed to cut the rope. But he had never faced a warrior with endowments and was therefore unprepared for what he met.

The small man raced up the rope so swiftly that when he hit the battlement, he seemed nearly to have been hurled into the air by some invisible force.

The wyrmling grunted in surprise, then swung his battle-ax down, trying to slice the man in two and cut the rope in a single blow. But the little warrior sidestepped the attack, swung up with a short half-sword, and plunged it deep into the wyrmling's throat, slicing through his esophagus and severing his spinal cord.

The wyrmling guard dropped without so much as a grunt, and lay for a moment, staring at the stars, bright and inaccessible, as his life's blood oozed from his throat.

Dark shadows passed before his eyes as human runelords flitted into the tunnels.

Bells began tolling in the Fortress of the Northern Wastes, deep bells that reverberated through stone, carrying their warning through Crull-maldor's feet. She stood in the Room of Whispers, a perfect dome lit only by glow worms along the ceiling, a room riddled with miniature tunnels in the walls. Each tunnel contained a glass tube, a special glass designed to conduct sound. And each tube went to a different reporting post.

At each end of the tube, the glass flared wide. By talking into the tubes the wyrmlings could communicate the entire length of the fortress.

"They're coming!" a messenger shouted, his voice emitting an urgent whisper from the tube. "Humans have breached the tower!"

There were shouts of challenge, the clash of arms, roars of pain, the sounds of wyrmlings dying, followed almost instantly by more reports from another tube, urgent whispers: "Enemy spotted, Tower Post Two!"

"Death Gate One—humans coming!" a third voice cried.

In the perfect acoustics of the Room of Whispers, it seemed that the voices came from everywhere and nowhere, like the distant hiss of the sea. It was as if the guards were incorporeal, like Crull-maldor herself.

Crull-maldor smiled inwardly. She had anticipated this attack, but she had not thought that it would come for another day or two. She had underestimated the runelords.

Two hours past midnight, bonfires had begun to blaze upon the nearest hills, summoning the small folk to battle. Within minutes fires had burst forth upon distant peaks all along the coast.

The runelords came. They raced through the night more swiftly than Crull-maldor had anticipated.

She'd thought that they would first attack at the Death Gate, as the previous men had done, but they had surprised her by scaling the watchtower. To wyrmlings, with their huge bulk and clumsy fingers, the tower looked unclimbable.

At Crull-maldor's side, her new captain reported, "Their numbers outside are great. We cannot see them all for the fog, but their numbers are easily in the tens of thousands. Their elite troops have scaled the tower, but a larger force is rushing the tunnels."

"Perhaps their numbers *are* great," Crull-maldor mused, "but if all that you could see from the tower was their fires . . . ? It is an old trick, to try to dismay an enemy by building many fires in the night. By having your troops sing loudly, five thousand can sound like fifty thousand."

She spoke comfortingly, but Crull-maldor knew that the humans really did outnumber her troops. They might even be strong enough to overwhelm her wyrmlings.

Yet she hoped that powerful runelords would lead this group so that she could decimate them.

No humans had escaped from the warrens alive in the first assault. So the small folk would have no choice but to send stronger forces.

The humans would not be prepared to face a wight. She wanted to crush the spirits of the human inhabitants of the island, and thus begin her dominion over them.

"Milord," a wyrmling reported, the voice rising in a whisper. "Human forces have secured the tower level."

The news came unexpectedly quick. It had not been a minute since the alarm had sounded. Five hundred wyrmling troops, destroyed like that?

Some of these runelords must have many endowments of metabolism, Crull-maldor realized.

But the small folk still had no idea what resources Crull-maldor had at her command.

"Drop all of the portcullises in the tower corridors," she said, so that the humans would not be able to escape. "Then light the tar fires in level two. These runelords may be tough, but they still have to breathe."

"Milady," the captain began to argue.

At that instant Crull-maldor felt a presence seize her consciousness, a sense of heightened intelligence filled with malicious intent.

It was a sending, a message from Emperor Zul-torac. *Deliver all of the corpuscite that you find to Rugassa,* he whispered to Crull-maldor's soul. *Send your wyrmling troops to scour the Northern Wastes in the search.*

Crull-maldor raised a hand to silence her captain, lest he disturb her further.

It was not the most opportune time to be receiving messages from the emperor.

Crull-maldor did not want her superior to know what she knew, so she envisioned a wall between herself and the emperor, a wall of stone, impenetrable. She made her mind a fortress against his probes.

Corpuscite? Crull-maldor feigned ignorance. *Did you ask for corpuscite?*

The emperor evaded the question. *Time is short. Do as you are told.*

Crull-maldor reported, *Humans have entered the fortress, humans swift and deadly. We are under attack!*

I cannot send my scouts out now! The emperor's dark mind brimmed with smug satisfaction at the news. There was nothing that Zul-torac would like more than to see Crull-maldor humiliated.

Take care of it, the emperor warned. *This is your first priority. The time has come to prepare for a great war, a war unlike any other. Lord Despair commands that you raise production on your arms and armor. Every man and woman over the weight of four hundred pounds must be fitted for war by the end of the week.*

Crull-maldor smiled grimly. A male wyrmling could reach four hundred pounds by the age of ten years. Despair was ordering that women and children be armed for war?

Making the armor alone would be all but impossible. Every child would have to be pulled from indoctrination classes and put to work carving the bones of world wyrms.

Surely Despair does not fear the small humans so much, Crull-maldor mused. But she began to wonder. With endowments, a woman or a child could be fearsome indeed. In fact, some of the human fortresses might be difficult to penetrate for a wyrmling—a large one would not be able to fit through doors. But a child . . .

Despair has no fear of the small folk, Zul-torac replied. *We are preparing to conquer the heavens. Despair is opening doors to far worlds, and our troops shall overwhelm them all!*

Crull-maldor considered the implications. The emperor was demanding all of the blood metal in her realm—blood metal that Crull-maldor would need to ready her troops for the coming invasions. She dared not deliver it.

Yet the promise of a coming war was a heady thing.

Crull-maldor had seen some of the beasts that the emperor had brought through doors in the past.

There were treasures to be plundered. Crull-maldor did not care for gold or silver. She was far more interested in the treasures of knowledge that might be gained on far worlds.

I will do what I can to obtain corpuscite, she promised. *But it is exceedingly rare here in the North. A few stones we might find, but I cannot guarantee that we will find much more.*

The emperor snarled and ended the communication abruptly. The sense of heightened awareness—and great corruption—both broke off with a nearly audible snap.

All around the room, whispers were rising. The sound of portcullises falling came from a dozen holes, metal sliding over stone, bolts being thrown so that the portcullises could not be raised. Shrieks and howls were coming from Death Gate where human forces had overwhelmed the wyrmlings.

But all too soon the humans would find themselves trapped.

Crull-maldor smiled inwardly. So, Zul-torac had already learned the lore of the runelords and how to form corpuscite into forcibles.

Crull-maldor had wrung the secrets from the dead earlier, and now she saw a great opportunity.

For nearly two hundred years she had been banished to this waste, and in that time she had ranged far across the barrens. She could not recall where every single stone of corpuscite lay, but she had seen them from time to time, and remembered one decent outcrop not sixty miles to the northeast. Though the humans encompassed her fortress, they had not yet discovered the secret gate, which exited into the hills some twelve miles to the north. Already Crull-maldor had sent troops to recover the corpuscite.

A great war was taking form, Crull-maldor realized. She intended to win it, to dominate the humans in her realm. She intended to put them to good use. As slaves, they could work the wyrmling mines and reap fish from the sea and caribou from the plains. Their skins would warm the wyrmlings during winter nights when the air grew bitter cold. They could provide meat in a pinch, and their glands could be used for harvester spikes.

All that Crull-maldor had to fear was that the humans would gain access to the blood metal.

There would be small pockets of it elsewhere here in the barrens, she knew. The island itself was four hundred miles across on the southern tip. To the north, the boundaries were often blurred, for in the winter the sea froze over, creating a continuous mass that stretched off into the bitter cold. But some years the ice would melt along the eastern shore, giving hints of the island's shape.

So the island itself was vast, some eighty thousand square miles at this time of year.

The greatest danger that Crull-maldor faced was that the small humans would retrieve the metal before she did.

She felt reconciled to the fact that they would get some of it, but she intended to take the majority.

The humans were too many and were spread too far and wide for her to control perfectly. They'd stumble upon a few stones here and there, perhaps even a rich vein.

She'd have to take it from them. The blood metal was too great a weapon. She couldn't let it fall into the enemy's hands.

In the room of whispers, suddenly she heard human cries from the tubes in the ceiling above, cries broken and muted by coughing and hacking.

Metal clanked upon metal as the small folk tried to break through a portcullis with their war hammers. The blows rang swiftly at first, but the humans with their boosted metabolism not only lived faster, they died more quickly.

All too soon the clanking slowed and became broken by shrieks of fear and shouts of despair as good men begged the Powers that be for air.

Crull-maldor bent her ear, bent her whole will upon the whispering sounds of death that drifted into the room, and imagined the humans in the tower crumpling in ruin upon the floor.

The battle at the Death Gate was just ramping up. The warriors racing down the long corridor were not powerful runelords apparently. They moved far too slowly for that, and they made far too much noise, singing and shouting, hoping to strike terror into the hearts of the enemy.

The wyrmling troops were eager to engage. It had been far too long since they had been able to prove themselves in a pitched battle.

The captain was listening to a distant whisper at a hole. "Spies at the Death Gate report fewer than five thousand humans have breached the corridors. Our troops have fled before them, down into the labyrinth. They await your orders for the time and manner of the ambush."

"Very good," Crull-maldor said. She could kill the humans with fire, or perhaps take them herself. But her troops needed battle, the good clean smell of blood. So she ordered, "Unleash the wyrmling horde."

❧ BOOK II ❧

*THE WARLORDS OF
INTERNOOK*

❧ 12 ❧

THE PROPHECY

No man can know the future, for the future is malleable. Having foreseen disaster, we can often take steps to avert it. Thus, when we look upon the future, we see only a future that may be.

—*The Chaos Oracles*

Darkness engulfed the great fortress of Rugassa. A roof covered the world, a roof of made of swirling clouds so thick that they blackened the sky.

The clouds did not smell of wetness or rain. Instead, they filled the air with fine sediments of soot, giving the air an acrid tang, as if a volcano had exploded, sending ash to mushroom out for as far as the eye could see.

The winds high overhead screamed, night and day, a distant piercing whine.

Sunlight could not penetrate the storm, yet light exuded from it: brief flashes of lightning that strobed high up among the dust and debris, lighting the heavens from time to time in strange colors—the green of a bruise, the red of flame.

The storm was centered over Rugassa, but its effects

covered the land for a thousand miles in every direction, sealing all of Rofehavan beneath shadows, eternal night.

Thus it was that nine days after the binding of the worlds, the lich emperor Zul-torac took his first walk in the daylight in nearly three hundred years, venturing out of the fortress to explore his lands.

He feared no danger. No sunlight could touch him, and no enemy could strike him down. In the nine days since the binding of the worlds, the wyrmling hordes had crushed all human resistance—destroying armies, enslaving nations. With a mountain of blood metal at their command, the wyrmlings were unstoppable.

More importantly, their leader was unstoppable. Lord Despair now marched at the head of the wyrmling armies, and with his vast powers and wyrmling runelords, he was invincible.

Even now, Lord Despair had taken his armies to a far world, to the One True World that had existed from the beginning, where he hunted now for the Bright Ones and the Glories, destroying those who had the greatest chance to strike him down.

Rumor said that the war went well. The enemy was fleeing from Despair, desperately seeking escape. Zul-torac's master had slain thousands of them, and now his troops were searching the wilderness, trying to corner the last of them, though they hid from him like foxes in their dens.

Yet there was a worry upon Zul-torac's mind that had nothing to do with assassins or armies. It had to do with his daughter, the princess Kan-hazur. She had fallen ill, and it looked as if she would die. There were certain rites he hoped to perform this coming winter, rites that required the lifeblood of his only child. He could not allow her to die before the solstice.

The lich lord was dressed in a robe made of black spider cloth with powdered diamonds sewn into it, so that he glimmered as he floated above the ground.

Thus he made his way up a long, winding road, out of the fortress, traveling a tunnel that ran through the cone of the volcano.

Suddenly, there was copious light ahead, thrown by the magma at the volcano's core. So high up, the winds' piercing howl grew to a keening wail; Zul-torac could taste dust upon the remains of his tongue.

He followed the road along a steep path. To slip off the side would send him plummeting into the molten ore.

Ahead, the path leveled out into a plain that had been gouged out of the mountain. Huge columns of black stone had been arranged upon the ground—not in any pattern that a wyrmling could discern. Some of the pillars stood upright, others canted to the side, as if a great temple had fallen.

There was a sense of order to the ruins, but not a pattern.

Circling this plain were dozens of doorways to other worlds, each an archway made of shimmering light. Zul-torac peered through them. In one world he saw great beasts wading amid a swamp, using their broad faces to gather algae from the scum-covered surface of the water. Another door opened into a world covered in bitter snow. A third showed an impenetrable jungle of odd vines. Through that door came two wyrmlings bearing a huge leather bag, sopping wet.

Inside it, some nameless evil growled and thrashed about.

The wyrmlings grinned as they passed, and warned, "Watch yourself. This one is nasty! Bog crab, we'll call it. Got more teeth in its mouth than I have hairs on my arse."

"What are you going to do with it?" Zul-torac asked.

"Throw it in a swamp on the borders," one wyrmling replied, "and let it eat anything that happens by."

The two carried their thrashing burden past Zul-torac.

The bog creature was but one of Lord Despair's new recruits. Through these doorways, tens of thousands of creatures had passed during the week—Darkling Glories that rode the night winds, giant walking hills from a planet called Nayaire, and nameless monsters from a hundred other realms.

But now Zul-torac focused on the plain before him. Amidst the black pillars, the chaos oracles hid—both from themselves and others. The creatures were so hideous, it was said, that the sight of one unveiled would drive a man mad. So the chaos oracles twisted light away from themselves, cloaking themselves in shadows the way that a wyrmling might wear his armor of bone.

Still, the thought of seeing one unveiled was tantalizing, and so Zul-torac peered.

Gloom had gathered around them, black shadows thicker than the mists in the sky above, darkness that swirled and eddied, sometimes parting just enough to reveal the tantalizing hint of a form, then just as quickly gathering again to immerse their masters in blackest night.

The chaos oracles were not of this earth, not of any

earth that Zul-torac had heard of. They liked it here by the volcano, relished the taste of sulfur in the air.

The shadows parted from around one an instant, and Zul-torac caught a tantalizing glimpse of a hunched back covered in horns, and twisted limbs, and one bright golden eye that peered at him, filling him with horror.

His blood ran chill and his breathing stopped.

Then the shadows coalesced, and thankfully the chaos oracle was cloaked again.

Zul-torac saw flashes of memory from his childhood as a chaos oracle accessed his mind. He could feel something, a presence, moving through his brain—from the right temporal lobe, to the left, then back down to the brain stem.

All of his secrets were laid bare.

"You come because you fear for the life of your daughter," an oracle whispered in his mind.

"Yes," Zul-torac said.

"You wish to know how to save her. . . . This I cannot see. Time is like a river, flowing toward eternity. Yet there are eddies and swirls. I cannot see all, but I see your death."

An image flashed into Zul-torac's mind: a darkened corridor, where glow worms lit the tunnel like ten thousand gleaming stars. In the distance was a light, a torch, but its flames boiled and sputtered as it rushed toward him. A man was coming, a man blinding in his speed. He raced toward Zul-torac in a blur. Zul-torac sought to flee, but his opponent was too fast. A dozen endowments of metabolism he might have had, and there was no escaping him.

He came in a blur. Zul-torac could see little—a simple

rounded helm of steel with a broad nose guard. Feral eyes filled with death. A red beard streaked with gray.

Then the man was on him, swinging a war hammer. At the touch of its spike, he felt the spells that bound his spirit to its wasted flesh shatter, crumbling, and all of his power drained away.

Worse, there were spells upon that blade, spells that brought banishment to the very spirit.

The warrior shouted in glee and for one instant he held still long enough so that Zul-torac could see his face. It was a human, a large man with the nubs of horns common to the folk of Caer Luciare. His grim countenance turned to exultation, and he opened his mouth wide, baring his fangs as he gave a victorious shout.

Zul-torac cried out in pain as his desiccated corpse exploded in a cloud of dust.

Suddenly the vision cleared, and Zul-torac stood before the chaos oracle, filled with a terror so visceral that he'd never felt the like.

Worries preyed upon Zul-torac's mind. Lord Despair had seized control of the world; now he was using it as a platform from which to conquer the heavens. Despair's powers made him invincible. He could use his Earth Powers to "choose" his warriors, warning them how to save themselves in the battles to come.

But Lord Despair could not use his marvelous gift to save a lich. Zul-torac's body was too wasted, too far gone toward death.

Zul-torac's mind raced. There was no one to save him, no champion to protect him.

But I have wyrmling warriors by the thousands, Zul-torac thought, and blood metal aplenty.

Despair had ordered Zul-torac to send some blood

metal to that evil wight Crull-maldor. Zul-torac had hesitated, not wanting to strengthen his old enemy. Even now he could not bring himself to send her the required forcibles.

The rest of the wyrmlings were growing in power, moving toward the Ascension.

But perhaps it is time, he thought. I can send both—a little blood metal along with enough champions to stop an army.

"He comes for you!" the chaos oracle warned. "He comes—a champion from the north! He rides now upon the water, bringing death and carnage!"

Zul-torac turned his back upon the oracle in a hot rage. "Not if I can help it," Zul-torac said. He headed back down the mountain, back to the safety of the wyrmling's indomitable fortress.

There he searched among the city's champions until he found the right wyrmling for the job: Yikkarga, a captain who had been put under the protection of Lord Despair. He was a huge wyrmling, well versed in battle, with a vicious reputation. Just as importantly, he had many endowments to his credit.

"I am sending you north," the emperor told him, "with a contingent of runelords. There is a human that needs killing. . . ."

❧ 13 ❧

THE BORROWBIRD

*To forgive another brings peace to an offended soul,
and is far more beneficial for the offender than for
him who is offended.*

—*Emir Owatt of Tuulistan*

That first night, Draken took the rudder once Aaath Ulber succumbed to sleep, and sailed his little ship up north. The voyage across the ocean to Mystarria normally took six weeks, but their little vessel was light and swift. Being a new ship, it had no barnacles on the hull to slow its progress, and since the vessel carried no cargo, it sat light on the water, and when the sails unfurled, it seemed to fly.

Thus, Sage named the ship the *Borrowbird*. The name seemed appropriate. The vessel was white, like a borrowbird, and the birds were known for theft. They often raided the fruit trees, and were fond of trinkets. The males used bright stones to adorn their nests in the hopes of attracting females. The decorations often spread for several feet in a circle, and were wondrous to look upon, for the birds arranged stones and flowers by size and color and shape, creating collages that were lovely and bizarre, as if formed by the minds of gifted, otherworldly artists.

In the early spring the birds went about stealing

pebbles from riverbeds, flowers from gardens, colorful bits of fruit or cloth, or shiny coins—anything that wasn't nailed down. There was even an odd report of a borrowbird going so far as to steal an earring from a woman's ear in order to get a glittering ruby.

With so many people wanting to steal the ship, the name was doubly appropriate. Draken didn't like the name, for the association with theft was a constant reminder of how Aaath Ulber had killed Owen Walkin, and so Draken suggested a dozen other monikers that day.

But Sage was the youngest in the family now, and so her name stuck.

That first day, while Draken was at the helm, his mind was filled with wonder. He could not remember when he'd sailed to Landesfallen as a child. He'd been too young.

Now he was going back, but to what?

His mother came up to watch the sunset with him. She sat next to him at the rudder, staring out to sea. The ocean had been rough and wind-driven part of the day, but now it calmed. The smell of salt was thick in his nostrils, and he wondered, "What do you think we'll find when we get to Mystarria? Will it be as bad as Father thinks?"

Draken had only a vague notion of the threat imposed by the wyrmlings. He really couldn't even envision what they looked like. But if Aaath Ulber was frightened of them, then he imagined that they must be terrible indeed.

"I think, we are sailing to war," Myrrima said. "It is not just a suspicion. Water has called me to battle. I hope that this is the last time."

Draken knew that his mother had faced terrors beyond imagination. She'd founded the Brotherhood of the Wolf and slain a Darkling Glory in her youth, and had fought reavers by the thousands. She'd battled Raj Ahten at the height of his powers.

Yet she seemed older to him and a just a bit frail, like a shirt that was growing threadbare from too much washing.

"To war with the wyrmlings?" he asked, and was surprised to find that his mouth went dry, and he had to lick his lips to moisten them. "Water has called you?"

Myrrima nodded slowly. He knew that it was an odd thing.

"Mother, surely there are water wizards on the far side of the world who could be of better service."

Myrrima glanced at him, turning away from the sea. "I may no longer be strong in battle, but I am strong in wizardry; perhaps that is what we need in this war."

"Father says that the wyrmlings may have a mountain of blood metal," Draken objected. Sage came out of the galley and sat down with them.

"I wish that it were not so," Myrrima said. "I don't want the wyrmlings to have it. Certainly I don't want to fight them for it.

"I wish that there was no more blood metal. It is an evil thing, the way that men use each other, the way that cruel men try to force their will upon the rest of the world. Men should not wield so much power.

"For the past few years, I have been glad that the mines in Kartish had played out. It seemed to me that it gave the world a rest, allowed mankind a chance to settle down, offered people a chance to work their gardens and raise their children.

"Your father and I have been content, more at peace than I had ever imagined."

The sun was plunging into the water out on the distant sea, a bright golden orb dipping below the horizon. Draken saw a tear in his mother's eye, something that he'd never witnessed before.

As a young man, he sometimes dreamt of war, imagining how he might prove himself on the field of battle. He'd never considered what a great gift peace could be.

Taking on firewood turned out to be as easy as sailing inland. The great tidal wave had deposited huge rafts of deadwood all along the coast, and in only a couple of hours the family was able to wrestle enough free for the entire voyage.

The greater worry was insufficient supplies. Draken had not been able to buy an ax in town, so he had nothing to cut the wood with. His father's war hammer could be used to split the logs, but it was a poor substitute for a good wood ax.

Nor did he have a decent stone to sharpen his blades with, so he picked up an assortment of rocks to use as grinding stones.

There were other things that the family wanted— proper cups and plates, spices, leather to make shoes and boots, a good large skillet, grease for frying, and so on.

But Aaath Ulber insisted that they would have to do without.

Draken dared not argue. He found that he was uncomfortable in the giant's presence. Aaath Ulber was an imposing figure, towering over everyone on the ship. And Draken had seen what happened when Aaath Ulber lost his temper.

Even now he could hardly look at the giant without having the image of Owen's death flash through his mind. Draken often found himself wondering what misspoken word or deed might set the giant off again.

Myrrima saw what was happening, and she told Rain. "Now that we know Aaath Ulber's problems, we must face them."

"Face them how?" Rain asked.

"There are runes that I can draw on him—runes to bring forgetfulness from hurtful memories, runes to help calm him, like a troubled sea."

With that, Myrrima got a bucket and threw it into the sea, then pulled up the rope.

With the seawater, she went to Aaath Ulber, who was at the helm, and drew some runes upon his brow to help soothe his mind—not that he seemed any great threat at the moment.

Though Rain tried to avoid Aaath Ulber, she couldn't do so completely. Late in the morning on the third day he grabbed Rain just after breakfast.

"Right, then," he said, staring at her as if she were a brood mare. He grabbed her thin biceps, squeezed, and then smiled. The effect was chilling, for his oversized canines showed as if he was baring his fangs. "Let's see what we've got here, girl."

Aaath Ulber had Rain come to the captain's deck; there he gave her a heavy chunk of wood and had her lunge with it, practicing sword drills in order to strengthen her arms. He made her swing until Rain fell into tears, and then he stopped and let her rest, warning, "The wyrmlings won't give you a break, child."

When she was rested, he forced her to go through

various routines of lunges and dodges, until she felt as if she'd faint.

"Too little food, and too little exercise," Aaath Ulber had said gently. "But we'll get you toughened up."

Rain was furious with him, certain that he sought an excuse to criticize her. But Aaath Ulber forced everyone in the company to join in battle practice that first day.

He began his lessons by telling them, "Fighting a wyrmling isn't like fighting a man. They'll outweigh you by five or six hundred pounds. So you won't be fighting level, eye-to-eye. Nor can you hope to take a blow from one and survive. You can't parry their attacks—they're too strong. A strike from a wyrmling ax will shatter every bone in your body.

"So you'll have to begin by forgetting everything that you know about how to fight.

"Your best and only defense is to avoid getting hit. We'll practice evasive tactics—dodges and leaps to help you get away from your opponent.

"You won't wear heavy armor—a little silken armor would be best, if you wear any at all. Chain mail or plate will just slow you down, and it won't do much to soften a wyrmling's blows.

"But better than defense is a good offense.

"Wyrmlings have long arms. Their strike zone is larger than yours. So you must perfect your lunges. Your goal will be to lunge in, strike quickly, and get back out of the wyrmling's strike zone before the monster can ever deliver a blow.

"More than that, your attacks must be effective. You must make certain that when you strike, you don't just draw blood. Try to make every blow a killing blow, or at least a crippling blow. You'll strike for the arteries in the groin, or a kidney, or a blow to the lungs. You want to fight with economy and grace, because as soon as you take down one wyrmling, the chances are that another will charge in behind to take its place."

"What if a wyrmling just comes out swinging?" Rain asked. "I mean, you said that they put harvester spikes in their necks and then go into a killing rage."

"When that happens, you must figure out how to steal the initiative. A feint, a shout, a misdirected gaze— any one of these can cause your opponent to freeze for just an instant, and in that instant you must strike."

So Rain practiced lunges hour after long hour, day after day, until her thighs and calves ached from hard use, and her arms felt as heavy as lead.

They were under full sail, following the coast northward.

The captain's cabin, being the finest room aboard ship, was given to Rain.

That left Myrrima and Sage in the crew's quarters, while Draken slept in the hold with his father and the goats, when he could sleep at all.

But Draken could not rest, he found that first day. It wasn't his father's snoring that kept him awake, nor was it the goats nibbling on his clothes.

It was Rain that kept him awake, his desire for her.

He'd been in love now for two months, and he looked forward to the day when he could marry.

As was the custom in Landesfallen, he'd promised himself to the girl when he was young, but it would be years before they could wed—three or four, at the least.

He needed to purchase his own land, build a house, dig a well, then plow and plant his fields for a couple of seasons, in order to prove that the ground could grow crops. He needed to plant trees and berry bushes, and it would take a few years for them to mature so that they'd bear enough fruit to support a small family.

He needed to accumulate livestock—a milk cow, some pigs and chickens. If he was lucky, he might even be able to afford a horse.

Three years it would take to prepare for a proper marriage, maybe four or five.

But the world had turned upside down.

He couldn't see himself buying land anytime soon, or planting crops. It was as if his dreams were slipping away, moment by moment, like the land that slipped behind them with each passing mile.

Draken's father steered the ship through the daytime, while Draken took the rudder at night.

He found himself yearning to be alone with Rain. So he was glad that night when she came to him in the early hours and sat cuddling against him "for warmth."

He wrapped his arm around her protectively, and struggled gamely to resist the urge to make love.

Draken broke out in a sweat as his desire for her grew; he often found his heart pounding.

As they sailed, the ocean lit up from beneath. Large gray squids had gathered in a huge school that spanned miles, and as they rose from the water, they would flash fluorescent blue and actinic white, driving the fish from the lower depths up to the surface.

So the ocean was alive with the sounds of fish leaping and slapping their tails in the water, even as the squids put on their light show.

Draken supposed that this was some new wonder in the world. Perhaps these squids hadn't existed in the oceans before the great binding. Perhaps they had come from the shadow world.

Yet the spectacle was peaceful, beautiful. Sometimes entire fields of light would burst up at once, as hundreds of squids strobed. It was like watching a lightning show down in the water.

As Rain cuddled against him, she looked longingly to the east for a bit, to the dark woods of Landesfallen.

"You know," she said. "You and I could get off this ship still. We could go inland and make a life for ourselves. We could forget about my family and your family, and just start over. *We* could be a family."

There was such yearning in her voice that Draken wanted to agree. The idea had its attractions. They could try to live off the land, eat burrow bears and rangits.

It sounded like a grand adventure.

She was willing to forgo the comforts of civilization with him, the amenities that most girls demanded.

But as a young man, Draken had patrolled the inland with the Gwardeen, flying over the wastes upon the back of a giant white graak.

Landesfallen was a remarkably inhospitable continent, rocky and hot in the interior, with vast deserts of red sand that blew in raging sandstorms during the summer. The only habitable places had been on the coasts, which were now underwater, and along the banks of a few of the larger rivers. That prime farming land had all been claimed hundreds of years ago.

But there were folks who made a living in the interior of the continents—crazed treasure hunters who went exploring the deep caverns where the toth had once lived a thousand years before. Then there were the gold seekers and opal hunters who went scrabbling over the rocks all year long, living off of lizard meat and desert tortoises and the grubs that they dug up from giant termite mounds.

Draken couldn't imagine himself and Rain doing that. But there were more immediate concerns.

"I couldn't do that," Draken admitted. "My father and mother need my help. Besides, my brothers and sisters might be in jeopardy."

"What are the chances that they're even alive?" Rain asked, leaning in to rest her head upon his chest. He could smell her sweet hair. The scent was intoxicating. "I mean," she apologized, "think about it. You said that they were going deep into the Underworld, to a place called the Lair of Bones, to find the Seals of Creation, so that Fallion could use his powers to mend them, to bind the worlds into one.

"But if he just bound our two worlds together as an experiment, to see what happened, what are the chances that he lived through it? Half of Landesfallen crumbled into the sea. Surely there were earthquakes there in Mystarria. The reaver tunnels . . ." She spoke softly now, apologizing even as she tried to reason with him. ". . . would have caved in. I fear that Fallion would have been crushed."

Draken's heart sank. "You're right," he said. "Trying to save him, it's a fool's errand. But I have to try. You don't know Fallion, or Jaz, or Talon or Rhianna. They raised me. They were my best friends. I know that if I were in danger, they'd do everything in their power to come to my aid—even if it meant crossing an ocean and fighting their way through reavers."

"If Fallion was alive," Rain objected, "wouldn't he unbind the worlds?"

"I don't know," Draken admitted. "Think about it: He's down in the Underworld, and reaching the surface could take weeks. Once he does, once he sees what a mess he's made of things, he might wish to reverse his spell—if he can. But that would mean another perilous journey, weeks or months in the making. He could be alive. I have to hope that he's alive, and at the very least make the effort to come to his aid."

Rain just shook her head sadly. "I wish that he would unbind the worlds. I wish that we could turn about, get back to living our lives. . . ."

Now she switched the subject. "Aaath Ulber doesn't care about all of this, about your brother. He has other designs, I think. He wants to fight the wyrmlings more than he wants to save Fallion."

Draken wasn't sure if that was true. "I think his loyalties are divided. He's two men—Borenson, who has children in danger, and Aaath Ulber, who has a wife and family in need."

"So who will he put first?" Rain asked.

Draken knew the answer. He'd look in on his wife and children at Caer Luciare. If the ship took port at the Courts of Tide, they'd have to make their way inland for hundreds of miles. The fortress at Caer Luciare would be on their way.

But he had to wonder, was that the right thing to do? Who was in greater danger, Aaath Ulber's wife or Draken's brothers and sisters?

Suddenly the seas pulsed with light ahead and salmon began to leap from the water, their backs flashing silver beneath the powdered starlight.

The squids were driving the fish to the surface. He got up, walked to the railing, peered down, and witnessed a giant squid flash in the water, with long arms and tentacles. He had heard tales of luminous squids before, but he'd never heard of any this big.

Draken realized that he should get a spear and go to the prow of the boat, try to bag a couple of the fish in order to make their stores last.

But he hated the taste of salmon, and he wanted to stay here and cuddle with Rain.

Rain stepped up and grabbed him then by the collar and kissed him so passionately that it took his breath away. She pressed her entire body against his, so that he could feel every inviting curve. He could sense her longings, and he had never had a woman who so wanted to make love with him.

At that instant his mother softly cracked the door to her cabin and stepped on deck. She cleared her throat and suggested sternly, "Don't tempt yourselves!" Rain scrambled to get clear of Draken's arms. "We have a long trip ahead. And don't let Aaath Ulber catch you."

Myrrima stood staring at them in the starlight, with a crescent of moon riding the sky at her back, until Rain retreated to her cabin.

Myrrima sat next to Draken and gazed at him until he was forced to admit, "I want to marry her, Mother. I want to marry her *now*. I've never wanted a woman so much. I feel like I'll die without her."

His mother did not answer for a moment. The only sound was that of the ship as it bounded over the waves, and the splash as a fish leapt in the air. The wind sang in the rigging, and waves drove against the hull.

Myrrima stared in wonder at the flashing lights in the water.

"There are squids down there," Draken said. "Giant squids."

"Yes," she said. "I can sense their . . . hunger." She turned to look at him. "And I understand yours. You won't die if you don't have her. I know. I felt that way about your father."

But Borenson had changed. The notion that she could feel anything for the giant Aaath Ulber was repulsive.

"I want to take her to wife," he said. "I want her to be the mother of my children. It feels . . . so healthy, so right."

"No doubt," Myrrima agreed. "Young love is always that way. But you must not make love to that girl, do you understand me?"

"Father is the captain," Draken suggested. "He could perform a marriage." It felt wrong somehow, imagining that his father would marry them.

"You knew your father," Myrrima said. "He wouldn't have allowed it. I cannot imagine that Aaath Ulber will be any more eager. Hold off for a few years."

Draken suspected that his mother didn't understand. He sometimes found himself growing dizzy with lust, and he knew that Rain felt the same way as he did. "But Mother—"

"No!" Myrrima said firmly. "You can't make a future with that girl now. We are going to war. If you were to bed her, she'd find herself with child inside a week.

"What if we get to Mystarria and find it overrun with wyrmlings? What if we find ourselves battling for our lives? What if you were killed, and left Rain pregnant, struggling to bring a child into the world and care for it?

"We have nothing, Draken—no home, no money, no safety. When you can offer Rain those things, then you can permit yourself to marry."

"I love her," Draken objected.

"You *crave* her," Myrrima argued, "and that is only the beginning of love. If you really love her, you'll wait until the time is right to be together, and that is how I'll know that your love is true. You'll prove your love by showing restraint."

Draken knew that she was right, and so he told himself that he would obey. Yet he craved Rain that way that a drowning man might crave water.

"Is there a spell that you can put upon me," he asked, "the way that you used to ease my mind when I was a child and I woke from nightmares?"

Myrrima studied him a moment, her mouth tightening into a hard smile. She seemed to focus on something behind his eyes as she thought.

"Magic shouldn't always be our first recourse when we are confronted by a problem," Myrrima said. "I could help ease your mind, make you forget your desires for Rain. But you'll grow more by struggling against those desires."

Draken resisted the urge to swear, but he wanted to. He was a drowning man, and his mother wouldn't throw him a rope.

"How long must I wait to marry her?" Draken begged.

Myrrima considered. He knew that she had no idea what they might be facing, how long the coming war might last—whether it would be over in a matter of weeks or stretch out for a lifetime.

None of them knew what they were getting into. They only knew that Gaborn had warned that it was urgent for Aaath Ulber to go to battle.

Myrrima shook her head. "Years," she said at last. "You will have to wait for years—perhaps only three, but ten would not be too long to wait for someone you love."

Draken took a deep breath and prepared himself to wait.

When Rain got up the next morning, she felt embarrassed. She could hardly look Myrrima in the eye.

So she went to work. She went into the hold where Aaath Ulber snored louder than an army, and milked the damned goats, then fed them some of the grass that she'd gathered the day before. Then she went topside to the galley and boiled some oats, spooned a bit of molasses over it, and served everyone breakfast—even daring to wake the giant.

She now felt determined to win Aaath Ulber's respect. In the few days that he'd known her, she felt he'd hardly said a kind word to her.

So she handed him a giant's portion of breakfast and waited for him to say thank you.

Aaath Ulber sat groggily on the side of the bed, scratched his chin, thought for a moment, and said, "Thank you, child." He studied her a moment, as if assessing the glare in her eyes, the anger in her stance. "You know I'll expect a lot from you. You'll have battle practice each day, of course, but there is plenty of other work to do. There will be sails to be mended, decks to be swabbed. You can start by taking the bucket and emptying the water from the bilge each morning. In a few days the wood in the hull will swell up and seal tight, but until then you'll have to keep ahead of the leaks."

"Yes, sir," Rain said.

She got the bucket, filled it, and spent the next two hours emptying the bilge. Then she practiced swordsmanship for an hour. When she was done, she opened a bale of linen undergarments that the men had salvaged earlier, unbundled them, and found that the seawater was ruining them. She could smell mold growing.

So she took all four bales of garments topside and boiled the undergarments, then strung them out to dry, so that for the next four days linens were strewn over every spar and tied to every rope that held every sail.

Thus there were underskirts flying like pennants from the crow's nest, and breast bands in the rigging, and dainty night blouses that young newlywed women liked to wear to please their men all strewn across the deck.

She'd never really get them dry, she suspected at first. The salt spray thrown up from the whitecaps kept everything moist, but she discovered that when she climbed the rigging and got high enough, she was able to dry out the clothes.

Thus she was able to salvage hundreds of garments which she imagined were worth a small fortune, but got hardly a word of thanks from Aaath Ulber.

Any free time that she had, Aaath Ulber put her to work in battle practice, and so she discovered that she was trying to stay out of the giant's way, trying to avoid his baleful gaze.

She realized that she couldn't visit Draken at night anymore, couldn't try to find time alone. Aaath Ulber and Myrrima wouldn't approve.

Draken steered them through the night and was up well after dawn, and Rain had to be content to serve him breakfast, earn a smile and a thank-you.

Soon, Rain's muscles ached constantly from the toil of battle practice and from scrubbing the decks; she wished that Fallion would unbind the worlds, undo the damage that he'd done.

The sun rose bright and clear each day, and the skies were hardly marred by clouds. The winds drove them mercilessly toward Mystarria.

In the far north of Landesfallen, the company stopped once again to obtain firewood, get more forage for the goats, and refresh their water supply.

They set sail to the west.

Over the days, Rain's relationship with the giant did not improve. There was a wall between them, a wall so high and thick that she could hardly see over it, see Aaath Ulber for what he was. She kept expecting him to blow up, lash out at her in a senseless fit of rage.

A week out on the voyage, Rain was on her hands and knees, swabbing the deck, when Aaath Ulber bumbled past, stepping on her hand.

She let out a scream of pain, for the giant weighed well over three hundred pounds, and she heard fingers crunch as he plodded on them.

She lifted her hand instantly, found that it was swelling and bleeding. She worried that he'd broken her fingers, for pain was lancing up her arm.

She pulled her hand away, sat up, put it under her armpit and squeezed.

"Sorry," Aaath Ulber said.

"Sorry for what?" she demanded.

His brow scrunched. "Sorry for crushing your hand."

She knew that she'd never get an apology for the rest of his faults, but she had to ask. "You didn't have to kill my father. You left those men in Fossil alive. Why couldn't you have left him alive?"

Aaath Ulber shook his head. "Oh, child, I didn't think of it in time," he admitted. "He pushed me too hard, too fast, and then the world went red. I—don't know how to ease your pain. . . ."

The giant choked up, then hung his head. "The man is dead. He was a fool to fight me."

That's when Rain saw the truth of it. Aaath Ulber was afraid to apologize. His emotions were too strong, too close to the surface.

The words he had just spoken were the closest thing that she'd ever get to an apology.

"I thought you hated me," Rain said.

"If I hated you," Aaath Ulber said, "I wouldn't be working you so hard. I wouldn't be so eager to keep you alive. I . . . don't know you well, but my son loves you, and that counts for something."

Rain broke into tears of relief to know that he did not hate her, tears of frustration that he had hurt her so—then rushed to her room to bandage herself.

Draken called at the door later, but Rain did not open it. She decided that she would comport herself with complete decorum from now on. She would not seek Draken out, or go to him at night. Instead, she would avoid him.

That night, the first autumn storm blew in, a hurricane. The sky became dark, the clouds the sickly green of a bruise. Then the winds and hail struck, and lightning lashed the heavens.

The men were forced to stow the sails while the storm blew the ship backward, far from its course.

The ocean swelled, and enormous waves rose up, threatening to smash the vessel. They slammed over the railings, and drenched the decks.

Thus, the hard times began in earnest.

Yet it was not the wind or the weather or the storms that bothered Myrrima most—it was the loss of her family.

From the time of his change, Myrrima had not slept with her husband; they were growing further apart by the hour. Aaath Ulber spent his days at the rudder, eyes cast toward Mystarria and his wife there.

The children, too, seemed lost. The whole family was torn apart. Sage had lost her sister along with all of her friends. She cried in her sleep at night, haunted by the memories of rushing water.

Meanwhile Draken barely spoke to anyone, and had become so morose that he spent every free hour huddling in the hold. When he wasn't asleep, he was feigning it, Myrrima felt certain. He too pined for his sister and for his friends. But most of all he longed for Rain.

Perhaps, Myrrima wondered from time to time, we should have left them both back in Landesfallen.

But Draken would not have been happy there, either. He would not have fit in among the Walkins. He was bright enough to recognize that.

But most of all, the children seemed to miss their father.

In the first few days of the ship's voyage, Myrrima still saw traces of her husband in the giant—in the way that he held his head, or the way that his blue eyes sparkled when he smiled.

But over the weeks, Aaath Ulber asserted control. He began to show a gruffness that she'd never seen in Sir Borenson. He quit smiling, quit his jokes.

After three weeks Sir Borenson was all but gone. Aaath Ulber became a driven creature, and desperate.

❧ 14 ❧

RUMORS OF A HERO

Do not fear mankind. They cannot withstand the might of Lord Despair.

—From the Wyrmling Catechism

"Damn these humans," the wyrmling lord Yikkarga growled as he knelt near a pit on the side of a small creek, the full moon shining brightly upon his pale face. "They've gotten to another cache!"

Crull-maldor stood on a levy behind the lord, some nineteen days after the binding of the worlds. There had once been an outcropping of blood metal by the creek—red stones, soft and heavy and coated with small particles of metal the consistency of sand. Crull-maldor recalled having seen a few stones on the surface here several decades ago, but obviously the humans had been digging at the site. The pit here was twenty feet in diameter now.

She tried to calculate the loss. A dozen pounds of

blood metal, she suspected. That was all that she remembered seeing on the surface here. But the pit might
have yielded more ore. A great deal of dirt had been
removed. There might have even been a ton or two
deposited here underground—enough to make tens of
thousands of forcibles.

The threat provided by so many forcibles was incal-
culable.

Over the past three weeks, Crull-maldor had begun
creating her own army of wyrmling runelords, twenty
thousand strong.

Victory over the humans had come rapidly, it seemed.

After the binding, the human runelords had spent the
greatest part of their strength attacking her fortress. But
Crull-maldor's counterattacks had been swift and brutal, decimating the humans until none had the strength
to openly defy her any longer.

She'd taken throngs of the small folk captive—
marching them down into her fortress where they were
either butchered for meat or put to the forcible.

The young men were the first to go—those who were
strong in arms and firm in their courage, those who had
no wives or children and therefore had little to lose.

Some had been taken slaves, sent to work the mines.
Others were forced to gather cattle, horses, and fish
for the wyrmling hordes, thus freeing her wyrmlings for
the more important duties of guarding Crull-maldor's
empire.

The humans' weapons had all been seized—as much
as Crull-maldor had been able to find; their gold and
treasures had all been looted.

Thus, her armies had subjugated the vast majority of
humans in the Northern Wastes.

But her hold was tenuous. There was far too much to do. The women and children in her tunnels were struggling to carve their own armor. The smiths at the forges kept their hammers ringing night and day. Her troops were grappling to hold on to the human territories—even as her scouts raced to relieve the small folk of their blood metal.

The emperor was being stingy with his blood metal, keeping her weak.

Often, a new slave will strain at the bands that bind him, and that was an ever-present danger.

She could not afford to let the humans gain an advantage.

Not three hundred yards away, a dog was barking and snarling furiously at the edge of a small village, distraught at the scent of so many wrymlings nearby.

Crull-maldor knew that one of the humans from the village must have discovered the ore, probably within hours of the binding. Crull-maldor had sent her troops to mine this outcropping twice already; and both patrols had come back empty-handed, unable to locate the trove. Now she knew why.

"We should destroy the village," Yikkarga suggested.

Crull-maldor scowled. She didn't trust Yikkarga. He was the emperor's man. It had only been six days since his ship had arrived from the mainland, and already he was seeking to wrest control of her troops from her.

Rumor said that Yikkarga was someone special. He was more than a runelord—he was under the protection of Lord Despair himself, and "could not be killed."

Crull-maldor did not know if that meant that she was forbidden from killing the wyrmling or if it was literal—the wyrmling Yikkarga could never taste death.

There were strange tales coming out of the South since the binding, and Crull-maldor did not know what to believe. It was said that the Lord Despair had taken a new body, that of a human. It was also said that the Knights Eternal had captured the wizard that had bound the worlds, and Lord Despair now employed strange creatures to guard his captive.

Great things were afoot. History was in the making, and it was a grand time to be alive.

But she did not trust Yikkarga. The emperor was obviously grooming him to be her replacement.

Already Yikkarga had sent some of his spies back to the emperor, to warn him that Crull-maldor was creating runelords of her own. She imagined how he would snarl and rage when he heard the news. Perhaps he would even report her insubordination to Lord Despair. If the emperor did, Crull-maldor would point out that she was only trying to empower her troops, prepare them for battle.

What would happen next, she could not guess. Perhaps she would be punished. Perhaps she would be praised.

Either way, a battle was coming.

"Don't be too hasty to deal out death to the humans," Crull-maldor told Yikkarga. "We shall have vengeance in time, but first we must recover the blood metal."

"So much of it, it will probably be hidden nearby," Yikkarga suggested. "I can have my scouts sniff it out." Yikkarga had brought a small contingent with him. His scouts had taken endowments of scent from dogs.

"Good idea," Crull-maldor agreed, "get to it." Secretly, she hoped that his scouts would fail to find the cache. She wanted to humiliate Yikkarga. He was hasty in the way of those who have taken endowments of metabolism, but Crull-maldor's troops would be willing to take days in a concerted search. Given time, her own troops could find the treasure.

Yikkarga's scouts rushed off to hunt. With a jerk of her head, Crull-maldor sent her troops swarming toward the village.

There were over a hundred wyrmlings in this band. Most of them were Crull-maldor's men, but four of the scouts and a captain served under Yikkarga.

If the humans had hidden the metal, it was going to be a race to see who could find it first.

Crull-maldor was becoming adept at rooting out hoards of blood metal. In the past week, her troops had recovered ten pounds of the precious stuff hidden beneath the stones of a hearth, and another bagful secreted beneath a pile of cow dung on a farm.

She knew that a man could be counted on to hide his treasure near.

But another three hoards had gone missing completely, had been spirited away—far from the site where the blood metal was mined—and her troops had yet to find them, though she was sending scouts out on a nightly basis.

In moments the barking of the dog was cut short by a yelp, and the wyrmlings swarmed into the village. They did not enter the homes by doorways or windows, but instead simply tossed the thatch roofs off or put their shoulders to a wall. They grabbed toddlers from their cribs and pulled women into the streets by their hair. Any man who dared defy them quickly succumbed with one blow from a meaty wyrmling fist.

The humans, perhaps four or five hundred strong, were gathered in the village square beneath a great sprawling oak.

Crull-maldor floated to them. She could not easily question the humans. She hadn't had time to master the small folk's speech, but Yikkarga spoke it well enough. The big wyrmling had taken five endowments of wit, and now remembered everything that he heard.

He went among the folk of the village, growling at the head of each family, demanding to know where the blood metal had gone. Men shook their heads, muttering the word "No!"

It was one of the few words that Crull-maldor understood in the speech of these small folk; she'd grown weary of hearing it.

The wyrmling troops hesitated now, encircling the humans. Crull-maldor's scouts were rushing through the town, sniffing at each hovel, sometimes rummaging under a bed or scrutinizing an attic.

It took nearly twenty minutes for Yikkarga's captain to report, "The blood metal is not hidden here in the village. We found a wagon that smells of it, though, out behind that barn." He jutted a chin toward a large building on the road north of town, near a small manor house.

"Go and search the woods and fields nearby," Crull-maldor suggested. "You have done well. You shall be rewarded."

Yikkarga had already found the owner of the manor, a ridiculous-looking man in a nightcap. His plump wife clung to his arm, while his three children groveled and tried to cower away.

The wyrmling lord Yikkarga loomed over the small folk, and stepped on the hand of a young boy of five or six to keep him from crawling off.

"He denies knowing anything about the blood metal," Yikkarga shouted to Crull-maldor. "Shall I torture them?"

"I will handle it." With a thought, Crull-maldor went whispering over the dry grasses of the field, using her powers to pull life from all around. The wyrmlings were masters of torment, but they could assault only the flesh. Crull-maldor could do more. As she neared the humans, the air grew frigid, and their breath steamed in the cold night.

The humans shrieked in terror and sought to back away. Crull-maldor wore a new robe of spidery black gauze, so that they might see her there in the moonlight, a hooded shadow.

She stopped near the family, reached out an ethereal finger, and pointed to the man's youngest child. "Tell me where you took the blood metal," she commanded. Yikkarga translated her demand into the human tongue; the fellow sat with pale eyes made round by terror, pleading, "No! Please, no!"

His wife grasped his wrist and squeezed subtly, a warning for him to be strong, to keep silent. She glared up at Crull-maldor, determination in her piggy eyes.

Crull-maldor marked the woman for death. She was the strong one in the family, the determined one.

"Take the woman," Crull-maldor said. "Let your men humble her."

Yikkarga grabbed the woman by the arm and jerked her from the little family circle. He tossed her into the street, ordered some men to begin carving off her knee-caps.

Cries of outrage rose from the humans. Women and children wept bitterly and turned away, while the little man in his nightclothes gibbered and cursed.

Suddenly Yikkarga dodged aside, just as an arrow came whizzing from the darkness.

There was a shout of warning, and Yikkarga pointed toward an inn. A dozen troops rushed the house, caught the assailant, and dragged him into the street. It was a young man with a longbow. He'd hidden in an attic.

It was a brief incident, and hardly slowed the woman's torture, but Crull-maldor marked it.

It is said that Yikkarga cannot die, that he is under Despair's protection, she thought. There was no warning that an arrow would come from the darkness. His back was turned to it. Yet he *knew*!

Now she knew, too. He could not be killed.

The wyrmlings turned their attention to the piggy woman, who was on the ground, wrestling with a couple of brutes.

"Tell them nothing!" the woman wailed.

Crull-maldor nodded to one of the men. He took a club and struck the human on her mutilated knees, causing such intense pain that the woman blacked out and fell silent.

The small human lord seemed to screw up his face, gather his courage, as if he imagined that he could withstand such torment.

Crull-maldor looked among the family members,

searching for the next victim, settled on the youngest boy. There are things worse than physical torment. There is anguish that goes beyond heartbreak. Crush a man's hand and you cause him pain, but some tortures are profoundly more difficult to endure than physical discomfort.

Crull-maldor reached out to take the child, rend his spirit in front of the whole family, when suddenly a young woman leapt into her path, a girl of twelve or thirteen, hatred burning in her eyes.

"Kill us all, if you want," she shouted. "You'll never find the blood metal! It's gone—far away from here. And someday a lord will come, a powerful lord who will rid the earth of your kind! The oracles have seen it!"

Crull-maldor hesitated briefly, allowing Yikkarga time to translate.

"It is the prophecy again," he said. "The humans have heard of it, a tale of a hero who will bring down the emperor. They have stolen the blood metal in the hopes of bringing it to pass."

Crull-maldor peered up at Yikkarga. He couldn't be trusted. He served the emperor—him and a hundred runelords more powerful than any that she had kept.

The emperor had sent them out of fear. Apparently, things had changed in Rugassa. Lord Despair had begun creating gates to the shadow worlds, assembling a vast army. Great swirling clouds of darkness now blanketed the entire southern realm, and beneath those clouds creatures called Darkling Glories flew, scouring the land for signs of enemies, while troops from a dozen worlds kept watch upon the ground.

Amid those troops was a race of hideous creatures

called Thissians, led by their chaos oracles, who could catch glimpses of the future.

They had seen something, a threat coming from the north, from her realm: a warrior bold and powerful bent on destroying the emperor, with a pair of sorcerers at his back.

Forewarned by prophecies of his doom, the emperor Zul-torac had sent these crack troops to the Northern Wastes, instructing them to find the human champion—and kill him.

But when Crull-maldor asked for a description of this warrior, Yikkarga was evasive.

He's trying to make me look bad, she thought.

It was an old trick. The emperor could not demote Crull-maldor without giving a just reason. Lord Despair would never approve it.

So the emperor was trying to embarrass Crull-maldor. The emperor had demanded that Crull-maldor hunt down and execute the humans' hero. Yet he sabotaged her efforts.

"He is a large man," Yikkarga had reported, "with red hair."

But here in the North, red hair was nearly as common as teeth. Millions of humans had it.

Yikkarga was withholding information, Crull-maldor felt sure. He knew more about this warrior, much more.

So the emperor played his little game. When the emperor's men caught their champion, Crull-maldor's humiliation would be complete. The emperor would remove Crull-maldor from her post. Yikkarga would replace her.

But more was going on here than met the eye.

The emperor is a fool, Crull-maldor thought. In the

process of hunting for a human hero, by asking too
many questions, Yikkarga's men were about to empower
the very man they were sent to destroy.

For now the small folk were seeking out blood metal
and hoarding it, saving it for the day when their savior
would appear.

The girl stood defiantly before Crull-maldor, as ide-
alistic children so often do. The lich ordered Yikkarga,
"Ask her if this warrior has a name."

The girl answered, and Yikkarga translated, "The
hero has no name, but she says that her people will
know him when he comes."

Crull-maldor wasn't so sure. Even if Yikkarga had
learned something important, he would not reveal the
information.

Indeed, that was the problem. Any information that
these humans revealed would benefit only the emper-
or's men.

So Crull-maldor reached out and seized the young
woman, placing a shadowy thumb and pinky finger each
on the girl's mandibles, the middle finger in the sacred
spot just above and between the eyes, and a finger each
upon the girl's eyes.

Instantly the young thing froze, and a whimper
wrenched from her.

The humans all cried out and mourned, some back-
ing away while the father fought to draw near, to comfort the girl.

Then Crull-maldor took her. A thin wail rose from
the child's throat, even as spirit matter escaped through
her nostrils in a streaming fog. Crull-maldor drew out
her hopes and dreams, all of her secret ambitions and
her love—emptying her like a bowl.

The child whimpered and trembled as Crull-maldor drained her, but she could not break away. She was trapped like a boar upon the end of a spear, trembling and straining but unable to escape.

The energy from the child was sweet, as sweet as flesh fresh after a kill.

She died with a feathery wail rising from her throat, her lips quivering, beads of sweat upon her brow, and a haunted look in her eye.

Crull-maldor broke off the attack early. The girl had died inside, but Crull-maldor left her with her heart still beating.

The girl managed to sway on her feet for a moment before she crumpled to her knees. There she just stared forward in a daze.

She was a hollow shell. She would never speak again, never eat.

Her family would try to restore her, to feed her, but it would take days until she died.

"Raze this village as an example to the humans," Crull-maldor growled.

The wyrmling troops cheered. Even Yikkarga rejoiced, and the sound of it brought a smile to Crull-maldor's lips.

Raze the village, Crull-maldor thought, and the people will scatter and tell what we have done. The humans will become even more enraged, more determined to destroy us, and perhaps they will create the very hero that the emperor fears.

Thus, I will turn the tables on him, and see him destroyed.

*   *   *

It was on the lonely march back to the fortress that Lord Despair communed with Crull-maldor—for the first time in nearly two hundred years.

The lich lord was floating among pale gray boulders that glowed eerily in the light of a thin moon. A slight breeze blew, so that she could nearly catch it and float on it, propelled by its strength alone. In the distance, foxes yipped and barked, while nearby the mice rustled among the thin grasses. The land was dying, succumbing to the curse of the lich lords, and so the stalks of wild oats were dry. As the mice scrabbled about, the reedy voices of grass betrayed their presence.

Then Despair came. He took Crull-maldor's mind, much as she might seize that of a crow, and he filled her consciousness with a vision of his presence.

Despair could take many forms, Crull-maldor knew. Male, female, old, young, human, wyrmling, beast. They were the same.

He came to her in the guise of a human this time, one of the true humans of Caer Luciare, with nubs of horn upon his brow. He was clean-shaven, with flashing eyes and a regal look, and he wore bloodred robes with diamonds sewn into them, so that they caught the starlight. He stood upon a parapet, upon a tower in Rugassa, so that in the distance forests loomed above the castle walls, dark and brooding.

He smiled in greeting, and peered right through Crull-maldor's soul, penetrating all of her evil designs, all of her little schemes and betrayals, and then dismissing them with a shrug.

"I know you, little lich lord," Despair whispered.

"Though you feel alone and forgotten, I remember you still."

Immediately, Crull-maldor dropped to the ground, prostrating herself before her master. "As I remember you," Crull-maldor hissed, "and honor you."

"Is it honor to spar with your emperor?" Despair demanded; fear lanced through Crull-maldor. "Is it honor to withhold the blood metal that he demanded?"

"Forgive me, milord Despair," Crull-maldor said. "I kept back a part of the blood metal only to serve you better, so that we might conquer the humans in this realm."

Despair glared at Crull-maldor for a long moment, then broke into a hearty laugh. "You amuse me, my pet," he said. "Long have you and the emperor sparred from a distance, and in this you have done well. Both of you are stronger now because of it.

"But the time has come to put aside your differences. A war is coming, one that will span the universe. You are my great wizard, and I will lean heavily upon you.

"In securing the North, you have done well. But more needs to be accomplished. I need warriors, runelords of great power. I will need weapons and armor by the score. Your people must work faster. Give endowments to all of your people—to every man, woman, and child. Give them ten endowments of metabolism each.

"Begin with your facilitators, so that they might grant endowments more quickly. Then move to your warriors.

"Do you have enough blood metal for this task?"

Crull-maldor thought quickly. She had seventy thousand wyrmlings under her command. It would take a pound of blood metal for each ten forcibles. She would need seventy thousand pounds just to grant metabolism. But her warriors would need more than just speed.

"My lord," Crull-maldor confessed, "I have but twenty thousand pounds of blood metal."

"Fear not," he whispered. "I shall send more soon. I must secure Rugassa and the blood metal mines at Caer Luciare first. Then you shall receive your rations.

"Go in among the humans, and harvest them as you have been doing. Strip them of endowments, so that even those who are unwilling to serve me shall find themselves converted to our cause."

Crull-maldor was struck by a thought. "Milord, if our people take ten endowments of metabolism each, it will create vast logistical problems. With seventy thousand wrymlings here in the North, we struggled to feed ourselves. But with so many endowments, our people will need ten times as much food to eat. . . . The land cannot support it."

The more that Crull-maldor listened, the more frightening Despair's proposition sounded. By granting all of his people endowments of metabolism, he would give them great speed. The endowment itself would boost all of the metabolic processes. It would speed up the body so that the wyrmling runelords would move at ten times their normal speed. Thus, in one year they would accomplish as much as they might have in ten years.

But they would age more quickly, too.

And they would need to eat ten times as often. Thus, they would have to harvest caribou and elk, wild oxen and seals. But there was not enough game on the island for that. In a month or two, all of the animal population would be decimated, and the wyrmlings would face starvation.

"There is much to eat on the island now," Despair said. "There is not just game—there are the horses and cows and sheep that belong to the humans, and then there are the humans themselves.

"Take endowments from the humans," Despair said. "And as you do, seize their livestock to feed yourselves. By the time that the livestock is gone, the small folk will be too weak to fight you, and you can harvest them. . . ."

Crull-maldor considered the plan. It was monstrous in nature. Despair would create a nation of runelords, something that—as far as she could tell—had never been tried before.

Among the humans, such a plan could not have worked. The humans were farmers and herdsmen. They relied so much upon their harvests that they could not have attempted anything on this scale.

But the wyrmling armies that swept across the worlds would move so quickly that they would be impossible to stop, and they could simply feed upon their enemies.

"I see," Crull-maldor whispered. "We shall be the devourers of worlds."

"You see but a glimpse," Despair corrected. "For now, your people shall each take ten endowments apiece, and in doing so they shall *ascend* above all other races.

"But in a few weeks, they shall get ten more endowments of metabolism, and ten more—until each has a hundred. Thus each wyrmling will be born and die within a year, and conquer much. The work that we are set to do is vast indeed, so vast that it could take millennia to perform under normal circumstances.

"Yet within the year, your people will begin populating a thousand new worlds, breeding and multiplying.

Inside a few decades, we shall not rule one world, but all worlds."

Crull-maldor smiled, unable to fathom what this might mean. "Milord," she whispered, "what place will you find for me to serve in such a vast kingdom?"

Despair gazed at her thoughtfully, and whispered, "You may choose a world, the finest jewel that you can find, and there you may reign."

❧ 15 ❧

WATER

There seems to be an unwritten law to the universe. Whenever you determine to do something great, something extraordinary, your fellow men will mock you and combine against you.

—Gaborn Val Orden

For six weeks the *Borrowbird* plowed through a sea that seemed to Aaath Ulber to be made of stone. For much of the time, leaden waves, as rough as boulders, tumbled into the ship under heavy gray skies. Three times great storms arose, battering the ship, driving it mercilessly.

The ship's meager supplies soon began to give out. The barrels of food dwindled, the water became depleted.

Aaath Ulber never caught sight of land, but six weeks into the journey Draken raised a shout in the nighttime, having spotted sails ahead. They were massive red sails of a wyrmling fleet, some twenty warships strong.

Aaath Ulber stood on the deck in the early morning and peered off in amazement: he hadn't known that the wyrmlings had such fleets.

So much about the wyrmlings was a mystery. They lived underground, and often sought to hide their numbers. Their capitol was at Rugassa, but there were tales of other large cities elsewhere—in the lands that Sir Borenson had once known as Inkarra and Indhopal.

But fleets of warships?

"Where do you think they're going?" Draken asked, while the rest of the family stood at Aaath Ulber's back.

"To introduce themselves to the folk of Landesfallen," Aaath Ulber said. The sight of the ships left him sick. "The wyrmlings must have learned of it."

But how? Aaath Ulber wondered. He could come up with only one answer: The folks in Rofehavan must have alerted the wyrmlings.

Aaath Ulber didn't want to alarm the children, but the sight of the fleet filled him with foreboding.

The wyrmlings have already taken Rofehavan, he reasoned. They wouldn't send out ships if they felt that there was still a threat to their home front.

They could only have gained such complete control, Aaath Ulber reasoned, if they got to the blood metal at Caer Luciare.

Otherwise, the folk of Mystarria would have overrun the wyrmlings.

My wife Gatunyea will be dead, he realized. As will my children there.

The wyrmling ships drew near, and Aaath Ulber had to run to the north for several hours to evade them. But his small vessel, so light and free, quickly outpaced the black ships.

The water ran out completely a day later. Just when Aaath Ulber needed a storm, none came, and his barrels lay empty.

The family could not go long without water—a couple of days if the temperatures stayed cool, fewer if it grew hot.

He wrapped a little goat hair around a hook, creating something that looked like an eel, and threw his line out behind the ship, hoping to lure a fish, hoping for just a bit of moisture.

They caught a striped bass that way, and Aaath Ulber ate it raw, but the moisture in the fish tasted as salty as seawater, and it only made his thirst worsen.

There were tales of water wizards who could turn seawater into fresh pure drinking water, and so he asked Myrrima if she would give it a try. But she had no knack for it.

They sailed through the next night without water, and a third day.

By then, Aaath Ulber's tongue felt swollen in his mouth, and he was beginning to grow sick with a fever. Little Sage was worse off. She fell into a swoon that morning, and when she woke at all, she kept calling to her dead sister, "Erin? Erin, where are you?"

Rain took some of her linen and draped it in seawater, then made a compress of it and put it on Sage's head, to try to slow the fever. But upon feeling the moisture in the rag, Sage kept trying to pull it into her mouth.

"We need water," Aaath Ulber mourned when his wife drew near. "Could you summon a storm?"

She just shook her head weakly. "I've never had a gift for that kind of thing."

The day was cool, but the sun beat down on Aaath Ulber as he sat at his tiller, drying his skin. His lips were chapped and caked with sores. He felt light-headed.

This sun will be the death of me, he realized.

Every muscle felt weak. He doubted that he could make it through another day.

But Draken has steered through the nights. He can carry on when I'm gone.

If someone is to die, he thought, it is right that it is me. I'm the one who brought them here.

Such was the parade of his thoughts, plodding in circles through his frenzied mind, when suddenly Myrrima came from the galley.

"Head straight into the wind," she said. "I smell fresh water."

Aaath Ulber turned the rudder just a bit, and Myrrima adjusted for him. Then she saw how weak he was and told him to move aside, as she sat and steered.

He peered off toward the horizon, looking for signs of land, but saw nothing.

"Get into the hold," Myrrima told him. "This sun will be the death of you." Aaath Ulber chuckled, for he'd been thinking the same all day.

Groggily, he made his way into the hold, where he lay having fevered dreams. Sometimes he thought that he was Gaborn's bodyguard again, and that they were traveling up the coasts of Mystarria to survey the realm. Other times he thought that he had been wounded fighting reavers, and that someone had put him in a death wagon by accident.

Draken put a cool compress on Aaath Ulber's head, and after a time he began to recover.

For hour after hour, Myrrima steered, gradually moving farther and farther south. It was near dusk when Rain finally spotted the source of the water and let out a shout. Aaath Ulber found the strength to struggle up from the hold. The red sun on the horizon cast its light upon a snow-covered hill far in the distance, staining its peak red. A great blue fog spread out from the mountain's base, so that Aaath Ulber could not see the island's shore.

"There!" Myrrima cried.

Aaath Ulber grinned, and cheers went up from Rain and Sage and Draken.

But a moment later Aaath Ulber finally caught a strange scent—metallic and bitter.

It's not a hill, he realized. It's an iceberg!

But ice is water, fresh water. And we're saved.

So that night in the fading twilight, as the half-moon rode upon the backs of the stars, the two men rowed their little away boats up to the berg.

As they drew near, the heavy fog obscured the stars. They could hear the sounds of the ice, splitting and cracking, and every few minutes some ice would rumble and go cascading into the water, starting an avalanche.

Getting the ice would be dangerous business. Even drawing close to the berg was to risk one's life.

"Perhaps we should wait until morning," Aaath Ulber suggested. "When we can see what we're doing."

"I'm not sure you'll last until morning," Draken said, as a loud crack split the air. "How about we get in and out quickly?"

Aaath Ulber grinned. "Spoken like a warrior."

So they lit a torch, and then rowed close to the berg. The ice seemed to rise straight from the water a hundred feet, and Draken stood for a long moment, waving his torch from right to left, looking for a path.

They turned south and Aaath Ulber began to paddle for a moment. Behind them there was a cracking sound and boulders of ice came raining down, just where they had been.

"Hah," Aaath Ulber jested, "if we'd only known, we could have just held our barrels out."

But the blocks of ice that bobbed in the water now were contaminated with salt.

So the two rounded the berg until they found a gentler slope, one where loose ice lay like boulders.

Here they tied their boat to an outcrop of ice and disembarked.

Draken carried the torch and scaled the berg's rough sides, while Aaath Ulber hoisted an empty water barrel under each arm and made his way behind.

When they were a hundred feet above the sea, and Aaath Ulber felt that the water would be pure and fresh, he used his war hammer as a pick, gouging out great blocks of ice.

With bare hands, Draken shoved the ice into barrels; then they hammered on lids and took them down to the boat in a rush, lest an avalanche fall upon them.

Three trips they made, hearts hammering in fear.

When the iceberg was silent, it seemed deathly silent.

And when the ice cracked in the least, it sounded like doom.

On the last trip, Aaath Ulber carried two barrels up, and felt too weary to hammer the ice, so Draken took a turn. He had only clanked the hammer against the ice lightly, when Aaath Ulber heard movement above.

Chunks of ice began to roll down. One pinged off of a nearby ledge.

"Avalanche!" Draken shouted; he turned and began to slide downhill.

But Aaath Ulber paused. It was only a few chunks; he hoped that there would be no more.

He lifted his torch and looked up—toward the peak of the iceberg three hundred feet above. He saw something white in the darkness—huge, rushing toward him.

A boulder of ice! he thought. He heard a snarl as it came to life.

A bear rushed past him, a great white bear!

It dwarfed the enormous bears that had haunted the Dunnwood in his youth. This breed could stand thirteen feet tall and weigh well over a ton, and this particular specimen strained the limits for size.

Aaath Ulber shouted a warning, but Draken was already running, and his flight attracted the predator. It bounded atop him. The weight of the bear drove Draken down onto his belly, and the two of them began sliding over boulders of ice, sledding toward the water amid the frozen scree.

But the bear was eager for a kill.

Draken screamed in terror, tried to scrabble away. The bear roared and lunged for Draken's neck.

By blind instinct, Draken managed to get on his

back. He shoved his arm up into the bear's mouth, far enough so that it got behind the monster's teeth, and kept it there, trying to keep the bear's jaws from clamping down. The bear slapped at Draken with a big paw, raking his side with its claws.

Aaath Ulber roared, hoping to startle the beast, and went rushing down the slope waving his torch.

He saw the war hammer that Draken had been digging with, and grabbed it as he ran.

Draken had nothing to fight with but his eating dagger, which was strapped to his hip. Draken shoved the bear's head back with one hand, pulled the blade and stabbed, thrusting it into the bear's neck.

The bear gave a yelping roar, whirled its head to the left to see where the pain came from.

Then it snarled and chomped down on Draken's face. Its teeth were like a vise, and it shook its head savagely, trying to rip the young man's flesh, or perhaps break his neck.

Aaath Ulber reached the pair and shouted, "Aaaagh! Get off of him!"

The bear looked up, saw Aaath Ulber. There was madness in the creature's eyes, an endless hunger. Aaath Ulber realized that it had been stuck on this iceberg for weeks with little or nothing to eat. It was desperate, and would give no quarter.

Draken slammed his knife into the bear again, and the monster barely registered the pain.

So Aaath Ulber swung with his might, adjusting the blow in mid swing so that his war hammer, slammed the bear between the eyes.

The bear fell upon Draken, a sodden weight.

"You killed it!" Draken shouted, panicky, trying to

shove the monster's weight off of him. "You killed it!" he cried again, relief and glee mixed in his voice.

"Yes," Aaath Ulber said dryly. "I killed it. But *you* get to skin and gut the beast!"

❧ 16 ❧

THE SPIRIT BAG

We define our own greatness. Envision the kind of person that you would most admire, and then set down the path to become that man.

—Emir Owatt of Tuulistan

A whisper of a thought came from the emperor. *Lord Despair desires Knights Eternal to lead his armies. You will begin creating and training them.*

Crull-maldor was down among her sorcerers, hundreds of liches and wyrmlings who struggled day and night to meet Lord Despair's growing demands, for the wars that he was about to wage were straining every resource.

No longer was the Fortress of the Northern Wastes a sleepy little outpost. In the forges, hammers rang night and day. Ax and spear, helm and shield. Crull-maldor's wyrmlings were struggling to meet the new orders.

War was imminent, Crull-maldor knew, a war so vast that the wyrmlings had never dreamed of the like.

World upon world her people would be called upon to conquer.

But now this?

Knights Eternal? Crull-maldor demanded. *How many will Lord Despair want?*

For millennia the wyrmlings had only three. A few hundred years ago, Crull-maldor had participated in creation and training of three more. But Crull-maldor had recently learned that some of those had been killed. Obviously, Despair would want to replace them.

It was a great labor to create and train the monsters, a labor that Crull-maldor despised—especially now, when so much more was required of her troops.

Our lord desires a hundred thousand of them, the emperor whispered. *It will require much from all of us. We will begin immediately. The rut is on. You will speak to the spirits of the babes in the wombs of your females, begin their instruction, and strangle all who are born this breeding season.*

Crull-maldor was stunned, and could think of nothing to say, but the emperor cut off contact with her mind, relieving her of the burden of speech.

She hesitated a moment, wondering why the sudden need for Knights Eternal in such vast numbers. The training of such a monster took hundreds of years, hundreds of thousands of hours.

For the next few centuries, training them would require all of Crull-maldor's time, all of her effort.

I am a nursemaid to the undead, she thought. That is all that I can be.

This was the end of her life, she knew. There would be no honors, no vaunted position. She would never become emperor, for with a call for so many Knights

Eternal, even the emperor Zul-torac would be demoted. He too, would become a nursemaid.

Why would Despair need so many of them? Crull-maldor wondered. But the answer was obvious. Despair had begun his great and last war. He was sending troops through the doorways, into the far reaches of the universe. He would conquer one world at a time, until the heavens groaned under his rule.

He would need servants to dominate these worlds—the most powerful servants in Despair's arsenal.

The Knights Eternal had gained Lord Despair's favor. That was the only possibility. It was said that they had taken endowments. Their living flesh allowed them a boon that Crull-maldor could never receive. That was the rumor, at least, and Crull-maldor believed it, for it was the only thing that made sense.

The Knights Eternal shall rule the heavens, Crull-maldor realized . . . and I, I will die being their nursemaid.

The very thought made her seethe.

I am more powerful than they, she thought. I am more powerful than the emperor.

And an idea struck her.

The only reason that the Knights Eternal had gained favor with Lord Despair was because they could garner endowments.

But what if *I* took endowments?

It was an intriguing idea. The endowment process worked only among the living, she knew. If a runelord took endowments and died, then the attributes returned to those who had given them. And if a Dedicate died, then the attribute was stripped from the lord who had taken it.

For this reason, it was imperative that a runelord guard his Dedicates, keep them safe, lest the lord's enemies kill the Dedicates and thus strip the lord of his attributes, leaving him weak and powerless.

But what is life? Crull-maldor wondered.

It was a mystery that she had studied for hundreds of years. As a lich, she defied death every second. She lived half in the world of the flesh, half in the world of the spirit.

Life is not an absolute, she told herself. Between life and death are infinite gradations, shades of gray. A body survives only so long as its spirit clings to its flesh, and most men who feel themselves to be alive are closer to death than they would like to believe.

So why would a Knight Eternal be able to take endowments, and not me? she wondered. The Knights Eternal are deader than I am, for I still cling to the remains of my own body while they only inhabit the shells left by others.

But that was the difference, she recognized. The Knights Eternal clung to flesh.

For ages she had trained the creatures, telling them that they had no spirits, that it was only the power of their minds that allowed them to seize a corpse and inhabit it.

But that was not true. The Knights Eternal did have spirits, powerful spirits. Crull-maldor lied to the creatures only so that they would fear oblivion all the more, so that they would cling to any flesh that they could, like a drowning man clinging to a raft.

It was true that their spirits were not whole, undefiled. As part of their preparation, before birth Crull-maldor would damage them, remove the spirit tendrils that formed their conscience and gave them their will. By doing so she made the Knights Eternal ill-suited to become abodes for the loci. Thus, the Knights Eternal could not communicate across the leagues with other loci, as Crull-maldor did. That had always been their weakness. That was why Despair had never shown them favor.

But much had changed with the binding of the worlds.

Much has changed, Crull-maldor thought, and much more shall yet change. . . .

Less than an hour later Crull-maldor trundled into the Dedicates' Keep deep in the wyrmling fortress. She wore her cloak of glory.

The cloak was not made of material; it was fashioned from skin, Crull-maldor's own hide, skinned from her while she was still alive. By wearing it, Crull-maldor could walk about in her wyrmling form, rather than appear as a spirit. She could manipulate things with her hands, if she so desired—bearing a spear into battle, or adjusting an ocular.

There was life in the hide still. It breathed on its own, and required nourishment. She kept it in a vat by day, soaking in blood, seawater, and various nutrients.

The skin had aged over the centuries, becoming wrinkled. Growths had formed over it—warty things—and patches of it were discolored.

The skin had eye holes but no eyes, mouth holes but no teeth. Crull-maldor could move about in the skin, but she had no flesh and bone to give her proper form.

Instead, she walked with a hunched back, barely able to hold her head up, her knuckles sometimes dragging on the floor. She was unsightly.

But the cloak of glory had its uses. The eye holes and other orifices could all be sewn tightly shut, so that Crull-maldor could inhabit her old skin and walk about in the daylight, as she had need.

Now she hoped that it would provide another use.

The Dedicates' keep here was a vast hall where dozens of sorcerers coaxed attributes from human Dedicates and bestowed them upon the wyrmlings. Hundreds of people filled the hall—terrified human women weeping and begging to be spared, wyrmling soldiers eager to taste the sweet kiss of a forcible.

The wyrmling troops were drawing attributes as quickly as they could. Mostly they took metabolism from the humans, thus speeding up the troops while leaving the Dedicates in a magical slumber. Human workers sweated and grunted as they lugged the sleeping Dedicates off for storage.

The room was filled with the deep songs of the facilitators, the screams of pain from Dedicates. White lights flashed as forcibles came to life, and the odor of burned skin and singed hair filled the room.

Crull-maldor limped to her chief facilitator, and commanded in a harsh whisper, "Give me an endowment."

The facilitator stared at her a moment, and a scowl of revulsion crossed his face. Obviously he did not think that her experiment could succeed, but his answer was contrite. "Which endowment, O Great One?"

"It matters not," Crull-maldor said. "Metabolism is easy. Give me metabolism." She imagined how it would be to speed up, to move faster than other liches, to think twice as fast as the emperor. There were so many possible advantages. . . .

So the facilitator waded in among the humans and

brought back a likely Dedicate, a small young man with a weak chin. The boy dodged and kicked, trying to break away. He did indeed seem to be a child with a gift for speed.

The facilitator spoke to the boy in his own language, soothing him, calming him, promising life in return for his gift. A few slaps to the face left the boy with a bloody nose and a firm conviction that giving up his endowment would save his life.

Then the ceremony began; the facilitator picked out a forcible and began singing to the boy in his deep voice, a wordless song meant only to mesmerize the child, get his mind off his fear. Then the facilitator pressed the rune end of the forcible to the boy's neck, and it suddenly grew white-hot at its tip. The sound of sizzling skin filled the air.

The boy whimpered then, but did not break away. Instead, he sat stoically, glaring at Crull-maldor, as if daring her to take his gift.

The facilitator continued singing, brought the forcible to Crull-maldor. He twirled it in the air, and thick white lines of light held in the air wherever the forcible went, creating a serpent of light that coiled through the room.

But when the glowing forcible touched Crull-maldor's skin, the white hot metal did not burn it. The serpent merely hung in the air, as if waiting to strike elsewhere.

The facilitator grew nervous, tried touching Crull-maldor in various places—her belly, her neck, a healthy-looking patch of skin on her forehead.

But nothing worked. Beads of sweat began to break upon his brow as he considered how she might punish him for his failure.

"Master," he begged, "a lich cannot take an endowment. . . . You are too far gone toward death."

It was as Crull-maldor had feared. She had tried an experiment, and failed.

It is because I do not cling to my flesh, she realized. I am a spirit inhabiting a bag made of skin, nothing more. I have the form of a living being, but I am not like the Knights Eternal.

She thought for long seconds, and answered the facilitator. "Oh, I can take endowments. But first I must take a fitting body. . . ."

❧ 17 ❧

THE BARBAROUS SHORE

No man is a barbarian in his own eyes, but often is seen as a barbarian by others.

— *Warlord Hrath*

Six days later the soft cries of gulls wafted above a still, fog-shrouded sea. In the gray dawn, the water barely lapped against the hull of the *Borrowbird*, the waves looking for the entire world like molten lead.

Myrrima peered overboard, and tasted the salty air. Land was not far off. She could smell a hint of it—autumn fields and wet earth, not too far away.

Fifty-two days it had been since the family had fled Landesfallen.

Fifty-two days was a long time. Much can change.

Myrrima was filled with burning questions: What will we find in Rofehavan? Where is Talon? What has befallen my other children?

The sea gave no answers. Myrrima was a wizardess, but unlike some who were gifted with aquamancy, she could not foretell a person's fate by gazing into a still pool.

For a moment, she thought that she caught sight of a shadow on the water—a fishing coracle. But it disappeared through the fog as silently as it had come, and she wondered if it had been a dream.

Her ship lay as silently as a log in the water. She'd lowered the sail an hour ago, and then bade the ship be still. A small spell kept a dense fog in place. It was not hard to do. There was no wind, and it would have been a foggy morning even without her help.

Aaath Ulber stumbled up from the hold and wiped the morning sleep from his eyes. He took the rudder by long habit, though there was no need to steer.

"We've got land nearby," Myrrima told him. She didn't know exactly where they were. No one on board was a navigator. But they had known that if they sailed west long enough, they'd run into a continent. But how far north or south had they come? To the north was Internook, home to the savage warlords. That was the most likely place for them to beach. But if they had drifted south far enough, they might beach in Haversind or Toom—lands that would be more hospitable.

The giant drew a deep breath, taking a long draught

of air. "There's a port," he said. "I can smell cooking fires."

He has a good nose, Myrrima thought. The warrior clans bred like hunting dogs, and they gave him a good nose with all the rest.

"Aye," Myrrima said. "If you listen close, you'll hear foghorns braying in the distance." She shot him a worried look.

Aaath Ulber stood silently until a horn sounded, long and deep. "Internook," he said softly. "We've landed in damned Internook."

He gave her a worried glance. They'd had nothing but bear meat to eat for the past few days, an old boar, sour and rancid.

Myrrima said, "I think that I should go ashore, purchase some fresh supplies."

Aaath Ulber held his tongue for a moment, peered at her from the corner of his eye. She knew that he would argue. He loved her too much to let her take the risk.

"I'll be the first to go into town," he said.

"Why you?" Myrrima demanded.

"I'm the biggest," he said. "If anyone gives me trouble, I'll be able to squash them."

She had known that he would make that argument. "You're the biggest—and the easiest to spot," she said. "You'll attract too much attention."

"Your dark hair will attract almost as much attention. And you speak with a Heredon brogue. I've always done a fair impression of an Internook accent."

"Fair enough to mock the warlords at a drunken feast, but this isn't a feast, and these are not our friends. They'll spot you in minute!"

"Last that I heard, it wasn't against the law in Internook to be a Mystarrian," Aaath Ulber growled.

"Last I heard, the warlords of Internook were using Mystarrians for bear bait in the arena."

"Let them," Aaath Ulber said. "The last bear that I tangled with didn't do so well."

"Maybe we should just keep sailing," Myrrima said. "I have an ill feeling about this. In two more days we could be in Toom."

Aaath Ulber stood over her, put his huge hand on her shoulder. He was trying to be gentle, she knew. He was trying to ease her mind. But it felt clumsy and wrong somehow. His hands now were as big as plates. They felt like the paws of some animal. There was a distance between them that could not be crossed, and when he touched her now she felt more isolated than ever.

"We need ale," Aaath Ulber said, "at the very least. I've heard that we cannot trust the water here. Ale, a few vegetables, a couple of hens. I can go to the morning market and be out in an hour. I won't talk much, just grunt and nod and point."

"That was my plan exactly," Myrrima smiled.

"Mmmm?" he asked. He pointed at her, jutted his chin, and grunted, as if to say, "I want that one."

Myrrima laughed.

"See," Aaath Ulber said, "I've been practicing all month. I've got it down to an art."

Myrrima didn't agree to let him go. Aaath Ulber simply went to one of the two away boats, lowered it over the side, and climbed down in. When he settled into it, he looked far too large for the small vessel. It threatened to sink under his weight.

Rain came rushing out of her cabin at that moment. "Wait," she cried. "I'm coming with you."

"You?" Aaath Ulber asked.

"You shouldn't go alone," she said. "With my blond hair, I'll fit right in."

Aaath Ulber opened his mouth to argue, but Rain shushed him. "I'll follow you, keep a good distance. And if there is trouble, I won't intercede. I'll just let the others know."

Myrrima studied the girl. She had the right hair color, but she wasn't big-boned enough.

Rain's plan made sense, but a wave of foreboding stole over her.

As Rain scrambled to get into the boat, Myrrima said, "Maybe I should come, too. . . ."

Aaath Ulber said tersely, "The others need you more than I do. Keep a fog wrapped around the boat, like a fine gray cloak. I'll be back soon."

He took the oars and began to paddle away, toward the distant bray of a foghorn. Myrrima demanded. "How will you find us when you're done?"

"Easy," Aaath Ulber said. "I'll just look for a broad patch of mist on the ocean, and aim right for the heart of it."

He smiled up at her, then pulled hard on the oars once, twice, three times—and the mist swallowed him.

Aaath Ulber rowed toward shore on the little ship's boat, with Rain seated in the back of the boat, doing her best to look brave.

"Don't worry," Aaath Ulber told Rain. "Everyone will be looking at me. No one will be looking at you."

He considered how very little the young girl knew,

and realized that Rain could use more instruction. "When we get to the dock, wait until I've gone a good hundred yards before you begin to follow. Understand?"

"I'll be fine," Rain said.

Aaath Ulber recognized that Rain seldom had to be told a thing more than once. She had a keen memory, and a good wit when she wasn't too shy to speak. But right now, her life would depend upon how well she performed.

For a moment there was little sound, only the splashing of oars as he dipped and pulled, dipped and pulled. Then a great horn sounded off toward shore. Other than that, the only sound was the waves lapping against the boat, and the only sight was the gray fog above and the waves beneath as they lifted the boat gently and then let it fall. The water was clear, with a bit of kelp floating here and there, and some small yellow jellyfish.

"When you follow me, keep your head down, and your hood up. This may not be the largest village in Internook. The men and women of the place, they'll think that you're some girl from the outskirts of town or a nearby village. But folks your own age—they're the ones you have to watch out for. They'll mark you as a stranger.

"Don't speak to anyone. Try not to look like you're following me. That means that you don't watch me. You might stop and look in the windows of a shop, or stoop over to tie the straps to your boots, or pet some stray dog. But you don't follow me with your eyes, understand?"

He waited for Rain to nod.

"Now, tell me what you're going to do when we get into town?"

Rain repeated the instructions nearly perfectly.

Yet he worried. Rain's face was pale with fear. Bone-white skin was common up here in the North, and so he figured that she wouldn't look too out of place. Her hair color and eye color were right. The folks here all had yellow or red hair.

What bothered him was the fear in her eyes, the tight lips, the way her shoulders hunched in on themselves, the way her breath came shallow.

"I want you to try not to be afraid," he suggested. "Your fear is what will give you away. Keep your head down but your back straight and tall, your shoulders wide. When you see someone, smile as if you were greeting an old friend. And when you walk along the streets, think of better days, and happier times ahead."

Now he had to broach the subject that most concerned him. "The warlords of Internook aren't bad folks, if you're one of them. But they breed like rats, and so for five hundred years they've been eager to hire their young men out as mercenaries. There are families here so poor that they raise children just to sell them. When a young man goes to war, he only receives wages after a campaign has ended, and if he dies in battle, that payment goes to his family. Many a father and mother have sent out their sons hoping for nothing more than to get gold from it, and to see their children all slaughtered.

"So the folk of Internook have gained repute over time for their brutality, for their warrior's spirit. The rest of the world sees them at their worst. But I think that in their own homes, they may not be so bad. . . ."

Rain spoke up, choosing her words slowly and carefully, her voice hinting at barely subdued rage. "What the warlords did to us cannot be forgiven or ignored. Their reputation for brutality is well earned. What's more, I do not believe that such folk could go to Mystarria and act like monsters without losing something of their souls. War hardens a man, and in Internook, their folks have been growing hard for generations." She gave Aaath Ulber a stern look and said, "You do me a disservice by telling comfortable lies."

Aaath Ulber was surprised by her impassioned outburst, but he was learning that there was more to this girl than met the eye.

"Don't worry about me," Rain said. "I've taken the worst that the warlords are likely to dish out."

Aaath Ulber peered into her clear eyes and saw something frightening there: death.

She's been raped, he realized. Probably more than once.

Aaath Ulber felt more than a little worried. Had he known what she'd endured, he would not have allowed her to come.

So he rowed on in silence. The folks of Internook were great eaters of fish, and as the boat neared land, he saw many a fisherman's coracle hugging the shore. The fishermen didn't dare go far in the thick fog.

The blowing of the horn guided him to port, and at midmorning he tied up at the docks.

The port was like many here in Internook. A river had carved a channel into the bay, a channel broad and deep. But the barbarians had hauled in huge rocks and blocked most of the old bay off, forming a funnel that pointed into the shallows. The mouth of the funnel ended with several iron columns interspersed about two feet apart.

In the summer, leviathans—great serpents of the deep—sometimes came in near shore, driving large schools of fish before them: salmon and cod, mackerel and bass. The fish would swim for safety toward the shallows, and be driven down the long throat of the funnel into the bay. Once they were in, the barbarians could drop boards through slats, locking the fish in while the iron bars kept the great serpents out. Thus, the fishing grounds here in Internook were remarkably bountiful.

The fog still held, and so Aaath Ulber was shielded from faraway eyes. He got up and whispered, "Remember, keep well behind me. When you can't see me any longer, that's the sign to start following. I'll take care to make plenty of noise, so that you'll know where I am."

He checked his head wrap, then lumbered out of the boat, onto the docks. He began to whistle an aimless tune as he strolled, his heavy feet thumping on the wooden planks.

Here near shore, the sea smelled differently. The fishermen would gut their catches in the afternoons, tossing the offal to the crabs in the bay. So the clean salt smell of the sea had heavier overtones of death and decay.

He passed a few women mending fishing nets on the docks, and as he did, all eyes peered up at him. As he feared, no one as massive as he could hope to make his way through town undetected.

He nodded politely, grunted as he passed, and his face flushed as he felt their stares follow.

At last the wooden docks met the land, and stairs climbed some fifty feet, scaling a rock embankment. He thumped up the stairs. There were fish stalls all about, the heart of the village's market, and people filled the streets in droves.

For barbarians, he decided, the village was surprisingly well kept. The streets were clean and well cobbled, and the market stalls were painted in bright colors—canary, crimson, deep forest green. Each stall served as the front of a home, and the houses were so close together that many of them shared common walls, thus conserving heat. Wildflowers seemed to sprout up from any little patch of dirt at the front of the houses.

But farther up on the hill, enormous longhouses could be seen shrouded in fog, each ringed with tall picket fences. Cows ambled about up there, while chickens and geese scratched in the yards. Each longhouse was made from huge beams, and served as a fortress for the families that lived inside.

Aaath Ulber bumbled through the market, peering at giant eels that hung from hooks in one stall; he stopped to watch one merchant toss a load of crabs into a huge boiling pot. Everywhere, fishmongers called out, "Cod, cod—so fresh he's still wiggling!" or "Shark, shark—eat him before he eats you!"

But it wasn't fish that Aaath Ulber wanted. He was looking for fresh vegetables, perhaps a young piglet.

He stopped for a moment, heard voices up the street to the north, other merchants hawking their wares.

He worked through the crowd, trying not to step on anyone. Everywhere, people stopped to gawk. Most didn't even bother to hide their stares.

So he strode along, still whistling. He stopped for a moment at a cross street, took an instant to look back, to see if he could spot Rain. But there were too many faces in the crowd, and he didn't dare search for long.

So he moved forward, hoping that she could see him well enough.

At last he reached a vendor who sold produce—fresh blackberries from the woods, wild mushrooms, hazelnuts, honeycomb—and a smattering of herbs from the garden—leeks and parsnips, carrots and tulip roots.

He grunted and mostly pointed at what he wanted, feigning an accent when he was forced to barter. He paid too much, giving the woman a plain golden ring for a good deal of food, then tucked it in a makeshift rucksack.

He moved on, stopped to buy that piglet he'd been hungry for. He found a nice fifty-pounder, traded it for some steel, and then tucked it up under one arm. The pig squealed like mad. It had been castrated in the not-so-distant past, and apparently feared that Aaath Ulber might try it again.

There is nothing that attracts attention like a giant in the marketplace holding a squealing pig, Aaath Ulber discovered. Every eye turned to him, and it seemed that folks two hundred yards down the street all stopped to stare.

So Aaath Ulber held the pig and scratched its head, trying to soothe it with a few soft words.

He wanted to get back to the boat now, but there was so much more that he wanted here in town. He was hoping for some nice pastries for Myrrima, or perhaps a new dress, anything to put a smile in her eyes. And he wanted cloth to make new clothes for himself and everyone else on the ship. But mostly, his family needed news—and weapons.

So he quieted his piglet, then kept on walking. After

purchasing four loaves of bread, which went straight into his rucksack, he found that his piglet stopped squealing altogether and amused himself by sniffing at the sack and grunting quietly.

At last he found a man in a stall who sold knives of all kinds. He stopped.

The man was old—astonishingly old. His face was lined and wrinkled, and his red hair had all gone silver long ago. He wore a beard cropped short, and dressed in robes appropriate for a merchant—not so rich as to garner envy but not so poor as to earn disdain.

Yet there was wisdom in his eyes, and he moved quickly enough when Aaath Ulber stopped to study his wares.

"Do you sometimes feel that something is missing from your life, good sir?" the merchant asked. "Perhaps it's a knife—something to butcher your pig there? Or would you like to see something larger, something more appropriate to a man your size?"

Aaath Ulber peered at the merchant's wares. There were long knives with notched blades for cutting bread, and small knives that a woman might use for peeling apples. But what interested Aaath Ulber most were the knives against the back wall. There was a pair of fine dueling knives—not too fancy, mind you. It wasn't the polished steel that you might find in Heredon, with silver finger guards and scenery etched into the blades. They were cheap, sensible—the kind of knives that some warrior lad might take into battle.

"Do you have anything larger?" Aaath Ulber asked. "A man my size needs a blade to match."

The old merchant eyed him for a long moment. "It's

not pigs that you're wanting to kill," the fellow mused. "I don't have much call for real weapons, you understand, but I have something that might interest you. . . ."

He turned and went to the display case on the far wall, then pulled out a hidden drawer beneath. It opened to reveal a tall sword, the kind that the barbarians here favored—nearly seven feet long. Few men were big enough to wield such a blade, but Aaath Ulber thought it just a bit too short. He knew that he couldn't afford it.

Yet the old man laid it on the display table in front of him. "You'd have to travel many a mile," he promised, "to find its equal."

Aaath Ulber nodded, but did not pick it up. Between a rucksack over his shoulder and a pig under one arm, there was not much that he could do.

He peered down at it appreciatively.

"You've an accent," the old man said. "Where do you hail from?"

Aaath Ulber grunted, "To the east—Landesfallen." He glanced back over the crowds, spotted Rain's dark green cloak. The girl was standing near some boys who were play-fighting with sticks. Aaath Ulber turned away quickly.

The old man fixed him with a stare, and nodded appreciatively. Aaath Ulber prepared for the old fellow to hit him with a barrage of questions: "How are things on the far side of the world?" "Did you have a pleasant voyage?" That sort of thing. But the old fellow simply got worry lines in his eyes, leaned forward, and whispered, "They're looking for you, you know."

Aaath Ulber was certain that the old man had him confused with someone else.

"For me?" Aaath Ulber asked. "How could that be?"

"Don't know," the fellow whispered secretively. "There's a giant—sailing from the northeast. That's all that I've heard. But they're asking for you." Then he peered straight into Aaath Ulber's eyes and urged, "Take the sword!"

"I . . . don't have that kind of money," Aaath Ulber said honestly.

But the old man smiled gamely, the look of a soldier who had fought for far too many years. "The price is cheap, to the right man. All that I ask is a wyrmling's head!"

Aaath Ulber wasn't surprised that the man had heard of wyrmlings. "What news do you have of them?"

The old man's eyes suddenly went wide, and he hissed, "Watch your back! They're here!"

A woman cried out, perhaps a hundred yards behind, and a deep growl rumbled through the crowd—a wyrmling curse.

Aaath Ulber straightened, whirled. Two wyrmlings came striding through the crowded market like small hills.

Wyrmlings in broad daylight! Aaath Ulber realized in dismay.

He'd never seen such a thing. The sun blinded wyrmlings and could burn their pale skin.

They wore helms and ring mail ornately carved from the bones of a world wyrm, so that it was the color of yellowed teeth, and their flesh and hair was as white and as unwholesome as maggots.

They'd seen him already, and one shouted in the tongue of Caer Luciare, "You!"

The wyrmlings rushed him, shoving commoners aside, and the crowd could not part fast enough.

They have endowments! Aaath Ulber realized. Each of them had at least two endowments of metabolism, he guessed, by the speed of their movements.

He didn't have time to run. He could hardly hope to fight. The wyrmlings streaked toward him.

He dropped his rucksack, reached behind himself, and grabbed a wicked fish knife from the table. Its blade was narrow and long. He figured that it would fit nicely between the chinks of a wyrmling's armor.

He grabbed the handle, held it in his palm, with the blade flat against the inside of his wrist.

His heart was pumping loudly in his ears, and Aaath Ulber's thoughts came swiftly. He studied their weapons. Each had a battle-ax sheathed to his back, and each wore a pair of "daggers" on his hips—each dagger the size of a bastard sword. One carried a long meat hook, and both had heavy iron war darts tucked into their belts. Aaath Ulber noticed how the wyrmlings peered about, their heads swaying from side to side. They were alert for danger, watching the crowd warily. Though they homed in on him, he could tell that they expected trouble.

I can use that fear against them, he thought.

I can't hope to beat two wyrmling runelords using normal tactics.

He didn't have an endowment to his name anymore. He couldn't match these monsters—not in speed, not in size, not in strength. But perhaps he could hope to outwit them.

Sir Borenson had studied the fighting styles from a

dozen countries, and had mastered them all. Aaath Ulber suspected that he'd have to pull from Borenson's hoard of knowledge to win this fight, show these wyrmlings some tricks they'd never seen before.

The wyrmlings neared him. It had not been five seconds since he'd spotted them.

"You there!" one of the wyrmlings shouted. "Come with us!" He reached behind his shoulder to grab the huge battle-ax sheathed on his back.

Aaath Ulber picked that moment to strike. He hurled his pig at the monster's head. The pig squealed in terror, lofted into the air. The wyrmling's eyes went wide, and he reached up to swat the pig away.

At that moment, Aaath Ulber lunged, throwing all of his speed and strength into one terrific burst, his hand blurring as he sought to strike.

The wyrmling was fast. He roared a battle challenge and knocked the pig out of the air as easily as if it were a pillow. He reached back and slid his ax from its sheath, twirled it as he threw it in the air, and then caught the handle—too late.

Aaath Ulber's diversion had served him well. He slid his long fish knife into the wyrmling's armor—prodding for its kidney, then twisting. Black blood spurted from the wound, warming Aaath Ulber's hand. The wyrmling roared in pain and surprise, then tried to step back. Aaath Ulber placed a foot behind the monster's heel and threw his shoulder into the creature's chest, using the wyrmling's momentum against it, so that it tripped and fell.

Aaath Ulber grabbed one of the monster's poisoned war darts and palmed it as the creature dropped.

The second wyrmling had already gained his weapon. This one pulled his "knife" from its sheath and halted for a moment, warily.

Already Aaath Ulber had palmed his knife again, and now stood with both hands in fists, so that the creature wouldn't know which hand held a weapon. But of course, at the moment, Aaath Ulber had a weapon in each hand.

The Muyyatin knife tricks, Aaath Ulber thought. That might do it.

The Muyyatin assassins had made an art of hiding weapons, of pulling daggers from hidden folds in their clothing, or switching weapon hands as they whirled about, seeking to gain the element of surprise.

The wounded wyrmling roared in frustration and scrabbled up from the ground. Aaath Ulber hoped that the creature had only seconds to live, but he couldn't be sure. The wyrmling was enormous, over eight feet tall, and the fish knife might not have reached all the way into the monster's kidney.

I'll know soon enough, Aaath Ulber thought.

If he'd hit the kidney, the monster would go into shock within seconds.

His companion raced up behind and roared like a lion, urging the fallen wyrmling into battle. All around, the folks in the marketplace were screaming, fleeing, so that a battlefield was opening up around them.

The second wyrmling swatted with the back of his hand, slapping aside a woman who was carrying a small babe. The blow took her head off and sent a spray of blood over the crowed. People shouted in terror and lurched back.

In that instant, it seemed that a curtain of red

dropped before Aaath Ulber's eyes. He drew a breath in surprise, and his heart pounded, so that he heard a distant drumming in his ears.

He lost all conscious thought as a berserker's fury swept over him.

❧ 18 ❧

WULFGAARD

From where the sun stands and from this day forward, I swear to fight evil where ever it may be found—first in my own heart, and then in my fellow man.

—Oath of the Brotherhood of the Wolf

The morning sun could not quite penetrate the patches of mist that veiled the village, and Rain felt as if her old clothes were becoming too worn, too insubstantial to keep out the chill. But when the wyrmlings appeared, she felt a thrill run down her spine bitterer than the cold.

She heard the deep growls behind her, like something that might come from a frowth giant, then turned to see the wyrmlings.

Her first thought was that they were beautiful. They had carved on their bone armor and helms for thousands of hours, gouging in strange pictographs and various knots, so that their work rivaled the finest scrimshaw carved into ivory that she had ever seen.

But then she saw the wyrmlings' eyes—soulless and cruel, a pale green that made them look like pits of ice. Their cheekbones were thick and their foreheads were thickened, as if over the millennia they had bred armor into their own bodies, and their mouths with their over-large canines were impossibly cruel.

All of her perception of them was gathered in a split second as the monsters raged past.

Then people in the marketplace began to shout. Vendors threw blankets over their wares, while townsfolk sought to escape.

A big man shoved Rain in his hurry to reach an alley, throwing her down. She still hadn't gained her land legs yet, and so her balance was off.

Children were screaming, but the townsfolk didn't clear a path fast enough, and flecks of blood rained through the air as one of the wyrmlings knocked a woman out of the way.

Rain leapt to her feet just in time to see Aaath Ulber attack. He had no endowments to his name, but he had a lifetime of training—no, she realized, two lifetimes of training.

He moved with blinding speed, stabbing. He seemed to leap into one of the wyrmlings, slugging it, but then Rain caught a glimpse of a flashing knife. The second wyrmling burst toward him with blinding speed, wielding a huge ax.

Aaath Ulber met him with a scream, a strange animal howl that Rain hadn't heard since he'd butchered her father.

Now he took his rage and lashed out at a wyrmling

that towered above him. The wyrmling's ax fell in a blur, and Aaath Ulber reached up and grabbed it. As he did, he leapt in the air and kicked with both feet, crushing the wyrmling's knee.

The wyrmling fell back, snarling in pain. His companion had been knocked over, but now he regained his knees. He lunged, swinging a meat hook down low, and caught Aaath Ulber in the calf of his left leg. Viciously the wyrmling jerked, pulling Aaath Ulber down.

After that, Rain didn't see much of what happened. The crowd was screaming, and several people rushed in front of her, making for the alley.

"Run!" some woman shouted. "The guards will be down on all of us!"

Just then, Rain heard a strange clacking sound— bone on bone—and peered down the street. A dozen more wyrmlings were rushing around a corner.

She heard Aaath Ulber snarling, while wyrmlings shouted and roared, and she suddenly realized that Aaath Ulber could not hope to win against so many.

A wise man might have run, but Aaath Ulber was in his berserker's fury, striking out blindly against wyrmling runelords, though he didn't have a chance in the world.

Many of the townsfolk stood riveted by the spectacle. Some men even dared shout words of encouragement to Aaath Ulber.

Rain put her back to a wall and stopped for a moment, staring. The crowd opened enough so that she saw Aaath Ulber on the ground, grappling with a much larger foe, struggling to rip the wyrmling's throat out with his teeth.

But one wyrmling, bleeding furiously from the face,

had leapt to his feet, and now he kicked Aaath Ulber in the ribs so hard that Rain heard bones snapping.

Aaath Ulber rolled into the street, snarling and furious, bereft of weapons. The bloodied wyrmling blurred into motion, leaping on Aaath Ulber, grappling with him, throwing punches with a steel gauntlet.

He struck Aaath Ulber in the face, once, twice, then gave a mighty blow that felled the giant, so that he dropped limp to the ground.

The wyrmlings then turned on the crowd and took vengeance upon those who had urged Aaath Ulber on. One of the wyrmlings grabbed up a great sword from the booth and swung, decapitating two men in a single blow.

By then the rest of the troops were arriving, and they circled Aaath Ulber, kicking and growling like a pack of wild dogs, while others fell upon the townsfolk.

It appeared that even being here, even watching Aaath Ulber fight, was deemed a crime worthy of death.

The townsfolk were rushing away. Merchants had ducked behind their stalls, often with women and children leaping in to seek cover.

A young man raced past Rain, grabbing her wrist. He pulled her toward the alley, and she resisted. He yanked her so hard that it lifted her from her feet, and he half-dragged her around a corner.

"Come on!" he said, his voice full of terror. She stumbled and ran, trying to keep up, as he raced across the street, into a stable.

"This way!" he urged as he pulled her toward some horses. The horses neighed in fear, while a few chickens that had been strutting about squawked and raced under the horses' legs.

The young man reached a small ladder that led to a hayloft, ten feet in the air, and shouted, "Up—go up!"

She climbed the ladder swiftly, found that there was a huge mound of hay, and scrambled to get over it.

The young man raced up behind her, urged her over the hay, and then pulled the ladder up and set it behind the pile of hay. Then he just lay back for a moment, panting from fear, and tried to still his breathing.

Rain did the same. Her heart was pounding hard, and it seemed to her that she saw everything in preternatural detail.

There was little light in the room. Most of it came from a small open door above them, so that sunlight streamed through the gloom. Motes of dust hung in the air, floating upon every breath of wind.

Aaath Ulber is dead by now, Rain realized, and despair dropped on her with a massive weight.

That can't be, she told herself. The Earth King said that he has to help Fallion, he has to help bind the worlds.

Has he failed already? Did he fail so easily? Was it dumb luck that brought him here?

"What, what will happen to that giant?" Rain asked.

She looked at the young man. He had long golden hair with a hint of crimson, almost the shade of cinnabar. His chin was strong, his nose narrow, and his eyes smoldered a deep blue.

"He's dead," the young man whispered, putting a finger to his lips, warning her to be quiet. "He's dead. And anyone who walks the streets now will die with him."

"But, but . . ." Rain tried to imagine Aaath Ulber dead. She leaned back in the hay, fear tightening her stomach. Involuntarily, she began to twist the ring on her finger. It was an old habit, each time she felt in danger.

"You're from Mystarria," the young man said. It wasn't a question. "Did you know that . . . giant?"

Rain wasn't adept at lying. She hesitated. The man had saved her, and she hoped that he was an ally.

Would he turn me over to the wyrmlings if he knew?

"I didn't know him," she said, too late.

"Your lips lie, but your body tells the truth," he said. Rain found that she was trembling in fear, and that it was everything she could do to hold back her tears.

"They knew that you were coming," the young man said. "For weeks the wyrmlings have been searching for a giant, a man with red hair, a man that they fear." There were shouts in the street outside, the sound of running feet, and the growl of a wyrmling. A man screamed as the wrymling took him.

The young man peered over the pile of hay, making sure that no one had entered the stable, and whispered, "There are two wizards with you, yes? We must get word to them, before the wyrmlings find them."

Rain shook her head, trying to make sense of this. There was only one wizard in her group. Yet she suspected that he was right. The wyrmlings were looking for them. There *were* two wizards in Draken's family, and that was so rare that Rain had never heard the like. "How could the wyrmlings know that we were coming?"

We told no one, she wanted to say.

But the young man simply said, "How do they do anything? Their leaders can talk to each other even though they are a thousand miles apart. They have wrapped all of Rofehavan beneath a swirling cloud of darkness, and they send blights to destroy our crops.

They know things . . . things that they shouldn't." He peered about nervously, obviously distraught at being here. "We will have to keep our heads down."

"For how long?" Rain asked. She desperately wanted to get back to Myrrima.

"As long as it takes—hours at least. The wyrmlings—"

The clanking of bone armor sounded outside the stable, and for a moment the two fell completely silent. A wyrmling trudged inside, and the horses neighed and stamped nervously at the smell of blood.

Rain didn't dare move. She held her breath, heart pounding as if it might burst, and pleaded with the Powers that the wyrmling might leave.

But the monster plodded through the stable for a moment, then stood below them, sniffing at the loft.

He's taken endowments of scent, Rain realized. She trembled all over. She wished that she'd thought to pull some hay over her, perhaps mask the smell of her sweat.

Shouting arose down the street, a man roaring a battle challenge. "You killed her!" he cried at some wyrmling. "Damn you for that!"

At the sound of clanging metal, ax on ax, the wyrmling rushed from the stables.

The young man leapt up and grabbed a beam, pulled himself higher, then peeked out the open window. Stealthily, he peered down one street, then back into the market.

He let out a sigh of relief, but there was sadness in his voice. "That man buys our lives with his own." He jumped back down into the hay, nodded toward the market. "Your giant killed two wyrmlings, but they did not take off his head. They always take the heads of those that they kill. . . . Unless I miss my guess, he's still alive. We must do what we can to save him. But we cannot make a move until the wrymlings have cleared from the streets."

Rain shook her head in wonder. Eight weeks ago, she'd wished the man dead. Now she was to be his savior?

The young man waited for a long moment, then whispered, "My name is Wulfgaard."

"That is not a name I have ever heard before," Rain said. The young man was handsome in his way. He looked to be no more than twenty or so. She wondered if he had been watching her on the street a few minutes ago, but realized that she had seen him: a young man who walked with a hunched back, pulling a game leg, as he hurried to keep up at Aaath Ulber's back. She'd worried at his motive. She'd thought him perhaps to be a simpleton, awed at the sight of the giant, but she'd also worried that he might have darker designs.

"It is not the name I was born with. I took it when I joined the Brotherhood of the Wolf."

Rain knew of such men, sworn to fight evil no matter how great it might be or where it might rear its ugly head. She knew that he would protect her with his life, if necessary.

"You were following Aaath Ulber," she said. "I saw you."

"I knew that he was the one," Wulfgaard admitted in a whisper. He strained to listen for a moment, as the clacking of armor drew close again. The sounds of battle down the street had gone still. "I knew him as soon as I saw him." Wulfgaard's voice became husky with emotion. "I need . . . we *all* need his help."

THE INTERROGATION

Hope nourishes courage the way that food nourishes the body. Never give your enemy cause to hope, lest he grow the courage to resist you.

—From the Wyrmling Catechism

Not all of Crull-maldor's troops had wyrms in them. Only a dozen of her captains were evil enough to earn the parasites that fed upon their souls.

So she had strategically stationed these captains across the island. One of them was in Ox Port, and thus he could speak to her across the miles. The captain's name was Azuk-Tri.

His mind touched hers but lightly, and she heard his voice as if it was a distant shout. *We found him. We found the one!*

Crull-maldor was in the Room of Whispers, attending her daily duties. She was ever vigilant, worried that at any moment an uprising might occur. The humans were restless.

She whirled at the call, and sent her consciousness across the miles, seizing the captain's mind.

Suddenly she saw what he saw, knew what he knew.

His men were dragging a limp body through the streets by the feet. The man was a giant for a human—a giant with red hair and small nubs of horns upon his plated brow. He was from Caer Luciare, a "true man" as they called themselves.

Blood covered the man's face. An ear had been torn off, and both eyes were swollen. He had puncture wounds in his leg from a meat hook, and he struggled mightily to breathe.

You've nearly killed him, Crull-maldor whispered to her captain's soul.

He fought like a madman, the captain whispered. *He has the berserker's rage. Never have I seen such a warrior. He killed two of my troops. Even when we had him down, even after we thought him subdued, he rose up and killed our men.*

Crull-maldor was impressed. The emperor would want the berserker's head.

But Crull-maldor did not want to give the human to her enemy—yet.

The berserker has fought well, Crull-maldor mused. And now he was in enemy hands. His deeds are the kind that makes a man a legend.

Yikkarga will hear of him, Crull-maldor suspected.

Crull-maldor knew that Yikkarga had bribed some of her troops to be spies. She couldn't hide the berserker for long.

She wasn't sure that she wanted to. Much was at stake. Lord Despair had promised a great deal for Crull-maldor's service, and she did not want to jeopardize her future.

But Crull-maldor had her own spies, and she knew that the emperor was still plotting her demise, seeking some way to sabotage her, and eventually replace her. A feud that had lasted centuries was not likely to be set aside now. Indeed, the emperor had more to lose than ever before, and even his servant Yikkarga recognized how high the stakes had become.

Over the past three weeks, Crull-maldor had learned a great deal about Yikkarga—and the power that preserved him.

Lord Despair had "chosen" the wyrmling, and in the City of the Dead, Crull-maldor had sought diligently to understand just what that meant.

She knew now that there was some kind of link between Yikkarga and Lord Despair, a link that warned him when death drew near.

So she could not kill the wyrmling. She could not take his life directly. But there were things that she could do to sabotage his efforts, and Crull-maldor had the beginnings of a plan.

So she rode the mind of Azuk-Tri as her wyrmlings dragged the berserker for nearly a mile, until at last they reached their makeshift fortress—a longhouse, confiscated from the humans. It was set upon a hill, and made of logs from giant fir trees. Because the previous owners had been rich, the logs were bound in copper, to keep them from taking fire, and the roof was made from fine slate and imported copper shingles that had turned green with age.

Enormous logs framed the door, and all along the top, antlers of caribou spread wide. At the very center, the antlers of a giant bog elk spread, some twenty feet across. It was an impressive trophy.

The wyrmlings dragged the human into the house, which was open and spacious. A hearth was banked with huge slabs of carved basalt, taller than a man, while rows of sturdy benches and a table made from slabs of wood filled the great room.

Crull-maldor whispered to Azuk-Tri, *Lend me full use of your mind*.

The captain calmed himself, let his thoughts roam. In that instant, Crull-maldor seized the man, crawling into his skull and taking possession the way that a hermit crab fills a shell.

It was easy, surprisingly easy—as easy as riding a crow. The feat had not been nearly as easy weeks ago before the great binding, and Crull-maldor found that she liked this man's mind. It was filled with interesting tidbits of information about this human settlement.

Crull-maldor ordered her men, "Bind the human to the table."

The wyrmlings lifted the man onto a huge table that was made from planks that were six inches thick. The man's feet were already tied together. Now the wyrmlings used ropes to truss him to the table, and the human groaned in pain, showing the first signs that he might revive.

When he was secured, Crull-maldor reached down into the captain's belt, into a compartment in the waistband, and pulled out a harvester spike—an iron spike about six inches long. The spike was rusty at one end, but its tip was black with glandular extracts.

Crull-maldor rammed it into the human's leg. Within seconds, the warrior's muscles spasmed and his eyes flew open.

"Yaaaaagh!" He screamed a battle challenge and began to struggle to break the ropes that held him to the table.

Crull-maldor pulled out the spike. The glandular extracts could give a man great strength, but they tended to blank out his mind, free him from all reason.

"Now, do I have your attention?" Crull-maldor spoke in the human tongue of Caer Luciare, a language that she had mastered more than three hundred years ago.

The human's eyes had gone bloodshot in but a few seconds, and he peered about dazedly, straining to see the wyrmlings in the room.

He's counting our numbers, Crull-maldor thought, in the hopes of winning a fight.

"Do I have your attention, human?"

The man let his head fall back to the table, then lay panting a moment. "Yes."

"Why are you here?" Crull-maldor demanded.

"I am Aaath Ulber, and I'm going to kill you all!" the human raged, straining at his ropes. His back arched off the table, and he jerked his arms mightily. Sweat had beaded upon his brow, and his eyes were filled with desperation. Not fear, Crull-maldor decided, but a desperate need to wage battle.

Crull-maldor knew that Aaath Ulber spoke the truth. The glandular extracts filled a man with rage, and in such a state, a man would speak the truth boldly, daring his enemies to defy him.

"Aaath Ulber . . ." Crull-maldor translated, "The Great Berserker?" He would be one of the humans' darlings. "You killed two of my men today. For that, you must die."

Crull-maldor held the thought for a moment. If she did the emperor's will, she would execute the human now. Yet she could not do it. If this man really posed such a threat to the emperor—well, perhaps he would deliver himself.

"But I cannot just take your head," Crull-maldor

explained reasonably. "You killed my men in public. Other humans saw what you did. Hope in an enemy is a dangerous thing. We must kill their hope, by executing you . . . in front of them."

Aaath Ulber shouted a berserker's cry full of passion and murder. He strained at his bands, throwing punches at the air, until the ropes around his wrists cut through his flesh and were soaking in blood.

The lich lord patiently waited for him to calm. It took long minutes before the warrior lay panting and exhausted on the table, sweat staining his shirt, eyes peering up at nothing.

Now Crull-maldor planted a seed. "You have come a long way," the lich whispered, "but you have accomplished nothing. Your people at Caer Luciare have all been killed or captured. Emperor Zul-torac has seen to that. The land is covered in darkness, and all of it is under the emperor's power. The woman you love is no more. Any children that you sired have likely been eaten. Your friends and comrades—both those whom you admired and those whom you held in contempt—are gone forever.

"There may yet be a few who survive, deep in the dark recesses of Rugassa. Some have been reserved for torture, no doubt. Others have been put to the forcible.

"So perhaps your woman still lives on. Perhaps your children cry in the night, hoping that you will come.

"But you cannot save them. To even try is vain. You shall die tonight in front of those you thought to free . . . by the *emperor's* command."

The berserker Aaath Ulber roared at that, and once again he strained at the cords, his knotted muscles bulging, his face twisted with rage and desperation. Though his wrists were cut deeply, he struggled against the ropes, striking at hallucinatory foes, until the thick wooden slats beneath him cracked under the tremendous stress.

Aaath Ulber's eyes were glazed from rage and pain. Speaking to him any longer would accomplish nothing, for he was past hearing.

Instead, with the fury of a wounded animal he continued to bellow and moan, eager to break free from his bonds, hoping to fight his way south.

In his dreams, Crull-maldor thought, he is already in Rugassa, emptying the dungeons of the emperor.

Crull-maldor leaned back and smiled in deep satisfaction.

❧ 20 ❧

THE DUEL

Ah, there is nothing that I enjoy more than the arena, where so many great hearts lie beating upon the floor!

—The Emperor Zul-torac

For the first three hours after Aaath Ulber left, Draken managed to keep his composure. A slight wind arose, worrying the sea. Long swells began to rise up and whitecaps slapped the hull, but Myrrima used her powers to keep the fog wrapped around the boat.

Twice in the morning other vessels drew near, but gave Draken's ship a wide berth.

Draken had spent the night guiding the vessel, but he could not sleep, so he stayed topside to peer out into the fog.

It was autumn, and with the coming of fall the salmon had begun to gather near shore. Draken saw huge ones around the boat, silver in the water, lazing about, finning in slow circles. The sight of them only sharpened his hunger. He'd never liked salmon, but it was better than the rancid bear he'd been eating.

Myrrima spotted some olive-green kelp floating by, and she used a staff to pull it in, then sat on the railing and began chewing it.

She offered some to Draken and the others but they all declined. Draken found that salty food only made him thirsty.

Sage amused herself by singing softly, and for long hours the family waited.

After four hours, Draken told himself that Aaath Ulber must have stopped at an inn for a drink, as his father was known to do.

After six hours, his lips drew tight across his teeth with worry. By midafternoon, he was sure that there was trouble.

Of course there is trouble, he told himself.

"When's Father coming back?" Sage finally demanded, well into the afternoon.

Draken was angry by then, angry at himself for letting Rain go into town without him. He felt weak from lack of decent food, and the weakness left his nerves frayed.

"Soon," Myrrima promised. "If he does not return by nightfall, I'll go find him."

"Not without me," Draken said.

Myrrima gave him a hard look, as if to say, "If I don't come back, you'll need to take your sister and flee." But then her face softened as she realized his predicament. His betrothed was out there somewhere.

"Your sister's safety comes first," she said.

Draken didn't dare voice his own thoughts to Sage. Why can't the child see? he wondered. Her father is never coming back.

At sunset Myrrima let her cloak of mist blow away in the evening breeze, and then waited until darkness had fallen before Draken lowered the away boat. The evening fog rose from the water, creating clouds at the limit of vision. A waxing moon was just cresting the horizon like a glowing white eye in the socket of the sea. Stars danced upon the glassy waves. A slight breeze had come up from the south, surprisingly cool, like the touch of the dead. Draken almost imagined that he felt spirits on the water.

As soon as the boat was lowered, Draken dropped into it. His mother shot him an angry look, but he stared her in the eye. "You can't ask me to stay," he said.

Myrrima hesitated, as if to voice some argument. "Will you follow my orders?" she demanded.

"Yes," Draken said.

"Then I order you to get out of this boat and take care of your sister."

"Perhaps in going with you, I would take better care of my sister. We don't know what kind of trouble you might be walking into."

His mother stared hard at him, and at last sighed. The truth was that neither of them knew what was right. "You'll keep your head down."

Myrrima gave Sage some final instructions. "If Draken and I don't come back by dawn, take the ship south to Toom or Haversind. Don't come looking for us."

"I won't leave you," Sage said, as if by will alone she might hope to save them.

"Promise me you won't try to come for us," Myrrima said. "If we get in trouble, then I doubt that you could help, Sage. You have a long life ahead of you. If we don't return, know that we love you—and know that above all, I want you to make the best life for yourself that you can."

Sage jutted her chin and refused to promise.

I suppose that I should not be surprised if my little sister is hardheaded, Draken told himself, considering who we have as parents.

Draken took the oars. Myrrima drew some runes upon the water to ease their way, and Draken began to row.

He could smell the smoke of cooking fires on the water, and as he drew near to shore, he spotted a large village rising upon a nearby hill; he was surprised by its size. It sprawled north and south along the shoreline for as far as he could see.

Internook always did have an excess of people, he thought.

A pair of beacons had been lit on the arms of the bay. The fires themselves burned in censers held by statues of men with the heads of bulls, carved from white stone. The firelight gleamed upon the surface of the stone, turning the monstrous statues orange-yellow, so that they could be seen from afar. Their horns looked to be covered in gold, and they spread wide and nearly circled the pyre like bloody crowns.

Draken recalled hearing once that each port had its own symbol, its own effigy at the mouth of the bay, so that ships passing by night might better navigate.

He knew that the word *vagr* was old Internookish for port. But he could not guess at the word for *bull*.

"Do you know where we are?" Draken asked.

Myrrima shook her head no.

Draken made his way by starlight toward the docks, pulling his cloak up to hide his face. As he drew nearer the village, he studied the rocky beach. He could see no wreckage as there had been in Landesfallen.

Internook, it appeared, had actually risen a bit, rather than sinking into into the sea.

What a shame, Draken thought. The world would have been better off without the barbarians.

He silently rowed up into the bay, and the reek of a town grew strong. He could smell fish guts and dead crabs, the leftover of the day's catch. Sea lions barked somewhere among the rocks along the shore, and that surprised him, given the warlords' penchant for wearing boiled sealskins as armor when they went to war.

Lights shone all through town—wan lights that only yellowed the thin hides that the barbarians used for windows. There were no lanterns placed upon the darkened streets, as he would have seen in Mystarria. The houses looked strange and widely spread. There were huge longhouses upon the hill; each was a dark, monolithic fortress with forty or fifty acres of farmland surrounding it. Dozens of families might live in a longhouse.

It made the village seem surprisingly . . . desolate, Draken decided. It was spread over a broad area, and each longhouse squatted like a small keep, an island in its own private wilderness.

No one walked the streets that he could see. There were no rich travelers with torchbearers, as you might notice in more civilized countries. There were clean bright houses down near the docks, but he could not hear any travelers at the inns, raising their voices in song.

The entire village was preternaturally quiet.

This is not the Internook of legend, Draken thought, where warlords drink and gamble through the long nights, while their dogs are made to fight bears for sport.

He pulled up to the docks in the starlight, climbed from the boat, and pulled his hood low over his face. His mother took the lead.

They climbed onto the wooden decks, which creaked and trembled under the onslaught of small waves, and made their way up toward a steep ridge, where he could see stairs climbing into town.

Hundreds of small fishing boats were moored at the docks, and as Myrrima passed one, she grabbed an empty sack, stuffed in some rope, and slung it over her back, as if hoping that in the darkness she might pass for some fisherwoman, bringing her catch home from the sea.

The ruse worked with the cats at least. A dozen hungry dock cats came rushing up to greet her, tails raised high and twitching in excitement. Some of them mewed sweetly, eager for fish. But when Draken peered down at one orange tom in the moonlight, he saw that its face had been clawed by other cats until it was swollen and disfigured. One eye was closed with pussy wounds, and as it mewed, it sounded vicious and threatening, as if it was accustomed to demanding fish rather than begging.

Myrrima stomped her foot, shooing the monstrosities away, and climbed the stairs into town, with Draken at her back. They came out of the darkness onto a deserted street, and peered both ways. The cold wind gusted suddenly at Draken's back, and once again he felt that odd chill creeping up his spine, like the touch of the dead.

It seemed early for the streets to be so barren. No one walked them, not a solitary man.

Sailor folk live here, Draken told himself. That's why the streets are barren. They'll need to be up at dawn, to sail with the tide.

Yet that answer didn't entirely satisfy him. He'd seen the docks at the Courts of Tide in Mystarria, where sailors caroused to all hours.

Perhaps it is unsafe to walk the streets at night here, he wondered.

Myrrima halted, and spoke, her voice shaking. "This is odd. It's almost as if the town is deserted."

Then Draken heard something, a bit of music carried on the wind, the distant sound of singing, like men carousing in an alehouse.

"That way!" he said. "I hear something."

Myrrima looked baffled, but followed his lead.

There was a sort of wooden porch that ran the length of the streets—made from rough planks laid over the mud. Draken crept to the side of a building and stood in its shadow, then padded along quickly toward the inn. The walkway let him travel in complete silence.

As he drew closer, the noise of the place became louder. There was roaring and cheering from men, as if a great celebration was going on. Drums and pipes pounded a steady rhythm while drunken men sang some folk song in the ancient tongue of Internook that had long ago fallen into disuse. A bear roared, mastiffs woofed, and the cheers became frenzied.

Perhaps it is a holiday, Draken reasoned. That's why the town is abandoned. Everyone has gone to the celebration.

He considered how best to keep a low profile.

I'll find a dark corner or nook, and then crawl deep into it, he told himself. I'll keep my ears open and my mouth shut. Surely someone will mention Aaath Ulber. It is not every day that a giant wanders into town.

Soon he reached an alehouse, but it was unlike any that he had ever seen. In his home country of Landesfallen an alehouse or an inn was seldom much larger than a cottage. Indeed, most alehouses simply were cottages owned by some widow who made her living by brewing ale. At night, when a batch was ready, she'd open her doors, throw a keg on the table, and let folks come and enjoy a mug at her hearth. If she had talent and could sing, all the better. If she was fair to look upon, finer still.

But this place was no cottage. He'd never seen a building so large, not outside of a castle. It was all made of wood, with enormous beams black from age. It was built much like a longhouse, but it seemed that all of the houses on the hill could fit inside. It had no windows, but high up, where the ceiling reached its apex at about forty feet, there was a broad opening in the wall. There, Draken could see light and the smoke of torches leaking through the breach.

The building looked like a castle, he decided, a fortress all made of wood. He went to the great front doors, which were wide enough so that a wagon might be pulled through, and yanked on one to see if it would open.

It swung outward a bit, and immediately he regretted his deed, for there was no way to open that door discreetly. Still, he saw no other way to enter.

So he pulled it open just a crack, and tried to see inside.

He nearly made it. A young man was standing with his back to the door, and as it swung outward, the young man was thrown off balance. He was a dirty creature, perhaps in his mid-twenties, with grime on his face. He had the blond locks so common to men here, cascading down his back, and a deep yellow beard covered his stony visage. He wore a jerkin of gray spotted sealskin, but bore no weapons.

He glanced at Draken suspiciously, seemed disinterested, and then craned his neck to see over the crowd. A bear bellowed, and the men roared and cheered.

They're watching the dogs fight, Draken thought, and strode into the great hall and tried to see over the crowd. The men in front of him were so large that it was like trying to peer over a wall.

The building, it turned out, housed more than an inn. It had an arena. A shallow pit, perhaps twelve feet deep and eighty feet in diameter, filled the center of the room. Tables circled the pit in rows, each row elevated a little higher than the last so that Draken found himself peering down into a little amphitheater.

The place stank of Internook ale, dark and sour and as rank as stale piss.

Warriors sat at the tables, drinking and feasting and carousing, laying down bets. There must have been five hundred men in the place, all with light hair. Some were blond going to gray, or pure silver. Some were more of a burnished gold or even a light red.

The men were all so much alike—burly barbarians with strong chins and deep brows, and great bushy beards that hid their mouths—that they seemed like brothers and cousins. Men with faces creased by wind and sun. Some wore their hair braided in corn rows, while others tied it back with rags.

It was not a bear in the pit. Instead, two great white bears were chained with iron collars to some support beams, and thus loomed above the pit. Several of the barbarians in the crowd had dogs with them, and the dogs growled and barked at the bears.

Down in the pit stood Aaath Ulber. His eyes were so black and swollen that Draken wondered if he could even see. His right ear had been bitten off, so that dried blood colored his hair and seeped down his shirt.

The giant had no weapons, and he was ringed by three wolves.

One of the wolves lunged, jumping for the giant's throat. Aaath Ulber dodged, caught the wolf in his fists, and hurled it against the wall, snapping bones and sending droplets of blood flying onto the dinner guests. The barbarians cheered and roared their approval, banging tin mugs on the wooden tables, even as another wolf lunged in and bit into Aaath Ulber's hamstring.

The giant kicked and flailed, until the wolf yelped and leapt back, then stood blinking.

Draken spotted more dead wolves on the ground, and realized that Aaath Ulber had already beaten them. There wasn't any fight left in these two.

A tiny portcullis opened behind the wolves, and

Aaath Ulber rushed them. The wolves went fleeing into a dark tunnel.

A warlord shouted, "Round one goes to the giant! Praise be to the Powers!"

He blew a war horn, and the crowd roared in approval.

But the wolf fight was not the only entertainment. The room thrummed to the sound of drums and pipes and lutes. A band was stationed on a platform so high that they seemed to be playing in the rafters. Men sang drunkenly and laughed at the tops of their voices.

Draken spotted a man in a fool's cap, wearing a cloak made of particolored patches of rags—scarlet and daisy yellow, sky blue and sea-foam green, plum and bone—weaving in and out among the tables. He had an enormous swan upon a platter, cooked with its feathers still on, its neck hanging over the edge of the plate. He made a great show of trying to work his way among the tables, smiling at guests and greeting them, all the while knocking over mugs and stepping on people's feet. He stopped at one table and held up the swan's head, then worked its mouth open and closed as it told jokes to the guests.

The place stank. Old ale had spilled onto the tables and floors for generations. But worse was the odor of the men in their jerkins made of sealskin and pig leather. They smelled of putrefaction and grime. Only the fairer scents of roasting meat and new-baked bread made the place bearable.

The young man who had seemed disinterested in Draken a moment before now stepped up behind and whispered in his ear. His voice was soft, his tone low and threatening. "Here now, little brother, you shouldn't be here. This is for elders of the clan."

He took Draken by the biceps, and began to steer him out. Draken reached for his knife, in case the fellow tried to get rough.

"Wait," Draken said. "I want to watch!"

Down in the pit, the announcer shouted. "Now, for the main challenge: Aaath Ulber the giant, scourge of the North, shall fight the wyrmling hero Lord Gryzzan-thal!"

The shouting and cheers rose to a fever pitch, and the young fellow that had taken hold of Draken seemed unable to help himself. He stopped, then glanced toward the action.

A door flew open down in the pit, and out strode a creature neither quite man nor monster. The creature was massive; it stood a good nine feet tall and could not have weighed less than eight hundred pounds. It was broad at the shoulder, almost impossibly so, and its skin gleamed sickly white; Gryzzanthal's face was hideous, with bony ridges upon his brow and armored plates upon his cheeks and jaw. The scowl upon his face could only have belonged to something that was pure evil.

The wyrmling was dressed in full battle regalia—with helm, armor, and sheath all ornately carved from bone. The helm was decorated with the tusks of a great boar that curled up near the bottom, forming chin guards. Gryzzanthal bore a round shield of yellowed bone with a black circle painted on it that showed the Great Wyrm in red.

His only weapon was a wyrmling blade, a strange heavy sword that ended in two long prongs.

The wyrmling banged sword on shield and growled

a challenge. Aaath Ulber stepped back, roaring like an enraged animal, and the two began to circle, looking for an opening.

It wasn't a fair fight.

Aaath Ulber had no armor, no weapon.

Draken wondered what the giant had done to deserve such a fate. And he wondered why the warlords of Internook would keep a wyrmling to fight in the ring.

Myrrima had crowded close to the door, and now she let out a soft yelp of recognition. Myrrima whispered, "That's him!"

The elder gasped. "Shhh . . ." he urged, opening the door, trying to push them out of the building. "Quiet. It's not safe for you here."

Down in the arena, Aaath Ulber lunged toward the wyrmling's weak side. The monster responded by swatting with his shield.

The crowd roared as Aaath Ulber grabbed the shield and pulled, trying to rip it from the wyrmling. But the monster tried to yank it back.

In seconds somehow Aaath Ulber got behind the creature and worked an arm under its chin guard. Aaath Ulber leapt in the air, throwing his weight into a lock, and tried to strangle the wyrmling.

The wyrmling flailed about, but its sword was useless. He swatted back with his shield, equally useless. The great monster whirled and threw himself backward, crushing Aaath Ulber into the wooden posts that ringed the arena; for a moment Aaath Ulber's eyes rolled back in pain as the wind was knocked from him. But Aaath Ulber clung to the wyrmling like death, and the audience went wild, shouting, "Ride him! Ride him to the ground!"

The young elder shoved Draken again. "Run!" he warned. "Head for the woods. The streets are not safe!"

Draken turned to leave. The rising moon glanced off the cobbled streets, and not a hundred yards away he saw something.

It was a great boar, like those his father had hunted far to the south in the Dunnwood of Heredon. It was a huge shaggy beast, with hair on its chest that swept the ground, and massive curling tusks that glinted like skeletal teeth.

Atop the boar was barding that gleamed like silver in the moonlight—chains across its back, and a fearsome helm that covered its head and snout.

But it was not the great boar that took his breath away, it was the creature riding its back.

"Wyrmling!" Myrrima breathed in warning, and Draken thought to run. But the wyrmling leapt from its mount in a single fluid movement and seemed to flow toward them with superhuman speed.

Eight endowments of metabolism it has, Draken thought, perhaps more.

And a sudden realization hit home. The warlords of Internook were not keeping pet wyrmlings. The wyrmlings were keeping pet humans.

Draken tried to whirl and flee into the crowded arena, but the doorman grabbed him from behind in a choking hold.

"I have him, milord!" the doorman cried.

In the flutter of a heartbeat, the wyrmling grabbed Myrrima and pulled her upward in the air, nearly snapping her neck in the process, as if she were no heavier than a doll woven from straw.

Then its free hand grabbed Draken and hurled him against the wall. Lights flashed behind his eyes like exploding stars, and he heard bones crack.

He sank into pain and forgetfulness.

❧ 21 ❧

BROTHERHOOD

The call of the wolf is the call of the Brotherhood. When you hear it, know that your brothers are in danger, and evil is near.

—Code of the Brotherhood of the Wolf

Three times during the day, Rain had tried to follow Wulfgaard from the stable. But each time, their attempt was cut short.

The wyrmling patrols came often. Sometimes they'd march by three minutes apart. Sometimes the roads would be clear for half an hour. But regardless of how seldom patrols came by, it was clear to Rain that the streets were not safe.

The markets did not reopen. No fishmongers called from their stalls. No one wandered the streets.

Rain and her newfound cohort could not sneak out.

"The wyrmlings have all the advantage," Wulfgaard told her. "They can stand on a hill two miles off and watch the streets with ease. With their endowments of sight, nothing misses their attention. With their endowments of metabolism, some of them can run a hundred miles in an hour. If we walk into the open, they'll rush down upon us, and there is no escape."

The young man did not talk loudly. His voice was all whispers, lest a wyrmling be within hearing range.

The power of a great runelord of course was legendary, and evil men with such power were the stuff of nightmares. But the wrymlings were doubly frightening.

"We must wait until the wyrmlings give the townsfolk the all-clear. Then we can blend in with the crowds."

So the two waited, Rain biting her lip, sometimes twisting her ring nervously. The hay that they lay in smelled fragrant. It was a mixture of grasses—fescue and oats, with sweet clover and a bit of alfalfa. It had been harvested only recently, weeks before, and so did not have the underlying odor of mold. Rain and Wulfgaard had covered most of their bodies with it, to hide their scent. They left only their faces exposed, so that they could breathe, and speak.

"You said that you need help," Rain asked once when the streets were dead quiet, and they did not fear the wyrmlings. Even then she whispered softly, so that her words barely carried to Wulfgaard's ear. "What makes you think that you need Aaath Ulber?"

"The wyrmlings fear him," Wulfgaard says. "They do not fear anyone else, even the greatest of our lords. . . . So the Brotherhood has been searching for blood metal."

"You found some?" Rain asked.

"We did—a stone here, a small cache there. The wyrmlings have managed to get most of it, but there are stores of it hidden away. . . . We have forged our forcibles in secret, and there are many who are just waiting for the hero to arise."

"You think Aaath Ulber is that hero?"

"He's a giant, sailing from the north—a man who knows the wrymling strongholds . . . and their weaknesses. Who else could it be?"

No one that Rain knew. But she couldn't reconcile her feelings. Aaath Ulber was dangerous to the wyrmlings, but he wasn't the kind of man she'd pick to be her hero.

"We've been preparing for weeks," Wulfgaard said. "The wyrmlings have taken many of our people, our best fighting men, and marched them down into their fortress to harvest their endowments, or sent them to the mines to work in chains. I am one of the few who has escaped attention. I feign a bad back, so that they will not take me.

"Each day, our people grow weaker and the wyrmlings grow stronger. We cannot afford to wait. . . ."

"Would your people grant him endowments?"

"Some would," Wulfgaard said hesitantly. "Perhaps many will rally to his cause."

"What would stop them from giving aid?" Rain asked.

"The wyrmlings are everywhere. Their scouts are on guard for those who have given endowments. Those who are too sick to walk or to work, are culled. A man who gives endowments . . . I do not think he would last a week."

It would take great courage to give an endowment under such circumstances. Rain wondered how many might really do it. But no one doubted the warlords of Internook. For generations their barbarian hordes had been trained to rush into battle against runelords with more endowments and better armor, and throw themselves against their enemies' spears. No warriors in the world had greater courage.

Rain asked, "You said that *you* needed Aaath Ulber's help. . . ."

"There is a girl," Wulfgaard said, "my beloved. The wyrmlings took her. For the past six weeks they have been demanding thralls—men and women to be stripped of attributes. The wyrmlings put them on ships and sailed them to Mystarria, under the eternal clouds.

"None that have been taken shall ever return.

"But I am not the only one to lose a loved one," Wulfgaard added. "Tens of thousands have been taken, and nearly everyone in the land feels the loss. They may have been deprived of a brother, or mother, or perhaps a friend."

"Why would the wyrmlings want your betrothed?" Rain asked. "Grace, glamour, metabolism?"

"Glamour," Wulfgaard said. "She is very beautiful."

Rain wondered. Would a wyrmling care about taking an attribute of glamour? She suggested softly, "Aaath Ulber said that the wyrmlings eat human flesh."

Wulfgaard was stricken, and he barely muttered, "We have suspected as much, but I hoped that it was not true. They do not have fields or gardens. . . ."

"Because they don't need them," Rain confirmed. "They eat only flesh. And there is more. The wyrmlings cut the heads off of people and extract glands from them, to use in making their weapons. They are called 'harvester spikes.' They are nails that the wyrmlings push into their flesh before they go into battle. Have you seen them?"

By now, Wulfgaard's face had gone pale indeed. He was trembling. He shook his head no. He had not seen the spikes.

Rain felt for him. The best that he could hope was that his beloved was still alive and had only been forced to give up an endowment. If she had given glamour, there would be no beauty left in her. Rain imagined that instead of honeyed locks, the girl's hair would be limp and colorless. Instead of bright blue eyes, her orbs would have turned yellow and sickly. Gone would be her smooth skin, and the surface of her face would look weathered and papery.

Instead of a beauty, the girl would be a horror.

"You know what the wyrmlings will do to this girl of yours. Do you imagine that you will love her still?"

Wulfgaard tried to hide his own uncertainty. "She was raised in the longhouse next to mine. We have been best friends since we were children. In some ways, she is more like a sister to me than a wife. Yet I love her as I love myself.

"Besides," he added, "I plan to kill the wyrmling that took her glamour."

"That is easier said than done," Rain said. "The wyrmlings are roving wide. We saw ships full of them heading for Landesfallen."

"Still, I must try," Wulfgaard said. "Think of it. The wyrmlings are trying to enslave us. At this moment, their burdens are light. But already we see the shadows on the wall. The wyrmlings do not care for us any more than we care for a pig that we shall butcher. They will use us—for our attributes, our glands . . . and if you are right, for food."

"They must be stopped," Rain said.

"They must be eradicated," Wulfgaard corrected.

Outside, there was the familiar clank of wyrmling armor, bone against bone. A soldier came within a hundred yards of the stables and stood for a long time, as if straining his ears.

Wulfgaard and Rain fell silent, and waited until well after dark. At sunset a great horn blew five short blasts, repeated five times.

"That is the wyrmlings calling," Wulfgaard said. "They will assemble at the moot hall."

"Do they do that often?" Rain asked.

Wulfgaard frowned. "Only twice before: Once when they took over the village, they told us the rules. The other time—it was to punish some men who would not give up their children."

He did not have to say it. Rain immediately suspected that the wyrmlings would dole out punishment to Aaath Ulber tonight.

"What did the wyrmlings do to those men?"

"I don't think you want to know," Wulfgaard said.

Only when the horns had stopped sounding did Wulfgaard dare stir, to creep from the stable out onto the street.

Before he left, he warned, "Only men will be allowed at the moot, I fear. You must stay hidden, until I return. . . ."

Wulfgaard crept down from the loft, then slipped out the door.

Rain wondered. Men were on the streets, and with her breeches and tunic she was dressed much like a man. She pulled up her tunic, tightened her breast band, and then made her way into the streets.

Boldly she trod down the center of the street in the dusk as the men of the town joined her.

But where do I go? she wondered. A wyrmling guard was on the street, not far ahead. She avoided eye contact, tried to keep an even pace.

If I head down to the docks, I will be seen. The wyrmlings will have me before I get far.

So she strode forward to the moot hall, hoping to learn Aaath Ulber's fate.

"When were you going to tell me that you found their champion?" Yikkarga demanded of Crull-maldor.

It was just past sunset. The wyrmlings were stirring in their dens, and the Fortress of the Northern Wastes was coming alive. Crull-maldor was in the Room of Whispers, and from every listening post she could hear the trod of heavy feet and the growls and snarls that made up the wyrmling tongue.

"I was going to tell you when I was certain," Crull-maldor hissed. It was a game between them, hiding information. "I know only that a large human was caught, one with red hair. I doubt that it is your hero."

"Why do you doubt?" Yikkarga asked. "He killed two of your men."

"He is not one of the small folk," Crull-maldor said. "He is a true human, from Caer Luciare."

Yikkarga snarled in outrage. "He is the one. I must take his head, immediately."

Crull-maldor gave him a sidelong look. She had suspected that he had been withholding information. Now he had confirmed it. "You never mentioned that you were searching for a true human. How many weeks have my men spent searching in vain for some phantom hero? Through your foolishness and ineptitude, you have placed the entire realm in danger. Or was it sabotage? The emperor fears this human. Are you *trying* to get the emperor killed? That would be treason! I am going to have to report your . . . indiscretion to Lord Despair."

Yikkarga had begun to turn as if he would race off to find the human, but now he whirled on Crull-maldor, fear in his eyes. Crull-maldor had him now. Most likely, Yikkarga had been ordered to hide the needed information by the emperor himself, in order to discredit Crull-maldor. But the emperor could never admit that to their master, Lord Despair. So Yikkarga would be left to shoulder the blame, and he would face the tormentors in the dungeons of Rugassa before this was through.

The huge wyrmling hesitated, then gathered his courage. "You are bluffing. You don't have Despair's ear."

"Six weeks ago that was true," Crull-maldor said. "But the world has changed. We have many enemies here in the North, and a surplus of humans that are of much worth to Despair. He whispers to my soul now, asking for frequent reports."

Yikkarga could not know that Crull-maldor was lying. Those who had wyrms could talk from spirit to spirit across vast distances.

"I . . . I am under orders to take the head of this human myself!" Yikkarga said.

Ah, Crull-maldor thought, of course. The emperor fears the human champion, so he sent an assassin—a warrior who could not be killed. Who better to make sure of the humans' champion?

"That won't be necessary," Crull-maldor suggested. "I have arranged for his public execution tonight, in the arena in Ox Port. He will fight a wyrmling—a runelord fully armed and armored."

A fool of a runelord, Crull-maldor thought. The wyrmling that she'd sent had taken endowments of speed and brawn, but he was a bumbling lack-wit. Aaath Ulber had already slaughtered better wyrmling troops on the street. If Aaath Ulber managed to take this one in combat—a broken and wounded human slaughtering a wyrmling runelord in full battle armor in front of an entire city—Aaath Ulber's reputation would be sealed.

Yikkarga immediately saw the danger. "This man has already slain two of your troops in combat!"

"True," Crull-maldor said, doing her best to sound addled by age. "Yes, now I see the wisdom in it. Perhaps you *should* go!"

With that, the wyrmling's champion was off, rushing from the room, disappearing in the blink of an eye. He had to have at least eight endowments of metabolism, and thus he could run some eighty miles in an hour. Ox Port was some eighty-seven miles away.

With any luck, Yikkarga would reach the arena just in time to see Aaath Ulber slaughter the wyrmling's slow-witted champion.

Crull-maldor smiled. She was a wight, and thus was not bound by the physical limitations imposed by mortal flesh. She could not travel at the speed of thought itself, but she could still cover a hundred miles with great haste, when need drove her.

She shucked off her spider robes, in order to gain more speed, then headed up through the dark tunnels toward the surface. Almost instantly she flew out of the opening of the watchtower, a shadow blurring through an evening sky lit by only the first star.

Below, she spotted Yikkarga, racing down a winding dirt road.

She willed herself ahead, gathering speed until she rode through the sky faster than a ballista bolt.

She would be in Ox Port to greet Yikkarga when he arrived.

The wyrmling stood before Aaath Ulber, sword at the ready, poised for battle. It was studying him, refusing to make a move.

The arena was lit by a circle of torches, in sconces high up on the wall. Aaath Ulber's eyes were nearly swollen shut, and the smoke made them water. He blinked away tears, trying to get a better look at his foe.

Every breath was bought with pain, for Aaath Ulber had more than one cracked rib. He took a deep inhalation, and laughed. "You're the one with armor and weapons, yet you're afraid of me." Aaath Ulber danced to the side, and the wyrmling blurred to intercept.

Quick, too damned quick, Aaath Ulber realized.

"I do not fear you," the wyrmling roared in challenge. "I shall roast your flesh on the end of my sword, and your blood will run down my chin this night!"

Aaath Ulber couldn't guess how many endowments the wyrmling had. His speech gave a hint. He spoke quickly, an octave too high.

But it was his breathing that gave him away. A man with metabolism draws breath more quickly. By counting the seconds between breaths, one can estimate how many endowments of metabolism a foe might have.

On average, a man draws about one breath every three or four seconds.

The wyrmling was drawing one breath every second.

No less than three endowments of metabolism, Aaath Ulber suspected, but perhaps no more than four . . . unless, of course, the wyrmling was purposely slowing his breathing, in order to hide the number of endowments that he had taken.

That was the problem when facing a runelord. You could never be certain how many endowments they might have. A smarter wyrmling might have refused to react just a moment ago. He might have tried to keep Aaath Ulber guessing whether he even had endowments.

But this wyrmling was dumb. It wasn't just his lack of strategy that convinced Aaath Ulber. It was the vacant look in the creature's eyes.

This fight is rigged, Aaath Ulber realized. The enemy wants me to win.

But why? To get rid of one useless warrior? That made no sense.

Unless this battle is only meant to warm the crowd, Aaath Ulber thought. Perhaps another wyrmling is waiting in the wings, ready to fight, hoping to expand his reputation.

That felt like the right answer.

Which means that I must conserve my energy, Aaath Ulber thought.

He took stock of his wounds—swollen eyes, blood loss from his ear and leg, broken ribs.

And everything else hurts, too, he thought.

It is possible to fight a man who has more endowments of speed than you, Aaath Ulber knew. A man who is well trained in battle, who acts and reacts without thought, can sometimes beat a man who has taken several attributes of speed. That is because a runelord with such attributes learns to use them as a crutch. They imagine that they are so much faster than a commoner that they can decide how to attack or defend when the battle is upon them.

But Aaath Ulber had been practicing to fight faster opponents all of his life, and he was going to teach this wyrmling a trick or two.

He shouted and lunged to the wyrmling's left, keeping clear of its blade. He grabbed its shield and jerked, pulling the wyrmling toward him, then used his momentum to get behind the monster. With a single bound and twist, he was on the creature's back. He worked an arm down beneath the wyrmling's chin and put the creature in a choke hold, then just dug his knees into the creature's back.

The wyrmling bawled, like an enraged bull, and struggled to shrug him off, batting his shield back uselessly, then spinning in an effort to throw him off.

For two seconds Aaath Ulber rode the monster. Suddenly it realized that Aaath Ulber could not be dislodged, so it threw its weight, all eight hundred pounds, back against the logs that lined the arena.

Aaath Ulber's ribs cracked, and the air went out of him. He wrenched his arms up tighter, and clamped a hand over the wyrmling's mouth and nose.

To strangle a man properly took time—two or three minutes. But a man could go unconscious in as little as thirty seconds. A man who was exerting himself in battle might go even faster.

But this wyrmling had endowments of metabolism. He burned through his air more quickly than a normal man.

Ten seconds, Aaath Ulber told himself. I only have to hold on for ten seconds.

The wyrmling stepped forward and then leaned to hurl himself backward once again. Aaath Ulber knew that he could not take another blow like the last.

He kicked off against the wall, seeking to throw the wyrmling off balance. But the wyrmling did not fall. Instead he spun again.

He is not thinking clearly, Aaath Ulber realized. He's craving breath.

The wyrmling shook his head, trying to break free of Aaath Ulber's grasp, and tried to bite Aaath Ulber's hand. He was almost out of the fight. His movements were slowing.

He reared back, tried to bash Aaath Ulber into the wall once more. But he was weakening, and when he drew back, he staggered. Aaath Ulber kicked backward striking the wall, and broke the wyrmling's momentum.

He clutched all the tighter, and suddenly the wyrmling seemed to remember that he had a sword. He reversed the grip, struck blindly overhead, trying to slash.

But Aaath Ulber threw his own weight forward and used his elbow to impede the wyrmling's attack. The sword blow never landed.

The wyrmling staggered forward and then fell. Aaath Ulber became aware that the crowd was chanting: "He-ro, he-ro, he-ro!"

He held on, kept strangling even though the wyrmling was down. When the creature went still, Aaath Ulber quickly grabbed its sword from the floor and lopped off the wyrmling's helmeted head.

He raised it high as the crowd of barbarians chanted. Blood flowed liberally from the severed head, splattering down over Aaath Ulber's shoulders. Many a man threw up his mug of ale, in toast to Aaath Ulber's battle prowess.

Not that I'll live long, Aaath Ulber told himself. I might be able to take a dim-witted wyrmling with only three endowments of metabolism, but the enemy has better warriors waiting in the wings.

"Toast!" the barbarians shouted, mugs held high. "Toast! Toast!"

They want me to drink from the wyrmling's head, Aaath Ulber realized.

He paraded around the ring, blood dripping down upon him; he spotted Rain in the crowd.

A door suddenly opened in the wall, a man-sized portcullis that led into a dark corridor.

The men were still cheering, urging him to drink. Aaath Ulber opened his mouth and raised the head high, as if to let blood pour down his throat.

Then he smiled in jest and flung the wyrmling's head into the crowd. He grabbed up the creature's sword, took a torch from its sconce, and strode into the dim recesses, armed to meet his fate.

Rain had been dazzled by the spectacle. She huddled against a back wall, as far into the shadows as she could get, and now searched frantically for Wulfgaard.

She hadn't been able to spot him earlier among the crowd. So many of the men looked similar.

She spotted Wulfgaard on the far side of the room, high in the shadows. He was huddled with several men, who cast their eyes about, as if they feared being watched.

They were a rough crowd, most of them younger men with murder in their eyes.

"Good show!" one old warlord muttered as he got

to his feet. "That giant is fast. No wonder the wyrm-lings want him."

Another murmured, "Reminds me of myself, in my youth."

There were guffaws, but no real laughter. The men looked worried, beaten. One of them glanced up toward Wulfgaard and whispered, "Do you think they can save him?"

"Don't know if I'd want them to save a blackguard who wouldn't drink to me," the oldest of the men said.

So, Rain realized, Wulfgaard's plan is an open secret.

She arose, and as the crowds thinned, she made her way across the room.

Wulfgaard looked up and fixed her with his eyes as she neared. He left his small band of warriors.

"A woman and a young man were taken by the wyrm-lings tonight, during the moot. They were strangers to our town, both with dark hair. . . ."

Rain fought back a frantic impulse to scream. "That would be Draken and Myrrima," she said in clipped tones.

Wulfgaard bit his lower lip, peered down at the floor. "We will have to work fast if we are to save them."

"But the wyrmlings," Rain said. "How will you fight them?"

"With these," Wulfgaard said. He pulled up his shirt-sleeve to reveal white puckered scars upon his arm—runes of brawn, grace, stamina, and a single endowment of metabolism.

It was not much to fight a wyrmling with, but Wulf-gaard's cohorts looked both dangerous and determined.

"When will you strike?" Rain asked.

Wulfgaard studied his men. There were seven of

them. The arena had nearly cleared. He gathered his courage and said, "What better time than now?"

With that, he nodded to the men. A huge warrior with blond locks stood up, pulled a short sword from his boot, and strode down toward the arena. He glanced back at his men. "Right, you men saw how it's done: no hesitation, no standing about. Now let's go free these wyrmling gents from the cruel vicissitudes of their mortal existence."

The others produced weapons from the folds of their sleeves, from inside vests and boots, then followed in line, swaggering killers out for a night of fun.

"Wait," Rain said before Wulfgaard could follow them. "Don't you have a plan?"

"There are already men outside the doors to make sure that no wyrmlings escape," Wulfgaard said. "We know the ground. Most of us have been playing in this arena since we could crawl. Grab a torch."

When they got to the fighting pit, each man took a torch, then jumped into the arena. One of them picked up the dead wyrmling's shield, and the men made their way into the dark passage, running swiftly and silently, hot on Aaath Ulber's trail.

The passage was a simple affair chiseled through sandstone. It led some hundred feet from the arena, climbing up a gradual slope to a large room littered with cages. Some were mere boxes that might hold a wolverine. Others were huge affairs massive enough for a snow ox.

Aaath Ulber could not recall having been here before. The wyrmlings had dragged him to the arena in a daze, and then wakened him by jabbing a harvester spike in his leg.

The only light came from his torch and from the powdery stars that shone through a high open window. Four wyrmlings were in the room, all dressed in battle armor. One jutted his chin toward the largest cage, which was taller than a man and made of thick iron bars. Bear dung littered the bottom of it.

"Into your cage, human," the wyrmling muttered.

Aaath Ulber stood for a moment, sword in hand, and considered his alternatives.

"You're good," a wyrmling said, giving a feral chuckle, "but not that good."

Instantly the wyrmling blurred, moving so fast that he defied the eye. Before Aaath Ulber could react, the sword was plucked from his hand. A simple shove left him tumbling into the cage, sprawling into the bear dung, and then the iron door clanked shut.

The wyrmlings laughed.

Aaath Ulber got to his hands and knees, looked up at the wyrmling that had shoved him. The creature had to have eight endowments of metabolism, more than even Aaath Ulber could hope to best. Aaath Ulber picked up his torch from the floor and asked, "You sent a fool to fight me! Why?"

"Everyone in those seats has seen a man die," the wyrmling answered. "We want them to see *hope* die. But it hurts a bit more, if it is nurtured first."

A cold wind suddenly swept into the room, sending a chill up Aaath Ulber's spine. It was a sensation he'd felt only three times in his life. A wight had entered the room.

He peered up, licked his lips, searching for the creature. But he could not see the ghost light that sometimes announced the dead. This one was keeping to its shadow form.

The wyrmlings in the room seemed not to notice. They were accustomed to the presence of wights.

A wight, Aaath Ulber reasoned, will be their leader. . . . It will keep away from the torch.

Aaath Ulber looked toward the torch. It had begun to gutter, as if in a high wind, struggling to stay lit.

"I don't plan on dying easily," Aaath Ulber said, rising to his feet.

✖ 22 ✖

THE ESCAPE

In battle, one must always seek opportunities to strike, but a wise man creates his own opportunities.

—*Sir Borenson*

Crull-maldor reached the arena only moments before Yikkarga, and spotted humans outside the door ready to ambush any wyrmling that sought to escape.

She flew in unnoticed above them, drifting through the high open windows, floating like a wisp of fog, then rose up into the rafters to hide among the huge oaken beams.

Cages were strewn everywhere down below, making many a dark nook for her to hide in, and wyrmling guards surrounded one iron cage in particular. There, with a torch in hand, squatted Aaath Ulber.

Crull-maldor tucked herself into a shadow in the rafters above the door. For several minutes, she was entertained by the wrymling guards below, as they ridiculed and tormented the human. But true to their orders, they did not harm him.

The attack on the guards came swiftly. Nearly a dozen humans rushed silently out of the arena tunnel, their torches blazing a warning to the wrymlings.

Her troops instantly took a defensive stance. Wyrmlings drew their weapons and roared in warning. As they did, the guards at the door opened it a crack and rushed in, so that the wyrmlings were set upon both before and behind.

Rain was the last in line, and though she sprinted with all her might, Wulfgaard and the others drew far ahead. She heard shouts and metal ringing as sword met sword long before she reached the cage room.

By the time that she did, the battle was in full swing. One wyrmling was down, one human beheaded, and two men wounded. The men were attacking in a well-ordered pack, four humans to a wyrmling. Some were striking high, others low. They went at it with a fury she'd never seen before, men screaming and throwing themselves into the fray, taking no thought about how to attack or where to defend.

There was no hesitation. Rain could see that despite their evident lack of planning for this specific battle, they'd been training for weeks, preparing for the time when the confrontation would come.

Yet one of the wyrmlings surpassed all their skill. As Rain entered the room, a wyrmling captain roared a battle challenge and swung a mighty ax.

Two men dodged the blow, but a third took it full in the chest. The others leapt in, trying to eviscerate the monster, but it was so fast that it merely swatted the men aside.

Two other wyrmlings had their hands full, and this one roared and struck out with an iron boot, the motion a blur, and snapped the back of one warrior from Internook.

The huge wyrmling roared in delight, then stepped back, leaving a clear killing field before him, and with a snarl invited his three remaining opponents to do battle.

The men hesitated, and in that moment two more men went down. The battle was quickly turning.

Wulfgaard raced toward the captain, threw his torch at the monster's face. The wyrmling stepped back, and in that moment Aaath Ulber struck. The wyrmling had drawn too close to Aaath Ulber's cage, and Aaath Ulber lunged through the bars and grabbed the monster's belt, then pulled with all of his might.

The wyrmling was thrown off balance. Instantly Wulfgaard lunged in and struck with his long knife, slicing into the wyrmling's groin. Blood boiled out from the captain's leg. Wulfgaard had hit a femoral artery.

The wyrmling batted with his shield, and Wulfgaard went hurtling some thirty feet and crashed into an iron cage. The wyrmling howled then, a primal scream of fear, and his men lunged in, trying to get closer. With the three of them side to side, they presented a fearsome wall.

But now Aaath Ulber reached up and got the captain in a stranglehold. The monster threw down his sword and struggled to use his free hand to break Aaath Ulber's grasp.

The human warriors in the band hurled themselves on the wyrmlings, stabbing and roaring. One man reached the wyrmling captain and plunged a poniard into his side again and again, striking through his ribs. The other wyrmlings were similarly wounded, but managed to stand and fight.

Suddenly there was a snarl at the door, and a huge wyrmling in full battle array filled the doorway.

Three young guards were there, and they whirled to confront the beast. In an instant the monster used a meat hook to grab one young man by the neck and jerk him from his feet. He used a heavy curved blade to slice through a second man, then ran the third through and lifted him into the air.

He hurled the corpses across the room, knocking one of the human defenders away from his target.

Eight endowments of metabolism he has, Rain thought. There was no way that we can defeat such a horror.

Her heart sank, and the blood seemed to freeze in her veins. Time stood still. She saw the huge wyrmling, imperious and cruel, seeming to grow as it took in the battle before it.

It spoke in the human tongue. "Fools! No man can kill me, for I am the chosen of the Earth King."

Rain did not do it consciously, but she sank to her knees, hoping that the wyrmling might see some reason to spare her. Of the humans in the room, she alone had not struck with her weapon. She had no place in a battle among runelords.

But in that instant, as all hope left her, she saw a shadow descend from the rafters. At first she thought that a black cat was leaping onto the wyrmling, but suddenly the shadow shined—a blue-gray ghost light revealing the form of a woman. She landed beside the wyrmling champion and leered down upon the battlefield.

Instantly, the temperature in the room dropped by fifty degrees, and the breath fogged from Rain's mouth.

The wight was smaller than the wyrmling champion, almost dainty in comparison. She was ancient, with flabby breasts and forearms. Her flesh was rotting from her body, but it was not her physical appearance that caused much alarm—a sensation of intense malignant evil filled the room, as if all the maliciousness in the world was made flesh in this creature.

"Wight!" Aaath Ulber shouted in warning. The humans all stepped away from their wyrmling opponents to face this darker foe.

None of the men in the room had weapons that could harm a wight. It took cold iron to wound one. A weapon blessed by a water wizard would sever it from the mortal realm, but such a blow could only be struck with a price—for the man or woman who struck the blow would likely die from touching the wight.

Rain's weapon had been blessed by Myrrima.

She pulled her dagger, shouted to the other men, "Get behind me!"

She couldn't hope to take on both a wight and the wyrmling lord, but she couldn't refuse the challenge.

She shifted her weight, tried to relax, and made ready to spring at the slightest provocation, as Aaath Ulber had taught her.

But at that instant the wight turned and smiled up at the wyrmling lord, a feral smile filled with hate. As swift as thought, she reached up and touched his shoulder.

"Yikkarga," the wight whispered. "Come!"

The wyrmling lord lunged backward, stricken, and snarled like a wounded dog. The touch of a wight could kill most men. But it only wounded the wyrmling. Its arm fell and dangled uselessly; the meat hook dropped from its hand.

Ice rimed the creature's bone armor, bright as frost, and its hot breath steamed from its nostrils. It froze, stunned for a second, and the wight leapt to attack.

She rammed her hand into the wyrmling's face, a thumb and pinky touching each of its mandibles, the middle finger between its eyes, directly over the brain, and the remaining fingers each covering an eye.

The wyrmling tried to swing its sword, but did so in vain. Its sword arm waved feebly, the wight swaying from its reach, and the behemoth stood in a daze, then dropped to one knee.

A thin green vapor began to pour from its mouth. The wight leaned forward and inhaled briefly, draining the life force from its victim.

Then she backed away. The wyrmling lord's eyes were as white as ice, soulless and empty. Its face was slack, devoid of consciousness.

The enormous wyrmling captain was all but dead.

The wight turned to Rain and whispered, "Finish him, my pet. Banish his spirit with your blade, lest he report your deeds to his master, even in death."

Then the wight turned to Aaath Ulber. "With this gift I free you, as a token of my goodwill. The emperor fears you. He fears the death you bring. Go now, and take it to him. Serve me well, human, and you shall be rewarded."

In that instant she faded, the dim light going back to

shadow, and it seemed to leap through the doorway and go vaulting up to meet the stars.

Rain trembled, and the hand that gripped her knife felt weak.

If the fallen wyrmling lord had spoken the truth, he was under the protection of an Earth King. Rain tried to understand how such a thing might happen, but all reason failed.

One thing she knew—the wyrmling before her was wounded. Perhaps it could have fended off an opponent bent on its demise, but it hadn't been able to fight off a wight—one who did not seek its death, but only to wound it.

Perhaps the wyrmling has a locus in it too, Rain reasoned. Or maybe the touch of this blade really will destroy its spirit.

"Do it!" Aaath Ulber urged from his cage. Rain peered over at him. He was still gripping the wyrmling captain, holding him by the throat, though the wyrmling sagged in ruin.

The other two wyrmlings were failing, too. Both of them were down, bleeding from many wounds.

Human warriors lay ringed about on the floor. Blood was everywhere.

Rain held her ground, glared at Aaath Ulber. "Am I some lich lord's pawn? I'll not kill at that creature's command. It has a locus in it."

Draken and Aaath Ulber had both warned her of the dangers of the loci. To obey their promptings was dangerous, for she could easily find herself under their control.

The men were wrestling with the lock on Aaath Ulber's cage now, and Aaath Ulber peered at her through his bars, thinking furiously.

"We are caught in some larger game," he said. "The wyrmlings often hate each other as much as they hate us. . . ."

Some larger game, Rain mused. But what could it be?

Her only goal was to get through this campaign alive, but the wyrmlings and Aaath Ulber were fighting for a greater cause. They were struggling for control of a million million worlds.

Her mind could not quite grasp all of this.

"We fight for our own side!" Wulfgaard said. He had pulled himself up from the floor and struggled to stand. He wobbled to one knee, then came staggering to her. He had a drop of blood eeling down from his nose, but no other sign of a wound.

He reached Rain and snatched the knife from her hand, went to the big wyrmling. The fellow did not seek to fight or run. It merely stared ahead blankly. It did not even blink as Wulfgaard sliced its throat and stepped back, so that it could bleed itself dry.

Wulfgaard turned and peered at Rain. He was handsome, with his long blond hair fanning out over his shoulders.

"The spirits of the newly dead only remain with the body for half an hour," Wulfgaard said, all business. "If we are to cover our tracks with these lich lords, we must take the spirits of all—friend and foe alike."

Rain had never heard such a thing before. One of his own men laughed, "Hah! Where did you hear that—from some lich lord?"

"From my mother," Wulfgaard said. "She could see

the spirits of the dead." With that, Wulfgaard went to each of the wyrmlings and plunged Rain's dagger into them, then did the same with his own men.

She stood in shock. To kill a man's body was one thing. To banish the life of the spirit was another.

Can Myrrima's dagger really do that? Rain wondered.

❧ 23 ❧

THE SYMPATHIZERS

No lord can hope to control the thoughts of his people, for as soon as he tries, they will begin to plot against him.

—*King Mendellas Val Orden*

Draken woke in pain, a bit of water dribbling on his face. He sputtered, rousing from a dream of drowning, a dream in which a great wall of water was rushing through the canyon, sweeping away his home, his family, his life.

He flung his arms up protectively, and Myrrima whispered, "Be still. This is healing water."

Almost instantly it seemed as if the water began melting into him, and his pains started to ease.

He peered up at her through swollen eyes.

"Mother," he whispered through cracked and bleeding gums. He suddenly remembered the beating—

wyrmling runelords pummeling him with bare fists, biting him. It had been mercifully short before he passed into unconsciousness.

He tried to take stock. His right ear burned, and he could feel caked blood all down his neck. Both arms felt as if they were broken, and at least one tooth was gone. Both eyes were nearly swollen shut.

All in all, he couldn't find an inch on his body that didn't hurt.

Myrrima had blessed some stale water from a bucket, and now she trickled it over his wounds.

They were in a dark room, like a warehouse, so deep in shadows that only a bit of starlight beamed through the slat boards.

"Are you all right?" he asked. His mother touched the right side of his face, felt his ear, and her touch was as hot as a bee sting.

"I've been better," Myrrima said. "They bit off my right ear, too. Either wyrmlings like the taste of ears, or they're doing it to mark us. . . ."

"Slaves?" Draken asked.

A gruff voice came out of the darkness. "Shut up in there, you! No talking!" The voice was human, an old man.

A door squeaked open, and a codger came shuffling out of a darkened room bearing the stub of a candle in a mug. It hardly lit his way, but in its light Draken could see a row of cages to either side of him, each cage bearing three or four people. He'd had no idea that there was even one other person in the room, much less dozens. They looked to be young, most of them—girls and boys between the ages of twelve and twenty, at the prime of their lives.

"Shush your mouths." The old man glared through rheumy eyes. He had white hair as stringy as worms, and a scraggly beard.

"Hey, what's going on in there?" An outer door opened, and a second man came in, bearing a brighter lantern. He was a big fellow carrying a knobby stick.

"These two were talking—the new ones!" the codger said, pointing at Draken.

The burly guard strode into the room. "Well," he said, "did you tell them the rules?" The big man looked pointedly at Draken. "There's no talking, see, by order of the wyrmlings. Understand?"

The big fellow glared until Draken answered. "Yes," Draken said.

The knobby club came whistling between the bars, striking him on the shoulder hard enough to leave a bruise.

"Understand?" the burly man said. "Tell me again."

Draken held his tongue. He felt bitterly betrayed. Here were humans in the employ of wyrmlings. But one look told him that these weren't just any men. This fellow had a wicked gleam to his eyes, and he delighted in causing others pain. The meanness went so deep that Draken almost wanted to shrink away from the man's presence.

He has a locus in him, Draken suspected. That's why he works with the wyrmlings.

During the long ship's voyage, Aaath Ulber had warned the family about the loci. The wyrmlings sought to be possessed by them, and called them "wyrms." According to their mythology, every man could prove himself worthy to bear a wyrm. Hence they called themselves wyrmlings.

But it was Fallion who had warned Draken against the creatures first. Fallion had read about them in his father's diary. He'd said, "Beware of evil. Do no harm to any man, if you can help it, unless you are reproving another for his wrongs. Some men are so evil that they need to be swept from the earth—those who would enslave or maliciously use you. There is no wrong in defending yourself against such evil. But beware of shedding the blood of innocents, for to do so aggrieves your own soul, and leaves you open to the influence of the loci."

Draken peered up at his captors in silence.

"Ah," the burly guard said, "the boy learns quickly." He leered down at Draken for a moment, as if seeking some excuse to hit him again. He swung the club, and Draken dodged to the side.

"Hah!" the fellow laughed at his game, then spun and sauntered out the door, slamming it closed.

The codger with stringy hair stood thoughtfully for a moment, stared down at Myrrima. He whispered, "If you're nice to me, things will go easier for you."

Myrrima held her chin up, and Draken could see the blood crusting on her. It had run in rivulets down from her ear, following the line of her cheek, and all along her neck. She shook her head no.

The old man hissed at her, his eyes suddenly blazing with rage and madness, then went tottering away.

Draken felt it from the codger too all of the sudden, a darkness to the soul so profound that he cringed. The man had a locus.

For a moment, Draken used the retreating light to seek a way out of his cage. The bars were thick, and straps of metal were woven into the roof and floor below, reinforcing the wooden slats. It was the kind of cage that was sometimes used to haul pigs aboard sailing vessels, to be killed for meat.

There was no straw on the floor beneath them, nothing to lie on. But they lay down, each of them on their left, and Draken put his arm beneath his mother's head so that she could use it as a pillow.

They did not speak any longer.

In the distance, a dog was woofing aimlessly, as if to entertain itself, while closer by the waves lapped against the docks. At least he could hear the lapping from his good ear. The water nearby smelled of death.

To the south, a wolf began to howl, and in a few moments a chorus of them rose.

They sound as if they're on the very edge of town, Draken thought. There's not a goat or calf that will be safe tonight.

"What do you think they'll do to us?" Myrrima whispered.

Draken pointed out the obvious. "We're in a cage. They plan to ship us out."

"Aaath Ulber said that wyrmlings use humans as meat?" Myrrima asked.

Draken shook his head. "Not just humans. They'll eat anything that walks, swims, or slithers on its belly. Won't touch birds though—don't like feathers in their mouths. They won't be eating us," Draken said. "They're shipping us south, to harvest our endowments."

We're such fools, Draken thought. We should have known that there would be wyrmlings here. It has been weeks since the binding. That was plenty of time for the wyrmlings to create runelords and send warriors afar.

But the truth was that Draken hadn't been certain

what he would find. He'd hoped that his own people would make use of the blood metal. He'd hoped that the wyrmlings would have been defeated by now.

"Aaath Ulber's hopes are dashed," Draken said with certainty. "All of his people—gone. . . ."

"Don't give up yet," Myrrima said. "Until we have done all that we can do, we cannot give up hope!"

"How many guards do you think?" Draken whispered. "Have we seen them all?"

"Who knows?" Myrrima whispered in return. "Lie still. Listen, and we'll see what we learn."

Draken stilled his breathing. The wolves were howling closer now. They'd been concentrated to the south, but now he heard one chime in from the west, as if a huge pack of them were raiding the outskirts of town.

The sound made him shiver. He'd heard tales of the dire wolves that haunted this land. The creatures were cruel and ruthless, and many a man who raised a weapon to fight them was dragged off and eaten.

A long eerie cry went up just down the street.

The wolves are close! he realized. They're rampaging through town.

Suddenly there were shouts outside the door to the warehouse, the gruff guard calling, "Who goes there! What's the meaning of this?"

The old codger raced from his little guardroom in the warehouse, bearing his stub of a candle at nearly a run. He reached the front door, swung it open. Draken rose up, saw men in the street bearing torches and axes.

A familiar voice bellowed, "What kind of man betrays his own people to the wyrmlings?" Aaath Ulber reached the broad door, and the two guards barred his way.

"Wise men," the burly guard said, "men who aren't so dumb as to piss against the wind. You would do well to join us. . . ."

A crowd drew up behind Aaath Ulber, ringing the guards. Rain stood at his back, her face stern but pale with fright, bearing a torch. At the fringes of the crowd, young men were howling like wolves. Firelight gleamed from naked blades.

"Here now," the guard said, seeing the mood of the crowd. "Don't you dare touch us! You kill one of us, and a thousand townsfolk will die. The wyrmlings will raze this whole district!"

Someone in the crowd guffawed. "We've already done all the wyrmlings in town, and brought death upon ourselves. I don't suppose the wyrmlings will give a damn if we poke a few holes in your wrinkled hides."

"See these men?" Aaath Ulber roared, nodding toward the guards. "They tell you that they're wise, but I'll tell you what they are: wyrmlings. They've got the souls of wyrmlings. Not all wrymlings are monstrous to behold. Sometimes the monsters hide inside."

The burly guard lunged toward the crowd, sword flashing, and struck at Rain. She stepped back, and the blow went wide, slashing a young boy in the ribs.

That was the wrong thing to do. Aaath Ulber let out a primal shout, and his eyes lost all focus as he attacked in a berserker's rage.

He slashed with a wyrmling's ax in a great arc, sweeping the blade through the guards, lopping them in half just above the waist. Blood sprayed from the wounds, but before either man could fall, Aaath Ulber leapt forward, throwing his weapon down, and grabbed their torsos.

Holding a gruesome corpse in either hand, he shook the men, screaming incoherently at first, then shouting, "Where's my wife? Where are you keeping her? Where's my wife, damn you?"

Blood seemed to rain over the crowd, and the corpses spilled their guts. White intestines, wine-colored livers, stomachs and kidneys, spleens and lungs all emptied. Aaath Ulber hurled the corpses against the door of the warehouse and stood for a moment stomping and kicking the offal like a madman, roaring in his rage.

"Here now," some burly warrior called. "You've killed them, I think." His voice was soothing and calm.

Aaath Ulber stood for a long moment, trembling and shouting, muttering under his breath, until he regained his senses.

As one, the warlords of Internook let out a cheer, then Rain rummaged among the offal, looking for the keys to the cages.

But the townsmen didn't wait. They rushed into the warehouse with axes and fell upon the cages, chopping through locks, bending bars, doing whatever they had to in order to set their people free.

In the aftermath of the battle, Aaath Ulber returned to the arena and quickly began to strip armor from the wyrmlings. The creatures were so heavy that it took three men to get off their bone mail. Afterward, they pulled off the creatures' leather jerkins to see their chests. Aaath Ulber hoped to learn how many endowments each wyrmling had, and in what mix, so that he might better gauge the danger that they presented.

But a quick survey showed that the wyrmlings did not have the scars left by forcibles on their chests and backs. Instead, the marks were found on the tops of their feet, beneath their iron boots.

The mix surprised Aaath Ulber. Their leader had the most endowments—nine of metabolism, nine of stamina, three of sight, two of scent, two of wit, one of voice, and two of hearing.

It was an odd mix in some ways.

"Where is grace and brawn?" Rain wondered aloud.

"They don't need brawn," Aaath Ulber said. "They outweigh humans by six hundred pounds, and a swat of their hand will take your head off."

"Plus, how much more strength would they get if they took brawn from a common human?" one older barbarian asked. "Not much, I'll tell you. Nor would they get much grace."

That was true, Aaath Ulber knew. As far as the wrymlings were concerned, they wouldn't want to waste forcibles in taking endowments for so little return.

Each of the other wyrmlings in the group were enhanced only with a few endowments—two each of metabolism, two of sight, and a couple of stamina.

"They need our sight to see in the daylight," Aaath Ulber reasoned, "and they want our speed and stamina so that they can move fast and run far."

"Good news," one of the barbarians said. "They shouldn't be too hard to kill."

But Aaath Ulber saw the wisdom in their choice. Most of the endowments that they were garnering were lesser endowments—sight and metabolism. Taking the sight from a man would leave him blind—unable to fight, or to escape from the wyrmling dungeons. And taking an endowment of metabolism would put the victim into a magical slumber from which he could not wake until his lord died.

Such Dedicates required almost no care. Better yet, they presented no risk to those who guarded them.

Taking these attributes was easier on the Dedicates, too. A person had to give up his endowments willingly. He might do so under the threat of death or torture, or even with a sufficient bribe, but he had to give them willingly.

But it is almost impossible to coax an endowment from someone who fears that they might die while giving it. Brawn, grace, and wit were thus hard to obtain.

Yet the wyrmlings' mix left them weaker than they might have been.

One of the young heroes that had freed Aaath Ulber was staring at the dead wyrmlings in shock, horror written plainly on his face. Rain knelt next to him, and asked, "What is the matter?"

"The wyrmlings took no glamour," he said. "When they took my betrothed, they said that she was comely. They said that they wanted her glamour. . . ."

So the girl is dead, Aaath Ulber suspected. Most likely they wanted only her tender flesh. It was rumored that young women are tastier than men. Like an old boar bear or an aging stag, the meat of an old man takes on an unpleasant musty taste.

"They'll take her sight or metabolism," Rain said, trying to convince the lad that his love was still alive.

Aaath Ulber considered the magnitude of the threat that the wyrmlings posed. He'd faced Raj Ahten, who had tens of thousands of endowments of stamina, and dozens of endowments of brawn and grace. After fighting a monster like that, these wyrmlings looked as if they would be easy.

But something in his gut warned him not to celebrate too soon.

There were wights in the wyrmling fortresses, and Aaath Ulber had not even told his family about the Knights Eternal or other dangers posed by the wyrmlings.

The wyrmlings will have their Raj Ahten, he knew.

Aaath Ulber sat in a lord's hall not twenty minutes later with Myrrima by his side and Draken and Rain at his back. The entire town was astir. Odd shouts echoed up from the market district as folks called orders to one another. The townsfolk were preparing to flee, for they expected the wyrmling reprisals to be swift and vicious.

An old lord sat across the table, Warlord Hrath, a stout fellow with a broad face. His braided hair had all gone gray, and each braid was tied with a bloodied scrap of cloth. Time had chiseled regal lines in his brow and face, and left his skin withered, but otherwise he was firm. There was no weakness in him, neither in his flesh, in his mind, nor in his resolve. "What is it that you need from us, Aaath Ulber?" he asked. "Name it, and if it is within my power, I will grant it."

At Hrath's side of the table were some of his own stout sons, along with the men who had helped free Aaath Ulber from the wyrmlings.

"I'll need food for our journey," Aaath Ulber said, "just enough for me to carry south to the wyrmling's stronghold in Mystarria. Our ship is lying just off the coast."

"Done," Hrath said.

"I'll need good weapons, to boot. I mistrust using

your tall swords in wyrmling tunnels. A good war ax for an off-hand weapon, and a large dirk would be best. I'll want wyrmling battle darts, and spare weapons."

"Finding weapons fit for a man of your size will be hard," Hrath said, "but we'll scour the town."

Aaath Ulber stared hard at the old lord. His wife and children and extended family were all in the longhouse—grandmothers, and babes—packing goods swiftly, preparing to flee. Aaath Ulber hardly dared ask for more.

"I'll need endowments, if I can get them," Aaath Ulber said. "Some of your young men have taken them already. I don't know how much blood metal is available."

Aaath Ulber hoped for twenty endowments of metabolism at the very least. He couldn't fight powerful wyrmlings with any less.

With twenty endowments, he would be twice as fast as a wyrmling who had ten. That was an advantage, but it wasn't an insurmountable benefit. A wyrmling with well-honed instincts, excellent training, and ten endowments would still pose a considerable threat.

And if I meet a wyrmling with forty endowments of metabolism, Aaath Ulber worried, I'm in trouble.

Warlord Hrath held up his hand, begging Aaath Ulber to stop. He sat for a long moment, elbows on the table, and laid his head in his hands.

"I cannot easily offer you such a boon," he said at last, "unless you can give us something more in return.

"You talk about sailing to the south into Mystarria, to strike at the heart of the wyrmlings, and this makes sense to me: Cut off the head of the snake, not the tail.

"But there is still power in the tail. Regardless of what you do next, the wyrmlings will make us pay dearly for this night. My family might flee, but where could we hide? I do not know. The wyrmling scouts can track us down by scent, and no matter where we might go, the wyrmlings are already there. They're scattered everywhere across Internook, ten to this village, fifty to a city. You and your men slew but five. I don't even know where the rest of the city guard is tonight. Usually the number of guards is double or triple what we found. Perhaps they had trouble in the countryside. It is rumored that they go to search for blood metal at night sometimes, when the town is sound asleep. . . ."

"It's not just *our* town's guards," a young man added. He leaned forward, whispering as if a wyrmling might overhear him. "Many of the largest and most fearsome of the wyrmlings' runelords have been leaving the past couple of weeks. I've gotten reports from many villages."

"There's no mystery to that," Aaath Ulber said. "It's high summer—time for the wyrmling rut. Only the largest and most fearsome of the males are allowed to breed. They will have returned to their stronghold, deep within its recesses, down where the women are kept as breeders."

Aaath Ulber did not dare say it, but he suspected that the lich lord had purposely either called much of the guard back to rut or sent them on some fruitless errand.

For reasons that he did not understand, she had sided with him against the Wyrmling Empire.

Perhaps, Aaath Ulber thought, this lich hopes that when I slay the emperor, it will leave her in charge.

Or maybe she is merely mad.

Wyrmlings were not the most stable creatures.

But, he vowed to himself, whatever she wants, whatever she offers, I refuse.

Warlord Hrath pounded the table, gazed at Aaath Ulber. "We will give you what endowments we can, and we will send word far and wide that you have come. We can gather the blood metal that we need. But if we do this, we will need your protection."

Aaath Ulber was loath to make such an offer, but there were no good choices. If he took a few endowments and then left, the wyrmlings would likely hunt down his Dedicates and slay them, leaving Aaath Ulber weak and vulnerable.

But he did not want to spend the rest of his life here defending the barbarians on this island. Aaath Ulber sighed. "Just my luck," he said. "I come to town for a loaf of bread and piglet, and what do I get? A war!"

At that, the barbarians laughed, Warlord Hrath pounding his mug on the table.

"I suspect that you will need my help," Aaath Ulber admitted. "But you understand that the wyrmling presence here in Internook is thin? Their main stronghold is in a fortress called Rugassa, in the very heart of Mystarria. You have tens of thousands of wyrmlings here on this island. There are millions more down in the heartland. I intend to breach their stronghold."

"You intend to fight them? Millions?" Warlord Hrath asked. "Just you few?"

"I intend to do all that I can," Aaath Ulber said. "But I hope for more aid. There are men of my stature to the south, or there were before the binding. I do not know how many might yet survive, but my plan is to unite them against the wyrmling hordes.

"I cannot fight that empire myself, but a thousand warriors like me, men with endowments, we could make the foundations of Rugassa tremble. . . ."

"No doubt," Hrath said, chewing his lip thoughtfully. "So you think to sacrifice us?"

The warlord was testing him, Aaath Ulber knew. He was asking if Aaath Ulber would simply take endowments and march into war, leaving the island defenseless. Hrath needed a commitment that Aaath Ulber would leave them secure.

"A man who takes an endowment," Aaath Ulber said, "takes the greatest of boons that another may offer. I would not want to put the men, women, and children of Internook at risk."

"Yet it is what your people have always done," Warlord Hrath intoned. "Your rich lords in Mystarria have hired our children, put them at the front of their battles, and used them only to blunt the weapons of the runelords that they were fighting. I know this. I myself was one of those young men. I fought for King Orden against the Merchant Princes."

Aaath Ulber stifled a groan. He had been but a child when he learned of that fray. Gaborn Val Orden's father had been king at the time. The Merchant Princes had sought to establish a trade route down into the forbidden lands of Inkarra, and King Orden had defied them. The Merchant Princes were known cowards who never fought their own battles, and so they had hired heavy lancers out of Beldinook and wild hill men out of Toom.

King Orden was a pragmatist, and had not wanted to test the enemy's resolve with his own troops. So he'd hired mercenaries out of Internook, and ordered them to form a shield wall that took the brunt of the enemy's charge—all while he held off at a good distance and gauged which among Beldinook's lancers were most rife with endowments.

The lancers from Beldinook had taken more attributes than King Orden had surmised, and Orden's mercenaries were decimated.

"I am not King Orden," Aaath Ulber said at last, reaching his decision. "I will not leave you defenseless."

"Then what will you do—secure Internook in our behalf before you go?"

Taking Internook would be a monumental task. Doing so might require months or weeks, if the land could be taken at all. And every minute that Aaath Ulber spent here was one more minute of frustration, one more minute of aching to learn if his wife Gatunyea, his children, and his people in Mystarria still survived.

Myrrima leaned forward, touched Aaath Ulber's arm, begging him to help these folks.

Aaath Ulber was loath to accept such a heavy onus, but Myrrima said, "We can't just leave. This island must be secured. If we try to just sneak away, the wyrmlings here will attack. This village itself will be demolished. Our only hope is to secure this island, then go south."

"How many enemy troops are here on the island?" Aaath Ulber asked.

Warlord Hrath looked to a young man, one of the striplings who had helped free Aaath Ulber. "Wulfgaard?" The boy leaned forward eagerly. Warlord Hrath explained, "This young man has sworn an oath to fight the wyrmlings. His woman was taken by them within days of the binding."

There was a deadly gleam in Wulfgaard's eyes, the kind of determination that Aaath Ulber had seldom seen.

If his woman had indeed granted an endowment to a wyrmling, there was no way to know which wyrmling it might be. If she'd granted sight, she would remain blind until her lord was killed. If she'd granted meta-bolism, she'd be in a slumber. In either instance, Wulf-gaard would have to slaughter one wyrmling after another until his beloved revived.

"We estimate that about twenty thousand have shown themselves," Wulfgaard said. "But we suspect that there are many more in their main fortress to the south. As Warlord Hrath told you, those twenty thousand are sta-tioned all over the island, but half of the guards in any given city get switched once a week, and shock troops form roving patrols that travel the length of the land—"

"In squadrons of fifty," Aaath Ulber finished. "I think you're right. There will be many more below ground. The wyrmlings always hide their numbers that way. And though their head is in Rugassa, they have hundreds of smaller fortresses scattered all across the mainland."

Aaath Ulber didn't want to admit it, but his own people had never been able to calculate how many wyr-mlings might be about. He'd argued with the High King many times that they should take their people south, flee beyond the mountains, in hopes of escaping the wrym-lings. But the king had justly argued against it. Wyrmling fortresses were hidden everywhere, and flying into the face of one offered no hope—not when Aaath Ulber's own people might have found themselves fighting in the open, without walls or towers to protect them.

"How many endowments can you grant me?" Aaath Ulber asked.

"We have been gathering blood metal for weeks. In-deed, we have already taken endowments in your be-half."

"Taken endowments?" Aaath Ulber asked.

Warlord Hrath leaned forward. "I myself have taken

endowments of scent from three dogs. Other men have taken brawn, grace, stamina, metabolism, glamour, voice, sight, and hearing. We can vector endowments from a thousand people across the island within a couple of days."

Aaath Ulber leaned back, astonished. He had imagined that it would take a week to garner a hundred endowments. "How could you take them in my behalf?"

"The wyrmlings themselves announced your coming," Warlord Hrath said. "They have been hunting for a giant, sailing from the north. They've searched our houses, searched our fields, looking for a man with horns upon his head. At first, we thought that they were mad. But as they began to lay heavy burdens upon us, our disbelief turned to hope."

Aaath Ulber sat thinking furiously. He had long been hunting the wyrmlings, and he knew that their lich sorcerers had strange powers. But he'd never heard that they were prophetic.

So how could they have known that I was coming? Unless, he reasoned, their powers have somehow grown or shifted since the binding of the worlds. . . .

"You could have created your own champion," Aaath Ulber suggested.

"For what purpose?" Wulfgaard asked. He scraped his chair forward, so that a young maiden could pass, bearing an armload of pillows. "We might protect our own lands for a time, but rumors say that the real danger lies to the south, beneath the shrouds of darkness. Where would our champion go? Who would he strike? So we waited for you."

Aaath Ulber wondered at the phrase "shrouds of darkness." He had never heard of such a thing. "Tell me," he said, "what has changed in Rofehavan since the binding of the worlds. . . ."

"You don't know?" Warlord Hrath asked.

"I know that most of Landesfallen sank into the sea on the far side of the world, so I set sail to come here as fast as I could."

"Toom fell into the sea also," Warlord Hrath said, "as did Haversind and all of the land along the north coast. But the coastlines of Mystarria were raised, and much that was ocean is now land. Ships that were in the bay ended up on dry land. But here in Internook, the sea level did not alter much.

"When first the binding came, we did not look abroad. There were troubles on our own island, not far from here. A fortress was found, with tunnels that led into the ground, and a single dark tower.

"Women and children that went to explore it never made it out. Good men went to rescue them, and their tale ends the same.

"We sent what runelords we could, but it had been ten years since we'd seen a forcible in our lands. The men who went were not like the runelords of old. Some lacked brawn, some grace. None was hale and well-rounded. Though they had the speed of runelords, they were warriors of unfortunate proportion.

"So they scaled the wyrmling tower, but they did not get far inside, I think. No sooner had they entered than smoke began to issue from every vent in the wyrmling fortress. None of our men escaped."

"A wyrmling fortress is not something that one assails lightly," Aaath Ulber said. "The wyrmlings love traps. Even your runelords could not breathe in that oiled air. There are pits and false walls inside a wyrmling lair. The harvesters are present in every stronghold, but they are not the worst of your worries. Wraiths guard it, sorcerers of great power who fend off death and steal the life energy from those that they vanquish. And just as every hive has its queen, at the center of the wyrmling fortress there is a lich lord who can communicate across the leagues with their emperor."

"By the Powers!" Warlord Hrath growled. "We have no weapons against such monsters."

"I do," Myrrima said. "I can enchant your weapons so that they strike down even the most powerful wraith."

"That is why the wyrmlings fear you," Warlord Hrath proclaimed. "They fear your coming."

There was a scraping sound nearby as some of the folks dragged a heavy bench across the floor. Two young men pulled up a hidden door, then went climbing down a ladder into the recesses of some hole.

"Our armory," Warlord Hrath explained, "hidden where the wyrmlings could not easily find it." Seconds later, the men began hauling weapons up from the hole. Hrath raised an eyebrow and asked Myrrima, "Will you bless these weapons?"

"Take your weapons to the nearest stream; I'll do it as soon as I can."

All around, people were darting about, gathering food and clothes, preparing to flee into the night. Warlord Hrath jutted his chin, and the men began hauling the weapons out—spears, axes, shields.

"What more have you learned of the south?" Myrrima asked.

Warlord Hrath shook his head, as if to warn that he held tragic news. "A few days after the binding, ships began to arrive from the south, our folks coming back from Mystarria. They too had been overtaken by the wyrmlings—and worse things.

"They spoke of changes that occurred during the great binding. Giant men appeared, like yourself, at the Courts of Tide. They warned of dire things to come, but that fool Warlord Bairn made a sport of killing them, in the hopes of placating the wyrmlings and making some sort of compact with them.

"But then a winged woman came and told of mountains of blood metal to the east—"

"Wait," Aaath Ulber said. "You say that a winged woman came? Was she a normal human, or was she like me, or was she a wyrmling?"

"She was human in every way, but for her crimson wings," Warlord Hrath said. "She was young, beautiful."

Aaath Ulber considered this news. The only winged people that he had ever heard of were the wyrmling Seccaths—the greater lords. They wore wings that were constructed by means that no human had ever learned or could duplicate. Humans had sometimes won the wings—by slaughtering their wearer and fitting them to their own backs—but it was a rare occurrence, something that might happen only once every two or three generations.

The wyrmling Seccaths were few in number. They included the three Knights Eternal, a few members of the imperial family, and perhaps half a dozen messengers and scouts that the emperor employed—messengers and scouts who were also brilliant and accomplished warriors.

Who could have killed a Seccath? Aaath Ulber wondered. Few had such prowess in battle.

"This winged woman, did she give a name?" Aaath Ulber asked.

Warlord Hrath's brow furrowed in concentration and he looked about the crowd for help. "Angdar was there in the city that day. He heard the tale many times in pubs that night from those who saw, and so he knows it better than I. Did the woman give a name?"

Angdar stepped forward, a burly man with a greasy face. "I don't recall hearing that she gave a first name, but she did a last: Borenson. I remember because I have heard that name in song many a time, and I wondered if she was any relation to the great warrior."

Aaath Ulber leapt toward Angdar, and felt so grateful that he slapped the man on the back. "My daughter. My daughter is alive. When did this happen?"

"Just before midday, two days after the binding of the worlds."

Myrrima got choked up and began to sob, as did Draken, and Aaath Ulber just stood and hugged them for a moment.

"Talon?" Myrrima asked. "She has wings? But how?"

Aaath Ulber explained quickly. As he did, Myrrima's face lit up. It seemed that the fears and worries slid from her countenance, revealing a fierce hope that had been hiding inside her for weeks.

"Talon's alive," Myrrima exulted at last. "She didn't get crushed in the binding."

Aaath Ulber hugged his wife and son, but he wondered. How had Talon fought off a wyrmling Seccath? How would she have known how to take its wings? If Fallion had gone into the Underworld, how could he have returned two days later?

Some answers were obvious. Talon knew of the hill of blood metal at Caer Luciare. Somehow she had killed a wyrmling Seccath, and the folks there must have shown her how to take its wings.

But that left so many questions unanswered.

"Tell me," Aaath Ulber asked Angdar, "what precisely did my daughter say—as close as you can? What were her words?"

The burly warrior held his tongue for a moment as he thought. "She'd come for help," he said. "She warned Warlord Bairn of the wyrmlings, like the others had, and told him of a mountain of blood metal. She wanted help in . . . freeing some men from a wyrmling fortress, two men who were being held captive. . . ."

"Fallion and Jaz!" Draken exulted, and Aaath Ulber's heart pounded with newfound hope. He did not want to leap to conclusions, but who else could it be?

Myrrima muttered, "The wyrmlings must have learned that Fallion bound the worlds. Let us hope that their awe of him keeps him alive."

Fifty days in a wyrmling dungeon, Aaath Ulber thought. Few could survive so long. The wyrmlings were not gentle. But then, few men were as durable as Fallion Orden.

Aaath Ulber looked to Angdar. "What did Warlord Bairn answer when my daughter made her request?"

"He asked for the location of the mountain of blood metal. She told him, and then he ordered his archers to open fire upon her. She flew off, I hear, unscathed."

It was all that Aaath Ulber could do to keep from going into a berserker's rage. "Bairn is a fool."

"*Was* a fool," Warlord Hrath corrected. "No sooner

had the woman departed than he began to mount an expedition into the wilds above Ravenspell, seeking the mountain!"

"*Above* Ravenspell?" Aaath Ulber asked, and a fey smile crossed his face. Smart girl. His daughter must not have trusted this Warlord Bairn. She's sent him on a chase—right into the enemy's camp. "Well, I don't suppose I'll need to go seeking vengeance upon him."

"No one knows what happened next," Warlord Hrath said, "but Bairn's folly cost him dear. He and his men rode out hard, and none were ever seen again.

"But it is feared that he stirred up a hornets' nest. Darkling Glories began to fill the skies, winging above the castles in Mystarria, betraying our troops' positions to the wyrmling hordes. The wyrmlings attacked the Courts of Tide—but they used reavers as sappers, to knock down the castle walls.

"The wyrmling runelords decimated the land in less than a week."

"Our folks fled the southlands, and as they did, darkness filled the skies—great swirling clouds the color of greasy smoke, whirling in a maelstrom.

"It hovers there still, so that all of Mystarria is veiled in eternal night. The Darkling Glories fly in and out of it, and the only illumination comes from the brief flashes of lightning that rip through the sky.

"The heavens grumble and moan," Hrath said solemnly, "and the earth is troubled. That is why I have wondered, why we have all wondered . . . against such powers, what mortal man could prevail? Why would the wyrmlings fear *you*?"

Aaath Ulber suspected that he knew precisely why. It

wasn't his prowess in battle, it was something that he'd learned long ago, a bit of knowledge that he held dear—and had never told anyone.

"At the arena," Aaath Ulber said, "there was a wyrmling lord. He boasted that he could not be killed, for he was under the protection of an Earth King. Have you heard rumors of this before?"

Hrath leaned away from the table, his eyes wide with surprise. "An Earth King? A wyrmling Earth King? Are you sure? That would be a fell thing indeed!"

"That can't be true," Myrrima cut in. "The Earth Spirit would not grant its power to such a beast!"

"Are you certain?" Aaath Ulber asked. "The Earth Spirit cares equally for all of its creatures, the hawk as well as the mouse, the serpent as well as the dove. Perhaps the wyrmlings are in danger of going extinct *soon*. If I had my way, I'd make them extinct!"

Aaath Ulber thought furiously. It would make sense. If mankind posed enough danger to the wyrmlings, the Earth Spirit might protect them.

But Aaath Ulber couldn't imagine how he could pose such a threat to the wyrmlings . . . except. His mind went back to that bit of hidden knowledge. It was time to reveal the secret he had kept for over a decade.

He leaned forward. "There is something that I must tell you: Six months before he passed, the Earth King Gaborn Val Orden came to see me one last time. He was old and frail, and appeared outside my door in broad daylight one morning. The guards at the castle gate swear that he did not enter, that he simply materialized from the soil. . . ."

"I doubt that he materialized," Myrrima said. "An

Earth Warden can be hard to see, if he does not want to be noticed."

"In any event," Aaath Ulber said, "he stayed for two days, and when we were alone, he told me something that he wished to be kept secret until the time was right for it to be published abroad.

"He said that there was a way for a killer to circumvent his powers. He said that he had learned of instances where his chosen had died—by murder. He would sense their impending doom, sometimes weeks in advance, but as it drew near, he could not avert the event.

"He said that there was a secret order of men who were doing this to gain power, and he feared what it might lead to. . . ."

"How could this be?" Warlord Hrath said. "The Earth King's power to preserve was legendary."

"Slow poison," Aaath Ulber answered. "When a man takes it, his death may be secured, but it might not happen for days or even months after the poison is administered. Thus, Gaborn would sense impending doom hours or weeks away, and as the threat grew, he would hope that the Earth Spirit would tell him how to avert it. But by the time that he realized that there could be no rescue, the killer was long gone."

"So," Warlord Hrath asked, "you're suggesting that we *poison* the wyrmlings."

Aaath Ulber sat, pondering. That was exactly what had happened earlier in the night. The lich lord had incapacitated one of the Earth's chosen, it seemed. But it was the young Wulfgaard who had struck the killing blow minutes later.

If indeed the monster had been under the protection

of an Earth King, then it had done the creature little good.

Incapacitate first, then kill at leisure.

"Yes," Aaath Ulber agreed, "poison would be one way to go about it. . . ."

Aaath Ulber peered around the room. The villagers were preparing to flee, but he realized that the spectacle would only attract more wrymlings.

"Tell your people to stay in their houses," Aaath Ulber warned Warlord Hrath. "As well as we can, we must maintain the illusion that it is business as usual here. Give me endowments, and I can protect the village."

"But . . ." Hrath objected. "What if the wyrmlings find out what we've done and attack? We'll have no way to protect your Dedicates."

"We'll hide them in attics and cellars as best we can."

"And if the wyrmlings attack in force? We have no castle walls here to repel them. We have little in the way of troops."

"Just as a runelord who is mighty with endowments needs little in the way of armor, I will protect you. My shield will be your castle wall, and I will fight your battles."

Aaath Ulber still had blood on his hands and garments when he took his endowments that night. Rain watched as the warlords of Internook built a vast bonfire, and its ruddy light stained the hairs of the giant's head a deeper shade of red and accentuated the blood splatter upon his clothes. In the firelight the nubs of horns stood out upon his brow. As Aaath Ulber waited in the village street, a keg of ale for his throne, an old man brought forcibles from some hiding spot in a nearby village.

He'd wrapped them in oilskin and hidden them in a keg of cider vinegar. Now the skins stank, even from Rain's vantage point forty feet away.

"Those wyrmlings don't have a taste for vinegar," the old man explained. "Hide them in a keg of ale, and you're asking for trouble. But put them in vinegar, and a wyrmling will never bother them."

He laid out the forcibles—sixty of them, a surprisingly large number.

So the ceremony began. Rain had never seen an endowment ceremony before. Her father had been a lord, a wealthy man, but even in his days the mines of Kartish had been failing, so she'd never seen a forcible.

She watched in fascination as the ceremony took form. A huge crowd had gathered at her back, perhaps some five thousand strong, and folks peered eagerly. Some folks had come out of mere curiosity. Others had come to give attributes. All of them seemed to be prodding and pushing at Rain's back, trying to get a better view.

The evening was taking on a spectacle, as if it were a festival day and someone had brought fireworks from Indhopal.

Now the old man took out his forcibles and inspected each by firelight. The forcibles were rods, much in shape and size like a small spike, a little thicker than the heaviest wire and about the length of a man's hand. They were made of blood metal, which was darker red than rusted iron, and which tasted like dried blood to the tongue.

At the tip of the forcible was a rune, a mystic shape that controlled which attribute might be taken from a Dedicate and transferred to a lord. The rune was about the size of a man's thumbnail, and though the shape of the rune did not mimic anything seen in life, the shape alone had an aura of power about it, a sense of rightness to it, that defied understanding.

Each forcible was made from pure blood metal, which was so soft to the touch that a chance scrape with a fingernail could dent it. Thus, the runes at the head were easily damaged during transportation, and the wizard who used them had to make sure that the forcible was pristine and perfect, lest the endowment ceremony go awry.

So the old man studied the rune at the tip of each forcible, and sometimes he would take a file and pry a little here, or file a little there.

As he worked, Aaath Ulber got up and spoke, hoping to gain the hearts and approbation of the people.

"I am no common man," he called out to the crowd. "You can see that by my appearance. But what you cannot see is that I am two men, two who were united into one when the worlds were bound."

At that, the crowed oohed and aahed.

"One of those two men you may have heard of, for I was the bodyguard of the Earth King Gaborn Val Orden in his youth. I was Sir Borenson, and fought at the Earth King's right hand when the reavers marched on Carris. I guarded his back when Raj Ahten sent his assassins against our king when he was only a lad, just as I guarded his son, Fallion Orden, and kept him safe in Landesfallen for these past ten years.

"Foul deeds I have done in the service of old King Orden, deeds that bloodied my hands and soiled my conscience. You have heard that I slew Raj Ahten's Dedicates at Castle Sylvarresta. More than two thousand men, women, and children I killed—in order to save my king, and our world.

"I did not shirk from bloodshed. I did not offer sympathy or condolences to those I murdered. It was a deed that shamed me, but it was a deed that I could not turn away from.

"I killed men that I had dined with and hunted with, men that I loved as if they were my own brothers. . . ."

Rain wondered at that. It was not the kind of thing that she would have bragged about. She feared Aaath Ulber, feared his lack of restraint, his raw brutality.

And here this crowd was, urging him on, empowering him.

"But that is only half the tale," Aaath Ulber said, "for as I told you, I am two men bound into one.

"*Aaath Ulber* was my title on the shadow world that you saw fall from the heavens, a title that means Great Berserker. I was the foremost warrior among the men of my world, and more than two hundred wyrmlings have fallen beneath my ax and spear.

"Seven times did I plunge myself into the depths of wyrmling fortresses, and once when no one else survived, I made it out alone.

"I do not tell you this to boast," Aaath Ulber continued, "I tell you this so that you will know: I plan to kill our common enemy. I will show no compassion, spare no child.

"I am two men in one shell. I have trained for two lifetimes, and gained skills that neither world had ever seen.

"I am stronger now than either man was alone—faster, stronger, better prepared.

"The wyrmlings fear me because I am the most dangerous man alive. I speak their language. I know their ways. I have breached their fortresses time and time again. The wyrmlings shall have nothing from me—nothing from us—but an ignoble death!

"This I pledge you: Those who grant endowments to me this day will strike a blow against the wyrmlings. I shall not faint, nor shall I retreat. Death to all wyrmlings!"

At that the folks of Ox Port cheered and raised their weapons, shouting war cries. Some women wept openly, while alewives poured mug after mug, and the men raised them in toast.

What better way to gain endowments, Rain thought, than to take them from drunken barbarians.

As Aaath Ulber finished, the old man held up a completed forcible and called out its name. "Brawn? Who will grant brawn to our champion?"

"Does he need any more brawn?" some warrior shouted, and many men guffawed.

"I am strong," Aaath Ulber agreed, "but I go to face wyrmling runelords that are stronger still. A hundred endowments of brawn I need, no less! And I need them this night—for I must cleanse this island of our wyrmling foes!"

"Hurrah!" the men cheered, and a huge barbarian strode forward, eager to be the first.

The old man cheered and shouted, "Bless you! Bless you. May the Bright Ones protect you, and the Glories guard your back!" He clapped the barbarian on the shoulder and the ceremony began.

It was evident that the old man was not well practiced in the taking of endowments. His hands trembled as he began to sing, so that the rod shook. In some distant day, he might have been a facilitator to some warlord, a mage who specialized in taking endowments. But forcibles had become so rare in the past few years. Now he closed his eyes and began to sing a wordless song that felt strained and uncomely.

It was not words really, but repeated sounds—groans and humming, interspersed with sharp harking calls. There was music in his song, but it felt wild and unrestrained, like a driving wind as it coils through mountain valleys, blowing this way one moment, another way the next.

Rain grew lost in the song, mesmerized, until soon the chanting and humming seemed to be part of her, something flowing in her blood.

Just as she lost herself, she wakened to the smell of burning flesh. The old facilitator had taken the forcible and pressed it to the barbarian's bared chest, and during the course of the song the metal had turned white-hot.

Hair scalded and flesh burned. The barbarian's face was hard and stony, his eyes unfocused. He knelt, staring at Aaath Ulber while the facilitator branded him with the searing iron. Sweat streamed down the Dedicate's brow, and his jaw quivered from pain, but he did not let out a sound.

Then the facilitator danced away, held up the hot branding iron. As he did, the forcible left a white trail in the darkness, a worm of pale white light that hung in the air as solidly as if it were carved from wood.

The children cried out "Ah!" and marveled.

The facilitator waved his forcible in the air, creating knots of white light, like a giant rope. One end of the rope was anchored to the barbarian's chest, while the other end blazed at the tip of the forcible. The facilitator studied the light trail, gazing at it from various angles, and at last took the rod to Aaath Ulber.

The giant pulled open his own vest, revealing a chest that was much scarred—both from old battle wounds and from the kiss of the forcible.

The facilitator plunged the metal rod into Aaath Ulber's chest, and in an instant the trail of white light that connected the two broke. The worm of light shot out of the barbarian's chest like a bolt, and with a hissing sound it rushed toward Aaath Ulber. It struck the forcible, which turned to dust and disappeared, and for an instant the light seemed to well up in Aaath Ulber's chest, threatening to escape. A white pucker arose on his skin in the shape of a rune, and suddenly the air filled with the acrid odor of his singed hair and the pleasant scent of cooked skin, so much like the scent of pork roasting upon a spit.

It is said that receiving an endowment, any endowment, grants the lord who takes it immense pleasure, and now Aaath Ulber's eyes fluttered back in his head, as if he would faint from ecstasy.

His head lolled, and he nearly swooned.

But the fate of he who grants an endowment is not so sure. The giving of an attribute causes such agony that it cannot be described. Women claim that the pain of childbirth pales in comparison, and almost always the Dedicate who grants an endowment will wail in pain, sometimes sobbing for hours afterward.

But this big barbarian did not cry out. He did not even whimper. He merely sat stoically, beads of sweat breaking out on his brow, until at last he fainted from the effort of staying upright.

His strength had left him completely.

In a tense moment, everyone watched the barbarian to see if he still breathed. Too often, a man who gave his strength gave more than his strength: he gave his life. For when the strength left him, his heart might be too weak to beat, or his lungs might cease to draw breath.

But the barbarian lay on the ground, breathing evenly, and even managed to raise his arms, as if to crawl. He fell to his belly and chuckled, "I'm as weak as a babe!"

At that there was a shout of celebration, for if he could talk, then he would survive.

Thus the endowment ceremony began, with those who offered greater endowments leading the way. The greater endowments included brawn, grace, wit, and stamina, and granting them was dangerous business. A man who gave too much stamina was prone to catch every little fever that swept through a village. Those who gave up grace often cramped up on themselves; their muscles, unable to loosen, would either cause them to strangle for lack of air or to starve. Even those who gave wit might pass away, for in the first few moments after granting the endowment, a man's heart might forget how to beat.

Thus, courageous men and women came to offer up endowments, and with each successful transfer the celebration deepened, for it was proved that the old man knew how to transfer attributes without killing his Dedicates.

Rain noticed a young woman at the edge of the firelight thrown from a torch, spreading salve upon one of the injured warriors who had helped fight at the arena. Rain went and borrowed some salve from her, a balm that smelled rich from herbs, and took it to Draken.

Gingerly, she placed the salve on his ear, where his captor had bitten it off. Draken did not jerk or start away when she touched him. Instead, he leaned into her, savoring her presence though it cost him pain.

She teased him, "You Borensons, with that odd gap where your ear should be: I do hope that our children don't inherit the trait."

Draken smiled up at her, his eyes gleaming, and pulled her close for a hug. He glanced around. All eyes were on Aaath Ulber, so he pulled Rain into the darkness in the shadows of a building and kissed her roughly.

For weeks now, on the boat, they'd been unable to find a place to be alone, had not dared kiss. Now he made up for it.

He kissed her lips, her cheeks, and hugged her so tightly that it took her breath away. He finally pulled back her hair, studied her in the weak light of the stars.

"I'm glad that the wyrmlings didn't get your ear," he said. "I've been longing to nibble on it."

He leaned in, chewed on her ear, and the passion inside her flamed to life. He was hugging her, so that his whole body pressed against her. She felt his strong chest firm against her breast, and she ached to race off into the woods, into the shadows, to be alone with him.

But she knew that the time was not right. She wanted a proper wedding, with family and friends gathered around to witness. So after a time, they stole back to watch the endowment ceremony.

Myrrima was there, at the edge of the light, her face stony. She looked as if she had been beaten.

"Have you spoken to your mother?" Rain asked, wondering what was wrong.

"No," Draken answered, clinging tightly to her hand. "Why?"

"She looks so sad," Rain said, and suddenly she knew why. Aaath Ulber was taking endowments, endowments of metabolism that would kill him. It might not kill him in an instant, but they would shorten his life by decades.

"Your father's killing himself," Rain said. "He's sacrificing himself, and he didn't even ask your mother's permission . . . he didn't talk to you, or Sage."

Draken held silent for a while. "He has another family now, too. I guess that their need outweighs ours." Draken sighed. "He's sacrificing himself for both of his families."

Rain bit her lip, appalled at the sacrifices this system of magic required. A few moments ago she had feared that one of the Dedicates might die in this process, and she'd felt relieved to see him survive. But now she realized that Aaath Ulber was the victim this night.

He would die from his wounds, even if the wyrmlings didn't kill him. Nothing could save him.

Aaath Ulber grew mighty during the course of that night, and as he did, his appearance altered subtly.

With three endowments of wit, a new light shone in his eyes, a keenness to his perceptions. He would now learn more quickly and would not forget anything that he saw or heard.

As he garnered endowments of brawn, his back straightened and his massive bulk seemed to hang on him easily.

After taking endowments of stamina, the bruises and scrapes on his face began to heal in a matter of hours, and he grew more lucid despite the fatigue of the night.

With three endowments of grace, he began to move nimbly, with the ease of a dancer.

Two endowments of glamour made him seem younger and more handsome, so that even his scars appeared attractive; there was a new certitude to him, the kind of confidence that invites others to follow.

With endowments of voice, his tone seemed to become deeper and mellower, so that others were more inclined to accept his counsel.

After taking endowments of metabolism, his body began to speed, his breath quickening, his voice becoming higher. With ten endowments, he would be able run at a hundred miles per hour or more. With twenty endowments, he would even be able to run upon the surface of water.

But not all of the attributes he took that night produced a visible change. Some granted abilities that remained hidden.

Warlord Hrath himself gave up endowments of scent taken from dogs so that Aaath Ulber would be able to track wyrmlings and would be alerted to the presence of any that wandered near.

Endowments of sight would let him see more keenly than any owl so that he would espy enemies miles away, even in the darkness.

A few endowments of hearing would make ears sharper than a robin's, so that he might hear a call for help from great distances.

So the night went, the barbarians bestowing Aaath Ulber endowments one after another, as fast as the old facilitator could manage, until he'd granted all sixty.

The barbarians of Internook were turning Aaath Ulber into a weapon fashioned from flesh and bone. They hoped to aim him like an arrow to the heart of their enemies, but Rain could not help but think how often arrows went astray.

The Dedicates were immediately hustled off to secret locations, for if the wyrmlings managed to find a Dedicate and kill him, the magical bond between Aaath Ulber and that Dedicate would be broken, and Aaath Ulber would lose the attribute that he so badly needed.

Thus some were carted off in wagons while a couple were hustled down to the docks and loaded into boats. Still others managed to hobble back to their homes or off into the wilderness to hide.

Sometime in the night, Draken rowed back out to sea to give word to Sage. At the first light of dawn he brought her to town.

Sage got off the boat and stood on the land, peering about at the trees and dirt, inhaling the scent of the forests above the village. The touch of clean earth revitalized her, lifted her spirits. She was happy to be back on land.

With the coming of day, messengers were sent to the east and west along the coast to bear the news with a warning from Warlord Hrath. "Be careful who you speak to. There are spies in the wrymling employ. Tell the headman of each village and city what has transpired and beg their aid. But do not call for an open revolt against the wrymlings yet. We dare not alarm them. Instead, we need more forcibles here, and we need the lord of each village to send a champion to join us. We meet tomorrow at dawn!"

Rain's heart thrilled at the news, and she watched

the proceedings with trepidation. The barbarians of Internook had always been enemies in her mind but now
she found herself hoping for their success.

Lest a wrymling patrol happen through town, Warlord Hrath had the young men take posts, surreptitiously
acting as guards. They worked in barns and fields along
the roads, with orders to whistle a certain song if any
wyrmling happened along.

As the forcibles ran out and dawn blossomed, the
crowds thinned, and sun came up a ruddy gold, with
clouds on the horizon, their hearts blue and their edges
lined with molten copper.

The old facilitator was weary, ready for bed, but
Aaath Ulber had one more task for him. He pulled up
his pants leg to reveal a welt, red and scarred with age.
It was a rune that Rain had never seen before.

"When we get more forcibles, can you make a couple of these?" Aaath Ulber said.

The old facilitator knelt and studied the welt. He
began to tremble nervously, then to laugh, giddy with
excitement. "Is that what I think it is?"

"Yes," Aaath Ulber said. "I got it in Inkarra when I
was young. That, my friend, is the legendary rune of
will."

Rain studied the thing. It was an odd symbol that
reminded her of a drawing of a thistle—with a central
hub with many sharp spikes poking up from it.

A rune of will, it was said, multiplied most of a
man's abilities. Any man would be made stronger by it,
faster, fiercer in battle.

But what will it do to Aaath Ulber, she wondered, a
berserker who lost all consciousness in battle and became mad with bloodlust?

At that moment, there was a shout. "Leviathans! Leviathans in the bay!"

Everyone in town cheered and celebrated. There was a great blowing of war horns. The entire town turned out, rushing down the cobblestone streets.

Dozens of the great serpents were out in the water, eeling about. They roiled to the surface and the morning sun glinted off their silver scales, which were pocked with barnacles. The great males swam about with their fins rising up out of the water, some of their pectorals riding six feet above the foam.

Before the school of leviathan came the fish—huge schools that raced toward the shallows. As they neared the fish trap, they grew so close together that there was not an inch between them. Huge schools of red snapper and sea bass had gathered, their fins splashing the water white. Many of them leapt as much as a dozen feet in the air, struggling to get into the fish trap, and as always, not two hundred feet off shore, the leviathans circled ominously, thrashing and lunging as they took the largest fish.

Warlord Hrath studied the spectacle, beaming, and slapped Aaath Ulber on the back. "You've brought great luck to our village! We have not seen so many leviathans in years!"

Rain wondered how long the luck would hold.

❧ 24 ❧

A DESPERATE PLAN

Beware of making plans in desperation, for when you do, you are only reacting to your enemy. It is far better to think ahead, to force him to make the desperate plans.

—Hearthmaster Waggit

"Are you really going to attack the wyrmlings?" Draken asked his father that morning. "I mean, that wight of theirs, she helped you, right?"

"I'll not be beholding to a wyrmling wraith," Aaath Ulber explained to Draken. "She helped us for her own purposes, and I'll have none of it. In fact, since she wants to make me her pawn, I want all the more to get rid of her. I'll gut her along with the rest of her folk."

Draken shivered. Dawn had come clear and cool, so much colder than the mornings back home in Landesfallen this time of year. He tasted a hint of ice in the air, and a bitter winter ahead. The sun slanted in through the village, casting blue shadows, and the smoke from cooking fires in the longhouses clung near to the ground in the heavy air.

The men sat in the shade on the porch of an alehouse, with the morning sun beating down all around them. Old Warlord Hrath seemed to be the leader of the town, but for the purposes of plotting this war, he had relegated a great deal of authority to young Wulfgaard.

The young man had brought a map from his house written on heavy parchment. The map itself might have been drawn fifty years ago, the parchment was so old and worn, but there were new markings painted here and there, and small notes written with charcoal.

The map showed the island of Internook, with its rough coasts and frozen tundra. But of greatest value was the information about the cities. Each city and village was shown in an inked circle, and beside the circle was a number in charcoal which represented the quantity of wyrmling troops assigned to guard that town.

In addition, a wash made of thin red paint showed where wyrmling patrols had been spotted.

"Not all of the figures are accurate," Wulfgaard apologized. "I've got word from many of the towns along the coast, and from many of the farther villages, but I had to guess in some instances. Still, it is not hard to guess, if you know how many longhouses are in a village. The wyrmling guards number only one to every one hundred of us."

All in all, the map was a masterwork of intelligence gathering. Draken was impressed, as was Aaath Ulber.

But Draken had to wonder how one man might hope to secure the island, for it seemed that the island was covered in cities and villages. Hunting down the wyrmlings in each area might take weeks or months. And no matter where Aaath Ulber began his attacks, the wyrmlings would surround him.

But now Aaath Ulber put his finger on a dark blot some eighty miles south of them—the wyrmling fortress.

"Here," Aaath Ulber said, "this is the prize. This is where we must attack."

Some children ran past carrying buckets. Aaath Ulber held the map on his knees, drew a long draught from a huge mug.

Draken wondered how many great battles had been plotted on the porches of alehouses.

The village was a riot. The fishermen were out on their levee with nets and spears, harvesting sea bass in great quantities. The women in town had taken up knives, while the children took the filets and soaked them in brine. The whole town had turned out for the harvest, and there was singing and rejoicing.

A carrion crow flew to the top of a merchant's shop across the street and sat on a black iron weather vane. Warlord Hrath peered up at it and grimaced. The crow merely squatted on its perch, braving a wind that barely ruffled its feathers.

Aaath Ulber studied the map. "This wyrmling fortress," he asked Wulfgaard, "have you found the bolt-hole for it?"

"Bolt-hole?" Wulfgaard asked. "There is none. There is only one way in, one way out."

"The wyrmlings always have a bolt-hole," Aaath Ulber explained, "sometimes more than one. A wyrmling warren is like an ant hive. The air within it needs to be refreshed. So there must be a second entrance somewhere. It has to be large enough for a wyrmling to get through, so it will have a roof of four or five feet at least. The bolt-hole will not be in sight of the main entrance, nor can it be at a higher elevation. Usually, it will be on the far side of a hill—not less than two miles from the main entrance, but often ten miles or more."

"We haven't seen anything like that," Wulfgaard said. "Not a trace."

"I'll have to find it then," Aaath Ulber said. "The wyrmlings will have it hidden. Rocks or brush might cover the entrance. But if you follow the wyrmling's tracks . . ."

Aaath Ulber pointed out three large hills on a ridge to the west of the wyrmling fortress. "I'll check here, behind this tallest hill. That's a likely place."

"I'd like to come with you, if I may," Wulfgaard asked.

Aaath Ulber glanced toward Warlord Hrath, to get his input.

The warlord shrugged. "Wulfgaard here, he has a taste for blood."

Aaath Ulber made a sweeping motion with his hand, from the eastern end of the island to the west. "We have hundreds of miles of coastline—and we know where the wyrmlings are stationed inland. We can't clear all of this out. . . ." He frowned in concentration.

"Why can't we?" Wulfgaard begged.

"It would warn the wyrmlings in the fortress," Aaath Ulber said. "Each time that we kill a wyrmling, a couple of dedicates are freed. Those who have granted the dead wyrmling metabolism will wake from their slumber, someone who has given sight will regain his sight. This won't go unnoticed for long, and the wyrmlings would retaliate, mount a campaign."

Wulfgaard seemed not to have considered that.

"More importantly," Aaath Ulber said, "by killing the wyrmlings, we're endangering their Dedicates."

"How is that?" Warlord Hrath asked.

"What do you think that the wyrmlings will do to a Dedicate that revives?" Aaath Ulber asked. "A man can never grant a second endowment, so they're no use as

Dedicates. They might be of some use as slaves—but there is nothing that a human can do that a wyrmling can't. A slave would serve little purpose. But the wyrmlings have a taste for human flesh. I doubt that anyone who revives in the wyrmling dungeons will ever breathe fresh air again."

Wulfgaard's face paled in concern. "We can't just slaughter the wyrmlings then," he said. "Even if we wanted to, we can't rise up against them without . . ."

"Sacrificing the lives of every man, woman, and child that they have already taken from you," Aaath Ulber confirmed.

Warlord Hrath's eyes flickered as he glanced up to Aaath Ulber. "There is really only one course of action then," he suggested. "We should kill the Dedicates ourselves, take the wyrmling's endowments from them. If we did, we'd leave the wyrmlings sunblind, as slow as commoners, and vastly outnumbered. We could take them then—even our old men could take them."

Wulfgaard grabbed the map and threw it to the ground. "No!"

Draken looked up to Aaath Ulber. As Sir Borenson, he had killed Dedicates before, slaughtered them until the stairs on the Dedicates' tower at Castle Sylvarresta ran with blood. There were songs sung about it still today.

Aaath Ulber shook his head and growled, "Now who is talking about sacrificing the lives of your people? By a conservative estimate, the wyrmlings have twenty thousand troops here on the land. Each of them has at least two endowments. The wyrmlings must have taken at least forty or fifty thousand of your people down to their lair."

"More like a quarter of a million," Wulfgaard said.

"By the Powers!" Aaath Ulber swore.

The number was staggering. It hinted at vast forces of enemies down in the warrens.

Aaath Ulber had never entered a wyrmling fortress of this size. He wondered if it was even possible to clear the monsters out of such a place with as few resources as he had.

Yet if he was to attack Rugassa, he imagined that this would be a good trial run. It would give him a chance to explore the wyrmlings' lair, study their defenses, and learn more about the enemy.

Aaath Ulber asked, "A quarter million. Are you certain?"

"I've heard from people in fifty villages and cities," Wulfgaard said. "If my estimates are right . . . then it is a quarter of a million at the very least."

"So many can't have given endowments yet," Aaath Ulber suggested. "It would take four dozen facilitators working night and day to grant the endowments that have been given already."

Unless the facilitators had taken endowments, Aaath Ulber realized.

He wondered. How many facilitators might the wyrmlings have? How many wyrmlings are in that fortress? If each warrior has only two or three endowments, does that mean that they have over a hundred thousand warriors?

That seemed to be too large a number.

Perhaps the wyrmlings are harvesting these folks, or merely executing those who present a danger.

Myrrima suggested, "The wyrmlings might be holding people captive until they have enough time to take their endowments."

That sounds right, Aaath Ulber thought. It would accomplish two things: the wyrmlings could round up those most likely to revolt while ensuring themselves a stock of potential Dedicates.

But harvesting so many endowments would require forcibles. Did the wyrmlings have that much blood metal?

Aaath Ulber considered. They might be mining it here in the North, but it seemed more likely that they would rely on shipments coming in from Rugassa.

The thought sent chills through him. "If we could capture their forcibles . . ."

Suddenly, the worry over what to do with wyrmling Dedicates was shoved to the back of Aaath Ulber's mind. There were more important tasks at hand.

Aaath Ulber pointed at the map. "I came to save human lives, not take them. There is only one way I can see to save the Dedicates. I'll have to go down and kill their guards, then work my way *up* the tunnels, slaughtering wyrmlings as I go."

Draken considered the plan. That would leave twenty thousand wyrmlings on the surface, wyrmlings that still had endowments, wyrmlings that would need strong men to fight them.

"We'll need several champions," Aaath Ulber said. It would be hard on these people to grant more endowments, but they would have to make the sacrifice. They'd have to scour the villages and farms nearby to find the needed Dedicates. "I'll want good men with a hundred endowments each to go down inside—to guard the wyrmlings' hoard of forcibles, to guard the Dedicates, and to help me keep any wyrmlings from escaping. . . . Afterward, they can help clear the wyrmlings on the surface."

Draken dared hope that he might be one of those who were granted endowments. He'd been in training with his father for weeks, practicing to kill wyrmlings. From the time that he was a child, Draken's father had prepared him for this.

Warlord Hrath sat frowning, considering the plan. "This is dangerous," he muttered. "If the wyrmlings on the surface get wind of what you're doing . . ."

"They would wipe out entire cities," Aaath Ulber declared. "They *will* wipe out cities, and there is little that we can do to stop them. But if the wyrmlings have as many forcibles as I suspect, we don't have time to come up with a better plan. With every moment that we hesitate, they get stronger."

Hrath shook his gray head. "A good plan is one that has a high chance of success—"

He was correct, of course. A new thought struck Aaath Ulber.

"If my guess is right," Aaath Ulber said, "the strongest wyrmlings are down underground right now, giving in to their breeding frenzy. The wyrmlings have no love in them, but at this time of year a wyrmling bull becomes like a stag in rut. Its neck swells, its eyes become bloodshot, and its mind goes cloudy. The bulls fight each other for the right to mate with a woman, even if there are a hundred other sows waiting for the honor.

"With them in such a state, I should be able to slaughter their greatest lords wholesale. That means that the ones on the surface, for the most part, will be the weakest of their men, culls."

Warlord Hrath shook his head. "And if you're wrong?"

"Then maybe we'll all die," Aaath Ulber said, trying to make light of the situation. "But then, we're all bound to die someday."

He raised his mug of ale in salute and laughed heartily. The barbarians of Internook were a violent people, given to war. Hrath raised his own mug, and Wulfgaard did the same, and men all around gave a cheer.

"So," Hrath asked, "you hope to kill all of the wyrmlings down in that hole?" The old warlord could not keep the edge of doubt from his voice. For one man to kill so many, tens of thousands, did not seem possible. Even a powerful runelord can make mistakes. Even Raj Ahten himself was bested by lesser men.

"I do," Aaath Ulber confessed. The giant rose to his feet and paced a bit, deep in thought.

Myrrima peered up at him, her sharp eyes piercing. "Even their children?"

"Every lion grows from a cub," Aaath Ulber said. "I cannot leave any alive."

"Are wyrmlings lions?" Myrrima asked. "You told me once that they may have come from human stock—just like you, just like me."

"They have no love, no sense of honor."

"Will you slaughter the babes in their cradles?" Myrrima asked. Gorge rose in Draken's throat at the thought. "Or will you bash in the heads of their toddlers? You want to protect us, and that is good," Myrrima urged. "But where does protection end and vengeance begin? Where does honor meet dishonor?"

Aaath Ulber stood deep in thought. His face was a mask of revulsion.

He is a ship that has lost its mooring, Draken told himself.

Aaath Ulber looked to Warlord Hrath for counsel. The warlord shrugged.

"Leave the babes and the children," Hrath advised, "any child smaller than a grown man. Perhaps some folks of Internook can take care of the babes. If any of the older children need to die, we'll take care of it."

Aaath Ulber sighed. "All right, I will spare the children that I can—and gladly. But I'd hoped not to do all of the killing with blade work. The wyrmlings often have the makings of smoke or water traps in their warrens. I'd hoped to use their own infernal devices against them."

"Blade work will be the only way," Hrath agreed.

Wulfgaard said evenly, "I want to be the one to guard our people in the underworld! My betrothed will be among the Dedicates."

Aaath Ulber whirled. "If our warriors get killed down there, you understand that you can't just let the Dedicates live. Our fallback plan must be to kill them all, to strip the wrymlings of their advantage. Could *you* do that?"

Wulfgaard gulped, hung his head. "I could kill them all but one," he protested.

Aaath Ulber peered hard at him and whispered, "That's not good enough."

Draken pondered. Could I do it?

Cold reason suggested that he should be able to.

I wish these people no harm, he told himself, but neither do I know them. I would care for no one down there, and I would spare no one. A man who gives an endowment to my enemy is my enemy, and his life is forfeit. Every man, woman, and child down there knows that.

"Perhaps I should be the one guarding the Dedicates," Draken suggested.

The giant Aaath Ulber stared hard at Draken, his brow furrowed in thought.

"The boy has a good point," Warlord Hrath put in. "It would be better if it was not one of our people down there, lest pity stay their hands."

"Draken," Rain argued, "you can't do this. You can't leave me behind. You have promises to keep."

She was right, of course. He too was betrothed, and he could not just forsake Rain. He didn't dare take the endowments of metabolism needed.

"I'll go," Wulfgaard said. "It's not your battle. I'll go, even if it means that I must kill my beloved."

The wyrmling patrol reached Ox Port at eleven that morning.

They were announced by the town guard, of course. A young man pitching hay from a loft on the hill began to sing:

> "Mother take your washing off the line,
> For a stranger comes to town.
> And much will vanish for all time,
> When a stranger comes to town.
>
> Beware the wanton look, the shifting eye,
> The hungry stares of the passersby.
>
> So, Father, bring your children near,
> If a stranger comes to town.
> For many are hurt that we hold dear,
> When a stranger comes to town."

It was the signal that wyrmlings had arrived, and Rain's heart began to hammer.

But Aaath Ulber took the news in stride. He glanced up toward the loft, and the young workman jutted his chin to the west, dropped his hand by his side, and held down three fingers.

"Looks like it's time to earn my keep," Aaath Ulber said, as he rose from his seat on the steps of the pub. He dusted off his pants and told Warlord Hrath, "I'll need some rope."

"You're going to try to take them alive?" Hrath's disbelief showed in his eyes.

Aaath Ulber grabbed a rock from the ground. It wasn't large, perhaps only a pound, but his intent was obvious. "Every time I kill one of those wyrmlings, it frees several Dedicates—and sends them to their deaths. There are better ways to handle our enemies."

He'd hardly finished speaking when the wyrmlings came round a bend, striding down the cobbled road in full war gear, bone-white armor and helms. Their heads swiveled back and forth as they marched through town. They were obviously searching for the wyrmling guards who were supposed to be watching the village.

Aaath Ulber walked toward them casually, head bowed. Few folks were on the street. They were all down in the bay, catching fish, cleaning them, salting them, preparing them to smoke.

So it was that Aaath Ulber sauntered up to the three. They bridled when they saw him, recognizing him for what he was, and one wyrmling looked as if he might turn and run for help.

Aaath Ulber merely stepped aside so that they could pass. The wyrmlings seemed confused by his actions.

They halted, not daring to turn their backs upon him. One glanced ahead, as if fearing that more men of Caer Luciare might bar the way, when Aaath Ulber attacked.

He leapt in a blur, fists raining blows upon his opponents, pummeling them with no weapon greater than a stone.

Aaath Ulber didn't have his full complement of endowments yet. He wanted twenty of metabolism, but the town had only seven forcibles left. The others had all been used up, and he wasn't likely to get more soon.

But his endowments proved sufficient. Within two seconds he knocked all three wyrmlings down. One had a split helm, another gushed blood from his eye.

Aaath Ulber relieved the monsters of their weapons. One of them kept struggling to get up, and Aaath Ulber kicked him hard enough to break a few ribs, and put him back down.

It took nearly half a minute for Wulfgaard to fetch some rope from the pub. Then the men bound the wyrmlings and a dozen volunteers helped drag them back to the arena, where Aaath Ulber locked them in cages that had been made to hold bears.

"Shall we kill them?" Warlord Hrath demanded.

Aaath Ulber merely smiled. "Kill them? I'm going to take endowments from them. The brawn of three wyrmlings is not easy to come by."

❧ 25 ❧

WATER'S WARRIOR

There are paths that lead to happiness, but few people tread them. Instead, they hope to find shortcuts, or imagine that happiness can be found wherever they decide to squat. But true happiness comes when we attain worthwhile desires, not when we merely surrender desire.

—*Myrrima*

A mile upriver from Ox Port, Myrrima climbed into a clear freshet and washed the weapons for the folks of the city. It was early morning still, just past dawn. She'd slept little during the night, yet somehow she felt renewed. The touch of water often lent her strength.

Birds were in the woods around her, flycatchers dipping to catch linnets that erupted like droplets of amber from a fallen alder across the river, and nuthatches and songbirds that chattered in mountain hawthorns.

The rune that she drew upon each club and blade was not one that had a name. She'd dreamt it once, long ago, in a nightmare where she battled a wight.

The dream had come on the heels of her own encounter with such a monster, an encounter that nearly left her dead.

The symbol that she drew was a rune for severing ties—ties to family, ties to friends, ties to the flesh, ties to the world.

Myrrima had never shown it to others. Things of such weight, she felt, were sacred. They came from the Power that she served, and were given only to her, to help her fulfill her purpose.

I am Water's Warrior, she told herself as she blessed the weapons, and I have been called to war.

She wondered what her part should be in the coming battles. Her own weapon of choice had been the yew bow, a good length of strong heartwood, mottled red and white, with a bit of cat gut for a string.

For her arrow, she preferred a medium-sized shaft, one thin enough to get good distance but light enough to travel far. If she wasn't fighting reavers, she'd want one with an iron tip that flared wide, a broad head that could sever arteries and slice through flesh.

She had not practiced her bow skills in weeks, not since the flood had taken her home. Indeed, she'd more or less given up on archery practice over the years.

She wondered now if she had done wrong.

Water had called her to war, but what part was she to play?

Perhaps all that I need to do is what I am doing now, she thought—blessing these weapons so that others may fight.

She'd dreamt that she had left war behind. She was at a point in life where her children were nearly out of the home. She'd hoped to plant herself in her little valley back in Sweetgrass and let the children grow around her, building their own cottages on the borders of her farm. She'd looked forward to playing with her grand-babies and passing down the lore of child-rearing to her children and their spouses.

But my life is at an end, she thought.

Borenson was gone, gone as completely as if he were dead. The last vestiges of him were hidden somewhere inside the giant Aaath Ulber, and by the end of the day, Aaath Ulber would take his death in endowments.

Twenty endowments of metabolism he required. With so many, he would live his remaining years in a flash. Two or three years he might survive, as measured by the seasons.

But during that time, he himself would move twenty times the pace of a normal man. Each day would seem stretched to him.

He's gone beyond my reach, she thought. What once remained of my husband has left me forever, traveling not across the far reaches of the land, but across time, where I cannot follow.

Such thoughts filled her mind as Myrrima washed each axe and spear, dagger and sword, and then set them in the sun to dry, with the rune side up.

The sun needed to dry the weapons. The runes would be spoiled if wiped with a human hand.

When she finished, she stood with the sunlight at her back, and peered down at the mass of blades. Hundreds of them lay spread out upon the ground, all of the weapons in the village of Ox Port.

Among them were many fine bows, and whole quivers full of arrows.

Is this all that Water wants of me? Myrrima wondered. Or dare I go to war?

Already, Myrrima's magic had saved them twice on this journey. She wanted to go into the wyrmling lair, to fight by Aaath Ulber's side.

Yet she knew that she didn't have the physical strength or speed for such an ordeal.

A horse whickered, and she glanced up to the road. A pair of young men sat in a wagon, waiting for her to finish. They looked to be fifteen or sixteen, about Draken's age. Bright, young, full of hope. Their future stretched out before them.

She shouted up to the boys, "Almost done. When these weapons are dry, we'll be ready to load. When you pass them out, tell the owners not to wipe the blades before they go into battle—and not to wipe blood off of them in the thick of it."

The young men nodded, and Myrrima went to a plain bow that looked to be fit for her size. She picked up an arrow from the ground, the gray goose feathers of its fletching still wet. She smoothed the fletching, nocked the arrow to the string, drew the bow to the full, and took aim at a knot on the tree.

The bow felt too strong for her. She could not aim it easily.

Or perhaps I am just too weak, Myrrima thought. A few days of practice, and my arm would grow used to it.

She let the arrow fly, and missed her knot by only an inch.

Myrrima looked up at the young men and thought of Sage, only fourteen years old.

If Myrrima was to go with Aaath Ulber that would mean she would leave Sage behind, a child abandoned by both of her parents. There was Draken and Rain, too, and Myrrima hoped to see Talon and Fallion, Jaz and Rhianna.

I am a mother, she realized. That is not a station that I dare abandon. I made a pact with my children before they were ever conceived, that I would be their champion, their bastion and hope. I promised to be their guide and companion.

Aaath Ulber was leaving, forging ahead down a path from which no man could ever return, and Myrrima decided to let him go.

He had not counseled with her or the children before taking his attributes. He had not explained his reasoning to her.

Perhaps he plans to say good-bye before he goes into the wyrmling fortress, Myrrima thought. He'd need to say his farewells to Draken and Sage and Rain.

Time to let him go forever, she thought, while tears streamed down her cheeks and she added her water to the ground.

❧ 26 ❧

A GATHERING OF HEROES

> *Heroes are not found in dreams and legends, but can be discovered all around us, walking down the very lane that you live upon. Look at the old man who labors mightily to gather firewood to warm his wife on a cold winter night, or the young woman who faces death to bring a child into the world. Heroism is not an anomaly, but the normal state of mankind.*
>
> —Gaborn Val Orden

The day seemed longer than normal to Draken. Young men went out in the morning, and by noon none had returned.

Then folks began to trickle into Ox Port. One old farmer carried a load of horse manure on a cart drawn by a reindeer, and when he gained the inn, he reached into the muck and brought out thirteen forcibles.

Not long afterward, other gifts began to arrive. A young woman came into town riding a donkey, her hooded green robe pulled low, looking tired and haggard. She had no sooner reached the inn than she threw off her robe and leapt from the donkey's back, vaulting high in the air.

She was a runelord who had taken endowments in secret, of course, come from some nearby city.

Other heroes from surrounding villages and cities began pouring in that evening.

None of them looked like the kind of men that Draken had expected. Each nearby town sent someone, but the warlords of Internook required only three things from their champions: First, the champions needed to be the most skilled warrior in his or her village. Among the runelords, great strength was not required, for with a single endowment of brawn a man wanting for strength could be made strong. Similarly, a man who lacked for dexterity could take endowments of grace, and those who were slow might have metabolism bestowed upon them.

So the warlords sought out those who had developed their fighting skills.

The second thing that the warlords required was self-sacrifice, for as Aaath Ulber told them, "All who fight this day will die." Oh, they might not die in battle, but they would be forced to leave behind families. Fathers who aged twenty years in a single season would leave their small tots behind, orphaning them.

For those who had raised their families, the sacrifice was less. So it was best if the volunteers had no loved ones at all.

But the truth was that the warlords were unwilling to give endowments to a hermit or a recluse, for they believed that a man who had no connection to others of his kind was imbalanced, and was likely to become a danger in the far future.

Last of all, the champion had to be strong of heart. He or she needed to be merciless, firm in conviction.

So the heroes were chosen—nine in all. The folk of Ox Port chose Wulfgaard as their champion, and as forcibles began to dribble into town, the old facilitator granted the boy endowments.

Of all the champions, only Wulfgaard was young and male. The rest were older men, past their prime. But they'd spent many years dueling with the ax and spear. Three of the four older men were masters of arms who had schooled younger men for war, and the rest of the champions were young women who had been trained as bodyguards, for all across the world, the blade women of Internook were considered to be among the finest of warriors and were often employed by the wealthy to watch over young maidens.

So the wyrmlings, who did not send women into battle, had not properly gauged the threat posed by the women of Internook.

By nightfall, more than one facilitator had "wandered" into town. Folks from nearby villages and cities also came, "to help harvest fish."

So the facilitators went to work, granting endowments all night long, hoping that they could bestow enough attributes upon their champions to put a stop to the wyrmling threat.

Long the facilitators sang into the night, while forcibles flashed white hot and left serpents of light in glowing trails.

Aaath Ulber coerced endowments of brawn from two of his captured wyrmlings, and took sight from the third, while the old facilitator in town managed to file down nine forcibles of will, granting one to each champion.

By night, folks sneaked into town through the woods. Most came only to gawk. The great champion had come in fulfillment of the wyrmling prophecy—rousing the hopes and fears of the barbarians.

The mood in town was like a festival, with folks

singing, celebrating, and dancing in the streets. The townsfolk were cooking fish over an open fire, and selling muffins and hot roasted hazelnuts.

Someone even brought out a pennant and ran it up a pole—the red flag of Internook with a white circle, representing the fabled Orb of Internook that Garth Highholm had carried to war against the toth.

Warlord Hrath forbade the playing of pipes or drums, for it was too dangerous. As Warlord Hrath complained, "Loud music will attract attention. We might as well blow our war horns and sound an alarm for our enemies!"

He could not stop the celebration completely. The joy in town was like a strong winter's tide, eroding the stones of despair on the beach, pulling them back in to deep waters.

Surely, Myrrima thought, this bodes ill.

Yet no wyrmlings came before dawn.

In the wee hours of the night, well before dawn, Aaath Ulber selected the weapons that he would take with him into the wyrmlings' lair. He carried his old war hammer, the one that High King Orden had bestowed upon him ages ago. Along with it he took various daggers and wyrmling war darts, and a bastard sword that was too small for him.

Then he went to his family to say good-bye.

"Stay here," he said. "Keep well. I will have little Hilde remain in the village to protect you all from harm, but you'll need to be on the alert for wyrmlings too. Long and bloody will be this day, before I return, and when I do, I myself will see to the cities and towns hereabouts."

"And if you don't make it?" Draken asked.

"You will know the moment of my death when my Dedicates arouse. If you see that happen, know that I loved you."

At that, Sage's eyes welled up. "Don't I get a choice in this?" she asked.

"Sometimes life doesn't give us choices," Aaath Ulber said, cupping a shoulder in each of his palms as he stared into her eyes. "The folks of Internook are looking for a hero, and apparently they think I'm the one to follow.

"So I must lead. And lest you forget, I had children on the shadow world. What has happened to them, I do not know, but I fear the worst—as I fear for all of our people."

Aaath Ulber clapped Draken on the back. "Be strong," he said. The young man had not been given a single endowment. But like his father, he was ready to fight wyrmlings with only the strength and talent he'd developed himself over the years.

Myrrima wondered how long it would take to clear out the wyrmling fortress. With twenty endowments of metabolism for each warrior, Aaath Ulber's champions should each be able to butcher a thousand wrymlings in an hour. But how many wyrmlings would be in that hole?

And what kind of man would Aaath Ulber be if he returned alive? She had seen Sir Borenson after he slew the Dedicates in King Sylvarresta's Keep. The deed had left him only half alive, wounded to the core of his soul.

She could not imagine that this would be any easier, though he argued that he could do it.

She peered hard at Aaath Ulber and asked, "Why is it that when you runelords want to save a life, you feel that you must take a life?"

Aaath Ulber said sadly, "There is no other way to free the Dedicates, as well you know."

At five in the morning, with the clear stars still glimmering above, the champions headed east toward the wyrmling fortress.

Even as they left, the facilitators kept up their songs so that attributes might be vectored to Aaath Ulber and his warriors.

❧ 27 ❧

THE DOOR

There is no door that can withstand Despair. It enters every heart, breaks down every wall.

—From the Wyrmling Catechism

The wyrmling fortress was Aaath Ulber's goal. He let Wulfgaard lead them on a run through the starlight, racing a hundred miles in less than two hours. The roads along the coast twisted among hills dark with stunted pines.

A little inland, farms graced the land, longhouses built among the hills. The folk of Internook all had a few milk cows and goats to supply for their family's needs, and so there were trails aplenty.

The champions wore no armor, so they ran swiftly and easily through the night.

Aaath Ulber marveled at the power he felt. He was growing old. A couple of months ago if he'd thought of rising from his seat, he would have weighed his options to decide if he really needed to move. His age, his lack of strength, his lack of energy—all had been an impediment.

But with his new endowments, he found himself moving freely. With brawn and stamina, he had more than enough strength and energy to perform any task that he needed. With an endowment of will, there was no barrier to his desire. To think was to move.

To think of running was to run. So Wulfgaard led the champions through the hills, where they raced as quietly as possible, avoiding branches that might lie in their path. They bounded over brush piles and rocks like wild deer.

Years ago, Aaath Ulber had borne enough endowments so that he knew what to expect. When running at a hundred miles per hour, the body is often tricked. To him it seemed that he was merely sprinting.

But when he crested a small hill, his body would sometimes take flight, so that he would find himself leaping forty or fifty feet before he touched ground once again.

Often as they ran, they spotted deer and foxes along their trail, fleeing for cover. But they seemed to move slowly, as if in a dream, and Aaath Ulber could have easily brought them down.

No one saw them as they ran in the predawn. Wyrmlings were about, but as Wulfgaard had promised, they kept to the towns and villages and main roads, guarding the vast majority of the human population. They were not worried that men might be racing through fields and hills by night.

It was said that sometimes the wrymlings sent out roving patrols, but Aaath Ulber's champions met none. Perhaps the troops only moved in daylight now, when humans were most likely to be abroad.

Or perhaps Aaath Ulber was lucky.

When they neared the wyrmling fortress, Aaath Ulber paused and sent two champions to guard the front door outside the pinnacle, to keep the wyrmlings from escaping. By then, the sun was cresting the horizon.

Then the remaining six champions raced off through the countryside, seeking the wyrmlings' hidden entrance.

Aaath Ulber merely sprinted into the rugged hills where he suspected that he might find a wyrmling trail, some fifteen miles west of the fortress, and followed his nose.

It is said that a hound dog's sense of smell is sixty times more powerful than that of a man. Aaath Ulber had taken endowments of scent from three dogs, and like a wolf that can smell blood on the wind at five miles, he caught the odor of wyrmlings easily enough.

The scent carried him down out of the mountains, into a steep vale. By the time that Aaath Ulber reached it, the sun had risen, casting its silver light among the blue-shadowed hills.

The land here was almost too rugged for homesteads, but Aaath Ulber found a couple of rustic shacks that had belonged to goat herders and woodsmen.

All of the homes were empty. The wyrmlings had swept through the valley, ridding it of anyone who might have witnessed their patrols marching along the river.

At one shack, a pile of human remains revealed the fate of the poor inhabitants. Human arm and leg bones were scattered about in the front yard, the last resting place of a young family, and tooth marks showed that the wyrmlings had gnawed them well.

The wyrmlings' scent led the champions to a shallow river, its bed graveled with rounded stones. Northern pines brooded along the shore, dark and stunted, growing so close together that a man could hardly walk through them.

The woods were soundless. No squirrels scampered up trees. No jays ratcheted. No stags bounded from the deep grass by the river and went leaping into the forest with their antlers rattling among branches. The only sound was the occasional clacking of a dragonfly's wing as it hunted along the reeds.

"We're getting close," Aaath Ulber whispered to his champions. "The smell is growing strong."

So the champions stopped and fed in silence, pulling rations from their packs—good white cheese with hard rinds, fresh bread, cooked fish that was still warm from the fires.

To an onlooker, it might have seemed as if they paused only for a minute there, but as Aaath Ulber's body measured it, it seemed close to half an hour that they rested.

He knew that his men would need their energy. The coming day would be long and bloody.

When he finished, the champions ran. They did not run on the land, but over the surface of the water. With so much speed, it was easy enough to do.

Aaath Ulber had always wanted to try such a feat.

The water held beneath their feet well enough, but it

was hard to get purchase, and harder still to change course. One tended to slide too easily, and stopping was all but impossible. It was much like running on ice, or upon spongy moss, but after a few moments, Aaath Ulber caught the hang of walking on water.

It required him to plan his turns. He could twist his feet a little, use the soles of his shoes to turn like a rudder. Starting required that he take little stutter steps, digging his toes into the pliant water, so that he splashed all of those who ran behind. To stop, he learned to dig his heels in, so that the resistance of the water slowed him.

As he splashed about, the water erupted beneath his feet in slow motion, the droplets hanging in the air like diadems.

All in all, he found water walking to be both a challenge and a joy.

The river gave a decent cover for the wyrmlings' trail, for the water washed most of their scent away, and the stones in the streambed hid most of their tracks. But on the banks of the river one could smell dung and urine among the pine needles and leaf mold. In some places in the river, one could see huge footprints, twenty inches long and eight wide, there along sandbars and the muddy shore where the wyrmlings had marched.

So Aaath Ulber and his heroes raced over the water, negotiating the ripples of rapids, moving faster when the channel deepened into still pools.

Here and there, large brown trout fed, rising to leave rings of silver on the surface, and Aaath Ulber recalled days in his childhood when he would have had nothing more pressing than to sit and catch one.

The river channel led straight into the wyrmling

fortress, three miles from where he'd joined it. The river itself poured out of a cavern in the rocks. The hole was tall and wide.

At the opening, the rock walls were covered with deep green moss. Tiny fairy ferns erupted from the cave wall in abundance, wild clover honeyed the air while a few wild blue mountain orchids on the riverbank gave off a scent like night and longing.

The party stopped for a moment, and Aaath Ulber sank into the water as they searched for any sign of wyrmlings in the woods at their side, or in the tunnel ahead. Aaath Ulber saw none, heard none. But he could not believe that the path ahead was unguarded.

He stopped, and the morning air was still and quiet, in the way that only the deepest woods can be. A strong wind tugged at his back, racing down into the cavern. It was as if the earth was inhaling endlessly.

"There is an old saying on my world about wyrmling fortresses," Aaath Ulber told the others. "'If it's easy to get in, it will be impossible to get out.' Beware, my friends: There are traps ahead."

"Should we light a torch?" one of the champions asked.

Aaath Ulber shook his head. "It will foul our air. The wyrmlings use glow worms to light the ceilings and fire crickets to spark on the floors. The white skin of the wyrmlings themselves is faintly luminescent. We should have enough light to see by, even to fight by."

Each of the champions had taken five endowments of sight, four of hearing. Aaath Ulber hoped that it would be enough to match the heightened senses of wyrmlings that had been raised in the dark for generations.

They raced into the long tunnel for nearly a quarter

of a mile, running now on the water again. The channel was narrow and deep, the water as cold as ice.

Overhead, limestone formations dripped minerals, bands of yellow and white. Bats squeaked and clung to the roof.

Suddenly, a quarter of a mile in, a wonder was revealed: Aaath Ulber slowed and looked up in amazement. The cave widened into an underground lake, and overhead a great roof opened, perhaps fifty feet up. Glow worms by the tens of thousands lit the ceiling, and as Aaath Ulber peered at them with his wyrmling's eyes, they seemed like constellations of stars glimmering in an eternal night.

Almost he dared stop, but the water was deep and he did not want to sink. So he merely slowed, plodding at perhaps eighty miles an hour, lost in glory.

The channel continued on, three more long miles, before suddenly it stopped. The river came cascading from a freshet above, and went churning off down the channel. But beside it was a wide roadway that had been carved with pick and awl—a tunnel.

The sour stench of wyrmling flesh issued from it, as if it was the lair of an old boar bear. Aaath Ulber could smell rotting flesh and bones.

He halted, raised a hand to warn the champions behind him. He could smell wyrmlings near, too near. He almost felt that he should be able to reach his hand out into the darkness and touch them.

He rounded a corner.

He expected a door here, a portcullis perhaps, or maybe a sliding wall of stone.

But the door before him was made of flesh. Wyrmlings stood guard, a wall of them: tall men with axes and battle hooks. They were broad of shoulder and great of belly.

They glowed faintly from their own inner light, and Aaath Ulber felt surprised that he could see so well by it. There were glow worms on the ceiling and walls, and now that there was a floor, a few fire crickets erupted in sparks at his feet.

The guards were not dressed like normal wrymling warriors. They wore no battle armor carved from bone, no ornate helms or shields. They wore only loincloths to hide their ugly flesh—and their war scars, hundreds of scars from the kiss of forcibles.

Their leader halted, raised his ax to bar the way. "Halt," he said in common Rofehavanish. "You cannot pass."

Aaath Ulber had suspected that the wyrmlings would have their Raj Ahten, but he had not expected to find one so soon.

Yet he saw not one champion, but five of the wyrmlings ahead.

"Are you sure of yourself?" Aaath Ulber asked. "Certainly you've heard of the prophecy?"

"You have entered the lair of the lich lord Crullmaldor," the wyrmling said, "from which no man has ever returned. She knows your plans. She sat in on your councils.

"Did you not see the crow on the roof across the street as you plotted our demise? She saw your maps, heard your plans. While your pitiful little facilitator secured a few endowments for you, ours granted us thousands."

Aaath Ulber hesitated. These wyrmlings were dangerous. Among the humans, Aaath Ulber had been the greatest of their champions in personal combat. But his people had numbered only forty thousand. If Aaath Ulber guessed right, there were more than forty thousand wyrmlings in this hole.

"Did you come to parlay with us?" Aaath Ulber demanded. "Or to fight?"

"Both," the wyrmling admitted. "Crull-maldor bids you turn away from here. The emperor is the one you want. He has your people in thrall, those who are left alive."

"I understand," Aaath Ulber said. "She doesn't dare try to kill him herself, so she wants me to do it."

"Yes," the wyrmling said. "Here is her offer: Turn away now, and she will let your Dedicates live. She will take no action against you.

"But if you forge ahead, she will punish you. She knows where your Dedicates are hid in Ox Port—every boat, every barn and cellar. Forge ahead, and they will not live out the day, for already our champions are at their doors!

"Nor will your wife Myrrima, your daughter Sage, or your son Draken survive the day. Forge ahead, and Crull-maldor will lay waste to your family and to all that you love."

Aaath Ulber froze in indecision, and could have stood wavering for a year. He knew well that he could not turn back. There can be no bargaining with wyrmlings.

To accept their offer was suicide.

Yet he worried that to go forward would cost him dear.

They're bluffing, he told himself, more from hope than certainty. And even if they're telling the truth, I dare not turn back.

This is the moment that every man dreads, Aaath Ulber realized. This is the moment when all of the future hangs in the balance. At the end of this fight, either these wyrmlings will be destroyed, or all that I have loved most will be gone.

He feared that both might be true, that he could not really win this fight.

There is a saying in Caer Luciare: Frustration is the father of wrath. A killing rage awoke in Aaath Ulber.

The berserker fury had always been strong in him, but now it came as a flame blossoms when the bellows blow upon it in the heart of a forge.

It was hot, furious. Aaath Ulber feared this wyrmling, for the creature knew too much about him. Certainly, the wyrmling's threats held an element of truth.

Yet Aaath Ulber roared a battle challenge, held his war hammer high, and rushed into the throng of wyrmlings at full speed.

Behind him, five heroes gave a battle cry and charged in at his back.

❧ 28 ❧

IN THE DEDICATES' KEEP

*Every man's life, no matter how illustrious or how cra-
ven, must come to a close. Much is made of the Earth's
power to protect, but the time will come when even the
Earth seeks to reclaim what once it owned.*

—*Gaborn Val Orden*

Dawn came silver and splendid to Ox Port, yet Myrrima's heart felt heavy with foreboding.

The sun rose; the cocks crowed and strutted about on
the streets and the roofs of the houses. The cows lowed
and begged to be milked; the birds twitted in the bushes
and sang their morning calls, the males warning one
another from their trees.

But this was not to be a normal day. A war was
about to erupt, furious and deadly. Myrrima could feel
it in the pit of her stomach, a cold dread that left her
guts and muscles in a tangled knot.

She took her borrowed bow and an arrow, and stood
at the margin of the road, waiting for . . . something.

Each time a crow cawed in the trees, or a horse whin-
nied, it set her on edge. The mood was infectious.

The celebrations died abruptly after Aaath Ulber and
his champions left, and everywhere throughout town,
men and women by some instinct began taking up defensive positions, just in case. Thus archers hid in the
lofts of barns, while men loitered in their doorways

with clubs and swords handy, everyone casting furtive glances up the roads.

The facilitators were still singing in the town square, adding attributes to the heroes by giving endowments to their Dedicates, thus vectoring more attributes to the champions.

There was a sense of urgency to their songs. War was about to break.

Myrrima studied the scene and wished that there was some spell that she could cast. But she was a water wizard, and there was little that she could do but summon a fog to blanket the town.

Almost without thought she did it, pulling clouds of mist in from the sea. At first the mists sparkled in the sunlight, but so great was her fear that the fog soon became great indeed, blocking out the rising sun.

Shortly after dawn, when Aaath Ulber had been gone for an hour, Myrrima whispered into the ears of Warlord Hrath. He peered at her skeptically for a moment, then nodded.

Hrath turned to the crowd, clapped his hands, and called for attention. "People," he shouted, "people of Ox Port, lend me your ears! We have an announcement—" He turned to Myrrima.

She stood in the cold gray fog, her face tired and expressionless. Yet there was an inner peace that burned in her eyes, like a glimmering pool. She said loudly and evenly, "All who wish to live, spit on the ground, giving water to the earth, and come to the great hall."

A single tear streamed down Myrrima's cheek and fell to the ground, her personal offering. She turned and marched east along the cobbled lane, heading toward the arena.

Warlord Hrath called to his people. "Go. She was a favored friend of the Earth King. Go with her. Take the Dedicates as well, all that you can find!"

So townsfolk came out of the mists bearing hundreds of Dedicates—all those who could walk or be carried.

Myrrima met the folks at the door, and splashed them with water from a bucket. "The waves wash you," she said as she sprinkled droplets over the head and shoulders of each person. "The sea secure you. May water make you its own."

She made sure that each person spit, and then bade the townsfolk enter.

As each person passed the threshold, a mist rose up at their feet and followed them into the arena, creating a dense fog.

It was not until Myrrima saw the Dedicates all herded together—blind and lame—that she realized just how many endowments had been given. More than eight hundred endowments had been granted in a town that hadn't had many more people than that in the first place. Obviously, most of the Dedicates were from nearby villages and farms. But even the hundreds of Dedicates that gathered in town did not make up the full score. Dozens were still on boats, far enough out from shore so that they could not be reached.

"Get our Dedicates all together," Warlord Hrath said. "They will be easier to protect if they're all in one place."

So the townsfolk made up beds down on the arena sands and in the tunnels. Men took up guard positions at the doors, and Warlord Hrath set their little champion Hilde up in the midst of the Dedicates. She was ringed by men and women who were blind and deaf.

Those who had given grace were curled in little balls, their muscles spasming with no way to relax. Those who had given strength had gone flaccid and weak. Those who had granted their wit had become morons, drooling creatures that leaked into their own britches and found joy in the warmness thereof.

The arena became a madhouse, a sick ward, while mists and fog floated among the torches.

Children ran rampant.

No sooner had the doors to the arena been bolted and a few torches lit in their sconces than a cry rang out.

Some who had granted endowments of metabolism and fallen into a magic slumber suddenly wakened. Some who were blind could suddenly see.

"Lord Theron is dead!" a man shouted. "My lord has fallen!"

By ancient custom, when a lord died in battle, any who had granted endowments of wit to him would tell the tale of his fall, for such Dedicates had shared memories of their lord's last moments and could often recall bits and snatches of their lord's demise.

Thus, two men and two women rose up and cried, "Theron is dead, long live his memory!"

No sooner than they had spoken, than other Dedicates began to revive, and cries rose up. "Lady Gwynneth has passed!" someone shouted. "Lord Brandolyn is gone!"

Too fast, Myrrima thought. Our champions are dying far too fast.

"They died in a cave," one man cried, "while wyrmling giants towered over them."

A small woman, old and frail, called, "They came,

runelords of great power—five in number, to bar our lords' way."

"They knew the name of Ox Port!" a young woman shouted. "They breathed out threats against the Dedicates here. They say that their champions are coming to take vengeance!"

"With a meat hook they grasped our Theron by the throat," a handsome young man shouted. "With an ax they felled him."

There was silence among the crowd, astonishment at the news, and Myrrima looked to Warlord Hrath. His eyes darted about as he studied the entrances to his arena, like a cornered animal.

"Our lord was a kind man," the first of the sages said. "His last thoughts were of his wife and family. His last fear was for our safety."

There was a deep silence during which Myrrima could hear her heart pounding and little else. She looked around the room. Draken had a nice long sword that Hrath had given him. Myrrima had a war bow and some arrows. Rain had a short sword, and Sage had nothing at all.

For long seconds, Myrrima waited for more of the Dedicates to revive, but none did.

Aaath Ulber is still alive, she realized. He has made it past the wyrmling guard by now.

But she knew that she could be wrong. He could have been knocked senseless, left bound and gagged. The fact that he was alive did not mean that he was safe.

In the Room of Whispers, Crull-maldor took reports of the enemy movements. "They're nearing the laboratories!" a voice shouted through one glass tube, while another warned, "They're in the butchery!"

The reports came so rapidly on the heels of one another that they made no sense. "Which is it," Crull-maldor demanded, "the laboratories or the butchery?"

But neither of her captains answered. By then, she surmised, both had been slaughtered, and now new reports issued from the communications tubes, a myriad of conflicting whispers.

The human champions were moving through the fortress with maddening speed; Crull-maldor could not keep up. In less than ten seconds they had cleared the butchery, she suspected, and spent another minute racing through the halls. It had been fifteen minutes since they'd breached the entrance.

"Drop all of the portcullises," she said. "That will slow them down."

The problem was that the humans had come in through the back gate and now were charging up through the warrens, level after level. The wyrmling horde could not use smoke to defend themselves from such an attack.

Though she might close the portcullises, each level was controlled from the level below. The humans would soon figure out how to open the gates above, and her tactic would barely impede their progress.

But that was all she wanted at the moment: to slow them.

Crull-maldor had not anticipated this attack. She had expected Aaath Ulber to be reasonable. Humans loved their families, would do anything to protect them. That much she knew.

Yet by his actions, Aaath Ulber had sentenced his own wife and children to death.

Already the humans had moved through much of
the lower tunnels, slaughtering thousands of wyrmling
women and children. Soon, they might reach her Dedicates' keep.

The humans would slaughter the Dedicates, of course.
It was the rational thing to do, and once the Dedicates
were gone, her wyrmlings would be left defenseless.

This man could destroy me, Crull-maldor thought. All
of my years of work will have been wasted. Lord Despair will punish me, drain my soul.

Crull-maldor did not know what happened to the
consciousness of a spirit once it died. There were two
kinds of death, the death of a body and the death of a
spirit. Despair knew how to kill both.

Yet it was whispered among the liches that life never
ended. At the death of the body, the spirit wandered into
its own world. At the death of the spirit, it was said that
the consciousness traveled beyond the spirit world, into
a realm of mist. There, life continued, but a life unfath-
omable to her.

She did not know if she believed in life beyond the
spirit world. She suspected that the death of her spirit
would be the end of her.

Crull-maldor considered whether to attack Aaath Ulber herself, but dared not try it. He moved too swiftly for
her now, and he bore weapons that could destroy even
a lich lord. But Crull-maldor was poised to put an end
to the threat. All that she had to do was kill Aaath Ulber's Dedicates.

This is just a race to see who can slaughter whose
Dedicates first, she reasoned.

Crull-maldor reached out with her consciousness
and touched the mind of one of her fell warlords, a

man named Zil, who had hundreds of endowments to his name.

She saw through his eyes: a wooded glen of dark pines, just outside Ox Port. He was upon a tall slope, looking down, and Crull-maldor could see a great wall of fog overtaking the village, rolling in from the sea.

With Zil's endowments of hearing, the sounds of the town came preternaturally clear: the shouts of children.

All around him, his troops hid, crouching motionless in the shadows.

"Take your runelords into the village," Crull-maldor whispered. "Now is the time. Cut down every human in the village."

Zil barked one short command to his troops. "Kill!" and the wyrmling runelords went leaping out from under the trees, racing toward town, silent and deadly.

The red haze melted from before Aaath Ulber's eyes gradually, even as he continued to fight. He leapt on the back of a falling wyrmling soldier, slit the man's throat, and rode him to the ground. Wyrmling women and children were crying out in terror, trying to flee. But the corridors ahead were packed, and they could not run fast enough.

Indeed, they were like a wall before him, a wall of flesh that blocked his own progress.

His arms ached from fatigue, as did his lungs and back. Great hunger assailed him, and he nearly collapsed, his head spinning from exhaustion.

Instead, he dropped to one knee and just squatted, gathering his breath.

"Aaath Ulber," Wulfgaard whispered. "Are you hurt?"

Aaath Ulber checked himself visually; he was drenched in blood. He wiped it from his eyes, felt it running down his arms and face like sweat. At first he thought that it was all wrymling blood, but then he noticed a pain in his right bicep. A wyrmling had caught him with a meat hook. There were smaller slashes on his chest, scoring through his leather jerkin, and scrapes on his face and knuckles. He had enough endowments of stamina to withstand such wounds, and he would heal from them by sunset, if all went well.

"I'm good enough," he said, as memories washed over him. He recalled the threats made against his wife and family, and his stomach knotted. Beyond that, everything was vague—charging through tunnels lit by glow worms, the sound of screams, wyrmlings dying at his hands by the thousands, mothers and children with heads cleaved by the ax, babes dashed against the floor. "I am well," he said in despair. "I am well."

His muscles were quivering, trembling. He turned and glanced at Wulfgaard. A warrior named Anya stood at his back. Both were covered in gore.

Behind them the passage was choked with bloody bodies, wyrmlings bathed in red, many of them still twitching or flailing their legs.

"Where are the rest of our troops?" Aaath Ulber asked.

Wulfgaard ducked his head, peered at the ground, and whispered, "They now ride in the Great Hunt, may their spears be sharp and their aim be true."

"We need to stop and eat," Anya begged Aaath Ulber. "You were the one who said that we should eat and rest every hour or two."

Aaath Ulber grunted. He felt weak and wasted. He'd never imagined a hunger that ran so deep. A runelord can fight for hours on end, but not without food. It takes energy, and already Aaath Ulber's fat stores were depleted.

Anya threw off her pack and pulled out some bread, roast chicken, and blueberries. It would take only a minute in real time for them to eat, to catch their breath. But in that minute the wyrmlings would have some time to regroup.

"How long was I out?" Aaath Ulber asked. "How long have we been fighting?"

"Five hours, I think," Anya said.

"Six, by my guess," Wulfgaard answered.

Time was a relative thing for them. Each had a different mix of endowments, and each had his own sense for the passage of time. Down here in the wyrmling hole, there was no sun to measure time by, only wild guesses.

Aaath Ulber had never been trapped in a berserker's rage for more than half an hour. But this time he had been gone for hours?

I am undone, Aaath Ulber thought. Taking that endowment of will was unwise.

Yet he could not undo the damage.

It was too long to have gone without eating, and so the warriors fed.

"Where have we been?" Aaath Ulber asked.

"Endless warrens," Wulfgaard said. "There are several tunnels that run parallel to one another. Most of them house workers. We found the breeding cavern. You were right, there were thousands of wyrmlings in it, but they were not . . . properly attired for battle."

Aaath Ulber had heard the rumors of course—naked wyrmlings driven mindless with lust. But no human had ever really witnessed such a thing. The tales all came from captured wyrmlings.

Aaath Ulber only vaguely recalled the sight—wyrmlings by the hundreds, naked and wrapped in one another's arms and legs, mindless in their breeding frenzy.

"Our main goal," he said, "should be to find their Dedicates."

After the Dedicates were secure, he didn't care what happened to the rest of the wyrmlings. He'd try to set fire traps, let the smoke smother the wyrmlings in the chambers above.

"They can't be far," Wulfgaard reasoned. "You can't hide a quarter of a million people down here."

Aaath Ulber agreed.

So they wolfed down their food and chugged their ale. No wyrmling dared to attack. The creatures were running up the tunnels, struggling to escape. They screamed and trampled one another, leaving dozens injured and dead in their wake.

It made for less work for Aaath Ulber.

Inside five minutes as Aaath Ulber's body measured time, he finished feeding. The others were not done yet, and he studied them. They were moving slower than he.

The folks in Ox Port know of our plight, Aaath Ulber realized. They're vectoring endowments of metabolism to me. I'm moving faster than my companions.

How much faster? he wondered. Twice as fast? No, he didn't feel that he was moving that much faster. But it seemed that he had more endowments of metabolism than the others, five or ten more.

He glanced at a fallen wyrmling woman lying nearby. Her tunic had been slashed in the back, revealing her pale skin. A pair of scars showed on her back.

Aaath Ulber pulled at the fabric, ripping it, to display the scars better. Runes of metabolism had been burned into her flesh.

"All of them have endowments," Anya said, "even the babes."

Aaath Ulber took out a stone and began to sharpen the spikes on his war hammer, expertly pulling the oilstone at an angle.

He pondered the implications of wyrmling babes and mothers taking endowments of metabolism. An entire wyrmling hive living at three times the speed of a normal man? What would it lead to?

He imagined miners hauling ore from the ground at three times the normal rate, and smiths hammering out blades. He imagined babes growing at three times the normal speed, while mothers spawned two or three wyrmlings in a single season.

The implications were enormous. They'll outwork us, outbreed us. They'll create . . . a society that will overrun ours.

What had Gaborn said? "Their armies will sweep through the heavens like autumn lightning?"

And it would cost the wyrmlings virtually nothing. One does not have to feed a Dedicate who has given an endowment of metabolism. One does not have to give him drink or worry about his escape. Such folk simply fall into a magic slumber until the day when their master dies.

It is said that those who give endowments of metabolism still breathe, but it happens so slowly that Aaath

Ulber had never seen it. It is said that their blood still flows. But their rest is like hibernation, except that their sleep is deeper than that of any bear.

It took nothing to maintain such folk. All that you had to do was to make sure that the rats didn't gnaw at their flesh. A few rat terriers in the Dedicates' Keep handled the job.

The monumental horror of the wyrmlings' scheme struck him.

The only way that such a society could exist was if the wyrmlings continued to take endowments from the humans.

They'll take metabolism from us all, Aaath Ulber realized. That's what they're doing here on Internook: taking endowments as fast as their facilitators are able. They each have two endowments now, but in a week they'll each have three, then four or five. Where does it all stop? When the wyrmling cows are dropping nine of their calves a year, or ten?

In a month, he realized, we could reach that point. In three months, the wyrmlings could each have fifty endowments or more.

His people would not be able to compete against such monsters. There would be no war—not even a hope of war—not if a wyrmling child matured to adulthood in a single year and spawned a dozen more of its kind!

He looked to Anya and Wulfgaard in alarm, speechless.

"Yes," Wulfgaard said. "We see it, too. We found their armory, where they carve armor from bones. They use reaver horns to make their awls. The children were making armor for themselves, the women too. The whole wyrmling nation is preparing for war."

"What did you do to the children?" Aaath Ulber asked.

"We left the smallest of them alive," Wulfgaard said, "as planned. I didn't know what else to do."

With an edge of hysteria to her voice, Anya said "They'll put us all to the forcible. They'll take metabolism from each of us—from every man, woman, and child."

There were four million people in Internook. Aaath Ulber had imagined that he had enough barbarians to defeat the wyrmlings. But now he considered how the wyrmlings might see them. These four million people weren't rivals, just cattle ready to be slaughtered. Four million people were not foes, they were potential Dedicates.

The wyrmlings' plan was so diabolical that Aaath Ulber felt sickened. He realized something else. Thousands of men and women on the island had been forced to grant endowments to the wyrmlings' children, and those men and women could not be freed until the wyrmling children were dead. This bloody task would fall to him. The very thought of slaughtering babes—even wyrmlings—nearly left him unhinged.

Killing innocents, Aaath Ulber considered. Is this the subtle trap that Lord Despair has set for me?

How can a man slaughter a babe without doing irreparable harm to his soul?

Aaath Ulber closed his eyes. Will I be a hero if I do what must be done? Or will I become food for a wyrm.

He could see no way past this.

I'll have to go back and kill the children and babes, he realized.

But before I become food for a locus, he vowed to

himself, I will strike a blow against the wyrmlings from which they can never recover!

Aaath Ulber finished sharpening his blades and then leapt to his feet. "We must find the wyrmlings' Dedicates' keep," he said solemnly. "We cannot rest again until we have claimed it."

Wulfgaard's eyes flashed to Anya, as if asking if she would be up to the challenge. As one the three gave a cry and set off.

Aaath Ulber led the way, racing through the warren's tunnels. Some wyrmlings were on the floor, trampled and wounded. He left them to the care of Wulfgaard and Anya, and considered: He was searching for Dedicates, and housing a quarter of a million would be hard under normal circumstances. But a sleeping body doesn't require much space.

So he ran ahead, rounded a corner, and spotted citizens fleeing.

But off to his right was a wide side tunnel, and in some dim recesses he glimpsed a brilliant white light.

Aaath Ulber wheeled and raced down the tunnel, into a broad chamber. The limestone ceiling was hung with stalactites. Water was seeping along the walls, leaving the room humid.

Aaath Ulber felt a cool chill, the presence of wights. His breath came out as fog, and ice fans glinted on the ceiling. Across the room he spotted forty or fifty shadowy wights wearing nothing but shimmering black spider cloth.

Some began to whisper and hiss as they cast hasty spells.

He reached to his belt and pulled out some wyrmling war darts—heavy iron darts that weighed roughly a

pound each. He tossed four at once, letting them fan
out across the room.

The war darts screamed into the wights' ranks, ripping through robes and vaporous flesh.

A dozen wights shrieked at their touch, giving off a
piercing wail. A foul green-black cloud erupted as the
creatures unraveled. The cold iron blessed by Myrrima's
spells made for a fatal combination.

Several wights lunged toward a far door. Aaath Ulber pulled a dagger and hurled it into the crowd.

Two wights erupted in a foul smoke, while others
rushed away.

He raced into them, drew his longsword, and danced
among them, taking them with ease, careful not to let
one touch him.

He felt a cold wind at his back, whirled to find a
wight floating toward him, shadowy hands extended.

Aaath Ulber slashed at it, and the wight exploded into
noxious fumes. A cold wind seemed to drive through
Aaath Ulber, freezing his heart, but the wight was gone.

He whirled and peered about. He could not see any
more of the wights, but he wondered how he'd missed
that last one.

They could be tricky. A wight must hide from light
by day, but any shadow will do—a snake hole or the
crack under a rock. They can fold themselves into ex-
tremely small spaces.

Nowhere in this room was safe.

He studied the room: it was a laboratory where wyrmling sorcerers worked. There were iron spikes on one
table and crucibles filled with vile secretions nearby.
The wyrmlings had been making harvester spikes here.

Over on one wall hung a pair of artificial wings, in the process of completion. The bones of the wings looked to be carved from the bones of a world wyrm, but the wights had stretched the skin of a graak over their frame, and now long pipes made from arteries and veins climbed the wall like vines and carried blood to the wings, so that they might grow. The heart of some large creature was lying in a wooden tub half full of blood, pumping nutrients to the wings.

All of this Aaath Ulber took in during a single glance, but one thing above all caught his attention: a cloudy white orb that sat on a table, emitting a flickering light.

"The orb!" Wulfgaard called. "The Orb of Internook!"

Aaath Ulber did not know whether to believe it. He didn't trust such luck. The orb was a thing of legend, a relic said to hold tremendous power.

Erden Geboren himself had brought it from the netherworld in ages past and had bestowed it upon one of his friends.

But as with all relics, thieves had sought it. Hundreds of times over the centuries the orb had disappeared, only to be recovered a few decades later.

As far as Aaath Ulber knew, it had not resurfaced in the past century.

"Is it," Anya asked, "is it real?"

Aaath Ulber approached the thing, peered into it. The ball looked to be of clear crystal, shot through with clouds. But the clouds inside the ball swirled slowly, much as clouds will float on a summer's day.

If it isn't the Orb of Internook, Aaath Ulber thought, it's something equally as mysterious.

He glanced around the room, spotted dozens of artifacts in the making. He recognized all of the other wyrmling creations, but had never seen anything like this.

"It's the orb, all right," Wulfgaard said. "See, it sits upon a human cloak. The wyrmlings were afraid to touch it. So they brought it here to study."

Aaath Ulber peered down. A rich green cloak with hems of cloth of gold served as the resting place for the orb; the cloak had a gold cape pin upon it shaped like a hawthorn leaf. It was something that a fat lord might wear.

"The wyrmlings have been raiding our homes," Anya said, "taking everything of value—gold, weapons."

"Well," Aaath Ulber said, "it looks as if they found something better than gold."

He leaned close and studied the orb, saw that its surface was inscribed with fine lines—graceful runes that danced along the surface. But he'd never seen runes like these.

He grabbed the orb, wrapping the cloak over it protectively, and hefted it.

The orb sparked when his finger grazed it, sent out a pulse of bright light. The air crackled from static electricity as fiery butterflies whirled about him, then dove into his flesh. His muscles cramped and burned at their touch.

"It punishes you," Wulfgaard said.

The orb was not enormous. It seemed to be a foot across. But as Aaath Ulber bundled it tightly in the robe, he felt the ball shrink at his touch, as if fleeing from him.

In a moment it was only four inches in diameter, and it went as black as night.

"What did you do?" Wulfgaard demanded.

"Believe me," Aaath Ulber said, handing the thing off to Anya, who immediately pulled off her pack and began to stuff it in, "I have no idea what I'm doing. But we don't have time to figure out this mystery now."

"There are tales of the orb calming the seas for our warships—" Wulfgaard said.

"And hurling storms against enemy fortresses," Aaath Ulber said. "If you can figure out how to unleash a storm against this fortress, be my guest."

Anya whispered, "Tellaris used it to guide her daughter's spirit back from the land of the dead."

Aaath Ulber knew strange legends about the orb. There were hints of a curse. Too often those who sought to own it wound up dead.

Of course, he thought, the same could be said of any man who owned a fine horse, too. The world was full of thieves who would gladly slit your throat for something like this.

"Move on," Aaath Ulber ordered. "We've got to find those Dedicates, and time is wasting. . . ."

"Myrrima," Rain said, her face filled with concern, "I think that I should row out to the *Borrowbird*. A battle is coming. Sage should go with me. It will be safer there."

Rain's heart pounded. The revived Dedicates had warned that wyrmlings knew the name of Ox Port. That meant that they would be here soon. A man with ten endowments of metabolism could easily run sixty miles an hour. At such a speed, the wyrmlings couldn't be more than an hour and a half away. Probably, they would be here much sooner.

Can we even make it? Rain wondered.

Fleeing sounded like a good idea right now—not just for Rain, but for all of them.

"Won't you come with us, Mother?" Sage asked.

Myrrima smiled grimly and shook her head. With a jut of her chin she motioned toward the collected Dedicates. "I can't," she explained with infinite sadness. "These are your father's. Someone must protect them."

There was a runelord guarding the room, the young woman Hilde. But Rain understood what Myrrima meant. She couldn't just leave the Dedicates in a stranger's care.

Draken growled and drew his sword. "Nor can I leave."

Rain studied his face, so full of resolve.

"Aaath Ulber is not your father," Rain pointed out to Draken. "You don't owe him your life." She pleaded with Myrrima, "Nor is he your husband."

"You're right," Myrrima said. "Perhaps there is only a tiny piece of Borenson left in him, a small corner of Aaath Ulber's mind. But even if he is only a ghost of a memory, I must remain faithful to him. I know that now."

"As must I," Draken said.

He gazed into Rain's eyes, and there was so much pain in his gaze, so much concern. "Please," he said. "If you must go, go!"

Sage wept and she threw her arms around Myrrima, gave her a hug. She came to a decision. "I want to stay, too, Mother."

Rain glanced toward the door in a near panic. Time was wasting. She admired the family's dedication to one another, but she didn't want to die for Borenson's memory.

Myrrima looked at her daughter Sage; the love in her face had grown fierce. "Stay with us then. We can all watch your father's back together."

They'll die trying to save what is left of Sir Borenson, Rain realized. She wondered if Borenson had indeed been such a great man. Was he, or anyone, worth such a sacrifice?

A distant cry rose from far down the street, a woman's wail of fear and pain. The wyrmlings were coming.

Rain didn't trust Myrrima's magic. It was said that water wizards had uncanny powers of protection, but they were not foolproof. A powerful mage could see right through the wizardess's ruse, as could a person with a strong and focused mind.

Some folks in the arena cried out in alarm, they glanced about in a panic, as if seeking the closest exit.

Myrrima stood at the door and blocked their escape. "Hold!" she called. "No one may leave. The enemy is here already. They are searching the town. We are hiding, hiding in a mist of our own making. No enemy can find us here. Avert your eyes from your enemy, and they shall avert their eyes from you! They will not see you!"

Before she finished her last words, there was a boom at the door to the arena. A wyrmling ax cleaved through it, shattering the wood and creating a wedge of light.

Myrrima whirled to face the threat.

Faster than a heartbeat, a second blow rang upon the door, and then a third; the wreckage of the door flung open.

A huge bull wyrmling stood for an instant, glaring into the arena.

Children gulped in terror.

Myrrima faced him. She looked down to the floor, and the wyrmling's eyes followed.

The wyrmling was breathing rapidly. A dozen endowments of metabolism he had to have had.

The wyrmling bull peered about the room, and his eyes seemed glazed, unfocused, as if he wandered through a waking dream.

Suddenly a cry rang out in the arena. One of the Dedicates had awakened, and she called out in a wail, "Alas, our lady Anya has fallen in battle!"

Rain stifled an urge to curse and brought her short sword ringing from its sheath as she waited for the wyrmling to charge.

Aaath Ulber roared in pain as a wyrmling runelord's ax sliced into his scalp, chipping bone from his skull.

The blow knocked him back a pace, and he staggered, head reeling. He tried to find his feet.

He'd reached the Dedicates' keep. Unfortunately he'd found the wyrmling guards, too—enormous bulls who were scarred by hundreds of forcibles.

One of them rushed into the breach and lunged with a meat hook, snatching Anya from her feet. She writhed and her bright blade flickered forward like the tongue of a serpent, but the huge meat hook had caught her in the back of the neck. The wyrmling shook his fist, and neck bones snapped. Anya's head lolled crazily.

The wyrmling hurled Anya against the wall as Wulfgaard gave a battle cry. The boy lunged with his own sword and plunged it beneath the wyrmling's arm, so that it ran up the bone and bit deep into the creature's armpit. Hot blood erupted from the wound, and Wulf-gaard danced backward.

Aaath Ulber charged, knocking the dying guard away, and saw Dedicates ahead. In the dim light thrown by ten thousand glow worms on the roof high above, he saw men and women stacked like cordwood, three or four deep.

Alarm bells had begun to sound, huge gongs that tolled solemnly. The wyrmlings had tried to slow Aaath Ulber down by closing the portcullis gates, but he'd spotted gear boxes below, and soon discovered that he had to open each box in order to clear the level above.

But he'd found the wyrmlings' treasure.

The room was filled with Dedicates. Many were still sleeping, but others were now awake—men and women freed from their endowments.

Unfortunately, the keep was also filled with wyrmlings. The wyrmling workers were trundling about with great swords, taking the heads off of anyone unfortunate enough to rise.

Bodies lay thick on the floor.

With a rush of bloodlust, Aaath Ulber buried his war hammer into the chest of a wyrmling runelord, then leapt in the air and kicked the head off another.

The path opened.

Wulfgaard rushed into the room, eager to find his betrothed.

Aaath Ulber glared at the wyrmling workers, so intent on slaughtering the Dedicates as they woke, and a red curtain lowered in front of his eyes.

With an animal howl, he waded in among the dead and rushed the wyrmlings.

* * *

Warlord Zil stared uncomprehendingly into the humans' arena at Ox Port. It was a strange building, with thick walls all around but open to the sky.

Inside, hot springs rose from the ground in an emerald pool, with roiling mist rolling off in waves.

A few beech trees grew beside it, and wild birds flitted among the branches, chirping and singing.

Zil wondered at it. It looked like some kind of sanctuary, a walled bath where a human lord might soak beneath the trees and meditate.

Or perhaps the barbarians performed sacred rites here, made some sort of offerings to Water.

There were trees, he saw, but there was no place to hide. The bath was empty.

He heard a cry of alarm. Almost it sounded like a human voice, and he turned his head. At last he realized that it was only the warning bark of a tree squirrel.

The wyrmling bull sniffed the air like a dog trying to catch a scent, and Draken waited for him to charge.

Suddenly there were cries down the street. The wyrmlings had found some more victims. The wyrmling whirled and disappeared, blinding in his speed.

Other wyrmlings flashed by, half a dozen runelords at least, and few spared more than a glance into the arena.

Cries rent the air all through town as the wyrmlings took those who had remained in their houses.

But the death brigades passed by the arena—and the vast majority of the townsfolk.

Silence fell over the village, and a minute later the town's facilitator called out, "More endowments for

Aaath Ulber! Who will grant him speed for his journey this day?"

The rest of the facilitators also began to cry out, hoping to heap endowments upon Aaath Ulber in his moment of need.

In the Room of Whispers, Crull-maldor learned the bad news.

"The humans are gone?" she cried.

Captain Zil stood at the far east end of the village. His men had made their sweep. She could see through the captain's eyes as the men finished searching some longhouses, then peered off to the woods.

"The smell of humans along the roads is strong," Zil explained. "We think that they might have fled into the countryside.

"We have been through every house, every shop. The humans are gone."

Crull-maldor took the news and tried to remain stoic. The humans had already taken her Dedicates' keep. She could not hold them off.

Alarm bells were tolling. Her wyrmlings were fleeing the lower levels, seeking to escape through the main entrance. Her own people were opening the portcullises now, retreating mindlessly.

But the front gates were guarded too, and human runelords there slaughtered anyone who tried to escape.

Crull-maldor considered her options. "The humans cannot have gotten far," she said. "Search the woods to the east. Perhaps they have escaped to the next town."

With that, Zil and his wyrmling runelords bolted off

to the east in a vast line, sweeping the woods for any sign of the fleeing humans.

Crull-maldor broke off communications. Her wyrmling champions had been slaughtered, and she suspected that in a few moments, the humans would execute her Dedicates, weakening her grasp upon the island.

Dozens of her lich lords were already dead.

More importantly, the humans would find her forcibles there in the Dedicates' Keep, at least ten thousand of them.

She was only glad that there were not more. Lord Despair had promised to send them, but none had reached her yet.

I am undone, she thought. There is nothing left for me to save.

She had offered Aaath Ulber a trade, and he had refused. He had betrayed her hopes.

She took little comfort in the knowledge that Aaath Ulber would destroy the emperor.

Still, she thought, when the emperor is gone, I may manage to win his place.

The hope was faint, and even as the thought came to her it dwindled to nothing. No, she could not believe that she'd take the emperor's place any longer. Only one thing was left to her. She promised herself: Aaath Ulber . . . I shall take my vengeance.

THE LICH'S TOUCH

A winter's night in Internook is as cold as a lich's touch, and just as likely to take your life.

—*A saying of Rofehavan*

In the Fortress of the Northern Wastes streams of blood spilled down the hallways where corpses formed small dams and diversions.

After the Dedicates' keep was cleared of its wyrmling assassins, there was no one left to stop Aaath Ulber.

A cask of forcibles he found there, ten thousand, all stored in a box hewn from granite. It was a great treasure, enough to endow powerful champions, and Aaath Ulber dared hope that it might be the key to saving mankind.

Yet the wyrmlings were still strong. More than a hundred thousand Dedicates lay in a slumber.

Aaath Ulber stopped at the door while young Wulfgaard searched among the Dedicates for his betrothed. He found her at last, lying facedown upon the floor in a puddle of her own blood.

Wulfgaard flipped her onto her back. Her face had gone white, drained, but blood stained her lips.

A rune of metabolism had been branded upon her forehead. It sat in a circle, a shapeless mass that somehow still pulled at the mind, begging to be recognized.

She must have wakened, Aaath Ulber thought, when we slew the wyrmling that took her endowments.

Wulfgaard lifted her in both arms, then peered up to the roof of the cavern and let out a long wail. He held her body high, as if begging the world to bear witness.

There will be no winning this war for that lad, Aaath Ulber thought. He might take vengeance, he might kill the wyrmlings, but that will be the end of it.

Aaath Ulber gave him a few minutes to sob and to mourn, as measured by his body. But in that time the sun had moved less than a minute in its journey across the sky.

The moment was used in preparation. Aaath Ulber threw away some of his blades, and sharpened some wyrmling weapons.

As he did, he planned how to finish it.

The wyrmling fortress was designed much like an ant's nest. The lower opening, well hidden, let air vent into the warrens.

But the wyrmling bodies heated the atmosphere, so that warm air rose up through the tunnels—to finally escape at the upper entrance.

Killing the wyrmlings now would be an easy matter. All that Aaath Ulber needed to do was clear out the upper tunnels. He knew that the wyrmlings here defended their fortress with firetraps, and suspected that he would find such traps hidden on the floors above him. All he'd have to do was light them, and let the smoke carry death through the tunnels above.

Aaath Ulber ate his lunch, rested. Half an hour he gave himself. He needed no more than that. He had enough endowments of stamina so that he would no longer require sleep. Instead, he only stood as runelords do, staring away at some private dream.

With so many endowments of wit, he found that remembering was easy. Even incidents that had occurred before he'd taken his endowments seemed to be easily recalled.

So he stood in that room of death, eating a bit of cheese and bread from his pack, lost in a fond memory.

He recalled the first time that he'd met his wife Myrrima, in a small city in Heredon. She'd taken endowments of glamour from her sisters and her mother back then, endowments that had been all but impossible to purchase.

Thus, she'd combined the beauty and poise of four gorgeous women into one. Her hair had been dark and silky, and the pupils of her eyes were so dark they almost looked blue.

The sight of her had left him speechless with desire. He'd wanted to know her name. He'd wanted to hold her hand and walk with her.

But it was his lord, Gaborn Val Orden, who had introduced them, and had suggested that they marry. It was a strange moment, one that always left him with wonder.

Why did Gaborn do that? Aaath Ulber asked himself. It wasn't part of Gaborn's nature to go about acting as a matchmaker.

Gaborn himself claimed to have done it by inspiration. He'd felt that it was the Earth's will.

But why? How has our union benefited the Powers?

He could not be certain. He often felt that some grand destiny awaited him and Myrrima, but he knew not what.

Perhaps that destiny will not be borne out by me but by my children, he suspected.

Or perhaps the great deed is already accomplished. Myrrima and I protected both Gaborn and Fallion in their youth. We nurtured them, kept them safe from assassins. That deed was well done.

Yet he wanted something more. He wanted to know the very moment when he fulfilled his destiny.

Perhaps it would not be some great thing that he accomplished. Perhaps it would be a deed so insignificant that mortal men would not even note it.

He turned his mind from the thought. Nothing could be gained by pondering such things, and he feared that in doing so, he might be giving sway to false pride.

So he focused instead on the memory of Myrrima, as fair as a rising moon, as brilliant as a diamond. An old man's voice whispered in his mind.

> "I'm growing, I'm growing old.
> My hair is falling and my feet are cold."

Aaath Ulber woke, feeling invigorated. He judged that half an hour had passed by his body's time, and that was enough.

"Let's finish it," he called to Wulfgaard.

The young man knelt on the floor beside his betrothed. Tears streamed down his face, and a terrible rage filled his eyes.

I don't even know the girl's name, Aaath Ulber thought. I guess that it doesn't matter anymore.

Wulfgaard jerked his head toward the sleeping Dedicates. "Maybe we should kill the rest. Who knows what the wyrmlings are doing, or what they're capable of?

How many heroes might they have up on the surface? They could be laying entire villages to waste. And you and I are the only two men left down here to stop them."

That was the crux of the problem. Aaath Ulber's gut warned him that this battle hadn't been won yet. A lich can communicate across the leagues. The lich lord Crull-maldor knew that he was here. She'd warn her captains, and the wyrmlings would attack the cities and village on the surface.

The only way to stop them was to kill their Dedicates.

Aaath Ulber had rejected that plan once before. But he'd hoped to have more champions with him still. Now he recognized that he was walking on the edge of a knife, and he did not know which way he would fall.

"I didn't come down here to murder Dedicates," Aaath Ulber argued.

"I've sworn to clean out these warrens, and let the folks aboveground worry about themselves."

Wulfgaard glared. Aaath Ulber could see that he wanted vengeance, and he believed that the only sure way to get it was to slaughter their Dedicates.

"Are you weary of battle?" Aaath Ulber goaded him. "Are you so tired of fighting?"

"No!" Wulfgaard denied.

"The best way for you to get your vengeance," Aaath Ulber said, "is to kill the wyrmlings—not your own kind. I'm sure that many of the young ladies down here are betrothed to others. Would you do to their men what the wyrmlings have done to you?"

Wulfgaard looked fierce. Rage and pain had left him on the edge of madness. He refused to answer.

"Let's do this the hard way," Aaath Ulber said. He

wanted Wulfgaard to go out and slay wyrmlings, but he knew that they couldn't leave these Dedicates unguarded.

Aaath Ulber was the better warrior. That meant that he'd have to clear the warrens, leaving Wulfgaard here to watch over the Dedicates . . . and fester.

"You stay here with your betrothed," Aaath Ulber said. "Make sure that your actions honor her."

With that, he turned and plunged into the wrymling tunnels.

The next hours seemed to be a nightmare, with Aaath Ulber slaughtering all that came his way. He spared no one, and only one time did a wyrmling give him pause.

He was in the crèches, where wyrmling women tended their babes. He was forced to slaughter them all, the children as well as adults, for to leave the young ones alone, without adults to tend them would be to protract their deaths.

As he raced into a small side cavern, a woman who was tending a dozen toddlers whirled and spoke to him in Rofehavanish, with a strange Inkarran accent. "Please?" she begged.

He halted, expecting her to say more, but she seemed not to know any more Rofehavanish.

He wondered where she had learned that word. While tending the Dedicates? Or was she like him, two people united in one body?

He thought to ask her, but the answer would not alter what had to be done, so he slit her throat and moved on.

The cries of the dying followed Aaath Ulber into the Room of Whispers, where he halted, and stood warily.

All around him, he could hear voices—wyrmlings

crying in pain, wyrmlings shouting orders, the distant tolling of bells.

The room was empty now, a simple dome. Three glow worms on the ceiling provided a dim green light, and all around the room were little silver rings pounded into the stone. Glyphs surrounded each ring, and a hole in the center let sounds escape.

Through the holes, Aaath Ulber heard the whispers.

A cold chill shot up his spine. He whirled, expecting to find a lich at his back. A whisper came from one of the holes, some wyrmling commanders shouting to a panicked crowd, "Get back! Get back to your holes. There is no escape!"

The floor beneath him vibrated to the sound of a gong.

The room was chill.

He peered up, found the hole where the sound had come from. The ring around it was marked with the three glyphs—the Eater of Souls, the number two, and the naked skull.

Aaath Ulber's breath fogged from the cold, and he whirled again.

A wight was nearby. Nothing stood in the entrance.

He spotted a bit of glittering spider cloth on the floor and slashed it with his sword, lest the wight be hiding in its shadow.

Then he whirled again. "Show yourself!" he commanded.

A whisper came to him from one of the holes above. "You have seen me before," a wyrmling said in the tongue of the men of Caer Luciare.

"I know you," Aaath Ulber shouted, "Crull-maldor."

It was said that there is power in knowing a lich's true name, but Aaath Ulber did not feel powerful.

"Alas," the lich wailed in mock sorrow, "you know my name!" She chuckled softly, and the sound of her voice faded. Aaath Ulber knew which tube it was coming from, and he pulled a war dart, jammed the barb up the hole.

A moment later, he heard the whisper again issuing from another hole on the far wall. "You have touched me," Crull-maldor said. "You have pricked me deeply, and now I shall prick you."

Aaath Ulber whirled, for he felt a cold wind brush his back. But there was nothing there.

She's trying to get behind me, he reasoned. She'll come out from one of her damned holes. But which?

In the protracted silence that followed, he knew that she was moving, racing through dim hallways, struggling to take him unawares.

He began to circle nervously, his head swiveling this way and that, as he searched for a shadow that would rise behind him.

He caught a dark blur in the corner of his eye, whirled, and saw a mist rising into one of the holes.

"Come out here!" he roared. "Let us finish it now!"

"What is the hurry?" the lich asked reasonably, her voice a dim whisper from the far corner of the room. "They say that vengeance tastes sweetest when it is served stale."

Aaath Ulber circled slowly, whipped his blade behind him in a dance.

A whisper came from a tube. It was distant, so dim that a man without endowments could never have heard it. "Watch your back, little man. I shall touch you yet. In an hour when you are less watchful, in a way that you do not suspect, I shall freeze your heart. . . ."

Aaath Ulber hesitated, waiting for the lich to return, but the room began to regain warmth, and he felt certain that it was gone.

It would be hiding from him somewhere, coiled like an asp beneath some stone.

He turned and raced from the room, up a corridor. The level above was empty of wyrmlings. They were clearing out, fleeing for the surface.

Near one guardhouse he found a huge stone vat that smelled of tar. He pulled off the heavy lid and peered in. The tar was mixed with bits of some noxious weed. The odor was more than foul; it seemed to corrode his very throat.

There was a torch in the guard shack, and a piece of flint.

Aaath Ulber held his war hammer above the torch and struck the handle with the flint until a spark caught in the dry moss that was wrapped around the head of the torch. He blew it until the torch blazed to life, then threw the torch into the vat.

Flames leapt from it, licking the ceiling, and heavy black smoke boiled from the infernal pot.

Aaath Ulber turned and stalked down into the depths of the wyrmling fortress as the smoke boiled out, filling the tunnels above.

As he passed the Room of Whispers, he stopped for a moment, heard the hacking coughs of wyrmlings and the panicked cries from the rooms above.

He would let the smoke do his killing for him.

With a heavy heart, he turned back. There were

wyrmling children still down below, babes whose only crime was that they had been born wyrmlings, that they had been given endowments.

It was time to punish them for those crimes.

❧ 30 ❧

A SEASON OF PROMISE

Spring is a season of promise, and in the fall nature fulfills those promises.

                         —A saying in Rofehavan

The collapse of the Wyrmling Empire in Internook came swiftly.

As Myrrima had feared, the wrymlings took vengeance in some places. Wyrmling death squads marched through the streets in a dozen cities, led by powerful runelords, and wyrmling war horns announced the attack on the fortress all across the land.

But in the uprising that followed, the humans vastly outnumbered the usurpers. Most of the wrymling warriors had but three endowments of metabolism. They were fast, but not faster than a marksman's arrow.

From the smoke and ashes of the great fortress Aaath Ulber came, and he raced across the land, scouring the coasts to the east. Three other human champions survived, and they raced to the west.

Songs would be sung of them that night, about the giant Aaath Ulber who wore robes woven from blood and traveled the earth in boots formed of gore.

By midafternoon Aaath Ulber caught the wyrmling champion Zil some twenty miles east of Ox Port, where the wyrmlings were setting fire to a village.

It is said that Zil begged for his life, and offered to serve mankind. But Aaath Ulber would not trust the creature, and so he slew Zil with the sword, slicing his throat close against the jaw, so that the wyrmling's lying tongue plopped out and jerked about on the ground.

Then Aaath Ulber hurled the wyrmling champion onto a bonfire that raged, the remains of some lord's fine manor.

By dusk, Aaath Ulber was a blur racing through all the cities along the coast and headed north into the wilderness, to clear out the wyrmling mines.

With the evening, the barbarians of Internook were singing and feasting. The human captives were coming home from the fortress, and folks from Ox Port sent wagons drawn by fast horses to speed them on their way.

The evening came warm and clear that night, with stars raging in the heavens, and the folks of Internook thought to celebrate.

But Draken wondered aloud to Myrrima, "Why are they celebrating? Internook doesn't have enough forcibles to protect itself. The wyrmlings will surely come from their fortresses to the south, and they will punish these people."

Myrrima was at the feast, picking out bread for their journey. She anticipated that Aaath Ulber would be back by dawn. "Celebrate life while you can," Myrrima said, "for death comes all too swiftly. The folk of Inter-nook know this."

She picked up a loaf of barley bread from a table, the sweet color of dark honey, and squeezed it experimentally. Then she turned to Draken, and the words that came from her now seemed to be wrung from her heart: "You should marry Rain tonight. Prudence might tell you to wait, but my heart says that you should marry her and enjoy your time together while you can."

Draken stared at her in disbelief. He looked so young. He was fifteen, going on sixteen. He was hardly more than a child.

"But, I'll need to buy land, build a house, get everything ready to support a wife."

"That can come later," Myrrima said. "The two of you can work together. It will be hard, but it can be done."

"I'm not old enough," Draken objected.

"Age cannot be measured in years alone," she told him. "You fled the locus Asgaroth with us when you were but a child. You've flown with the Gwardeen, and faced the wyrmlings. Such things age a boy and make him wise before his time. You're more of a man than someone twice your age."

"Father would never agree," Draken said.

"Aaath Ulber? He's not here to stop you," Myrrima said.

She hated to admit it, but Draken's father was gone now. Borenson had been transformed into a monster, a hero, a creature of legend. Like a dragonfly emerging from the bones of its nymph form, he had taken a fearsome visage.

"Your real father, Sir Borenson, would have agreed

with me," Myrrima said. "He was a man who loved to see people happy."

Draken nodded slightly, "Yes, I think he would have agreed."

So Draken married that night at the feast, while Aaath Ulber was still scouring the wilds. He married in the style of the barbarians of Internook.

In front of the entire village, he and Rain stood next to the fire, and Warlord Hrath bound their wrists together with strong cords. He gave Draken a fine ax, for his right hand, and Rain a bottle of wine for her left, and then had them repeat their oaths.

Draken found himself shaken at the power of the ceremony. The nearness of Rain, the warmth of her touch, the anticipation that he felt—all combined to send him shivering. He hardly recalled the words of the oath. He peered at his mother on the far side of the fire, saw her eyes tearing with joy, while little Sage stood holding her hand.

Draken promised to love Rain for the rest of his life, and to bed no other woman. He promised to nourish her and her children, both belly and soul. He swore to protect her and sustain her, through daylight and darkness, through the warm spring rains and the bounty of summer, until winter's icy touch released him.

When Rain took her vows, they barely registered in his mind. They were much the same as his, but he recalled an odd phrase, one that he'd never heard in a wedding ceremony, for Rain swore to "scold him only when he needs it, and to nag him not at all."

When the vow was finished, he took her in his arms and kissed her. The townsfolk raised their mugs of ale and shouted a great salute. There were cheers of "Blessed be your bed!" and "Health to you; wealth to you; and great be your joy!"

Then he found himself striding away from the group, still bound to Rain. Warlord Hrath warned him, "Don't untie the knot until dawn. It will bring you bad fortune!"

So together they went down to the docks and got into their away boat, and with each of them holding an oar, they rowed at a leisurely pace out to the *Borrowbird*. The ocean was calm that night, as calm as a summer pool, and the starlight reflected from its muzzy surface.

They climbed into the ship, which was still at anchor, and peered up at the sky. A crescent moon hung above the water, and in the distance a seabird cried.

Draken kissed his wife then, and peered into her eyes.

Her face was not the most beautiful that he had seen, he thought. She was fair enough, but not like some of the great women of legend.

He did not love her any less for it. Instead, he yearned to hold her, to cling to her.

He kissed her, and in moments he found himself playfully tugging at her clothes. He could not get his own shirt off, for the ties that bound him to Rain kept them on.

"I think this is some sort of barbarian joke on the newlyweds," he said. "Let's cut the knot."

"No," Rain begged. "Leave it be. I like being bound to you." She hesitated for a moment and said, "Let's cut the clothes off instead."

And he did.

* * *

Aaath Ulber raced through the night from village to village, slaughtering wyrmlings as he went.

They could not have escaped him even if they had tried. With his endowments of scent from hounds, he could smell the peculiarly rancid odor of their fat, even from miles away.

So with each city or village that he searched, finding the wyrmlings was not hard, and with so many endowments of metabolism to his credit, dispatching them was no harder.

He had grown weary of killing. He longed to stop, but he had to tell himself that with each wyrmling that he slew, he was freeing another four or five Dedicates.

I have not found myself, as the Earth King asked, he realized. I am more lost than ever.

He only hoped that Myrrima might help him. The touch of a water wizard could heal a man—even his blackened mind. So many times in the night when he'd wakened in the past, suffering from intolerable dreams of slaughter, Myrrima had healed him.

He only hoped that she could heal him now, in his darkest hour.

For the rest of the world, it was only a single night. But Aaath Ulber suspected that he had some thirty or forty endowments of metabolism now. He could run two hundred miles in an hour, and time for him stretched on limitlessly.

The work of that day seemed to him to be endless.

Yet as he ran, each time that he stopped in a tiny hamlet to dispatch a single wyrmling, he wondered, What have I won?

I've wiped out a minor fortress in the frozen wastes,

he thought—one that was poorly equipped and run by a leader who was too evil and petty to be efficient.

It is not the same as what I will face in Rugassa.

In Rugassa they had mountains of blood metal. In Rugassa the emperor ruled, and beneath him there had risen some false Earth King. In Rugassa the skies were filled with Knights Eternal and Darkling Glories.

What we've won here, he thought, is nothing.

So he raced across the country through the long night, and his mind was not easy. His imagination conjured the nightmares he would have to face in Rugassa.

Sometimes he worried about Crull-maldor. The lich had managed to evade him, and even now he feared that she might rise up from the ground on the trail in front of him or materialize at his back.

She had sworn her vengeance.

Yet as the long night drew on, he finished his circle of eastern Internook, and raced back to the fortress one last time to meet with the other champions.

As he crested a hill a few miles from the fortress, he glanced out to sea and spotted a fleet of wyrmling warships—three in number, making their way toward shore.

The vessels were huge, with enormous square sails stained like blood.

Supplies for Crull-maldor, he wondered, or fresh troops?

It didn't matter. He would have to finish the wyrmlings, lest news of the uprising reach distant shores.

So he stopped for a bit and fed himself on wild blackberries, then he raced downhill, hit the rocky beach, leapt out from shore, and poured on the speed as he reached the water.

Running at two hundred miles per hour, he raced over the sea, slipping and thrashing. The sea felt springy under his feet, but it was more solid than the stream had been. He wasn't sure if the salt in the water made the difference, or if it was because he had more endowments.

So he raced over the uneven surface of the ocean, bounding over waves and flotsam.

The ships drew nearer, and the size of them impressed him. The planks on the hull were perhaps sixteen inches wide and looked to be four inches thick. The mainmast towered a full hundred feet above the water.

He could see the wyrmling steersman at the helm, and Aaath Ulber appeared so quickly that the creature was barely able to register surprise before Aaath Ulber leapt twenty feet into the air, up to the prow, grabbed on to the heavy railing, and sprang lightly to the deck.

In less than a minute he dispatched all of the wyrmlings aboard, turning it into a ghost ship.

While checking the hold, he discovered the ship's purpose: It carried treasure, stone boxes filled with forcibles, more than three hundred and fifty thousand of them. They were made of good blood metal, and the heads had already been filed down into runes of metabolism.

Of course, Aaath Ulber realized. The wyrmlings to the south are better supplied with forcibles. It took them weeks to send shipments to this worthless little outpost.

In exultation, Aaath Ulber raced to each of the ships, slaughtered the crew, and secured the treasure.

As he rode toward the rocky shore, he dreamt of what this might mean.

There were Dedicates to be had here in Internook, and there were warriors fierce and strong.

He stood at the helm of the lead ship, and shouted toward the shore, "The Wyrmling Empire shall be ours!"

Myrrima was treated to a room in the village inn that night, a fine room with a straw bed covered in quilts, and a pillow made from goose down.

The innkeeper, a matron in her fifties, built a small fire in the hearth, even though it was not cold, and she'd left wine and cheese on a nightstand.

It was long past midnight when Myrrima prepared for bed. She used a basin filled with warm water to take a sponge bath, and she promised herself a real bath on the morrow—in fresh clean water, out in the river.

She put on her night-robe and then sat before a bureau mirror combing out her long hair. She smiled to herself.

One of my children is married tonight, she thought. With luck, a grandchild will soon be on the way.

A cool wind blew through the room, and she suspected that the door must have blown open. She glanced toward it as a mist floated up through the crack.

A wyrmling hag materialized, her skin cracked with age, her body somehow formless and distorted.

In a panic, Myrrima pushed back in her chair. Her only weapon was her bow and arrows, arrows blessed to kill even a lich. But she'd leaned her bow upon the bed, on the far side of the room.

The wyrmling hag towered above her. Myrrima heard words in her mind: *Come with me, to the land of the dead.*

Myrrima thought swiftly. She had no endowments to her credit. Her spells were useless without water nearby.

But a touch from her blessed weapons would banish a wight. Myrrima grasped the handle of the dagger strapped to her hip.

The lich lunged, a shadow blurring in its haste.

Myrrima's dagger cleared the scabbard and she felt more than saw the wight's attack. A cold pain lanced through her wrist, freezing her hand at its touch, so that the blade fell from numb fingers.

Myrrima whirled and leapt across the room for her quarrel of arrows just beyond the bed.

A thrill of ice raced up her spine as the wight caught her, and then a dagger of cold seemed to impale Myrrima, cutting through to her heart.

With a gasp, she fell onto the bed, and all sight, all sound began to fade.

Sage! she thought, wishing for one last moment with her child.

It was not an hour past dawn when Aaath Ulber reached the village of Ox Port, along with the rest of the heroes in tow.

The morning sun blazed golden in the heavens, and a few clouds on the horizon merely caught the rays and seemed to lend the sky some of their own color.

The birds were singing in the trees, and squirrels and chipmunks at the edge of town raced about, hiding seeds in their middens in preparation for the coming winter.

The heroes came pulling handcarts, bearing treasures from the wyrmling hoard: forcibles from their ships, oculars to see afar with, gold, and more.

The handcarts could not hold it all, of course. Most of the treasure had been left behind, and much of value was still to come—hundreds of thousands of Dedicates rescued from the darkness.

Young Wulfgaard bore one of the greatest of the gifts: the fabled Orb of Internook, blazing in his hands so brightly that it looked as if he held a splinter from the sun.

Most of the heroes were glad of heart, laughing, and Aaath Ulber expected the townsfolk to erupt in song.

Yet as he neared the edge of Ox Port, he sensed that something was wrong, and when he saw Warlord Hrath looking grim and sullen, he knew before the words were spoken.

"There was an attack," Warlord Hrath said. "A lich came to town. The innkeeper heard your wife fall, and nothing more. When she went up to check on her, Myrrima was lying beside her bed with ice on her brow. Nothing could be done."

Aaath Ulber stood for a moment, shocked into disbelief.

"I am so sorry," Warlord Hrath said. "We initiated a search, all through town."

Aaath Ulber sank to his knees. No course of endowments now would make him strong enough to stand, and with his perfect memory he heard Crull-maldor's words ringing in his ears: "I shall touch you yet. In an hour when you are less watchful, in a way that you do not suspect, I shall freeze your heart."

She had touched him, he knew, and he feared that it was not over.

"Draken? Where are Draken and Sage?"

"I'm here, Father," Sage said, stepping out from the

crowd. "Draken is with Mother now, watching over her body. He's been with her most of the night."

His children were alive, at least for now, he realized. But it was only a matter of time before the lich returned.

"Take me to my wife," Aaath Ulber said. Sage grasped his hand and led the way.

With so many endowments of metabolism, it seemed that Sage moved as if in a dream.

Aaath Ulber could smell the sweet scent of Myrrima's skin long before they neared the inn.

His mind was black, and his eyes were blind with grief.

He felt lost, more lost than he had ever been in his life.

But he relished the touch of Sage's hand. Too soon this war would lead him to distant shores, to dangers that he could not fathom. He wanted to walk with her, hold the hand of his child, one last time.